WARLORDS REIGNING

BOOK 3 OF WARLORDS
AN ADVENT MAGE NOVEL

HONOR RACONTEUR

 RACONTEUR HOUSE

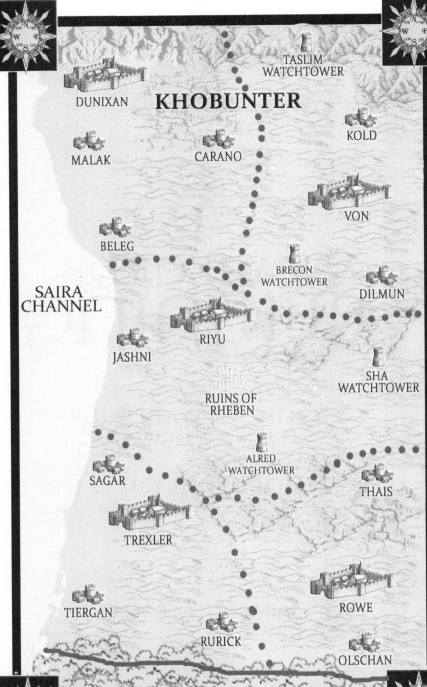

KHOBUNTER

TASLIM
WATCHTOWER

DUNIXAN

KOLD

MALAK

CARANO

VON

BELEG

BRECON
WATCHTOWER

DILMUN

SAIRA
CHANNEL

RIYU

JASHNI

SHA
WATCHTOWER

RUINS OF
RHEBEN

SAGAR

ALRED
WATCHTOWER

THAIS

TREXLER

TIERGAN

ROWE

RURICK

OLSCHAN

Q'ATAL

Published by Raconteur House
Murfreesboro, TN

WARLORDS REIGNING
Book Three of Warlords
An Advent Mage Novel #9

A Raconteur House book/ published by arrangement with the author

PRINTING HISTORY
Raconteur House mass-market edition/ August 2018

www.raconteurhouse.com

Other books by Honor Raconteur
Published by Raconteur House

THE ADVENT MAGE CYCLE

Book One: Jaunten
Book Two: Magus
Book Three: Advent
Book Four: Balancer

ADVENT MAGE NOVELS
Advent Mage Compendium
The Dragon's Mage
The Lost Mage

Warlords Rising
Warlords Ascending
Warlords Reigning

THE ARTIFACTOR SERIES

The Child Prince
The Dreamer's Curse
The Scofflaw Magician
The Canard Case

DEEPWOODS SAGA

Deepwoods
Blackstone
Fallen Ward

Origins

Vanya's jaw dropped and for the first time the man lost his cool aplomb. "You want to turn an entire country into some sort of magical garden?"

Trev'nor grinned at him. "Yup. It's going to take us a while, probably a lifetime, but we've got a good start on the project."

No one knew how to take this statement. Even the Remcar-ol were taken aback in surprise.

With a shake of the head, Casimir moved past this point. "Your goals are admirable, certainly. And after you are done conquering Khobunter, will you turn your full attention to this large-scale project of yours?"

Trev'nor took that to mean, 'after you've gotten a taste of conquering, you sure you're not going to turn your eye onto your neighbors?' "We will. Well, that and governing Khobunter itself, of course. I'll be heartily glad when all the fighting is done, personally. I'm more of a builder by nature. This fighting ill-suits me."

Vanya accepted this with a provisional nod. "And what of your co-ruler? Warlord Riicbeccaan, do you feel the same?"

"I do. Gentlemen." She planted a hand on one hip, expression one of exaggerated patience. "You do all remember that I'm a Balancer? That it's my job to literally fix the weather patterns of this world? I'm running a country in my spare time, here, and I need sleep at some point. One country is enough for me to manage, thank you very much, I don't want any more than that."

Trust Becca to bluntly state what everyone else danced around.

"Well." Gaidar regarded her with open amusement. "That was refreshingly honest and frank. Thank you, Warlord. I think you've addressed most of our fears, and while I find the concept of three teenagers conquering and ruling a country to be unorthodox, you're apparently doing a decent job at it. At the very least, you're doing better than your predecessors, and that's an improvement I'm happy to accept. I only have one more question that I need answered by you. What will you do about the remaining two provinces?"

Becca glanced at him, and Trev'nor signaled to her silently that he'd take this one. "We always send a message to the warlord ahead of time, listing out our intentions and demands, and give them a chance to negotiate with us. Honestly, Warlord Gaidar, we'd prefer to not fight if we don't have to. Khobunter's sand has soaked up enough blood, I think."

"I happen to agree." Gaidar relaxed back into his chair, body language more comfortable than before. "Thank you for the frank answers, Warlords. I am content with them."

Vanya cleared his throat. "I agree with my brother Warlord, but I do have an additional question. I wonder at the timing and urgency of this meeting. Why now?"

Nolan took this one, voice smooth and unhurried. "We received a report that Warlord Rowe had reached out to you, offering a peace treaty in return for troops. We did not want to drag another country into Khobunter's affairs or encourage the possibility of another battle."

"So by coming here, speaking to us, you hope to convince us to leave Rowe up to you," Casimir summarized, very careful to keep any inflection out of his voice and face.

Nothing about his reaction indicated how he felt on the matter.

Trev'nor really wished people would just state what they felt in negotiations, but apparently that was some major no-no in politics. He found it frustrating trying to read the man. "I came here hoping to prove to you that I'll be a good neighbor. I'm not interested in more conflict. Rowe is extending a hand out to you, trying to convince you that they won't attack in the future, that they'll be a better neighbor than I will. It's not true. I hope to prevent all of you from being dragged into our war by believing in that lie."

"The Warlords of Khobunter are willing to hammer out peace and trade agreements at this summit meeting," Nolan announced to the table in general. "They have no desire for further conflict, certainly not with any of you. My question to all of you is this: Will you accept Rowe's offer? Or will you choose the one we bring before you?"

"Of course we don't get an immediate answer to that question," Becca sighed some time later. Her hands idly scratched Tail as he lounged in her lap, him moving his head periodically to different angles so her nails hit the right spot.

They'd been very politely ushered into a suite of rooms nearby, offered a chance to freshen up, and had a variety of dishes laid out for them. Trev'nor liked the open floor plan of the place and the late afternoon breeze coming in through the open window, but found he couldn't really pay attention to the food. His stomach was a little too tight and nervous for that.

"I didn't expect one," Nolan offered, idly picking up a sliced fruit tart and nibbling at it. "They have to think about it. I got the vibe they liked what we said, though."

"So did I," Shad agreed. Of them all, he appeared the most relaxed, sprawled out on one of the couches with a leg crossed over another, his arms spread wide along the back of the couch. "I got the feeling Rowe demanded a lot and didn't promise much. And it doesn't give any of their neighbors much advantage to side with Rowe, tactically speaking. If they come to Rowe's defense, that means they'll be in near constant conflict with you and will have to always stand ready on Rowe's borders. That's very costly and time-consuming, and there's no real reward in it. Not when you're promising the same thing as Rowe: peace."

Nolan inclined his head toward Shad. "Exactly. I fully expect a favorable answer. I also fully expect us to be cooling our heels here for a few days before we get it. Such is the nature of politics."

"They better not take too long," Becca warned direly, her hands still moving along Tail's head. Even on the opposite end of the room, everyone could hear the cat's purrs. "We don't have that kind of time."

"I know that, you know that, it's convincing them to make a decision quickly that will be an issue." Nolan finally bit into the tart and smiled in delight. "These are quite good."

Trev'nor wondered if it was a lifetime of political maneuvering that made Nolan so immune to nerves in this situation. Likely so. He found it nearly impossible to stand still, choosing instead to pace back and forth in front of the window. A few days of waiting? Becca was right, they really couldn't afford to do that. Maybe one of them should stay, one of them return? Leaving Dunixan in charge of an unstable Riyu seemed highly unfair and they still didn't have everything done in Jashni yet. Close, but not quite. Maybe Becca could stay?

Although if Trev'nor returned without her, Danyal would pout. He could just see it now.

Something tingled his magical sense, and Trev'nor

focused out the window, frowning a little. What was that? Earth Path? Yes, someone was on the Earth Path and approaching at blazing speed. He tracked them for several minutes before the mage came in close enough that the distinct feel of his magic registered. "Shrieking hinges, Garth's here!"

"Wait, what?" Becca and Nolan demanded in unison, both of them bolting out of their chairs, Tail getting unceremoniously dumped to the ground. The cat glared at his person irately.

"Not here, here," Trev'nor hastily corrected, his eyes a little blind as he kept track of his mentor's progress underground. "But he's coming toward Ascalon at a break neck pace. I give it another few minutes before he arrives. Shad, do you know anything about this?"

Shad shook his head, eyes narrowed, and he sat up straighter on the couch. "No. But if he's coming himself, then something's happened that he feels he has to deal with personally. And I can only think of one thing that would bring him out of Strae right now."

It took a moment for Trev'nor to realize the obvious. Then he let his head flop back in resignation and exasperation. "The Trasdee Evondit Orra."

"It's the only thing he wouldn't want you kids to deal with on your own," Shad agreed slowly, a worried crinkle appearing between his eyes. "At least, that I can think of."

Trev'nor didn't like the sound of this, or the timing, but he had a sinking feeling Shad would prove right. "All of you wait just in case we get an answer," he threw over his shoulder as he strode to the door, "I'll meet him outside the gate."

"Bring him here!" Nolan called to his back as he left the room.

Trev'nor waved a hand in acknowledgement, his pace quickening once he reached the main street outside. Fortunately, none of the city-states in the Empire of Sol had any sort of imagination to their city layout, and Trev'nor could navigate this place as easily as Mellor. He ran through the city, dodging pedestrians as he went, and reached the main gate in short order.

"Magus Rhebengarthen is coming shortly and will appear in front of this gate," he informed the nearest guard.

"We're accustomed to him arriving there, sir," the guard responded with a reassuring nod.

Right. Sometimes Trev'nor forgot that Garth regularly visited Ascalon.

Garth rose from the Earth Path, the ground sloughing away from him like reverse quicksand. How odd. He looked entirely the same as he had the last time Trev'nor saw him, but it felt like a lifetime ago as so much had changed. He felt such a strange mixture of happiness, guilt, and relief, but mostly relief. There was very little in the world that could go toe-to-toe with the Advent Mage and come out on top. With his cousin here, Trev'nor felt like he had an army at his back.

Garth looked tired, dark circles under his eyes, and Trev'nor felt a little bad about that, as he knew he was the cause for quite a few of his mentor's sleepless nights. Still, Garth turned to him with a radiant smile, holding out both arms.

Without any hesitation, Trev'nor crossed the distance between them and hugged his cousin with all of his strength. "Garth."

"I'm so glad to see you well." Garth stroked a hand down Trev'nor's shoulder, returning the fierce embrace, before finally letting go and stepping back a foot. "Let me look at you. You're remarkably tanner than when you left home. Did you grow?"

"Maybe, my pants are a little too short these days," Trev'nor admitted. "Which drives my batman crazy. How are you? I know I sent you a lot of problems to deal with—"

Garth held up a hand, stalling any apology. "For good

reason, and I was very happy you trusted me to help, even if dealing with the influx of foreign students threw us all into a tizzy. You have nothing to apologize for, Trev'nor."

Relaxing, Trev'nor gave him a smile. "Still, I feel bad. I know you lost a lot of sleep because of it. Come in, we're all waiting in an apartment in the city. Did you hear that we've approached our neighbors for a peace treaty?"

"I did, thanks to Asla," Garth responded. "But I have someone for you."

Someone? Only then did Trev'nor realize that Garth had more than a bag at his feet, but also a portable crate. Bending down, he peered inside and felt his heart leap. "Priya!"

His meuritta stared at him with sharp blue eyes, icy with anger. Her calico coat stood up along her spine, showing her general displeasure, the smooth wings tucked along her side, the top of her long tail lashing. She proved that locks were not an issue, certainly not this flimsy thing on the crate, and popped it open instantly before leaping into Trev'nor's arms. He hugged her tightly to his chest, hearing her chittering and deciphering it as something between a scold for leaving her behind and joy that she had him again. Rubbing his chin along the top of her head, he crooned, "I know, I know, I'm a terrible friend. You're a good meuritta to wait patiently for me."

"She's been a terrible meuritta waiting for you," Garth corrected with a dark look at the back of Priya's head. "She let her displeasure be known far and wide. Berni wasn't any better, for the record. Chatta ordered me to take both of them before they brought the academy down on our heads."

"Now that sounds more realistic," Trev'nor admitted, unable to tamp down his smile. The other meuritta, a darker tortoise shell-coloring with black eyes and wings climbed out of the carrier, tail also lashing in displeasure. He extended a free hand to Nolan's meuritta. "Come on, Berni, let me take you to your master. Good boy, up you come, sit on my

shoulder. Excellent. Garth, I'm happy to see you, you have
no idea, but I'm a little worried about why you're here. Bad
news?"

"Potentially," Garth admitted grimly. Closing the crate
back up, he gathered both it and his luggage in hand. "Take
me to the others. I'll explain to everyone all at once."

Berni latched onto Nolan immediately once Trev'nor and Garth returned, tail wrapped around Nolan's neck, a chittering purr loud in the air. Garth hugged everyone but Shad, then turned to his friend with a dark look promising retribution. Shad had taken off without permission, leaving Garth in a lurch just as he needed all hands on deck at the Academy. Becca winced as Garth rumbled, "You and I will talk after this. You won't like how the conversation goes."

Shad shrugged, unconcerned.

Exasperated, Garth let it go for now and dropped into a chair. He looked and sounded a decade older and quite ready to take a nap right where he sat. "Guardians. I'm glad I got here in time."

"Trasdee Evondit Orra?" Becca guessed with a wince on her face.

Garth blinked at her. "You know?"

"Guessed," Trev'nor corrected, forcing Shad to move over so he could sit as well. "It's the only thing we can think of that would draw you out of the academy right now. What did they say?"

"Nothing, not to me directly, but I received an alert that they're on their way here to capture you three." Garth grimaced when they all burst out at once, incredulous and demanding details. Holding up both hands in a staying motion, he requested, "Don't yell at me, I'm just the messenger. I think—mind you, I'm probably right—they've been biding their time, waiting for you to come out of Khobunter. They don't dare come in after you. You have too much of a stronghold in there; it would take a war to get you out again. With you here, potentially for days, it gives them the time to come up and capture you."

"That's their thinking alright," Nolan growled. "There's only three things that can get Grandfather to openly swear, and the Trasdee Evondit Orra is one of them. Okay, so they're coming after us. Do you know how they're traveling or when they'll arrive?"

"Sadly, no. I only know that they've already left. They do have an Earth Mage at their disposal, my sister, but I don't think she'd do the favor of taking them up. So whatever method they're using for travel isn't as fast, but it'll surely be faster than conventional means." Garth sat forward, elbows on knees, meeting each of their eyes in turn. "I recognize that you are now warlords, you know how to handle situations like this, but I couldn't leave you to face them alone. You already have a very delicate peace treaty that you're negotiating. I can't let the Trasdee Evondit Orra crash into the city and destroy it."

Becca belatedly realized Garth feared that by coming, he stepped on their toes, or somehow undermined their ability. Hastily, she assured him, "We are more than relieved that you came to help us. You know the players better than we do and it's better that we have someone else backing us, showing that it's not just three rebellious mages running amuck."

"With you here, it proves that the rest of the magical world recognizes that we're doing the right thing and will support us," Trev'nor added in perfect agreement. "So we're very glad you're here."

"We are sorry you had to come out to deal with them, though," Nolan tacked on, absent-mindedly rubbing his meuritta's ears. "Everyone's alright at home?"

"No worries there, everyone's fine." As if remembering, Garth pulled out a stack of letters from his bag and passed them out to the correct parties. "I seem to be everyone's point of contact for a mail drop. Oh, and I have a letter from your wife, Shad. She's in the pique of health and ready to deliver at any minute."

A trace of a shadow crossed Shad's face.

Becca scooted in to sit next to him, leaning in to whisper, "Are you sure you don't want to go home for just a brief while? I don't want you to miss the birth of your daughter."

Hesitating strongly, Shad looked to her. "Can you do without me for a little while?"

"Nothing that will happen in the next two weeks will demand your expertise," she informed him. "And I'm as safe as houses, surrounded by dragons and mages and soldiers as I am. Go home for a couple of weeks. I'm sure Llona or Cat will happily take you and stay until it's time to bring you back."

Nolan's attention honed in elsewhere while Shad deliberated this before announcing, "Llona volunteered to take you. In fact, she's insisting—the dragons say that a birth in the clan is always a happy occasion and a father shouldn't miss it."

"I am absolutely positive that Xiaolang will step in and be the kids' military advisor if need be," Garth tacked on. "And I'll escort them back to Khobunter myself. I want to see what they've been up to before I return home. They'll be fine, Shad. I think you can go with no worries."

"But what about the Trasdee Evondit Orra?"

"I'm calling Raile in for help there," Garth informed him with a smirk. "Even they don't dare cross him."

Shad's hesitation cleared and he gave them all a smile. "Alright. I'm convinced. But no more than two weeks. Things are too unstable up there for me to be gone for long. Nolan, can Llona leave now?"

"If you saddle her, sure. She's been itching for a good flight after sitting around here for several days." Nolan shooed him on. "Go, go."

Shad planted a quick kiss on Becca's forehead before popping off the couch. "Remember, kids, be good or be good at it!"

Becca rolled her eyes at this parting, and watched with fondness as her brother bounced out the door. Part of her felt relieved for both his and Aletha's sakes that he would be there for the birth. Another part of her felt a little sad that she would miss it herself. Becca had anticipated what it would be like to be an aunt for her new niece, but with multiple countries now separating them, she wouldn't really be part of that little girl's life.

Shaking it off, she turned back to the problem at hand. "Garth, did you actually send Shad off so he couldn't kill the Trasdee Evondit Orra when they arrived?"

"More like so I wouldn't be tempted to murder them myself," he sighed, resuming his seat. "I know Shad would help me bury the bodies."

They all laughed, but it was short-lived. Becca could see on everyone's faces that they half-wished Garth wasn't joking. "Alright, so your report about them, did it mention who?"

"Yes, fortunately. En-Nelle of Tain and BycLewsh, with enough magicians to form a circle." Garth's eyes turned into a glittering, cold expression like chipped ice. "I think they plan to strip you of your magic on the spot before actually getting around to trying you."

In a way, Becca couldn't blame them for this plan. Who would want to try and keep three trained mages under wraps long enough to haul them into Hain for a trial? It would be beyond difficult. And they certainly had enough evidence that the three mages had been using their magic to conquer a country—the outcome of the trial had a very obvious outcome. Still… "They're very quick to break their own rules, has anyone else noticed that?"

"We all have, I think." Trev'nor stroked his purring meuritta while staring blankly at the far wall. "Garth. How many people know that our task was given by the Gardeners?"

"It's not widespread knowledge," Garth responded slowly. "Once I got your letter, I did inform everyone's parents, but not more than that. I didn't feel that the timing was right to inform the world in general. Just being a Balancer is enough to draw the wrong types of enemy to you. Or fame hunters. I didn't want to invite more trouble to your door."

"We do appreciate the caution," Nolan assured him. "I think Trev is wondering if just saying 'the Gardeners have appointed us to this task, don't interrupt' will get the Trasdee Evondit Orra to back off."

"I highly doubt it. Their argument will be that the Gardeners do not rule this world, and while they may guide us, we are still ethically bound to the oaths we made as mages." Garth's tone held a distinctly sarcastic edge. "What may or may not help our case is why you had to conquer Khobunter. If they know Chahiran descendants are in there as enslaved magicians, they might very well change their tune altogether."

"Because they are always greedy for more magicians," Becca concluded with a sigh. "At least they're predictable in that regard. But they really didn't know about Strae receiving a sudden high influx of students?"

Garth shrugged and eyed the plate of delicacies nearby with open interest. "I tell the Trasdee Evondit Orra as little as possible. Life is less complicated that way. Raile and Vonlorisen work off the same principle."

Becca edged the platter closer to him, and he finally gave in and picked up a tart, biting into it happily. "So, they have no idea we have so many untrained magicians. Garth, I'll be honest, I'd like to keep it that way."

"I don't blame you and I certainly am not planning to tell them anything in regards to your students unless forced to do so. It will just invite another argument." Garth popped the last of the tart into his mouth and reached for another one. "I'll handle the Trasdee Evondit Orra, don't worry about that. In fact, I'll make sure that word gets passed to me immediately when they arrive and they're stopped at the gate. Xiaolang will happily help with that. I have to ask, how are negotiations going?"

"Well, we think," Nolan replied, grabbing the last fruit tart before Garth could devour it. He handed a small part over to his meuritta, who happily munched on it. "They certainly like the idea of having new leadership in Khobunter."

"I think they're a little worried about us getting a taste for conquering." Trev'nor finally went for the food himself, although he barely nibbled at it. This lack of appetite spoke strongly of nerves. "Becca mostly waylaid those fears, though. It's times like this that I wish the Q'atalians were telepaths instead of empaths."

"Don't we all," Garth grumbled around a mouthful. Swallowing, he queried, "But you think they'll agree to a peace treaty?"

Nolan nodded. "Fairly sure. We're not sure of how long they'll deliberate before they give us an answer, and that's what we're worried about most at the moment, as we can't afford to sit here for long."

"How long is too long?"

Becca looked to Trev'nor, seeing his reaction as she ventured, "Three days?"

"I really wouldn't push it past that point," Trev'nor agreed instantly. "We left an ally in charge of Riyu, but that city's seriously a mess, Garth. Not in the physical sense, either. Their previous warlord was the scum of the earth and his people suffered from it. It's taking a lot on our parts to straighten things out. Besides, too much longer, Danyal's going to climb out of skin."

Becca glared at him. This was not the right time to bring up her love life. She toyed with the idea of teasing Trev'nor in return about his own love interest to retaliate.

"Danyal?" Garth looked between the two of them, catching their reactions, his brows climbing up into his hairline. "Commander Danyal? You've mentioned him in your previous letters."

"General Danyal now," Trev'nor corrected with a pointed smile at Becca. "Oh, and he's courting Becca."

Garth let out a low whistle, his full attention swinging to her. "You don't say. Shad knows about this? Really, and the man's still breathing. That's amazing in its own right. Aletha, Chatta, and I were taking bets on if you'd even be allowed to date before you hit thirty. Your letters gave me the impression he's a good man, but he must be more than that to gain Shad's approval."

Part of Becca really wanted to brag, another part felt a little shy about doing so. The boys, at least, seemed to encourage this so she unbent enough to confess, "He's amazing. Very smart, very kind, the type of person that inspires loyalty and confidence. It took me ages to get him to make a move, though. He was so concerned about bride prices and dowries that he hesitated for months."

"She had to openly dissolve the practice and announce there wouldn't be a bride price for her before Danyal asked her on a date," Trev'nor added. "You're right, Nolan, the sweets here are good."

"Aren't they?" Nolan shifted Berni off his shoulder and into his lap so he could lean back in the chair. The meuritta didn't care about the manhandling and went boneless in Nolan's lap. "I'll make sure you meet him when you come up, Garth. And we'll show you Rheben."

"I'm very interested to see Rheben. For that matter, I'm

interested to see all of it. How is the terraforming project coming along?"

Becca's attention gradually lapsed as the three men fell to discussing soil conditions, plants, and the like. She couldn't follow that sort of technical discussion and she didn't even want to try. Instead she focused on the one issue none of them really wanted to discuss.

How would Garth convince the Trasdee Evondit Orra to leave them alone?

True, he was an old hand at dealing with the magic council and their ridiculous agendas, but this wasn't on the same level as safeguarding Chahiran magicians from their clutches. This time, according to their rules, all three of them had violated the Mage Oaths. Garth's prediction that they wouldn't blithely accept 'a Gardener told us to' was likely spot on. The magic council accepted the statements of the Gardeners with a buffet sort of mentality—they only accepted the things they liked and skipped over the rest.

She studied Garth openly. Even though he smiled, his attention engaged in the conversation, the strain and tension in his body language didn't completely fade. He must have left home quickly, as his white hair wasn't in its usual sleek pony tail, but a little ruffled around the edges, and he still wore the dark brown professor robes. From the tight set of his green eyes, she guessed that part of him still worried about what to do when En-Nelle of Tain and BycLewsh arrived. That meant he didn't have a firm game plan, only some ideas. Would it get down to an actual battle with them?

Would they be forcibly cut off from the magical community?

Becca swallowed hard at the thought. She hated the very idea of it, but unfortunately the possibility could turn very real. If the magic council forced that outcome, it would lead to a very firm division of two sides. Coven Ordan supported them completely, and they already didn't like the council's agendas, so they would not come in on the Trasdee Evondit Orra's side. The same would be true for Chahir's magicians. It would lead to a brutal division with Hain.

Her own feelings for the Trasdee Evondit Orra aside, could they afford for that to happen?

Garth liked to think that after a decade worth of experience, he knew how to handle power-hungry people like En-Nelle of Tain. If nothing else, he'd certainly learned to call in reinforcements if he felt like the situation called for them.

This definitely qualified.

He went directly to Asla and Xiaolang's house after meeting with the kids—warlords. He really had to start thinking of them as warlords, and wasn't that a mental trip. Asla apparently expected him, as she answered the door very quickly when he knocked, a smile on her face. "Garth."

"Hello, my pretty sister," he greeted, giving her a hug. "I haven't seen you in a while."

"Several months," she agreed, hugging back. "And I'm glad to see you but worried I'm seeing you at this point. The kids?"

"Unfortunately," he sighed before stepping fully into the house. "The Trasdee Evondit Orra have already dispatched a team up this direction. Asla, I hate to ask, but—"

She put a finger firmly to his mouth. "Don't even start that, Garth. As if I'd let those power-hungry fools interfere with some of our own. What do you need?"

He really had done the world a favor, rescuing Asla all those years ago, even though it hadn't seemed that way at the time. "I need the use of your mirror. You're the only one with a powerful, stationary mirror that can reach far enough. I need to contact both Vonlorisen and Raile Blackover."

Asla stared at the mirror doubtfully. "I know I can reach Raile Blackover, we've done it before, but Chahir is a little…."

"Call Raile first," Garth advised, fully understanding her hesitation, as the mirror might not be able to connect that far. "I know for a fact he's put a scrying pool in Rheben, so he'll have the power to connect from that distance."

"Oh, good." Gesturing him fully in, Asla brought him to the mirror above the hearth and touched it lightly. "Raile Blackover. Wizard Blackover?"

After a moment a familiar, scratchy voice responded, "Yes, I am, and who is this?"

"De Asla," she responded politely. "I'm Rhebengarthen's sister and calling on his behalf. Go ahead, Garth."

"Garth, you rascal! Been a while since I heard from you."

"Not that long," Garth objected. "Not since I had to call begging for help. I'm sorry to say I'm calling now for a similar reason."

"You can't have my teachers. I need them all here."

"It's not teachers I need, it's you." Garth didn't know how to ease into this, so went with the blunt facts. "I've received a warning that the Trasdee Evondit Orra has sent a team, which includes a full circle, up here to Ascalon."

Raile let loose one of the vilest curses to ever breach the air. "They're after the kids."

"I'm afraid so. I'm in Ascalon now to help stop them, but I'm a little light on manpower to manage this. Raile, can I come up and get you?"

"Please do, Garth. No, better, I'll have Sallah bring me down. You're expecting them soon, aren't you?"

"I am, although my informant couldn't give me a firm itinerary. I'm not even sure how they're traveling up here, just that they had already left as of yesterday."

"So, very soon. Alright, don't you move. It's better you're at least on hand if they show up in the next hour. I'm coming as fast as I can."

"Raile, before you leave, I need you to connect us in a three-way call to Vonlorisen. I'm afraid it's come to the point where we need to make it clear we won't abide by the Trasdee Evondit Orra's rules anymore."

A long moment of silence ensued. "Garth. Are you sure?"

"No," Garth admitted frankly. "It's just a gut feeling. But I think this has been a long time coming, even if we don't choose to acknowledge it today. Raile, we've had to fight for the right to build an academy on Chahiran soil, we've had to fight to keep our Chahiran magicians in Chahir, and you know that once they learn of the rescued magicians, they'll want to take them all out of Khobunter and never give them back. The council has never really worked in the interests of the greater good."

Raile heaved a gusty sigh. "I'm afraid I have to agree with you. The amount of clout they've been throwing about the past decade has given me more migraines than I care to admit. Alright, hold on, let me see if I can contact Vonlorisen."

"Tell whoever answers that it involves Nolan and I guarantee he'll find time to spare for the conversation."

"Of course he will," Raile snorted, tone saying Garth had stated the obvious.

It took more than a few minutes, likely because they had to track down the king, but Vonlorisen's slightly out of breath voice came through crystal clear. "I'm here. Garth, what's this about Nolan being in danger?"

Garth succinctly summed up the situation as best he could. "Right now, I'm up here in Ascalon to help safe guard them while they're in peace talks with the other warlords in Sol. But I can't fend off the entire council by myself, especially if they've brought a full circle of magicians with them."

"Where do these dastards get the impression they can strip my grandson of magic?" Vonlorisen fumed. "Nolan has direct orders from a Gardener, for heaven's sake! They shouldn't be trying to interfere with him."

Garth personally agreed, but he didn't expect the magic council to be that cooperative. "I can possibly bargain these three free of the situation, but I don't like the possible concessions I'd have to make. It would include surrendering the magicians they've already rescued in Khobunter, which I know for a fact they won't agree to. It would also include them walking away from Khobunter completely and forfeiting what they've gained."

"They won't agree to that, either," Raile commented. "And for good reason. Vonlorisen, Garth has proposed that we stop catering to the Trasdee Evondit Orra."

Startled, Vonlorisen demanded, "Can we do that?"

"Yes and no," Garth explained a little tentatively. "No, we absolutely can't, because every magician must hold to some law, some greater power, to keep their greed in check. But that said, I don't feel like that greater power has to be the very corrupt magic council we've been dealing with so far."

"What he's actually suggesting, and a little too scared to say outright, is that he wants to form a separate magic council for Chahir and Khobunter, possibly Bromany as well." Raile had a bit of an evil cackle in his tone. "I think it a splendid notion. In fact, the more I think about it, the more I like it."

Vonlorisen sat on this for a few seconds before asking, "What are the cons?"

"We would no longer be able to ask for any assistance from Hain," Garth answered concisely. He'd spent most of his trip here thinking about this, so it took little on his part to rattle off the answer. "We'd have to negotiate any transfer of magicians and artifacts before they crossed Hain's border, and we'd lose immediate access to their research institutions and academies. Transfer students who are in Hain would have to be recalled immediately, and we'd have to lay some very strict ground rules with the Trasdee Evondit Orra before it would be safe to think about transfer students entering Hain again."

"That's not an insignificant loss," Vonlorisen acknowledged slowly. "But if I understand you two correctly, the pro to having our own magic council is that we would no longer be forced to obey their rules, cater to their preferences, or be forced to hand over magicians to them."

"And I'm personally not convinced that we'd lose all access to those institutes and academies forever," Raile tacked on. "The Trasdee Evondit Orra will not want to deal with our new council in the immediate future. They'll try to wrest back control, but I think within five years or so they'll give up and start bargaining with us."

"I'm of the same opinion," Garth admitted frankly. "I think we can do this. No, more to the point, I think it's high time we did this. My only real concern, truly, is who do we trust enough to put on the council? And you can't vote me, I refuse."

Raile cackled again, sounding pure evil. "Who said we wanted you? I want Chatta."

"Actually, Wizard Blackover, I quite like the idea of Rhebenchattaan being in charge of the new council. She certainly knows how to run an organization."

Garth shared a speaking look with Asla. His sister had a hand clamped over her mouth, tears leaking out of her eyes from the effort of not laughing. Garth just felt glum. When Chatta realized that he had more or less engineered her being volunteered to start and run a new magic council, she was going to skin him. The last thing his wife wanted was another job. "Can we designate her as a temporary placeholder? She already runs Strae Academy. I really don't feel like she has the time to hold two positions."

"Ah, that is a point," Vonlorisen acknowledged, as if just realizing this. "And she's a young mother, on top of it all. Very well, let's put her temporarily in charge while we think of personnel. Garth, I know that you don't have the time either, but I think you should be on the council, at least."

Relieved, Garth agreed immediately, "I'd be honored. Gentlemen, can I take it we're all in agreement on this?"

"I think we are," Raile responded, perky but also a little resigned. "Although it's sad that it's come to this point. For now, why don't we each withdraw and think about who to nominate. We'll try to think of at least five people each, then meet again in three days to discuss it in detail at that point. Vonlorisen, I'm heading to Ascalon immediately to support Garth, just in case."

"Thank you, Wizard Blackover, that eases my mind." Voice turning hopeful, he requested, "Perhaps you can have Nolan call me when he has a free hour? I'd dearly love to talk to my grandson."

"I'll make sure it happens," Raile promised. "Garth, see you soon."

"I'll wait by the main gate," Garth confirmed. As the magic on the mirror died out, he turned to Asla and warned her direly, "You are absolutely not to tell Chatta that I almost got her volunteered for that. She'll come immediately to scalp me."

"How about I tell her that a king and ancient wizard wanted her, and you talked them down to a temporary position instead, making you the smart husband?" she responded cheekily.

"I like your version so much better." It was mostly true, after all. "Alright, I have no idea what to call this new magic council, but I suppose an official name doesn't matter at the moment. I'll be a good friend and warn Xiaolang he might have a fight between foreign magicians in his city sometime this week."

"Please do," Asla requested primly. "And when you face off those idiots, I want to stand at your side."

This took Garth somewhat aback, as Asla wasn't really a fighter by nature, but one look at her face told him how upset she was. The situation had apparently tapped into her maternal instincts and ignited her ire, like a mother lion protecting threatened cubs. It might have surprised him, but Asla had proven to be a formidable witch in her own right the past ten years. He wouldn't turn down good help. "I'll make sure you are."

"Make sure Shad's there too," she included thoughtfully.

"Ah, we can't?" Garth gave her a shrug, smile lopsided. "He's on dragonback heading for Strae as we speak."

"For the birth, of course." Asla slapped a hand against the other, a very Chahiran gesture of recognition. "I'm glad that he went, although it would have been nice to have him with us, just in case."

"I have three other mages and two dragons. I'm not worried," Garth responded truthfully. "I'm only calling in Raile for political support. Help me request of the guards to be notified as soon as the Trasdee Evondit Orra arrive."

"Of course," Asla responded, immediately going to the hook near the door for her coat. "And we'll talk to my husband while we're out."

Trev'nor sat eating a rather scrumptious dinner with his two friends, none of them willing to wait for Garth to return. Who knew how long it would take for him to arrange everything as he wanted. Trev'nor realized that they hadn't introduced Garth to the dragons because all of them had been out hunting when Garth arrived, but they'd do that soon. Shad would miss the introduction, unfortunately, but

Trev'nor could always put the memory into a crystal so Shad could see it later.

He didn't know how long this conference would take but wasn't surprised at the lack of communication. Perhaps tomorrow they'd hear something.

Becca's head came up, a frown pulling at the corners of her mouth. She stood and went to the window, opening it and sticking her head out. "Odd. Someone's skirting just under my air currents. An Air Mage?"

"Coming from which direction?" Nolan inquired, sounding worried.

"Southeast. Almost due southeast."

"And someone else is coming from due north," Trev'nor commented, his head swiveling that direction even though he couldn't see it through all of the walls. "Earth Path, and coming in hot. I think it's Sallah."

"Garth mentioned calling Raile in for reinforcements," Becca said uneasily, still staring outside. "So Sallah's likely with Raile, right? But this Air Mage coming from the south, do you think that's the Trasdee Evondit Orra group?"

Nolan gave a grim nod. "Probably. Becca, how soon until they arrive?"

"Half an hour?" she offered. "They're relatively close and coming in very quickly."

"Trev?"

"Also about half an hour," Trev'nor answered, troubled. "That's not good. That means they'll arrive at more or less the same time, right?"

"Probably." Nolan stood, his chair moving a little jerkily against the carpeted floor. "I think we better call in our dragons, make sure this doesn't come down to a force of might right off the cuff."

Trev'nor eyed his friend, saw the determination and anger there, and knew what Nolan meant to do. "You don't think we should hide back here until Garth and Raile can get a word in edgewise."

"No. The Warlords of Khobunter have no reason to hide behind someone else's protection."

"Well," Becca turned away from the window with a feral smile, "when you put it like that, it's hard to argue. Let's go beat up the Trasdee Evondit Orra."

"Maybe try diplomacy first?" Trev'nor requested wearily.

"Now, now, Trev. When someone is selling a fight so hard, it's rude not to buy it," she chided him with a demented cheerfulness that reminded him strongly of Shad.

It was definitely obvious who raised her.

Becca hated the Trasdee Evondit Orra. She didn't hate much in life, but that group of greedy people made the top of her list. She hated them for being so difficult that they'd forced Shad and Aletha to choose a dangerous path when they rescued Becca as a child. She hated them for not supporting the magical community as they were supposed to, for making an already difficult situation even more difficult for Chahiran magicians. She especially hated them for being so blinded by politics that they never once even thought to question Khobunter's dangerous cultural climate.

Becca was spoiling for a fight with them.

That said, her mind was now politically trained to see the consequences of whaling on the Trasdee Evondit Orra, and she didn't know if they would come out better for cutting themselves off from that group. For all that they made life difficult, they also offered many resources that Chahir would otherwise not have access to. Becca was grimly aware that even if she could see why they should keep them, it might not be a choice left in her hands to make. It might come down to a matter of survival—hers or theirs—and never mind the political repercussions.

The three teenagers stepped out of their apartment and moved at a sprint through the city. The grey buildings on the grey streets became a monochromatic blur as they ran, the only variation coming from the brightly clothed people, moving around like a living rainbow. At this time of the day, the city's occupants were in full swing, and the streets had considerable traffic in them. The noises and conversations washed over Becca's ears in a slightly confusing muddle. Ignoring it all, she fought her way through, trying Asla and Xiaolang's house first, but not getting an answer. Nolan led them toward the main gate instead, calling for their dragons as he ran. The sky over their head darkened considerably as Becca's tumultuous feelings sparked her magic and gathered a storm. She recognized it but let the storm build anyway.

She might need it shortly.

Trev'nor kept glancing up at the sky then her, clearly worried, but also grimly aware of the situation enough that he didn't stop to argue with her about it.

Asla and Xiaolang's house sat not too far from the main gates, only six blocks, and they covered that ground at a dead run. Becca kept an eye on the soldiers stationed along the top of the wall but they didn't seem alarmed to see a storm abruptly shaping over their heads. They did seem more alert, though. Becca prayed that it wouldn't get bad enough that they felt the need to interfere. That would have international consequences she didn't want to deal with.

They hit the main gates, the guards on duty standing at ease, their attention fully on the outside road leading in. Becca and the boys barely got nods as they went past, and she soon realized why. Xiaolang stood not ten feet away with Garth and Asla. So he was there to help keep things in hand? Bless the man.

Becca's heart warmed to see Asla with the men, ready to defend them as well. Xiaolang turned sharply at their approach, then met them part way, already speaking, "Don't worry, we won't let them touch you. Becca, I promise you it won't come down to a magical battle."

"I'm not so sure of that," she riposted, coming to stop

near Garth's shoulder. "So I'll keep my storm on hand, thanks. Garth, brace yourself. Our dragons are coming."

"Ah, I'll be glad to meet them," Garth responded, expression torn between curiosity and resolve. "Although I wish it wasn't under these circumstances. How far out are they? You said they were hunting."

As if to answer his question, the strong flap of wings sounded from overhead. Becca's head jerked up, trying to spot Cat among the clouds. Her dragon must have broken speed records getting here this quickly. Nolan hadn't been sure they'd make it before the other two groups.

The clouds broke and both dragons darted out of the sky like streaks of living lightning. Both threw their wings out wide, abruptly halting their downward descent. They didn't crash to the earth like a meteor, but they landed hard enough to jar the humans nearby, nearly throwing everyone off their feet.

Jogging out to meet them, Nolan called out reassurances, "You came in time! No one's here yet!"

"Good," Garth the dragon pronounced in his deep voice. He strode in, tail lashing in agitation, steam curling out the sides of his mouth. He looked over the humans for a moment before noticeably calming, his head coming down to rest more at their level. "Fledgling. Family?"

"Yes, they are," Trev'nor responded, coming forward and scratching under that massive chin before turning to do the introductions. "This is my Aunt Asla, my Uncle Xiaolang, and this is Garth."

Garth caught the emphasis and pointed to himself in question, head canted.

"Garth," Trev'nor's eyes sparkled with humor as he intoned, "meet Garth, my dragon."

Xiaolang busted out laughing, hanging onto his wife's shoulder, who was wide-eyed and flabbergasted.

For several moments the two Garths just stared at each

other, then Human Garth managed, "I thought reincarnation worked only if you, you know, died."

Trev'nor lost it. He had a stitch in his side, trying to contain his laughter.

Xiaolang came up to sling an arm around Human Garth's shoulders, mock sympathetic, devilry in his eyes. "Did no one tell you that you were adopted?"

Recovering his balance, Garth played along. "No. Believe me, my mother has some explaining to do." Shaking himself, Garth came forward to properly greet his dragon doppelganger. "Hello, ah, Garth."

Garth's nostrils flared as he breathed in the other. "Greetings, Garth."

Lost and more than a little bemused, Garth looked to Trev'nor for an explanation.

"I literally had nothing to do with this," Trev'nor promised him. "It's just, the first few days we were up in dragon territory, we had a lot of explaining to do, right? And we kept mentioning you, and he figured out that you were a prominent, powerful man in our community. So he decided to take on your name. He has this idea it's appropriate."

"Is," his dragon maintained.

Not quite sure how to take this, Garth's easy-going personality came out and he started chuckling. "I think I'll take this as a compliment. Well, Garth, I am very happy to meet you. It's nice to meet Trev'nor's dragon partner."

"Same," Garth rumbled. Turning his head, he indicated for Cat to come stand at his side.

"This is Cat, my dragon," Becca introduced to the group. "And no, I didn't name her that either. The only one who got to choose a name was Nolan, oddly enough."

"Pleased to meet you, Cat." Xiaolang finally got hold of his laughter long enough to greet the dragons properly. "And you as well, Garth."

The dragons rumbled back greetings, getting good sniffs

and scratches from the humans in.

Normally Becca would have let this continue for a few minutes, but they didn't have that kind of time on their hands. "Cat, you remember how I said a few weeks ago that our magical leaders won't like what we've done in Khobunter? That they might come after us?"

"They come," Cat growled, each word accompanied by sparks. "Nolan said."

So he'd already explained the situation. Good, that saved them time. "Yes, they're coming. We're trying not to fight."

The dragon pointedly looked toward the sky and then back at her mage with an 'oh, really?' look.

"Alright, so maybe I want to pound sense into them," Becca admitted, hands clenching into fists at her sides. "But we should try words first."

"Then pound," Cat stated firmly, her tail impacting the ground hard enough to leave a rut behind.

And this was why Becca loved her dragon. They were firmly of the same mind when it came to things like this. "Absolutely."

"Peas in a pod, these two," Trev'nor mourned. "Alright, Garth—ah, I mean, Cousin Garth—"

"Knew that'd get confusing," Nolan commented to no one in particular.

Trev'nor ignored him and kept going. "—what's the plan? I assume you reached Raile, as I can feel him coming in even now."

Garth's eyes went to the sky, and the group coming in, and swore a little under his breath. "They'll arrive before he will. Short, dirty version is, we're cutting all ties with the Trasdee Evondit Orra and forming our own magic council."

Becca felt the bottom of her stomach drop out. Spluttering, she demanded, "W-why? Really? When was this decided?"

"An hour ago, really, and because we've had enough,"

Asla answered concisely, tone clipped. "Now brace yourself. They're here."

The Air Mage let his group down with no fanfare, just a straight drop, gentle enough to not jar anyone before he released the wind completely. Such fine control spoke of many years of practice and Becca realized with a sinking heart who it was: Tyvendor, one of her teachers. She'd thought the magic was familiar but hoped she was wrong.

Becca watched him come in with open dismay. She felt more than a little betrayed and hurt. Why had he assumed the worst? Why hadn't he reached out and tried to find out her version of events? Had he so quickly condemned her that he'd bring a full circle of people to strip her of magic?

Out of the seventeen people, several were familiar faces. As Garth's report said, En-Nelle of Tain and BycLewsh stood among them, older now, their age showing in the grey of their hair and the stark lines around their eyes and mouths. BycLewsh had always looked severe to Becca, but the man had lost at least thirty pounds since she'd last seen him, enough that his cheekbones and nose stood out prominently, making him almost scarecrow-like. En-Nelle's short frame had actually gained the weight her companion lost, and she looked like that scary aunt no one wanted over for family dinners.

Becca's eyes moved past them, but the only other person she recognized was Cora, who looked very torn on being here at all. Becca held out some hope that Cora, at least, was not there to automatically condemn them. It still smarted to see her standing on the other side, as if she'd joined the enemy. Had they brought a Life Mage to deal with Nolan in particular? Or perhaps they knew about the dragons, and thought another Life Mage a necessary precaution against them?

En-Nelle stepped forward in a swirl of black robes, dark eyes snapping. "Garth. You'll not protect these three, not after what they've done!"

"They've obeyed the orders given to them directly from the Gardeners," Garth retorted flatly. "So yes, I will protect them."

"Wait, the Gardeners?" Cora protested, her blue eyes going wide. Whirling, she demanded of En-Nelle, "You didn't tell me that!"

"What does that have to do with this?" the elderly woman snapped at her. "They have clearly violated their mage oaths!"

"Actually, no," Tyvendor disagreed, his long face drawing into a tight frown as he stared at his former student. "That casts this situation into an entirely different light. You told me that one of my students had violated the oaths and it was my duty to strip her of her magic. That's the only reason I'm here. Becca, what is actually going on?"

So Tyvendor hadn't fallen completely under the Trasdee Evondit Orra's spell, nor Cora for that matter. Eager to get them away from the group, Becca quickly started, "It's true, we had a Gardener visit us—"

"THAT DOES NOT MATTER!" En-Nelle screeched.

Cat whirled as quickly as a dragon that large could, snapping at the woman close enough to send En-Nelle stumbling back in panicked reflex. "You let Becca talk," the dragon commanded sharply. "You listen or I pound."

Becca did adore her dragon. Grinning at her, she gave her a pat on the leg before resuming, "The Gardener said that Khobunter is Trev'nor and Nolan's task. It was what they were prepared for, since they were young. It's mine as well, part of the reason why I was awakened early."

Cora came directly to her, staring deeply into her eyes, putting both hands on her shoulders. "Becca, I need you to answer this question honestly. You didn't conquer Khobunter for any other reason?"

Swallowing, Becca looked at one of her oldest friends

and answered truthfully, "We did. Cora, there are magicians in Khobunter. They're enslaved."

Cora went abruptly still, barely even breathing, too shocked to formulate a response.

Tyvendor blew past her, grabbing Becca's shoulder and yanking her a little around, his body nearly shaking in outrage. "What? How long? Who?"

"The third group," Nolan answered, his quiet voice cutting through the rising emotions like a hot knife through butter. "The third group that left Chahir over two hundred years ago went into Khobunter. It is their descendants who are enslaved."

The entire group froze, staring at him. Nolan faced them all calmly for a long moment before turning to En-Nelle, whose expression had become very calculating. He continued, "We were enslaved in the beginning as well—as soon as we crossed the border—and had to fight our way out of those chains. We conquered the country because we had no other choice."

"And before you get the idea in your head," Trev'nor came to stand toe to toe with En-Nelle, his superior height forcing her to crane her neck back to look up at him, "you will not have them. They are ours. Ours to protect, nurture, and guide. Do not think for a moment that I will allow you to put your hands on them."

Her thin lips peeled back from her teeth like a predator shark. "It is greed that motivates you after all! You all hear him."

"It's greed that motivates you into thinking you can pull them out of Khobunter," Raile commented idly.

Becca turned sharply, as she hadn't realized he'd arrived. Just how long had he and Sallah been here, unnoticed by them all?

Tyvendor immediately stepped back to give his mentor a bow. "Raile. I had no idea you would be coming."

"Obviously, otherwise you wouldn't have helped these fools get up here," Raile retorted sarcastically. "Ty, I am fully aware of the situation in Khobunter. Young Becca came and told me personally over a month ago and formally requested aid from Coven Ordan. Her request was granted."

Tyvendor's head jerked back in surprise. "You've helped them?"

"We now have forty-two Coven Ordan magicians in Khobunter either training all of the magicians freed or helping to rebuild the country into a more hospitable place," Raile informed him levelly. "I am among them. And before you start screeching, En-Nelle of Tain, may I remind you that I, too, am a Balancer? It is my task to raise and train the last of the lost magicians from Chahir. The Gardeners have kept me alive specifically to do this. So if you think that you can march in here and take these three to punish them for doing what they are supposed to, you will have to take me on as well."

That gave her pause as perhaps nothing else would have. En-Nelle looked about her and realized that of her own group, she'd already lost the support of two people. She had several upset mages in front of her, one witch, and two dragons who were steaming mad. Literally. That did not include the repercussions if she faced off with Raile Blackover, of all people. The whole of Coven Ordan would not take that well.

Her eyes latched onto Becca with a loathing so intense Becca felt almost physically injured from it. Becca held steady and reminded herself that while this woman was power hungry and calculating, she wasn't as evil and cruel as Riyu. In fact, she failed to even measure up to that man.

"It does not make what they did correct," BycLewsh finally interceded, his voice smooth. "They should have reported this matter to the council."

"Why?" Garth responded, already weary with the whole

argument. "So that you could conquer the country yourself and steal all of the magicians out of it? To what end? The oaths a magician takes are to protect and serve the people who need their help. You might not like their methods, but these three have certainly upheld their oaths in that regard."

"What you should have done," Raile informed the two of them, a visible tic in his temple, "was to come up here and ask questions. Not bring a full circle with you to act as judge and jury immediately. You are too accustomed to always getting your way, I'm afraid. It ends today."

As if they had planned this ahead of time, Garth smoothly took up the declaration. "We formally announce that Khobunter, Chahir, and Bromany will no longer recognize the authority of the Trasdee Evondit Orra."

En-Nelle spluttered so badly she couldn't formulate a single word in response. BycLewsh actually staggered back a step, his eyes wide enough to pop straight out of his head.

As if they had voiced an actual protest, Garth repeated, "Khobunter, Chahir, and Bromany will no longer recognize the authority of the Trasdee Evondit Orra. You heard me correctly. We're all tired of the politics, the bargaining, the senseless power struggles involved in that council. We're done. We'll form our own council to rule over the magicians. Once we have it properly formed up, I will visit Guin Braehorn—" he cut himself off, head jerking about sharply. Trev'nor's and Sallah's did as well, as every Earth Mage picked up on the earth magic heading at a blazing speed in their direction.

Trev'nor's options were very limited on who could possibly be using the Earth Path. Unless someone else from Coven Ordan had decided to join the party, they really only had one option. "Is that Aunt Kaydan?"

"Probably," Garth confirmed, orienting himself to face the latest addition to the party.

Trev'nor hadn't seen Aunt Kaydan in years, but as she rose from the ground, the earth cascading away from her, he realized she hadn't changed much. She looked remarkably like Garth, just a petite and feminine version of him, with her light blonde hair, green eyes, and oval-shaped face. She gave her brother a quick smile before stepping in and giving Trev'nor a firm hug. "Long time no see, cousin."

"Very glad to see you," he responded, hugging back, then whispered against her ear, "Did you seriously just bring King Guin with you?"

"I'm nothing more than a chauffeur for this," she informed him impishly. "I'll enjoy the show, though."

Guin Braehorn did not seem pleased to be there. At all. He didn't wear his crown or formal robes, but dressed in a more casual day suit of charcoal grey, suggesting he hadn't taken the time to change. The lines around his brown eyes and mouth deepened as he frowned at En-Nelle and BycLewsh. Everyone bowed to him except Nolan, and Trev'nor realized belatedly that he shouldn't either. As a ruler of Khobunter, he should be greeting Guin as another head of state. He kept his head up, glancing to the side to make sure Becca did the same. She fortunately did, although she managed a polite nod to him.

"King Guin," Becca greeted calmly. "I believe we've met only once before in person."

"We have," Guin responded politely enough, although his eyes narrowed as he took her in. "But you make a very impactful impression, Riicbeccaan. Or should I address you as Warlord?"

"Do as you wish," she invited, baring her teeth in what might, charitably, be considered a smile.

Guin took in a deep breath, glared at the now worried council members, and then faced Garth. "I received a report that your three students have conquered Khobunter. Is this true?"

"We have." Trev'nor put himself directly in the man's line of sight, forcing him to interact with Trev'nor and not Garth. Making Garth back them up with the Trasdee Evondit Orra was one thing, arguing with an old friend was another. He'd already burdened Garth and Trev'nor had enough experience with politicians now that he felt he could take Guin on. "We did so because it needed doing. Because Khobunter is the task given us by the Gardeners. If you wish to take issue with that, King Guin, then you can address those concerns to me."

Kaydan clapped and bounced on her toes. "Ha! I guessed right. Told you, Guin."

Half of the tension riding in Guin's shoulders abruptly released. "So you had good cause. Bless the Guardians. Yes, yes, Kaydan, you were right. I suspected you were, but I had to verify that for myself. Warlord Trev'nor—" he paused, mouth working as if he'd said something strange, something he didn't know how to swallow. "It feels very odd to address you like that. I still remember you as a five-year-old, running about and finding trouble."

"Still finding trouble at seventeen," Trev'nor admitted ruefully. "Just on a larger scale now."

"Yes, apparently so." Guin's eyes took in not only the magicians gathered around them, but the two dragons lurking behind the warlords.

En-Nelle couldn't take this back and forth anymore and bustled forward, a simpering smile on her face that pulled oddly at her cheeks. She was used to scowling, not smiling. "Your Majesty, whatever you might have been informed about the Gardeners, they cannot be used as an excuse. These three mages have violated their ethical oaths—"

With a downward slash of the hand, Guin cut her off. "En-Nelle, I am fully aware of what a Gardener is and what their task is. We have all felt the impact of their directions. Three of the people standing here have seen a Gardener multiple times and received instructions from them. You really think that you can just gloss over them as if they were a footnote? If a Gardener has come and issued instructions to those three, then I'd say that takes precedence over whatever rules the council made up."

Alarmed, she rocked back on her heels, jaw dropping. She tried again, more insistent. "But they can't just go around conquering countries, no matter what reason they have! It will incite other mages to overthrow everything they've been taught. That's clearly the case, as these three have already corrupted Rhebengarthen into thinking he should cut all ties with the Trasdee Evondit Orra."

Now Guin shared her alarm, stepping to the side to get a clear view of Garth. "You said that?"

"Guin." Garth sounded world-weary as he spoke, but he kept his chin up, shoulders braced. "I have literally had to fight with the Trasdee Evondit Orra on every single matter, insignificant or otherwise. They have half of our mages despite the fact they don't really have the personnel to teach them properly. And now they're showing up in a full circle without any sort of advanced warning with the intention of stripping these three of magic, skipping a formal hearing. Do you realize how many laws—their own and otherwise— they break on a regular basis to keep themselves in power?"

"That is outside of enough!" En-Nelle snapped at him, aghast, high spots of color in her cheeks. Her voice went so high that it made the magicians directly behind her jump. "The audacity of you to think that you can spout such nonsense! Who do you think you are?!"

Garth stared her down levelly. "The Advent Mage. Former Balancer of this world and Dean of Strae Academy. Have you truly forgotten who I am, En-Nelle?"

Trev'nor let out a low, soundless whistle. Garth rarely threw his political weight around, but when he did, it was a rather scary thing to behold. Very few people in the world had the ability to stand toe-to-toe with him and win. He was so laid back and easy to approach that many people forgot just who this man was. At least until they pushed him too far.

En-Nelle of Tain, despite knowing Garth even as a student, had clearly forgotten. Or perhaps it was because she was there at his beginning that she didn't give him his due. She saw it now, her eyes darting between every person, searching for the support she had lost. Even BycLewsh refused to look at her.

Beside himself, Guin rounded on her and hissed, "Have you seriously pissed him off to such a degree that he's cutting all ties with us? Don't you realize that by doing so you've likely damaged Hain's alliance with Chahir and probably Coven Ordan as well? Are you a complete moron?"

"No, but they broke the law—" En-Nelle hastily stated, her hands up in a warding gesture. The magicians behind her shifted uneasily, casting each other looks that spoke of doubt.

"Dean," BycLewsh addressed him with a carefully neutral tone, "I feel that such an announcement is perhaps immature at this stage. If we have overstepped, I offer my apologies. Can we not discuss this?"

"Your chance to discuss this was several months ago, when you received the report of what my former students were forced to do in Khobunter," Garth responded in that same level tone that sent chills of unease racing up and down Trev'nor's spine. "Your chance to discuss this ended the moment you came here in full force, trying to catch them unaware while they are in the middle of peace talks in a foreign land. Are you completely blind to the political ramifications of showing up like this, unannounced, in Ascalon? We have multiple heads of state visiting here. If anything happened to them, you would not only embarrass Ascalon, but invite the wrath of Warwick, Osmar, and Q'atal."

BycLewsh had clearly not thought of that and his already pale expression went ashen. A fine tremor started in En-Nelle, and she panted in short bursts, a panic attack threatening. A few of the witches behind her started sidling backwards, clearly not willing to stay close to the woman anymore. One wizard promptly moved away, closer to Garth, silently stating that he really had nothing further to do with the situation.

Trev'nor dared a look at the rest of the magicians and found them all staring at Garth, appalled and now worried.

"That doesn't take into account that one of the people you so casually think to strip of their magic is the sole heir to Chahir's throne," Guin continued where Garth picked up, only with increasing volume and wider arm movements. "And the other two are warlords of a country. I shudder to think of what would happen to any of us if a single strand of their heads is harmed. I truly do not understand what you two were thinking, rounding magicians up and hauling them here."

From the gate's open entrance a commotion started, quietly done, but when Trev'nor risked a glance he realized that some of the warlords he'd come to have peace talks with now watched. He swore under his breath and caught Xiaolang's eye, but the man waved him down, already turning to go and take care of it. Xiaolang moved at a quick jog and greeted them in a low voice. Trev'nor left it up to him to keep them at bay.

Garth moved to stand firmly at Trev'nor's side, ignoring everyone but Guin. "I will not have these three punished for something they're supposed to do. I will not have any more of my students be pawns in their power games. I'm done, Guin."

"Nope," Cora announced firmly and shifted so that she stood behind Becca. "I'm not getting in the middle of this. In fact—Garth. I request permission to re-enter Chahir."

"Granted," Garth responded promptly, sparing her only a glance. "Anyone else want to do the sensible thing?"

"Me," Tyvendor announced firmly. "In fact, Becca, I'm sorry I ever doubted you. I thought this might be a mistake, which is why I volunteered to come up myself, but I should never have brought these idiots along with me."

Becca gave him a sweet smile and darted in for a quick, firm hug, which Tyvendor readily returned. Cat leaned in to nuzzle both of them, joining in the hug. "You're forgiven."

Giving him a nod, Garth granted, "You're welcome back as well, Tyvendor. I spy one other Chahiran wizard here with us. What do you say, Charles?"

Guin opened his mouth, alarmed, ready to leap in and cut this off but unable to get more than a croaking sound out before the wizard answered.

"I denounce all ties with the Trasdee Evondit Orra," he announced firmly. "Busted buckets, but this really was the last straw. Don't look at me like that, En-Nelle. You deliberately twisted the facts and withheld information from us all because you wanted to take Garth's pet students down a peg. Well, they're his bloody pet students for a reason, you idiot. A Gardener? They had an actual Gardener give them instructions, and you choose to ignore that?"

"Twice," Becca corrected him mock-cheerfully, trying to shove her dragon off before Cat could accidentally knock her down.

Charles looked at her, grey eyes widening. "Twice?! That tears it. In fact—Warlord Becca, are you still looking for help up in Khobunter?"

"We never turn down help," she assured him.

"Then give me a week to pack up and I'll join you. I feel like I should help out for at least a month as an apology for this fiasco." Glaring at both En-Nelle and BycLewsh, he stormed past and planted himself firmly on the other side of the line.

Turning to look at him, Trev'nor assured him, "You'll be more than welcome. Thank you. Anyone else?"

No one else spoke, although they edged a little away from the council members. They all looked Hainian, so doubtless they couldn't just cut all ties even if they wanted to.

Guin put up both hands in a staying motion. "Wait. Wait, please. Let's not jump too hastily. Garth, I know you're upset, you have every reason to be. What if I promise to restructure the council myself?"

Green eyes narrowed as Garth locked gazes with Guin. "You'd do that?"

"I would much prefer to re-organize the council over upsetting most of the magical world," Guin promised faithfully, expression easing into hopefulness. "Especially as they're a thorn in my side on a regular basis. Give me six months to find better people to serve on the council and then we can discuss this again. That's all I ask."

Garth caught Raile's eye and got a nod of agreement, then he looked to Becca, Nolan, and finally Trev'nor. Trev'nor believed that Guin would be good to his word, and they really would do better working together as a magical community than having two councils battling it out. He gave Garth a firm nod of agreement. He'd much rather at least try and work things out.

Taking in a deep breath, Garth shut his eyes for a moment, thinking hard. He let it out in a steady stream before opening his eyes once more. "Alright, Guin. We'll try it your way."

Guin not so secretly heaved a breath of relief. "Thank you. I'll work on it the minute I get home. En-Nelle of Tain, BycLewsh, you are both formally put on standby until I can review everything you've done. Stand down immediately."

En-Nelle looked about her as if she couldn't understand what had gone wrong, or at what point everyone had turned against her. "B-but they broke the law...."

"They broke the law for very good reasons and did so with permission from the Gardeners themselves," Raile corrected her. "They broke the law to save lives. Sometimes, En-Nelle, you must face the fact that the laws are not always right.

Sometimes, you have to understand that laws were made to guard against wicked intentions, to protect innocents, and if they're doing the opposite, then maybe it's time to rethink those laws."

BycLewsh locked eyes with Raile for a long moment. "These enslaved magicians. You've seen them?"

"Seen them? Child, I've been teaching them, marrying them, and protecting them for the past month solid." Raile looked thoroughly put out by this question.

"They're really of Chahiran descent?" BycLewsh pressed, not in an argumentative fashion, but as if he needed this confirmed for himself.

"They are. It's undeniable."

Garth the dragon rumbled firmly, "Our magicians."

BycLewsh didn't say another word, but the look he shot his fellow councilwoman promised murder when there were no longer witnesses. Trev'nor knew why—if they had played their cards right, they might have gained a whole new crop of magicians and been able to influence them. Instead, En-Nelle's bullheadedness had cost them the opportunity completely, as well as losing them every magician in Chahir and Bromany.

Guin's head bounced back and forth as he listened to this exchange, his confusion mounting. "What magicians?"

Leaning heavily on his cane, Raile came forward, gesturing for Guin to come aside for a moment. "Come, I'll fill you in."

Trev'nor watched as the remaining magicians stripped the two councilors of their wands and slipped magic binding amulets over their heads. Numb, neither of them argued against this or protested. Trev'nor quite happily moved further away from them, standing with Nolan instead. Letting out a loud, pent-up breath, he stated, "I can't believe we managed that without a fight."

"I'm actually relieved we did, as fighting in Ascalon

right now would have hurt our chances of an alliance badly," Nolan stated with abject relief. "Good play, Garth."

Garth winked at him. "I do have my moments. Alright, everyone, let's go back inside and discuss what to do next. Garth, Cat, thank you for backing us up."

"I watch them leave," Garth the dragon announced, hunkering down to wait.

"Me too," Cat agreed, following his example.

Trev'nor personally felt like an escort for that group was wise and didn't even want to question it.

Kaydan sidled in next to him and murmured from the side of her mouth, "You know, your Uncle Roarke would be brilliant on the council."

In more ways than one. Roarke Kartal had always been politically savvy and ambitious. He had the skills to serve and the connections to do the job right. "Trust me, I'll recommend him."

"Good." With a wink, she gave the area in general a satisfied smile. "Well, that was certainly worth the price of admission."

"Shame you didn't have any popcorn," Garth drawled to his sister.

"Isn't it, though?" she agreed sunnily. "It was good seeing everyone, and I'd love to catch up, but later. I want this group back in Hain before they cause any more trouble."

Guin strode back to the group looking, if possible, even more outraged than before. "Kaydan, if you would, can you leave me here for a few hours? I wish to establish a proper alliance with Khobunter's new rulers. Since they're already in talks, now seems to be the opportune time."

"I agree." Nolan waved an arm toward the city. "We can't offer formal hospitality, being guests ourselves, but we'd certainly love to speak with you."

"I'll apologize to your hosts first for this—" Guin waved a hand toward the waiting group, "—brouhaha. Give me one moment, please."

"Certainly," Nolan assured him smoothly.

Trev'nor admired his friend's politician face. He'd have to work on his own.

As Guin left to issue orders, Kaydan gave everyone a quick hug, then strode over and took the Hainian magicians smoothly away, blazing a fast retreat southward.

Only with them gone did people truly relax. "Let's go back to our apartment, then," Becca offered to her hovering mentor.

"Please," Tyvendor requested. "I have—actually, I'm sure we all have—many questions regarding what's actually happened. I can't trust anything I've heard about the situation. I think we need to hear the story from the beginning."

"I will tell you," Trev'nor promised.

That evening passed with difficult conversations and vague feelings of unease. Since Hain didn't share a direct border with Khobunter, the alliance talks between King Guin and the new Khobuntian warlords were quick and painless. No one wanted to antagonize—Guin had known them all since childhood and there were no hard feelings or agendas on either side. Trev'nor wished that all talks would go that smoothly.

With an agreement settled between Khobunter and Hain, Guin turned his attention to the magic council for the rest of the evening. Garth, Guin, and Raile closeted themselves off to the side for most of it, speaking to each other in low tones, no doubt plotting on how to form a new council. Trev'nor put in a good word at the beginning for Uncle Roarke before retreating to join the others. He considered going back over and butting into the conversation until he remembered that

Garth was adamant that politicians and magicians should not mix more than necessary. Granted, Trev'nor had a leg on either side of that fence, but these days he weighed more on the 'politician' side.

Besides, did he want even more responsibilities?

Deciding it best to leave that alone, he let them discuss. When they reached a conclusion, they'd tell everyone and Trev'nor could wait until then. He chose instead to do some stretches and light sparring with Tyvendor, catching up with him, then retired for the night. By the time he headed for bed, Guin was gone, Kaydan having collected him at some point. Nolan wasn't in the house either, supposedly at Asla and Xiaolang's, talking to his father and grandfather.

Trev'nor woke up the next morning to a pounding on his door. After so many months of living in a quasi-battlefield, Trev'nor's eyes snapped open and he was out of bed before he could even question who it might be. Throwing open the door, he found Nolan on the opposite side. "What?"

"The warlords have an answer for us," Nolan responded, excitement and nerves warring over his face. "We'll convene in an hour."

Trev'nor promptly closed the door on him and dove for his last set of clean clothes. He really missed his batman Mose right now.

In half an hour he'd eaten a light breakfast, redone his hair, put on fresh clothes and fell to pacing around their living area waiting on the other two. Well, no, Nolan was ready to go as well. Becca had yet to emerge. Trev'nor wanted to make some sarcastic comment of women always taking longer to get ready, but she actually could get ready faster than he and Nolan combined, so he bit his tongue.

When she did emerge, Becca had her hair done in a rather elaborate five strand plait, Trev'nor's meuritta in her hands. Priya looked quite pleased with herself. Giving her an exasperated glare, Trev'nor demanded, "Is that where you've been? I could have used your help, you know."

The meuritta chittered at him dismissively, then leaped out of Becca's hands and bounded over to him, demanding to be picked up. Sighing, he bent to scoop her up and give her a rub. "You're being very capricious, as usual. Alright, everyone ready? Let's go. And no, missy, that doesn't include you."

"Might as well, it'll take ten minutes to walk over there, and it doesn't hurt to be a little early." Nolan gave the rest of the room a smile, as their mentors all looked a trifle anxious this morning. "It'll be alright. I think."

"You were doing really well until those last two words," Becca mourned. "Where's Xiaolang? We could really use an empath about now."

"Tell me about it," Trev'nor grumbled, putting his meuritta firmly in Garth's hands, opening the main door and stepping out of the apartment. "Wish us luck!"

"Luck!" four voices caroled back to him.

Trev'nor regretted eating breakfast almost immediately as his stomach started churning in uneasy knots. Why had he thought eating anything a good idea? He risked a glance at Nolan, but his friend looked rather calm about the whole situation. Becca, at least, shared his nerves, as she kept fidgeting with the hem of her coat, adjusting it over and over again. Then again, Nolan was an old hand at negotiations and diplomacy. He and Becca were the novices.

"I think I would rather go into a battle than another conference this morning," Becca whispered to him.

"You're not the only one," he muttered back.

Nolan had the gall to chuckle. "It'll be fine, you two. If it was a flat 'no,' we would have gotten the answer the first day. But they took a full day to think about it, which means they like the idea. They just want to hammer out a few concessions on our end."

"Is that what it is?" Trev'nor liked the sound of that.

A lot. But if that was the case… "Wait, couldn't you have mentioned this yesterday?"

"At what point did we have time to talk about this yesterday?" Nolan responded in exasperation, giving him a pointed look. "Besides, there's a small possibility I could be wrong. They could have delayed to talk further with Rowe."

"Lovely," Becca groaned. "I could have done without that possibility, thank you."

"Hey, sharing is caring."

"Is not," she sniped back.

Trev'nor ignored the bickering, staring at the square, grey-stoned conference building in front of them. His nerves hopped like a frog in a hot skillet. He really, truly, would prefer a fight over this. At least with battles, he knew what to expect. Swallowing bile down hard, he forced himself to at least look calm as they ascended the short steps and entered.

The inside looked slightly dimmer than the outside, largely due to the lack of natural light. Trev'nor spied An Meiling and Li Shen already seated and gave both of them a proper good morning. An Meiling actually gave him a hug, beaming up at him and whispering, "Don't be nervous, it's all good news."

And that was why he loved empaths. "Really? Good, my breakfast has a chance of staying in my stomach, then. Thank you for telling me."

"There's a few points you'll need to discuss and agree on," Li Shen warned, "but I don't think any of them are unreasonable."

Trev'nor really wanted him to define 'unreasonable' but they didn't have time to discuss it as Casimir entered with his councilors in that moment. Sensing his chance to talk one-on-one had ended, Trev'nor gave them both a nod and resumed his seat at the head of the table. Nolan and Becca looked up as he joined them and Becca leaned in to whisper against his ear, "What did they say?"

"That we don't need to be nervous," he whispered back.

Nolan let out a little hiss of triumph before turning and giving Casimir a civil, "Good morning, Warlord Casimir."

"Good morning, Prince Nolan," the Warlord of Osmar returned, equally cordial. "Warlord Trev'nor, Warlord Becca, good morning to you as well."

"Good morning," Becca returned with a winsome smile. "Good morning, Warlord Vanya, Warlord Gaidar."

"Good morning," the men returned as they entered and took up their own seats.

Trev'nor caught Xiaolang's eye and was reassured all over again at the subtle wink the man threw him. So even Xiaolang felt that they would be able to accept the terms the other warlords had come up with?

Vanya stood, looking around the table, and gave a grunt of satisfaction. "I see that we are all here. Excellent. Let's begin."

Becca lay flat on the couch in their Ascalon apartment, a cold cloth over her eyes. She didn't really have a headache per se, more like her brain wanted to leak out of her ears. Those 'simple negotiations' had taken at least nine hours. Her voice had nearly given out before her brain did. Trev'nor hadn't fared much better. In fact, the only one of them that seemed to think nothing of it was Nolan.

The Prince of Chahir could not be underestimated for his stamina.

Both meurittas and Tail took advantage of a stationary person and cuddled in against both sides with Tail on her thighs, contented purrs and chitters coming from them. Becca sporadically moved her hands between the three, rubbing behind ears, but even those movements taxed her brainpower.

Someone entered with a polite rap on the door. "Oh? You're all back. Did negotiations succeed?"

Becca knew she should probably sit up and answer Garth properly but didn't have the energy for it. "They did."

"Actually, they went very well," Nolan answered from somewhere nearby. "They asked for typical concessions, like peace treaties and trade rights, with a few extras thrown in. They asked Becca for more rainstorms in the northern area and requested that Trev'nor visit the main roads at least once a year and keep them in good repair."

"I told them I might not do it personally, but we have three other Earth Mages now in Khobunter, plus a trained Elemental Mage, and one of us would certainly do it." Trev'nor sounded past exhausted, his normally smooth tenor rough around the edges. Coughing a little, he stopped talking.

Becca lifted a corner of the cloth to peek out and saw not only Garth but Raile also join them, taking chairs. Both men looked tired as well, but then, they'd been involved in their own negotiations. "How fared it on your end?"

"We have an agreement with Hain on who should form up the new council. Not everyone on it was corrupt—Doss, for instance, and Odanne—but most of it will be replaced. If you two will agree to bring Khobunter under our jurisdiction?" Raile paused to get nods from them both before continuing, "Then we will form under the newly organized council. While we're at it, we're changing some of the laws that govern us, as some of them are just archaic. We've hammered out the basic laws and oaths that should govern our magicians and I'll put it in a more neatly written form tomorrow. We can't trust Garth's handwriting."

"Hey," Garth objected good-naturedly. "It's legible, isn't it?"

"No," Raile denied dryly, "it really isn't. Once I have it written up, take a while to review it, then sign. I need you both to sign."

"We're waiting on the official treaty with the other Sol Warlords to be written up as well," Nolan assured him. "So we'll be here tomorrow regardless. But we really have to leave after that; we can't spend any further time here."

"Understandable," Raile assured him. "But I'm very curious now. What will they do about Rowe?"

"They'll send an official message to Warlord Rowe that they've signed a treaty with us and that they won't take part in any internal conflict in Khobunter. Basically, they're throwing the ball back into their court." Nolan paused before adding truthfully, "I don't know how Rowe will react to that."

"Dunixan is of the opinion that Rowe has to be seriously pressed before he'll move," Trev'nor explained to them, pausing only long enough to drink something. "And I'm not sure if being denied by Ascalon is enough to press them to attack. We promised to send our own message to Rowe, which I suppose Nolan or Becca needs to write tomorrow."

"I'll do it," Becca volunteered, still firmly not moving. She had purring creatures to think of, after all. "Dunixan gave me an idea of how to approach them before we left, so I have a fair idea of what to say. I just hope that they won't react like Riyu or Trexler did. I'd prefer to avoid another fight."

"I think we'd all prefer that." Garth sounded a little amused as he asked, "How are you doing, Becca?"

"Just tired," she responded, half-honest. In truth, she missed Rahim fiercely. Right now, she wanted nothing more than to have him on hand for some much needed cuddles. But she didn't want to say that aloud, as the boys would surely tease her for it. Instead, she glossed over it. "I need to recover some brain power so that I can start those promised storms. It'll be a sign of good faith for our new allies."

"That's a good plan," Raile approved. "I wish I could help you, child."

"Me too," Becca groaned. There were definite drawbacks to being the only living Weather Mage. Sitting up, she let the cloth fall to her lap, as she really did need to participate in this conversation. The meurittas abandoned her when she did so, going to join their boys, but Tail shifted so he could stay in her lap. "Raile, Tyvendor made a comment earlier that puzzled me. Is he intending to come up and help with Khobunter?"

"He is. I mentioned to him that someone up there is

messing with the air currents, which was what sent you north in the first place, and he agrees with your assessment that it's likely an Air Mage. I think he wants to be on hand just in case your guess is right. He won't be able to come immediately, however, as he has a few personal issues to settle before he can move up to Rheben." Raile paused and added more frankly, "I think this is his apology for doubting you and not asking more questions of the Trasdee Evondit Orra."

"I'll take it." Becca frankly didn't care what motivated people as long as they came to help. "I won't ask him to fight, though, that's not his job."

"My dear child, if you think you can keep Tyvendor out of the fight, you don't know him well at all," Raile opined with a pointed look at her.

Alright, well, she couldn't argue that. Tyvendor was definitely of the proactive personality type. "I'm not saying I won't take the help if he offers, I just won't ask it of him."

"Another mage will help with the battles, although I'm still holding out hope we can negotiate the last two into an alliance." Trev'nor leaned over in his chair to snag her cloth and put it over his own eyes. He slid down to slump in a boneless sprawl. "I will be so glad when all the talking is over and we can go back to what we're supposed to be doing."

"Are you talking about planting or governing?" Nolan asked, amused.

"Yes."

Becca considered the timeline for leaving and the logistics of traveling back for a moment before double checking, "Garth, you still plan to go up with us?"

"I do, if only for a few days. I want to see everything you've done and do a little research in Rheben and Sha, see if I can't trace which ancestor it was who built the two places."

"We'd all like the answer to that," Raile observed. "You three don't need to worry about playing host for us, I'll show him around. I know you have enough to do as it is and not enough hours in the day to do it."

Wasn't that the truth. Alright, well, if Raile wanted to play tour guide for Garth, she wouldn't protest. "Then I won't wait for either of you. Trev, Nol, I vote we leave day after tomorrow, first thing in the morning."

"Agreed," Nolan said promptly with a nod.

Trev'nor waved a tired hand. "Fine, fine."

Maybe she could sleep on the way up? Cat certainly didn't need her guidance, after all, and the saddle was made to keep her in position. Becca felt tired enough right now that it actually sounded like a good idea. And didn't that say something. She glanced out the window, saw light, and decided that she didn't care if it wasn't late enough in the day. "I'm going to bed."

"Bed," Trev'nor said dreamily. "I like beds."

"You know you've reached adulthood when you're no longer interested in staying up until bird's hours of the morning," Garth observed.

Unable to refute that, Becca just stumbled toward her room.

If someone had warned her just how much paperwork went into running a country, Becca would have come up with a Plan B. Nolan surely knew, right? As a friend, shouldn't he have warned them?

It took another day and a half to finalize the treaties, sign everything, and get copies of them for their own records. Becca did not like the extra delay in leaving, which put them arriving in Riyu close to midnight. Fortunately, they didn't need to worry about Raile. Sallah had already retreated to Rheben, running the academy while Raile was gone, but Garth was kind enough to take Raile back. Having one more thing to think about would have sent her straight over the edge.

She at least had the energy to stay awake in the saddle on the flight back to Riyu. She spent the majority of her time getting her storm systems lined up for the next few days. Everyone got rain, but the areas that hadn't been reconditioned by Trev'nor and Azin only got a light sprinkling.

Riyu finally bloomed into sight. Unlike previous times, it didn't have the creeping inky blackness to it. The city had its own light. As they came in closer, Becca blinked behind her goggles, surprised at how much of the city now had street lights. They had to be street lights, they were too regularly spaced to belong to individual buildings. When had that happened?

Azin. It must have been Azin. No one else would have the magical ability to pull this off. They had her work with metal so often that Becca often forgot that flame itself lay within Azin's domain as well.

With a lazy back flap of wings, Cat landed on top of the wall, crouching low so that Becca could converse easily with the guard on duty. Becca saluted. "Fourth Guard, how is the watch?"

"It is well, my Warlord," the young man responded with a sharp salute to her. "Welcome back, my Warlord. May I escort you to the fortress?"

"No need, I dropped here just long enough to make sure there weren't any problems in the city. Nothing's happened while we were gone?"

Shaking his head, he assured her, "Nothing truly serious, my Warlord. Warlord Dunixan and General Danyal have managed things in your absence, although I'm sure they'll be glad you've returned so quickly."

"Yes, no doubt," she agreed with a quick smile, already readying for takeoff. "Alright, then, I'll head to the fortress.

Keep up the good work."

"Safe return, my Warlord," the guard wished her before stepping back and giving Cat the necessary room to take off again.

Cat covered the rest of the distance in minutes, landing on top of the fortress, as Garth rested on the lower perch and left her no room to maneuver in. Becca didn't care, it involved climbing stairs either way. Sliding down, she unbuckled the main cinch and took the saddle off Cat's back with a pat of thanks. "You flew well, my friend. Thank you. Go to the kitchens and order yourself a cow, alright?"

"Two cows," Cat immediately bargained.

Laughing, Becca agreed, "I think you've earned two. Off with you."

With a deep throated purr, Cat hopped off the side of the fortress, gliding down and around toward the kitchens. Becca took a moment to doff helmet and goggles, thankful to get out of the things, as it felt like she had no circulation left in her face because of them.

"Becca."

Whirling, she found Rahim at the top of the stairs, his uniform jacket still on even at this hour of the evening. Dropping the saddle and riding gear, she went straight for him, and he met her partway to catch her up in a firm embrace. Burying her head into his shoulder, she breathed in the scent of him, sunshine and musk. She felt herself relax for the first time in days. "Missed you."

"Missed you terribly," he whispered against her hair, his arms tightening. "I know that it made the most sense for you to go and for me to stay, but can we avoid that next time?"

"Like the plague," she swore vehemently. Pulling back, she caught his head in both hands and kissed him thoroughly. He kissed back, just as hungry to touch her, not at all willing to part.

They finally did, because air was rather important to

the breathing process. Becca didn't retreat more than a few inches. Rahim didn't let her go any further than that, either. His dark eyes searched her face in the failing light, looking for something and finding it. "You succeeded?"

"We did," she announced proudly. "We have a written treaty with Osmar, Ascalon, Warwick, and Q'atal that includes trading rights. King Guin of Hain came up and negotiated an alliance with us as well. The other warlords did ask for a few other things, like keeping up the roads near the border, and I promised to send more rainstorms their direction, but overall they were just really happy to have a neighbor that didn't want to conquer them."

He let out a breath of relief, the tension in his body leaving in a rush. "I'm so glad."

Worry had etched lines around his eyes and dark circles under them. Becca decided she would tell him about the clash with the Trasdee Evondit Orra tomorrow, after he'd gotten a good night's sleep. Instead she asked, "What happened while we were gone?"

"Thankfully, nothing dramatic. We finished rebuilding Jashni and did the upgrades to Riyu to make it safer here. We're still tracking down all of the criminal groups but we've made good progress, I think. Raja Dunixan has been very determined to get things done, as he doesn't want problems festering while we deal with Von."

"I think we all share that opinion." Linking her arm with his, Becca started down the stairs, her stomach grumbling petulantly for food. Aside from a midday snack, she hadn't eaten since this morning. "Have you eaten?"

"Earlier, but I'll keep you company. I take it you didn't eat on the flight here?"

"Not really, we were trying to get home as quickly as possible, as we had a late start this morning. Ah, before I forget, you'll be meeting two of my mentors rather soon. Garth came up to Ascalon—I'll explain why tomorrow, it's rather complicated—and he actually wants to take a quick tour before returning home, see what we've done up here. I expect him either tomorrow or the day after. Tyvendor will be here in another week or two. He's an Air Mage from Bromany and was one of my teachers when I was younger. He's very, very upset with what's happened up here and has volunteered to come help for a while."

Rahim paused at the landing, studying her expression. "You look incredibly happy that these men are coming."

"I want to show off a little," she confessed, cheeks heating in a light blush. "And Tyvendor is a force to reckon with. He's an incredibly strong mage in his own right, and I'll need his help later, I think."

Still not willing to continue their trek down to the dining area, Rahim's expression tightened into one of concern. "Why do you think so?"

"I mentioned before that someone's messing with the air currents up north? I thought I did, I forget who I tell what. Well, there's only two types of magicians that can directly impact air currents like that aside from me. Either Elemental or Air Mages. My money's on an Air Mage in Von. If I'm right, and I think I am, then I might need Tyvendor's help to deal with this person."

Far from being reassured, this alarmed Rahim further. "Why? You've managed fights before with magicians involved."

"Rahim…" Becca trailed off, not sure how frank to be about this. "Fights between mages are a different thing altogether. I only know of one fight between two mages in recent history, and it was between Garth and an insane Fire Mage in Chahir. It leveled several city blocks."

He jerked back, thoroughly alarmed now. "They're that destructive?! No, I suppose that makes sense, I've seen how much power you wield. Then you hope, what, that having another mage with you that can fight with air will help you subdue this person quickly?"

"And minimize the damage, yes, that's exactly what I'm hoping." Stifling a tired yawn, she tugged him back into motion. "But that's a different problem for another day. Feed me."

Snorting, he let himself be led downward. "As you wish, my Becca."

Trev'nor headed into his office the next morning while stifling a yawn. He'd gotten good sleep the night before, but for some reason, days on end of talking exhausted a man as much as hard physical labor would. He couldn't say he was glad to be home, as Riyu certainly wasn't that, but he was glad to be back in his usual routine. At least here, if he wanted something done, he didn't have to pass it through a committee first.

He sat in his office chair, reaching for the daily report on his desk, then paused as a knock sounded on the door. "Ah, Amir, you're back!"

"Yes, Raja, just yesterday. We came back a little earlier than planned." Amir had the content expression of a man newly married, every hair in place and his uniform starched to within an inch of its life.

Waving the man in, Trev'nor inquired, "Was it a good wedding? No problems, I hope?"

"A snag in my bride's hemline was the only disaster, and that easily remedied," he responded with a bright smile. "In all, both families were very happy we could finally marry. Thank you for the generous gift and time off, Raja. Without you and Raya Becca, this would not have been possible."

Trev'nor knew him to speak perfect truth but waved it aside. "It shouldn't have been this difficult to begin with. I'll ask on Becca's behalf: did your wife agree to come up?"

"She did, Raja; in fact, she feels very flattered to be considered for the position of lady-in-waiting. I believe she wants to speak with Raya Becca today and get started." Amir tactfully paused before asking, "Your diplomatic talks, did they go well?"

"Fortunately, they did. We had a little trouble with the magic council, but I'll brief you, Dunixan, and Danyal all at the same time. I'm waiting on everyone else to eat breakfast before we convene for a meeting and catch up with each other."

"I see. Then I will contain my questions."

"Trexler," Trev'nor pressed, truly worried that their daily check-ins weren't enough. "How was Trexler?"

"Still a little rough in areas," Amir admitted frankly, "but in better shape than when we left it. The gardeners sent that direction, and the two magicians from Bromany, have done a wealth of good in the province. I've never seen it so green and lush before. It looked like a garden."

Those words meant the world to Trev'nor and he fought to keep himself from grinning like an idiot. "Does it really?"

"Indeed yes, Raja, it was amazing to behold. The garden you started with the others, I thought it impressive, but it's now at the height of maturity. I'm also happy to report that your order to harvest the garden to feed the poor in the city is going very well. I double checked, but there have been no reported cases of death by starvation since we left."

Trev'nor punched a fist in the air, victory giving him a heady high. "Yes! That's what I want to hear. So their weekly reports really are the only troubles? Nothing else? Bless you, Amir, that sets my mind at ease."

"I'm happy to report good news," Amir admitted, grinning back at him. "They did have a request for you, however. They want to expand the gardens. You've mentioned before that you have plans to make all of Khobunter into a garden, but

I know other areas take priority. Do you have a timeline of when you can return to Trexler and expand the gardens?"

"Not right now," Trev'nor answered, wishing he could say differently. Sitting back in his chair, he thought about it, trying to think long-term for once. With so many emergencies demanding his attention, thinking ten or even one year from now sometimes proved difficult. "Our immediate plan is to put a garden around each city. After that's done, then the places that need more development will get made top priority and we'll tackle them in order. In your opinion, do they need extra help? I can request one of the magicians in Rheben to swing by, maybe treat the place like a class project."

Amir hesitated strongly before admitting, "Perhaps a little? They're managing, but I think they're barely managing, and having a little in storage wouldn't hurt."

"No, it wouldn't." Trev'nor thought about it some more, then nodded. "Tell you what, Amir. It happens that my mentor is in Rheben right now. I'll call him and ask for a favor, see if he can swing by and recondition the soil for me before coming up here. It'll only take a few hours for him. They have enough seeds and such on hand that they can handle the planting well enough."

Amir nodded, relieved. "I'll leave you to manage it, Raja."

Another knock sounded at the door, this time from Nolan. "Oh good, Amir's back. Congratulations on your marriage, Lieutenant."

Standing, Amir turned and gave him a bow. "Thank you, Raja Nolan. I'm happy it went well and am glad to be back on duty."

"We missed you," Nolan informed him, expression a little rueful. "We sent you off just when we needed you, but I'm glad for your sake you went. Trev, I think we're all ready for the meeting."

"Then let's go up." Trev'nor followed Nolan's lead and

went up to the third level and the main war room, Amir following along behind.

This early in the morning not much traffic filled the hallways yet, although Trev'nor saw a few people and exchanged greetings with them on the way. The war room doors were wide open, and several overlapping voices poured through. He recognized all of them, so wasn't surprised to see the group gathered inside. Simin stood on guard near the door, as usual. Azin and Ehsan spoke quietly together, not seated yet. Dunixan, Danyal, and Becca already sat at the table. In fact, Trev'nor would bet his left eye that Becca and Danyal held hands under the table.

Love birds. Seriously.

Ignoring that, he took a seat next to Dunixan, listening with half an ear as Nolan closed the doors and everyone else joined them at the table. "I appreciate you covering for us while we were down there."

"My pleasure," Dunixan responded, then grimaced and added truthfully, "Well, no, it was a headache, but I was glad to do it since you apparently achieved the impossible down there. Becca's shown me the treaties you signed. Good work. I don't think Khobunter's had a signed peace treaty with any state in the Empire of Sol in the whole history of the country. You even managed to get an alliance with Hain, which I don't think has ever happened."

"It has not," Danyal agreed with a proud smile at Becca. "It makes the achievement even more impressive."

Becca blushed prettily under his regard before clearing her throat and trying to look more raya-ish. "I think they were glad to have someone in charge uninterested in conquering them. Now, the thing that I haven't told anyone yet was about our clash with the Trasdee Evondit Orra."

"Who?" Dunixan asked slowly, his gaze turning inwards. "I feel like I know the name, but I can't quite place it."

"Magic council in Hain," Trev'nor explained for him,

Danyal, and Amir. "They managed all of the magicians who also lived in Chahir, Coven Ordan, and such, but…well, things happened."

"The reason why our mentor came to Ascalon when he did was because he heard a report that the Trasdee Evondit Orra had sent a circle up to intercept us and strip us of our magic," Nolan reported factually.

Danyal slammed an open palm against the tabletop, expression furious. "They did what?!"

"Is that even possible?" Ehsan asked incredulously. "Even with powerful mages like all of you?"

"With a full circle it's possible," Nolan confirmed darkly. Waving Danyal down, Nolan silently requested for him to calm while he explained. Trev'nor let his friend tell the story, as his throat still felt a little raw after so much talking. Was being able to talk for long stretches of time some sort of princeling training? Or did Nolan cheat with life magic? He'd have to ask.

By the time Nolan finished, Danyal, Ehsan, and Azin looked ready to ride off to war. Dunixan had his head in both hands. Trev'nor couldn't blame them, his emotions sat somewhere in between those two reactions. Even Simin's hand kept clenching and unclenching around her sword hilt, itching for a target to pound her fury out on.

Danyal turned to Becca with a distinct tic going off in the corner of his jaw. "You could have told me about this last night."

"I wanted to celebrate being back last night, not make you steaming mad," she responded, not bothered by this accusation. "Besides, Rahim, I think you missed the point. They didn't get their way. We won that argument."

"And we managed to keep it contained, so it didn't affect the talks. Xiaolang handled the situation for us, so the warlords were content to let us manage things," Trev'nor declared. "Or at least, they were willing to ignore it, as it never came up in the talks. Which I'm willing to take, really. Anyway, we mention this now so that you're aware that half the trouble we were expecting on a magic-political level just disappeared. The re-organized magic council is being formed as we speak, and eventually we'll have members of that council visit us formally, but I don't know when that will be."

"Likely not anytime soon. This sort of thing takes time." Nolan looked between the others, especially Azin and Ehsan, with a last warning. "But do not take them lightly just because they've taken our side this time. We still have a certain level of ethics to uphold, and they will not go easy on us if they feel we've crossed that line."

"Understood," Dunixan answered pensively. "We'll all bear that in mind."

"Good." Becca waved a hand, dismissing the topic. "Now, next topic, and this is the important one. I sent a message to Rowe this morning stating that we had no intention to march on them if they were willing to try negotiations first. I expect a response in the next week. But I think we should follow it up with a more formal declaration of our intentions and demands."

Dunixan nodded firmly. "I agree. In fact, I took the liberty of drafting something for you. Here."

Trev'nor took the page from him and read it through, finding that it was more or less a summary of the agreement they had with Dunixan. It gave Rowe the same position and power, subservient to their own, with the condition that they accept the new laws and free all the slaves. It was remarkably straightforward with little of the usual greetings and formal language that Trev'nor saw in such official documents. Then again, this was only meant to be a rough draft. Sliding it across the table to Becca, he let her have a chance to read it.

"I like it," she informed Dunixan, sliding it toward Nolan next.

"So do I," Trev'nor admitted. "It's more or less our agreement with you, which is what we want. But what are the odds that Rowe or Von will take it?"

"I give it even odds that Rowe will accept." Dunixan steepled his fingers under his chin, his black hair flopping a little too far over his forehead and into his eyes. The man needed a haircut. "You must understand, Rowe doesn't have the same military force as the others. They've been whittled down by Riyu over the years and we all gave it another two years, maximum, before Riyu took them in force. It's part of the reason why they approached Ascalon—they don't have the means to fight you off themselves."

"They took Rurick," Azin objected. "Doesn't that speak of military strength?"

Trev'nor shook his head and corrected grimly, "We unfortunately set them up for that. Rurick's guards were more or less wiped out by us, so even with the strong walls, they had no one to defend them. Rurick was prime for picking."

Dunixan laid a hand on his shoulder, squeezing once in a comforting way, his dark eyes sympathetic as they met Trev'nor's. "Unfortunately correct. They'd never have managed it otherwise."

"Makes sense," Becca allowed. "So, you think they'd rather negotiate than fight anyway."

"Especially considering what you do to a territory after you take it," Dunixan confirmed, turning to look at her more directly. "They'll be financially better off. The only thing that will temper the odds is their pride, which is strong. We'll have to be very careful how we word the offer to avoid slighting them. Still, I give it a good chance of succeeding."

"As do I," Danyal agreed. "But Von will not likely take it."

"No," Dunixan sighed, rubbing at his temples. "No, they likely will not. I suggest that we send messages to both before marching on them, on the off chance I'm somehow wrong and Von has the sense to accept your terms. They might, especially if you can convince Rowe to ally with us. It will mean the entire country is against them and surely even Von's general won't fight against such staggering odds."

Trev'nor found that last statement somewhat confusing. "I'm sorry, why are you specifically mentioning his general and not Von himself?"

"Ah." Dunixan's head swiveled back to him, canted a little in question. "Have I not told you about this? I can see I haven't. Von himself is not a particularly power hungry ruler. He's actually more humane than most of the warlords, mainly because he's following the business model of his predecessor, but he has little military ability. He's a bureaucrat, not a fighter. His general, Ajil, was appointed over all military affairs some ten years ago and he's as formidable as a lion. Nothing gets past the borders because of Ajil."

"And he has considerable pull with the warlord and won't like the idea of an alliance?" Becca guessed.

"Not by even one grain of sand," Dunixan confirmed darkly. "I know, I've tried to bargain with the man before. A wounded scorpion is more docile."

Trev'nor didn't like the sound of that at all. He hated the idea that they would once again have to battle it out with someone, force them to come under their rule, but it might well come down to that.

"Still, this sounds somewhat promising?" Nolan offered thoughtfully. "If Von is a different type of ruler than what we've seen so far—excluding you, of course, Dunixan—then that means Von itself won't be in very bad shape. We won't have to overhaul its economy like we've done everywhere else."

"There is that." Trev'nor liked this point a lot. Not just because it would save them considerably in terms of money and manpower, but also because it meant people weren't suffering needlessly. "Alright, Dunixan, you've dealt with them before, how should we word the letter to Von?

Aggressively?"

"No other way to do it," Dunixan assured him, mouth in a flat line. "If you try to be diplomatic, they won't take you seriously at all."

"Right. Then I vote we have Becca write the one to Von—"

"Just what are you trying to say, huh?" she challenged with a glint of humor in her eyes.

Trev'nor wisely ignored her. "—and we'll put our heads together to write something to Rowe. Amir, if you could help us translate after we're done? I think this had better be said in Khobuntish."

"Of course, Raja," Amir assured him. "In fact, Raya, may I aid you?"

"I will be glad to have your help," she informed him, waving him into the empty seat next to her.

Danyal would help her too, of course. Trev'nor wasn't worried about her, especially since they didn't think the letter would work anyway. But how to phrase this delicately so that Rowe would agree?

That was the question.

8

Becca could only take so much diplomacy for the day before she had to escape outdoors. Rahim went with her, their excuse being that she needed to get those storms formed up for their new allies, and he needed to properly safeguard her while she did it. Absolutely everyone saw the excuse for what it was, but they just smiled indulgently and shooed them on.

Becca headed for the new gardens, partially because it offered some privacy there, partially because she wanted to see the condition of the soil and judge just how much rain to bring in. They walked hand in hand, his calluses and skin warm against her own. They got looks from the soldiers, but she ignored those. Rahim did as well, which pleased her enormously.

The garden area outside the city had areas designated for crops, then another for an orchard, all of the plants half-grown in a state of maturity. So, Nolan hadn't encouraged them to full maturity before he left? Perhaps he'd been conserving magical power. Frowning, she knelt and put a finger straight into the soil, testing it. "Seems rather dry. I thought I sent a storm this direction on the flight up here."

"You did," Rahim assured her, looking out over the area, alert as always. "It stayed for only an hour or so, though."

"An hour?" Becca had intended for an afternoon.

Swearing, she stood up, brushing the dirt off her hand. "Curse that mage to the ninth circle. I meant for it to stay longer than that. I really shouldn't try to work weather and fly at the same time, I obviously can't do the two at once. Alright, new storm."

Rahim watched as she formed storm clouds, dark and heavy, his face turned toward the sky. "It always fascinates me watching you do this. Does it ever feel mundane to you?"

"Never," she assured him with a quick smile. "Because every storm is different. How were things while we were gone?"

"As well as to be expected. Raja Dunixan has a different way of managing things. It's not a complaint," he added hastily, "it's just that he has…hmm, how to say this? A more business approach to problems? You and Raja Trev'nor and Raja Nolan, you approach the heart of the matter."

"Ah. Well, that doesn't surprise me, he's a businessman at heart. But things went well enough, eh? Good." The storm above her became thick and saturated with rain. She made a few tweaks so that it wouldn't just gush, but fall in a steady and soft pattern. There, perfect for watering. "Alright, retreat."

They retreated to the gardening shed nearby, standing under the narrow porch, and she let the clouds loose. Rain fell in a soft mist, perfect for soaking the tender stalks of the plants, and they watched it silently for a time, just enjoying each other's company.

"How is your new batman? Batwoman?" Rahim frowned, puzzled over the term. "I believe she is normally a lady-in-waiting."

"I have no idea what to call her," Becca admitted cheerfully. "Nahla's equally confused. I only met her briefly this morning, but she strikes me as a very organized, go-get-'em type. I can see why she and Amir work together well as a couple, as they're both very work-oriented. She peppered me with questions, mostly on the logistics of how we move and how long we stay in a new area, what meetings and trips I had planned for the future, and so forth. I answered as best I could, but…" Becca trailed off with a splay of her free hand and a shrug.

"It's hard to predict," Rahim finished in perfect understanding. "Like this last trip you took down to Ascalon, none of us anticipated that."

"I think her plan is to keep a formal uniform pressed and ready at all times, just in case. Which, really, is the best way to go about it." Nahla had also delicately asked if Becca would need a wedding dress soon, which was a question she really wanted an answer to herself. She and Rahim barely had time to themselves, and they'd just started dating, so it likely would be pushing things to make any decisions just yet. Still, a part of Becca felt she'd already found the right person.

Studying him from the corner of her eye, she wondered: did he feel the same?

Oblivious to her thoughts, Rahim leaned his tall frame back against the wall, propping himself up comfortably. "I realized this morning that by the end of this year, you'll have all of Khobunter under your control."

She blinked, jarred by that statement. She hadn't thought that far ahead at all. "Busted buckets, you're right. Our battles for a territory never take more than a month, and if we can really talk Rowe into an alliance…we might actually have them both under control before the year is out."

Rahim's dark eyes studied her, mouth quirked up at the corner. "Are you scared or happy about that?"

"I'll figure it out and let you know," she responded faintly. Even if that had been her goal from the beginning, it hadn't hit her on an emotional level until that casual statement. Ye little gods and pink elephants, the idea of being a ruler for an entire country made her head spin.

Putting an arm around her shoulders, he leaned in to press a kiss against her temple. "Don't be scared. I'm with you every step of the way."

She leaned into him, snuggling. "The Gardeners did indeed know what they were doing when they sent you to me."

Rahim froze, grip tightening reflexively. "You think so too? That I was prepared to meet you?"

"I didn't even think of it until Shad said something, but yes, I believe he's right. Because you are exactly what we needed, in the moment we needed you most, and I don't believe in coincidences like that." Lifting her head enough to meet his eyes, she added frankly, "They might not have anticipated that our hearts would choose each other, but that's fine, isn't it?"

"It's fine," he assured her softly. "I don't really care how you came to me, just that you have."

Smiling, she snuggled in again, as she felt the same way about it. Struck by a thought, she asked, "Wait. I've been so focused on other things, I didn't think of this before, but you have family living in Trexler, don't you?"

"Ah, yes. My parents, a younger brother, aunts, uncles, cousins. I did send a letter home, telling them about us."

Shrieking hinges. If they really did marry, that meant Becca would inherit a whole new set of relatives. "How, ah, did they take the news?"

"With considerable surprise," he answered, chuckling. "I think my mother was half-convinced I wouldn't be able to marry at all. They took my rise in rank with much celebration, and my news of you with stunned surprise. I received many questions about how we came to be courting. I haven't answered their latest letter yet."

Making a snap decision, Becca asked, "Can I write a note to them as well?"

"You want to?" He tilted his head so that he could see

her face.

"I think I'd better at least say something now, don't you? It will make it easier to talk to them later if we know each other a little now."

This pleased him immensely and he gave her quick, chaste kiss. "Then please do. I'll help you translate it."

"Bless you." Becca had made great strides in being conversational in this language, but her writing skills still left a great deal to be desired. She just didn't have enough practice at it yet.

Something off near the gate caught her attention and she had the rain slacken a little so that she had an unimpeded view. "Oh! Garth's here."

"Where?" Rahim demanded, turning to look where she was pointing. "The man with the white hair?"

"That's him. It went white when he was seventeen and turned Jaunten." Becca moved off at a steady jog, waving her arm over her head as she went. "Garth! Raile!"

Both men turned toward her, away from the gate guard, and waved back.

"Why didn't you call ahead?" she asked, slowing to stand in front of them. "We would have let you in properly instead of making you wait around out here."

"Didn't think of it until we were halfway here," Garth admitted easily. "It's fine, I wanted a look at the gardens anyway. Who's your companion?"

Realizing she was being rude, Becca hastily made introductions. "Rahim, this is Rhebengarthen, Dean of Strae Academy. Garth, this is General Rahim Danyal."

Garth offered him a bow. "Thank you for the gift of your name, General."

"Harmony be with you, Dean," Rahim responded with full courtesy, taking Garth in with a head-to-toe sweep.

They'd told many a story about Garth to their new allies and friends, and Becca could see Rahim struggle to adjust the mental image he had formed of Garth to this man of normal stature with long hair and a kind smile. Of course, that was part of what made Garth so dangerous. No one expected trouble from him at first glance.

"Come see the gardens, then," Becca invited, half-turning to lead the way, adjusting her storm to cease for the time being. "Raile, if you wish to go inside and rest, I'm sure Rahim will escort you."

"No, no, I want to see what you've done as well." Raile waved away this offer.

Becca made sure to adjust her pace so that he could walk without straining. Leading the way, she fell to explaining how the battle to take this place played out, and what plants they put into the garden, allowing them to better feed the people of the city. Garth, of course, had spoken about this a little with the boys already, so he knew some of what they'd done. Still, he asked several more questions, curious and pleased with their work. Raile asked just as many questions, pointing out areas that could be improved upon as they kept expanding.

Becca tried not to feel like she was being graded on a project.

When they reached the end of the gardens, she invited, "Come inside, let's have an early dinner."

"I'd be pleased to," Raile accepted with a glance at Garth. "Although I should check with my ride home."

"That's fine," Garth assured him.

They entered through the side gate, the guards giving her sharper salutes than normal and taking in their guests with avid curiosity. Becca let them speculate; there was no harm to it.

They walked to the fortress, letting both men see the city. Becca saw it again through Garth's eyes as he touched the walls of the buildings they passed, commenting to her that some of them had been formed by hand, others by earth magic, a few places repaired by a witch. To her, all of the red sandstone looked the same, but as they navigated through the narrow, winding roads, she got quite the education of her city's architectural history. Garth especially liked the tall composite street lamps that Azin had crafted along the sidewalks. He paused with his hand on one, looking up at it thoughtfully. "I'm sure that when you get a proper wizard or witch up here, they can spell these to light themselves, but using the dragons to light them instead was a stroke of genius on her part. They're extraordinarily well-crafted. I'd very much like to meet her."

"I'll make sure you do," Becca promised.

They kept walking and Garth stepped in close to her to ask, "So that's your young man?"

She found that question funny as Rahim and Garth were near the same age. "Yes, that's him."

"I see now why Shad liked him. Everything about him screams soldier and he watches you like a hawk. I pity the fool who tries to attack you with him nearby." Garth gave her an approving nod. "You did well choosing him. How is his family taking this?"

"With considerable surprise, or so he tells me. I haven't met them yet, but I should probably make time to do that soon." Although how Becca would manage that, she had no idea. The demands on her time limited her movements. She'd barely been able to carve out these past two hours for a little time with Rahim, and even that had been interrupted. "Did you meet Parisa's parents in Rheben?"

"I did, and I'm heartbroken and pleased at the same time to see them. They never should have been up here in chains." Sorrow passed over his face for a moment before he shrugged it off. "Although I should take comfort in the fact they're safe now. They were astonished to meet me, to hear that they have yet other family members who are also Earth Mages. Trev'nor apparently mentioned to them they had more family but hadn't gone into detail. I want to bring them home at some point so they can properly meet the rest of their family."

He seemed to be asking permission and Becca hastily assured him, "I think that's a wonderful idea. Please do. Their world here in Khobunter is too small, they need to see outside of it."

"Yes, precisely what I thought as well. Good, I'll arrange it." Garth paused at a street corner and looked about him, taking in the new street lights, the pedestrians, the cart vendors with all of their spicy and baked goods. "There's considerable life to this city. Khobunter was not like this before. No city of it was," Garth stated cryptically.

"No, Dean, it was not," Rahim answered, coming up to stand at his side. "They would have only been like this during a festival before our new warlords took over."

"We still have some trouble in the city, as gangs took over part of it," Becca admitted frankly. "But we're slowly curing that problem. How do you know that, anyway? I thought you'd never been farther north than Ascalon."

"The outer walls used to be there," Garth turned to a point that they'd just passed, "not a hundred years ago. This city used to stand at a third of its size. Most of the buildings that stood then aren't around now, so they were flimsy constructs, not something that could last more than a decade. This used to be a far poorer city."

Oh. Becca was always astonished how much an Earth Mage could deduce. "I thought Jaunten knowledge told you."

Shaking his head, Garth denied, "Ascalon is as far as any of my ancestors made it."

"I've always been tempted to have you turn me Jaunten," Becca mentioned as an aside to him. "But Shad warned me it gets terribly confusing in your head sometimes."

"It does. Granted, that knowledge has saved my life on more than one occasion. Actually, I was turned Jaunten to give me the knowledge to survive. But there are times when I really wish I could give the gift back, as it can leave you with a migraine. Although Earth Magic adds to the confusion as well. Here, for instance, I see the city not as it is now, but also as it once was. Very confusing." Garth shook his head in an attempt to dismiss the overlay. "Well. Let's go eat dinner, and then I suppose I should head back home after that."

"So soon?" Becca objected. "At least stay the night, since you don't have a lot of day left."

"It's not like I need the light," he pointed out in amusement.

Ah. True. With his method of traveling underground, it didn't matter what time of day or night it might be. "Still, you'll arrive in the wee hours of the morning that way. Stay tonight, leave in the morning."

Garth hesitated strongly before shrugging and admitting, "I wouldn't mind, if Raile's alright with it?"

Waving this concern off, Raile assured him, "Perfectly. One more night can't hurt."

"I just don't want to leave Chatta on her own for much longer," Garth explained. "She's probably at the end of her rope by now. I left her with arranging substitutes for my classes, and dealing with three children." Garth winced. "If I don't get back soon and help her, she'll scalp me."

Raile chuckled. "With good reason."

"That's fine words, coming from you," Garth groused at him. "You tried to volunteer her to run a new magic council earlier."

"While safely out of her reach. Timing, Garth. You learn timing as you get older."

"Oh, sure, preach timing to me. You're not married to her." To Rahim, Garth confided, "Mark this for future reference. Being married to a magician has many wonderful advantages, but the downside is that they always have their own work pulling at them. Respect their time and energy, and you have a happy wife. Volunteer her for even more projects, she can and will attack you at range."

Rahim wore that inscrutable expression on his face when someone said something he wasn't quite sure how to respond to. He slowly nodded. "I'll remember that."

"He's already good at doing that," Becca dismissed airily, not wanting Rahim to read too much into that advice, "fortunately for my sanity. Alright, gentlemen, let's go eat."

Becca skipped into her rooms with every intention of quickly changing into warmer clothes and maybe pulling her hair up before it drove her absolutely crazy. The desert nights could be as cold as the day was hot, and she wanted an extra layer before she went out to have an after-dinner party with Garth and the boys. As she entered the room, she called out, "Nahla! Are you here?"

"I am, Raya!" her batwoman responded, coming out of her bedroom with two sets of uniforms draped over her arm. In the time since her arrival, Amir's wife had proven to be a godsend. She spoke multiple languages, had common sense, and knew how to be flexible with Becca's foreign upbringing. Amir had likely fallen for the woman because of her mind more than anything else. Not to say Nahla wasn't pretty. She just didn't have the delicate features and slim build that most beauties in Khobunter exhibited. Nahla had a strong bone structure, giving her a striking look instead of something soft and delicate. Her voice was a husky growl, not sweet and high, which Becca found pleasant to listen to. Pausing in the doorway, Nahla cocked her head in question. "What do you need?"

"We're doing a small get-together outside with Garth tonight," Becca explained, already striding for her room. "I need a warmer coat to change into and can you do something with my hair? I've got a storm coming in, so I can't divert the wind, but if I get a strand in my mouth one more time, I'll scream."

"Perhaps a braid?" Nahla offered. "Something tight that will wrap around your head."

"If you have an idea, roll with it," Becca encouraged. "Where's my thick wool jacket?"

Nahla followed her into the room, reminding, "It's at the cleaners after you got dirt all along the sleeve hem. Here, take the blue coat instead, it should be warm enough."

How exactly had she managed without a batwoman before this? "Alright, I'll grab that one."

"Sit first," Nahla encouraged her, moving around Becca so she could finish hanging the uniforms. "I'll do your hair."

Becca obediently sat in front of the mirrored vanity on the low, cushioned stool. As Nahla's fingers expertly undid the ponytail, combing through the tangles, Becca let her eyes drift shut, a sigh escaping her. She'd always loved having her hair played with. It sometimes brought semi-painful memories back to her, dim through the passage of time, of her own mother fixing her hair. Mostly she remembered Aletha or Shad doing it for her until she realized Shad was perfectly terrible with hair. Then she'd only let Aletha or Trev'nor do it.

A knock sounded at the door and Nahla dropped her hair to go answer it. With only one room between her and the door, Becca could clearly hear every word.

"Is Riicbeccaan in?" Carjettaan asked neutrally.

"Yes, she is. Step inside, I'll announce you."

Becca really wanted to send the woman off, as she was still uncomfortable with her, but Carjettaan only spoke to her when necessary. She shoved the feelings of unease aside and rose, moving into the small sitting room. "It's fine, Nahla, thank you. Carjettaan, is something wrong?"

The former Star Order Priest stared her right in the eyes,

her own filled with challenge. "I need to clear the air with you."

Nahla glanced between the two women, waiting for Becca to give her a cue. Unwilling, but seeing the necessity, Becca murmured to her, "Can you pass along the message to the boys that I'll be a bit late? They can start without me."

"Of course, Raya." With a polite duck of the head to Carjettaan, she slipped through the door, shutting it softly behind her.

Becca gestured for Carjettaan to take one of the chairs while she took the opposite, using every trick Nolan had taught her to make the space her own. She kept her chin up, shoulders relaxed, one leg crossed over another in a casual manner. Her stomach quivered and clenched with the desire to run for the hills, but she allowed none of that to reflect on her face.

Her guest did not look as poised or comfortable. Carjettaan sat on the edge of her chair, leaning forward, mouth tight. "Riicbeccaan. I know that you don't like me. I know that it's because of what I was. You have every right to feel the way you do, but if you can't trust me, you can't trust what I'm telling you. For this nation's sake, you must."

Becca had no argument to that. "I know."

"You know, but you can't seem to work your way past it." Frustrated, Carjettaan's hands clenched into fists as they rested on her knees. "What can I do? What can I tell you? There must be something."

Becca had never experienced the childhood fear of a monster under the bed. She'd faced her own boogeyman in a dark sea cave with nothing more than a fishing knife in her hand and a promise that help was coming. But she remembered the first time she'd gone into a fight against someone—the fear and nervousness—and Shad's advice to her had been: Understand your enemy. Figure out their motivations. Sometimes it's as simple as survival. Sometimes it's not. But if you understand them, you'll know how to defeat them, and the fear will be gone.

Her brother might be a pest and a tease, but he'd spoken good counsel to her that day. She'd proven it time and again, especially in this country. Perhaps she should apply that counsel here, too. "I don't understand you."

Carjettaan's fair brows shot straight into her hairline. "About what?"

Shaking her head, Becca repeated more forcefully, "I don't understand you. Why the Star Order? Why join such an evil group? You must have been an initiate when it fell. You had to know that Vonlorisen had changed the laws regarding magic by that point, so why?"

Slowly, Carjettaan straightened, eyes locked with Becca's as she studied the warlord's expression. "I was initiated six months before the laws were changed."

The shaking in Becca's gut stilled, her attention now riveted.

"And I didn't really have much choice in the matter," Carjettaan continued slowly, carefully, each word weighed out before spoken. "I didn't understand the reasons for it at first—that came later—but when my magic began to awaken, they approached me. Said that I had been touched by magic but not like the corrupt ones being born. I was touched with pure magic. I counted myself lucky. I was relieved. Because I had the right type of magic, I wouldn't be executed outright. My family was safe. I didn't question it.

"It was only later, nearly two years later, that I realized what they had meant. I didn't have the full magic talent that a witch or mage did. My talent was easy to change, as it was just magic-touched enough that they could influence it, corrupt it, to conform to their wishes. I was sixteen, Becca."

Becca's eyes swept shut in understanding. Sixteen. Garth's age when he'd escaped into Hain. Cora, Jarod, Krys, Helen, they'd all left about that age. She'd heard how terrified they had been. Being eight years older had not changed the fear. If the Star Order hadn't chased her, but instead offered to turn her into one of their own so she could stay with her family, would she have taken it?

Naïve and sheltered as she had been? Yes. Yes, she would have.

"I didn't understand," Carjettaan whispered. "I truly didn't until the Gardeners reached me. And then they showed me, directly in my mind, what my magic was supposed to do. What I'd been twisted and manipulated away from. And I felt physically ill but it was too late. I couldn't undo the damage already done. The best I could do was move forward. Becca."

She lifted her eyes back up to the woman she no longer hated. She felt nothing more than abject pity and empathy now because she finally understood that Carjettaan was as much a victim as Becca herself.

Carjettaan's voice was choked with emotion, eyes too bright. "When the Gardeners told me what you needed, that I could help, I leapt at the chance. I felt like I finally had the chance to make amends. You don't have to like me, but please, at least let me help you. Properly help you."

Taking in a deep breath, Becca wrestled with her own emotions, trying to push the words past a constricted throat. "I don't hate you. I finally understand you. You're as much a victim as me, Jetta."

Hearing her given name out of Becca's mouth drew Jetta up short and she had to drag her jaw off the ground and back into its socket. "You—you'll forgive me?"

"Forgive a teenage girl who was forced into the Order so she could survive?" Becca shook her head, ashamed now she'd ever doubted either Jetta or the Gardeners. "I wish we'd had this talk earlier. I wouldn't have wasted so much anger on you. I finally understand why Garth and Shad always called for the Gardeners when they found Star Order Priests. They saw what I didn't, apparently. Jetta, this country is filled with good people forced to do things against their conscience in order to live. I don't condemn them for it. I can't condemn you either."

A single tear tracked down the woman's face and she wiped it hastily away, her eyes averted toward the floor. "Thank you."

"I can't promise we'll be bosom buddies," Becca continued with a lopsided smile, "but I will listen. And I'll talk to you properly."

"That's all I ask." Jetta stood and gave her a deep bow. "Thank you."

Becca couldn't wrangle up another word as the woman left, staring at the closed door for several minutes after Jetta was gone. Her heart still hurt. And she hadn't let go of all the anger she still harbored for the Star Order, not by a long shot. But she no longer hated the Legend serving with her.

Nahla returned and helped with her hair. Perhaps sensing Becca's mood, she didn't ask any questions, just helped her into a coat and sent her on her way. Becca walked through the streets of Riyu, trying to calm down, but the walk did little to encourage that. She reached the outer walls and went through the southern gate into the garden the boys had planted. Trees now covered the landscape, most of them fruit or nut trees, and she used the pulsing light ahead to navigate by.

Someone had lugged an iron brazier out into the middle of the garden, stacking wood in it high enough to reach almost bonfire proportions. The two meurittas played hairdresser, and Garth, Trev'nor, and Nolan lounged on stone benches, laughing and at ease. She wished she could feel the same.

Nolan spotted her first, his wide smile of greeting fading as she came into the circle of light. "Uh-oh. What's wrong now?"

"Not wrong," Becca denied, coming to sit next to Garth,

as he had the only spot available. Tail leapt up into her lap as soon as she settled. "I just had a talk with Carjettaan."

Both boys shared a startled glance before they shifted around to face her more directly. Garth picked up on their reactions and asked slowly, "Why is this remarkable?"

"Jetta is a former Star Order Priest, reformed by the Gardeners and brought up here to help us," Trev'nor explained quickly, shifting Priya so he could face Becca more easily. "She's serving as our Legend. Becca's been wary of her since her arrival. Really? You two talked?"

"She told me an abbreviated version of her story." Leaning sideways, Becca looked up at Garth. "Is that why you tried to save them? Because you saw them as victims?"

"I knew they were," Garth explained gently. "I spoke at one point with a wizard named Kamik Dassan. He's a blood magic expert and he broke it down for me, exactly what the Star Order had done to them. It was beyond disturbing. I didn't hold out any hope for the older members—they were too hardened and corrupt at that point—but we tried to save the initiates whenever we could."

Rubbing at her forehead, Becca wished she'd thought to question Shad further about all of this. He'd surely known as well.

"You don't look all that…" Trev'nor trailed off, mouth searching for the right word to end the sentence with.

"Happy? Relieved?" Becca's expression twisted into a grimace. "I don't know what I feel. I feel bad that I didn't question everything before. I do feel better now that I understand Jetta and the others. It's a relief to no longer look at them and see the enemy. But at the same time… she confessed everything to me and I don't know how to carry that. It just adds to everything else I'm carrying and I don't…" she choked and had to stop, catching her breath.

Garth put a warm hand in the middle of her back, rubbing in smoothing circles. "I think you've hit the point we did."

There was a wealth of understanding in his tone. Becca leaned into his side, unable to meet anyone's eyes, but wanting the comfort Garth offered.

"I'm not following," Nolan admitted slowly. "What point?"

"You likely won't feel it, not here," Garth acknowledged, pulling Becca more firmly into his side, keeping an arm around her shoulders. "This isn't your country or your people. Shad and I always felt it the strongest when we were rescuing people out of Chahir. Xiaolang too, in his own way. We grew very emotionally attached to them. Their worries, their concerns, became ours as well. It added to the stress, became a burden, but we couldn't just set the feelings aside."

Yes. Yes, that was exactly what Becca felt now. As if she'd taken Jetta's burden onto her own shoulders. "How did you manage it?"

"You have to look at some of it and say to yourself, can I fix this? Can I do anything about this? And if the answer is no, you force yourself to set it back down. But sometimes you have to realize that you don't need to do anything. What that person needed from you most was your attention. They needed you to listen. The act of listening can be incredibly healing."

Trev'nor moved to sit cross-legged in front of them, his hands worrying at the end of his braid as he stared up at his mentor. "But how do you let go? I know, logically, that there's a lot I can't do anything about. It doesn't mean my emotions cooperate."

"It's hard," Garth admitted. "I found it easier if I could focus my mind on the things that I could do. I couldn't fix the Star Order Priests myself. I couldn't save them. But I could call for someone who could and I could trust them to do the job properly. If you keep chasing after things you can't change, you'll break down eventually. Focus on what you can do. It's the only way to manage and stay sane."

The man comforting her had escaped into a foreign country at sixteen, rescued people out of enemy territory for nearly four years, founded a magical academy, then served as dean while raising three kids. If there was anyone who understood how to deal with extreme stress, it was surely Garth. Becca believed he knew what he was talking about.

"This advice goes both ways," Garth informed them, squeezing Becca's shoulders for a moment. "You're carrying the responsibility of an entire country. Happiness and sorrow both for hundreds of thousands of people. I know you're overwhelmed at times. I know you're struggling. There're adults that can't pull off what you three managed here. You have extraordinary people around you, willing to help at any moment, and you must remember to talk to them. Even just venting your frustrations helps. The Gardeners set this as your task, but they gave you all the help you need, too. Don't lose sight of that."

Some part of her felt that because of her position, Becca couldn't show weakness to others. Hearing Garth say those words, she felt foolish for even thinking it. She couldn't go around bawling her eyes out in the streets, of course, but she had her own inner circle to confide in, didn't she? They were more than enough.

"So you're saying you never lost your temper during all of that?" Nolan asked doubtfully, mouth curved in a teasing manner. "Because we heard about what happened in Jarrell."

"One time," Garth groaned with a dramatic flop of the head. "I destroyed something one time and no one lets me live it down. You weren't even there!"

"Shad likes to tell the story," Becca admitted with a watery giggle.

"I have no idea why I'm friends with him," Garth growled, not sounding all that upset. "For that matter, I don't know why it's his favorite story, as he wasn't there either."

Becca blinked. "He wasn't? But he said he was."

"He was locked up in a crystal the entire fight, he didn't see jack," Garth stated vehemently. "Everything he knows, he learned secondhand."

"Really." It dawned on Becca that she had a very rare opportunity presented to her. She had Garth without any possibility of her brother interfering. "Garth, why don't you tell us what happened in Chahir while you were on those missions? I know we've heard the stories, but I think I'd like to hear your version of events."

"Tit for tat?" he countered with a quick grin. "I'd like to hear it straight from you what happened up here in Khobunter too."

"Deal." Trev'nor scooted in a little closer, his back to the fire, rescuing his braid from the meuritta doggedly determined to re-do it. "Why don't you start with exactly how Night turned Shad Jaunten?"

Trev'nor wiped a little sweat from his forehead before it could slide into his eyes. Today, for some reason, was far hotter than yesterday, despite the fact that Becca had called in shade clouds for him. Undeterred by the heat, he doggedly stayed outside the city wall, determined to expand the gardens further out. Garth had suggested a few things before leaving, ideas to help the water flow better and create shade for the more delicate plants, things that Trev'nor and Nolan really should have considered when putting the garden in the first time.

He tried not to feel like he'd been graded on a class project.

Let's see, the ground here could accept water now. He'd have to expand the irrigation lines a little further out, or get Azin to do it, so that they could put in more fruit trees. Dates would be nice, come to think of it. Or maybe—

"Trev."

Fishing the mirror out of his pocket, he asked, "What, Bec?"

"Rowe responded."

Trev'nor's attention immediately switched from dirt to mirror. "What did they say?"

"That they'd negotiate, but only in person. They actually suggested meeting at the border, on neutral ground.

Dunixan's opinion is that they're serious, and I agree. The meeting is in five days from now. Who do you want to go?"

That didn't require much thought on his part. "I'll go. You took the last one, after all, and if I separate you from Danyal again the man will murder me in my bed."

"It's nice to see you possess such finely-honed survival instincts. Alright, you go. Take Amir with you, though."

"I'll need him," Trev'nor acknowledged ruefully. He absolutely did not want to stumble into a situation where an accent threw his language skills for a loopty-loop and not have a translator on hand. Well, Dunixan of course would help, but it wasn't fair to assume that Trev'nor could take him. "I'd like to take Nolan with me if he's alright with that."

"He says sure."

So, Nolan sat nearby, eh?

"Ah, Dunixan wants to go with you as well. I'm not sure how large of a party should be part of negotiations, but you'll need help sorting all of the rescued slaves, too. Maybe have people standing by in Rurick? The meeting place is close to there."

It really was a good suggestion. He especially liked that Dunixan volunteered to go with him, for various reasons. "I like it. Form up some troops for me. I'll transport everyone down to Rurick and then go over. Actually, I might take the rescued slaves back to Rurick temporarily. It's a good place to go, there's enough space for everyone while we get them sorted."

"That, and you think the citizens of Rurick are in Rowe."

It wasn't a question but Trev'nor answered it anyway. "Yeah, I do. If I'm right, we might as well just take them home. Assuming we need to get everything ready, I say we spend the next two days prepping and then leave. That should give me more than enough time."

"And some to spare," Becca agreed. "Alright. You're finishing the garden first, right?"

"If I can. I'll need Azin's and Nolan's help, though; there's no way I can finish it myself in two days."

"Nolan's already headed your way. I'll contact Azin for you. And Trev, I'm saying this now, but if our missing people really are in Rowe, you'd better call me immediately. I want to see them too."

"Of course." Trev'nor wouldn't even dream of doing otherwise—she'd strangle him. Becca had consistent nightmares about not finding their friends, or not getting to them quickly enough to save them. He wouldn't torture her any longer than necessary.

Ending the call, he took a good look around him, at the freshly turned earth, the young plants already started, and the desert sand beyond that. Still a lot left to do. Just once, Trev'nor would appreciate being able to start a project without being rushed from start to finish. Sighing, he wiped the sweat from his forehead again and bent back to work, determined to get it done as quickly as possible.

It all sounded simple: form up two squadrons of troops with their marching orders, pack, transport them down to Rurick. So why did it exhaust Trev'nor and force him to stay up until midnight two nights in a row pulling that off? By the time he finally got everyone loaded on the earthen carpet, ready to travel south to Rurick, he was half-convinced that just getting everyone down there was the hardest part. Surely the negotiations would be a lark in comparison.

Nolan, Azin, Orion, and Garth all flew with them at a lazy glide, the meurittas flying circles around the slower moving dragons, chittering happily, but all of them keeping pace with Trev'nor down below. He appreciated it, as he still felt travel between cities in Khobunter had an inherent danger to it. They still had bandits out here, and scorpions, and poisonous snakes, to name a few. If it came down to it, Trev'nor could just drop everyone down to the Earth Path, but still he preferred having a flying escort overhead to watch out for potential trouble.

It took them nearly a full day to reach Rurick at his slower pace traveling along the top, and when they did arrive, Nolan had to drop in and take the wards down so they could bring everyone inside. Trev'nor entered the city with the strange swirl of emotions in his chest he always experienced here: grief and loss and determination. He'd never be able to rest in Rurick peacefully until he had the people restored here.

The soldiers still on duty in Rurick greeted them with happy smiles and immediately ushered everyone in to the right buildings, helping them settle in for the night. Trev'nor stepped into their dining hall long enough to eat but found himself too restless to think about turning in. Dunixan tried to catch his eye, gesturing for him to come sit and eat, but Trev'nor felt himself to be too poor company to sit and chat. As much as he liked spending time with Dunixan, his head felt too full of memories, most of them painful. He had to move, to try and exorcise the demons. He waved at the man, dredging up a sorry smile, and took to the streets instead.

The air felt cool against his skin, but not as cold as the ghosts haunting him. He'd killed people for the first time in this city. His hands still felt the weight of those souls even now, months later. Every corner seemed to hold some memory, good or bad. He walked all along the darkened streets, letting moonlight and memory guide him. As if his feet had their own will, they took him to the place where it had all started.

The slave pen.

Well, not that the building stood anymore. They'd all flattened it to little bitty gravel before leaving Rurick. Now only an empty lot remained. He stood exactly where the guards' doorway had been, once upon a time, and looked out over it without actually seeing any of it, lost in memory. The air grew colder and he shivered under it, regretting having forgotten his jacket. Or maybe he just felt colder, standing here and remembering what it had been like to live in chains.

"Trev'nor."

Startled, he jerked around and found Dunixan standing directly behind him. "Roshan. Problem?"

"No, people just got worried when they couldn't immediately locate you. I told them I'd find you." Coming up to stand beside him, Dunixan looked around but, of course, saw nothing more than an empty lot. "This place, it holds some significance?"

Swallowing, Trev'nor faced forward once more. A fine shiver racked through his body from head to toe and back again. He'd like to blame the breeze drifting down the deserted streets, but Trev'nor tried not to lie to himself. The sensation of iron bars pressed up against his skin felt vivid and stark for a moment, the tactile memory overwhelming. He explained quietly in a numb voice, "It's where we were first held as slaves. We destroyed the pens before we left."

"Ah." A wealth of understanding filled that one syllable. Dunixan studied him for a moment then doffed his own coat, pulling it over Trev'nor's shoulders and shushing him when he tried to protest.

Trev'nor felt too thankful for the man's body heat and presence to protest much. The coat helped dispel everything haunting his mind, the warmth chasing away the cold. He'd come out here for solitude but now he didn't want it. Walking with memories hadn't done him any good at all. He much preferred Dunixan's solid presence by his side instead.

Words low, Dunixan hesitantly offered, "I'm not sure whether I should ask or not...."

When he trailed off uncertainly, Trev'nor encouraged

him with a silent wave of the hand. There was little that he wouldn't answer when Dunixan asked him, especially when it came to Rurick.

"This place enslaved you, and yet when the three of you speak of Rurick, it's with great regret and determination. You're adamant about finding the people that once lived here." Hands lingering on Trev'nor's arms, Dunixan's head canted a little to the side. "I'm rather confused."

Yes, of course he would be. Trev'nor found it too hard to face him, the emotions still too raw to speak of casually, and his eyes returned to the lot once more. "The people who lived here were almost slaves themselves to the government. Trexler had half abandoned this place, letting the local leaders do whatever they wanted, and they were in constant fear. For good reason it seems. Once we broke out of the chains, and actually spoke to the people, we learned all that. We learned a great deal about Khobunter those first few days. Despite all of the cultural prejudices, they treated us well and became our friends."

"There is something about Chahiran culture that is similar to Khobunter's culture," Dunixan stated carefully, feeling his way through the words. "When you decide someone is your friend, he is your friend unequivocally."

"Precisely so." Trev'nor finally pulled himself completely free of the memories and turned his head to give Dunixan a quick smile, edged in sorrow. "It was the one thing we could relate to at the beginning. My friends are missing, Roshan. I want them back."

"Then by all means, let's get them back." Dunixan slid an arm around his shoulders, the one-armed hug meant to comfort and encourage. "I must ask this, though, before we go to meet them. Do you plan to exact revenge on Rowe?"

Blowing out a breath, Trev'nor leaned into the man's side a little. He let his head flop backwards, giving him an uninterrupted view of the night sky. Not a single cloud lingered, and the stars shone bright and brilliant in the inky depths of the heavens. The peacefulness of it settled over his mind even as he answered, "No. What good is it to take revenge on an ally? And honestly, the attack wasn't even about Rurick, it was to take advantage of Trexler. I won't try to avenge anything for that man's sake."

Snorting, Dunixan allowed, "I wouldn't either. Alright, I just had to ask before we start negotiations. If they give all the slaves back and accept your terms, you'll really treat them like allies?"

"Just like I do you," Trev'nor confirmed, tone firm. Then thought better of it and amended, "Well, alright, probably not."

"I'm relieved to hear it," Dunixan drawled.

Trev'nor bit the inside of his cheek to stifle a giggle. "We won't be as friendly with each other. I'm still upset with them, honestly. It will take some time on both our parts before we're actually on good terms. As long as they abide by the agreement and are good to the people, I won't complain."

"Hmmm," Dunixan said noncommittally.

That did not sound like agreement. Trev'nor quirked a brow up at him. "You think differently?"

Dunixan turned them both, encouraging Trev'nor to walk back toward their lodgings for the night. "I think it would behoove you to have many of your own informants in Rowe to make sure they really do abide by your agreement. Khobunter has always been a hotbed of trouble because they find it difficult to honor treaties. Often, they'll only do enough to suit their purpose, and when that's finished, they ignore it."

Sound advice, and Trev'nor would take it. He looked at Dunixan and thought of Garth's advice to him. Had he been blind to the full spectrum of possibilities in this man? He'd always sought out Dunixan's advice, his friendship, but it occurred to him that he could have more if he asked for it.

The burdens he carried would crush him if he tried to shoulder it alone. This silent support meant the world to him. Trev'nor leaned into the man a little, staying firmly tucked under his arm as they walked back along the silent streets.

They spent a full day revisiting Rurick and making the necessary repairs they hadn't had time for before. Nolan found yet more things he wanted to change in the garden, although he drafted Azin's power to help him this time. The morning of the fifth day, they mounted their dragons—Azin and Mose on Orion, Dunixan mounting behind Trev'nor for the trip. Amir and Simin rode Nolan, which was a funny sight in and of itself. Trev'nor let the soldiers stay in Rurick, as he didn't need them just yet. Or at least, he hoped that he didn't need them. Surely three mages and two dragons were enough of a show of force to make anyone behave. He made the meurittas stay behind—incorrigible creatures that they were—with the task to open all the locked doors in the city. They chittered so happily, he might as well have handed them a treasure trove with no time limit.

The border had nothing to indicate where Trexler's former territory ended and Rowe's started, except a rather decrepit sandstone post with writing half-worn away by time and wind. The dragons landed easily, and Trev'nor planned to leave Garth's saddle on, as he wanted a quick getaway if they needed it. He could see in the distance a party of people coming toward them, all on dragoo and moving in quickly.

So, they both decided to come in earlier? Well, that worked out fine. Trev'nor would rather have more time on hand to negotiate than be forced to camp out here. Not that they couldn't, they'd brought the necessary supplies, but he'd prefer not to. He slid down first, then reached up and gave

Dunixan a hand down, which the other warlord gratefully took.

Rubbing at his thighs, Dunixan admitted, "It's very different riding a dragon. Even that short stretch made it clear. I'm glad I rode with you."

"I figured you might feel it," Trev'nor acknowledged ruefully. "I haven't been riding Garth for so long that I don't remember the pain. Wait for Nolan to switch back and he'll be able to soothe the cramps out."

"I'll ask him." Determined, Dunixan hobbled Nolan's direction.

Since he had nothing to do but stand there, Trev'nor created a table and benches from the sand, a tall open pavilion of stone over it all to give them some shade. Coming up to his side, Nolan asked, "Are you sure that's a good idea?"

"What, openly using magic? Nol, they already know we're mages, we've nothing to hide at this point."

"Sure, but knowing something and having your face rubbed in it are two different things."

Urk. He might have a point. "Too late now. Either way, they're up."

Sighing, Nolan let it go and took a seat at the table. Azin slid in next to him, watching the approaching riders with a wary expression. Dunixan chose to stand, but he did move into the shade, as any sensible person would do.

Distance over the desert sands could be amazingly deceptive. What looked like a short span actually took the approaching riders another two hours to cross. Trev'nor sipped at his canteen of water and waited patiently, not about to try and hurry them along, as surely that would not go over well. When they finally did reach the border marker, everyone stopped and eyed the structure with some trepidation before dismounting. Nolan might have had a good point earlier. Still, Trev'nor could hardly have just stood around under the blazing suns for two hours just to make them more comfortable.

Without being signaled, Amir moved to stand just

behind him, ready to translate, just as the other party arrived.

In a creak of leather, a middle-aged man with a lean build and highbrow dismounted from his dragoo and stepped forward. He looked hot but still wore the formal white and grey uniform of Rowe, dusty though it was due to the roads. He offered them a respectful inclination of the head, dark hair swinging over his shoulder at the movement. "I am Farzin Rowe, Warlord of Rowe."

So this was him, eh? "I am Warlord Rhebentrev'noren. Harmony find you, Warlord Rowe. Thank you for agreeing to come and meet me. With me are Warlord Roshan Dunixan, Life Mage Vonnolanen, First Simin, Lieutenant Amir, my batman Mose, and Elemental Mage Azin. Our dragons are Garth and Orion."

Farzin didn't quite know what to make of being introduced to dragons, but he bowed politely nonetheless. "Greetings. This is my Minister of Finance, Gazsi, and General Shahin."

Gazsi certainly looked the part of an accountant with round spectacles perched at the end of a very thin nose. His manner and dress were austere, as if he wore a uniform himself instead of the loose robes men in court sometimes favored. General Shahin, in contrast, could be used as a model for a recruiting poster. Straight back, head neatly shaven, jaw square in shape. If he went head to head with a stone wall, the wall would lose. Trev'nor would swear to it.

"Come, gentlemen, sit in the shade while we talk," Trev'nor invited with an open arm toward the table. "We've brought some fruit, bread, and cheese with us. We can eat together while we negotiate."

This had been Dunixan's advice, to put them on a friendly footing, and it obviously worked. Every man relaxed a notch and Farzin even smiled at him. "We also brought some delicacies with us. Let us eat together, Warlord, and speak of peace."

"I'd like nothing better," Trev'nor admitted frankly.

Trev'nor found it a very strange experience to ride Garth and not fly. They'd little choice at this juncture, as Farzin did not feel comfortable enough with magic for him to take the Earth Path. And Trev'nor didn't want to outpace the man back into Rowe territory by simply flying. The whole party stayed grounded, moving at a loping gait that ate up the ground. People always said the dragoos were a cousin breed of the dragons, but Trev'nor had never understood why they thought so. Sure, their noses had the same shape, they shared the same body structure, but a dragoo's tail had nothing on a dragon's, and of course they were a third the size and lacked wings. But when he saw them run side by side, he finally got it. The gait and the way they moved along the ground was amazingly similar.

They moved at such a pace that comfortable conversation wasn't possible, and Trev'nor found that he didn't mind. He'd done nothing but talk to the man for the past four hours, and his throat wanted a break for a while.

Trev'nor had to wonder if someone else would have been a better choice to lead the negotiations, as Farzin seemed half-terrified of Trev'nor just based on reputation alone. He emanated the air of 'please don't hurt me' the first hour they spoke. It took considerable charm, and offers of help and food to get the man to settle down. Would Becca have had an easier time of it? Generally she wasn't as feared here in Khobunter, as this culture viewed women as the peacekeepers. Unless it was magic itself that Farzin feared, in which case Becca definitely was scarier.

At least they'd agreed to an alliance. Dunixan had been a tremendous help during the negotiations, as he offered examples of what his alliance with the trio meant, which eased Farzin's fears considerably. In all aspects, the terms were very favorable, with the possible exception of losing all of the slave labor, which would impact the economy—at least short term. Trev'nor offset this by promising he would stay long enough to put in multiple orchards, gardens, and an aqueduct system to help feed Rowe.

In the end, they struck an agreement, and Farzin made a verbal oath to adhere to the new laws. Trev'nor had taken Amir with him, anticipating the need to write something up on paper, but Farzin seemed satisfied with a verbal oath for the time being, stating they could put it down to paper and sign something when they reached Rowe. Trev'nor knew the promise to be legally binding and didn't worry about it much. From the corner of his eye, he studied Farzin's expression. The man kept glancing at Nolan, who was in dragoo form and running alongside them, then forcing his eyes away. Gradually they'd creep back to the golden dragoo of their own volition. Fascination or fear?

"Fledgling," Garth called back to him, tilting his head a little to see Trev'nor with one eye. "Becca say rain coming."

"Got it." They'd relayed via dragon Rowe's acceptance, and Trev'nor didn't have to be told how happy that made everyone up north. They'd all rather have allies than enemies to be conquered. He'd relayed a request to Becca to send a storm this way, as a sort of good faith gesture, and apparently she'd agreed it was a good idea.

Trev'nor hated the idea that the water would go to waste, though. Time to test what Farzin really felt about magic.

Taking a breath, he turned in his saddle to call back to Azin, "Becca's sent a storm! Let's start on the ground here. You take right, I take left?"

"Sure! What do you want to do with the minerals?" she called back.

"Pave the road with it!" Trev'nor didn't see why not, the road could use a little help.

She lifted a hand in acknowledgement, glowing to his eyes as her magic came to life.

Trev'nor relaxed back into his saddle, his own magic coming to play. He swept up the minerals and rocky bits in the soil, loosening it and preparing it to receive water, his magic sweeping out as far as the eye could see to the left of the road. He could feel, as well as see, Azin doing the same to the right. Both of them gathered up the loose minerals and packaged them into hard paving stones in the road ahead. Trev'nor focused well ahead of them, not wanting to throw anyone off by putting paving stones right under them as they tried to run. Still, it jarred even him when they finally hit the smoother section, as he'd paid no attention to the road aside from rebuilding it.

When he fell into a good rhythm, he dared a peek at Farzin and found the man staring ahead and to the side, a little dumbfounded. He didn't look afraid, though. Trev'nor took it as a win.

They had another four hours at least to go until they reached Rowe at this rate, which meant it would be quite late in the evening before they arrived. Trev'nor didn't know if he could keep this up for four hours straight before his magic tapped out and resolved not to try. He'd go until he felt tired enough to stop, then signal Azin to break off. No sense in them running themselves ragged at this point, especially considering how much they'd have to do when they hit Rowe's capital city.

Dark clouds rumbled overhead, gathering in strength

and size as they spread in from the east. Trev'nor realized belatedly that calling for a storm now meant he would get wet while traveling. Busted buckets, he had not thought that through. Why hadn't someone else pointed it out? Or were they all so tired of being hot that the idea of a rainstorm sounded blissful?

Becca certainly wasn't wasting any time. The air became heavy and humid with the promise of rain, the sky so overcast it felt like evening instead of afternoon. Trev'nor gave it ten minutes, tops, before they all got drenched.

Garth realized the problem quickly and bounded two leaps ahead before spreading his wings wide. "Everyone, under wings."

No one disobeyed, not even Farzin's party, who still looked a little askance at the dragons. The only ones that didn't immediately obey were the other dragons and Nolan, although everyone on the dragons dismounted to stand under Garth's massive wings. People scattered equally to either side, General Shahin huddling in with Amir, Azin, and Mose, the rest of Farzin's party on the other side. Trev'nor threw a leg over the pommel and slid to the ground, coming to stand in between Dunixan and Farzin.

"You did not think this through," Dunixan chided him, voice rich with laughter. "Why did you ask for a storm now?"

"I didn't think she'd send it the very same hour," Trev'nor protested. "I figured, you know, that she'd get one started and shoo it our way and it would hit sometime tonight. After we were safely in the city."

"Next time perhaps be more clear in your request?" Dunixan suggested archly, eyebrow matching his tone.

"Excuse you, I was relaying the request through two dragons," Trev'nor shot back, amused more than anything. "That's bound to lose something in process. Besides, it's fine. This way I can show Warlord Farzin what I meant earlier."

Fat drops of rain hit the ground, darkening it, first in a

splatter, then with increasing speed until visibility dropped down to twenty or thirty feet ahead. The dragons frolicked around in it, tussling playfully with Nolan, who gave as good as he got. Trev'nor, used to such a scene, largely ignored them. Drawing Farzin over to the side, he pointed to an area a little further ahead and to the left. "See that patch of ground there, where the water's forming into puddles?"

Farzin's dark eyes narrowed a little in concentration. "Yes, so I do."

"That's an area of ground that I didn't change," Trev'nor explained. "But see here, near where I'm standing? The earth accepts the water readily. All of those minerals we pulled out of the ground earlier to repave the road with, I did that for a reason. We have to change the very condition of the soil to accept water before we can even dream of planting something in it."

Taking this in, Farzin studied both patches of ground for a moment. "Your comrade—you introduced her as a different type of mage. All mages can do this, then?"

"No, not at all." Trev'nor liked the question; it proved Farzin attempted to understand them better. "Azin is an Elemental Mage, which means she can use all of the elements to one degree or another. Her strongest elements are earth, metal, and fire, which is why our talents often overlap. But only an Earth Mage or Elemental Mage can do work like this. Nolan is here to help me with the plants after we get the soil ready for a garden, as Life Mages are over anything living."

Farzin stared at the frolicking dragoo, head canting in perplexity. "Is that why he can…?"

"Change into different animal shapes? Talk to all of them? Yes, that's why. It's part and parcel of his magic." Feeling this was a good opportunity to expand a little on the subject, Trev'nor explained, "I can do more than this, you understand. I can build with stone and even travel with it."

Blinking at him, Farzin repeated, "Travel? Ah, you mean by building roads."

"No, I mean travel with it, as a means of travel itself. We call it the Earth Path. I can wrap us up in a cocoon of earth and magic and move within the earth itself. It's very fast, I think it's one of the fastest methods of travel known."

Proving to be shrewd on some level, Farzin's head tilted forward as he studied him. "You did not offer this earlier."

"You didn't act comfortable around magic, I didn't want to push you," Trev'nor countered truthfully, hands spreading in an open shrug.

Dunixan cleared his throat and offered, "You'll discover, Warlord Farzin, that your new warlords are not the type to push people about. They are too gracious for that. You'll also discover that it is alright to be blunt with them. They prefer it, actually."

That he did. Trev'nor found the double-talk of diplomacy and politics to be confusing and irritating.

"Blunt speech, you say? Alright, then let me try it for a spell." Farzin faced Dunixan squarely, chin lifting. "Have you traveled on this Earth Path before?"

"I have," Dunixan answered forthrightly. "I found it strange, but not unlike being in a cave. He's right, it's very fast, and if you will allow him to use it, we'll be in Rowe before you know it."

"Is that so." Farzin took in a breath and let it out again in a steady stream. "I suppose I should take a leap of faith at some point. Warlord Trev'nor, we are in your care."

That sounded like a go-ahead to Trev'nor. He grinned at the man before lifting a cupped hand to his mouth and calling to the puddle-jumpers, "Stop playing and come in close! We're using the Earth Path!"

They stopped splashing each other and came in, Nolan shifting to human form as he walked under Garth's wing. That distinctly unnerved everyone in Farzin's group, and the warlord himself was in danger of losing his eyes from their sockets, they popped so wide. Still, no one said anything and Trev'nor allowed them to take things at their own pace without comment. They'd come to terms with matters after enough exposure. He felt confident about that.

Wrapping earth around the group, Trev'nor dropped them down into the ground and then paused, waiting to see who would panic. He looked about the group, but no one screamed or fainted. Maybe they were all alright with such enclosed spaces. Relieved, he oriented himself for Rowe and set them moving at a good clip, calling out a warning as he did so. "Don't touch the walls, please, they'll hurt you! Otherwise you're fine to move around."

He didn't try to talk to anyone, as Trev'nor didn't know this part of Khobunter well enough to navigate and talk. But he caught the conversation going on behind him between Nolan, Dunixan, and Farzin.

Farzin: "We are moving, you say? But I don't feel that we are."

"That's the strange part about it," Dunixan agreed. "But we are moving."

"You see the light on the walls, the way it shifts?" Nolan waited a beat before continuing. "That means we're moving. When he's perfectly still, the magic glows a steady color and there's no movement."

"Oh. That's informative, I'll have to remember that. Is it safe to talk to him this time?" Dunixan asked.

"I wouldn't think so, otherwise he'd be answering these questions. Come to think of it, I doubt he's been in this corner of Khobunter before. He probably doesn't know it well enough to navigate and talk too. Better leave him be."

"How does he navigate?" Farzin asked curiously.

"He explained it to me once," Nolan answered ruminatively. "Let's see if I can remember it. He said it's mostly landmarks that help orient him. He can feel more than we can in the earth, such as the leylines, underground rivers, and so on. But he can also feel large structures on the earth itself when he's close enough, so he can feel cities. He uses all of those things to tell where he is and where he should go. In an area that he knows well, it's easy, and he can come up in a precise location. I think this time he'll just aim for some spot outside of Rowe's walls and count it good."

Considering Trev'nor had told Nolan that a good period of time ago, his friend had a good memory to retain all of that. Turning his head a little, Trev'nor called behind him, "We'll get there in about an hour."

"Roger that," Nolan responded cheerfully. "Oh, if we have that much of the day left, then let's do the important things first. Warlord Farzin, we didn't dare ask before, but you have the citizens of Rurick, don't you."

There was a pregnant pause before Farzin admitted, "I do."

A thrill shot through Trev'nor. He knew it!

"Release them to us first, please? Actually, most of the city are friends of ours. We've been searching for them for months. We'd like to take them home today and settle them back into Rurick."

"Of course, Raja Nolan," Farzin agreed readily, still with an air of caution. "You're truly friends with them? I'd heard that the people of Rurick captured you as slaves when you first entered Khobunter."

"No, the government of Rurick captured us as slaves," Nolan corrected swiftly. "The people were as much enslaved to them as we were. We realized that rather quickly. We've always felt bad that we left them so vulnerable to attack after we took the government out. It will ease our hearts if we can restore them home again."

"I understand." Farzin seemed to feel it best to take advantage of the way Nolan had delicately stated the matter and asked no further questions. "I can certainly authorize their release immediately upon our return. You will transport them home via this Earth Path method? I thought so. What about the other slaves?"

"Release them all, Warlord Farzin. I'll take them where they're supposed to go." Trev'nor dared to look over his shoulder, fixing the man with a firm look. "Rowe today, then Olschan and Thais tomorrow."

"Of course," Farzin assured him with spread hands, almost placating. "In fact, I will use the semaphores today to order everyone's release and give them a chance to bathe and be outside of the chains this evening. That way you can pick them up tomorrow at your convenience."

Trev'nor's convenience was daybreak. But that probably wouldn't go over well. "Thank you, Warlord, I appreciate that. Please do so."

"I have a thought," Dunixan offered. "Why don't I help Farzin re-organize the government here in Rowe, as I know very well what needs to be done, while you and Nolan deal with the people and gardens? If we start with the main city, and issue some orders from there, then Olschan and Thais should be a snap in comparison."

And this was why Trev'nor would kiss a Gardener the next time he saw one. Dunixan was indeed a wonderful gift from them. "You are the best ally ever. Please and thank you."

Grinning, Dunixan assured him, "My pleasure. Well, no, more like headache, but I prefer this headache over a fight any day. Farzin, be thinking about where you want gardens in your city. You haven't seen what they can do to an area yet, but trust me, it will be the most lush and green garden you've ever imagined. I've not seen anything to compare to it yet."

"And that's with our gardens half grown-in," Nolan noted in amusement. "Just wait until they reach full maturity."

Dunixan looked poleaxed. "Wait, there will be more?"

"Of course there will." Nolan chuckled, delighted by

his surprise. "Ah, I forget, you didn't see Coven Ordan, just Bromany. Just wait, my friend, it will be jaw-dropping by the time I'm done with it."

Nolan started detailing the rotation of plants, and what fruits and vegetables would be available, and then dragged Azin into the conversation to talk about irrigation systems and aqueducts. Trev'nor listened with a smile on his face, as to him, it painted a very beautiful picture indeed.

12

Rowe did not look like any of the other cities Trev'nor had seen in Khobunter, and yet did at the same time. It had similar architecture; the same building materials of sandstone, bricks, and wood; but something about the place cast a different feeling. Trev'nor finally realized it contained more life and spirit than he'd seen so far—Dunixan's territory aside. The people here were not downtrodden and they didn't duck their heads in an instinctive move to hide when their leaders passed them in the streets.

That spoke very well of the government and Trev'nor sighed a little in relief. Rehabilitating a city from the ground up was quite a process, and he would be very glad to not have to do it yet again.

Still, he did see multiple places that called for improvements. While the people might not be openly suffering from poverty, they certainly weren't doing well. City walls aside, almost every building needed repair of some sort, and Trev'nor still saw more than a few beggars.

Deferential to his new ally's wishes, Farzin led them directly to the slave pens once they breached the gate, Gazsi and General Shahin breaking off to attend to other duties. Trev'nor knew there had to be more than one pen location, but he contented himself with starting this one before moving on. The guards outside the pen gave their warlord sharp salutes and stared at the people following him with open curiosity. Trev'nor bore their scrutiny without comment, stepping inside the foul air of the slave pens.

No matter how many times he entered these places, the smell always hit him hard. The sensory input threw him briefly back in time to when he first entered this country. Trev'nor blinked the memory away but he couldn't blink away the filthy conditions these people lived in, the lifeless way they sat huddled next to each other, or any of the rest.

Seeing it, Farzin winced openly and gave Trev'nor a slightly apologetic bow. His mouth opened to say something, then closed again, as if he realized no words could magically make all of this better.

Trev'nor turned to the Elemental Mage standing at his shoulder and requested quietly, "Azin, will you do the honors?"

"I'd be pleased to," she responded tightly. Her magic flared out and every chain inside the pen melted off and away, gathering into ore bars neatly stacked near the front door. That, more than anything, got the attention of every person in the pens.

The magicians took one look at them, saw three powerful mages in their midst, and immediately stood, coming to stand at the front of their cages. Azin, without a word, undid the bars, freeing them so they could step out.

Clearing his throat, Trev'nor launched into what was unfortunately his usual speech in such situations. "My name is Rhebentrev'noren and I am Warlord of Khobunter. Under my rule there is no slavery. I'm here to free you, to take you home if you're a captive of war, or to take you to a safer place for training if you're a magician. We'll have the amulets off you soon, but please bear with them a little longer until I can transport you. Any injured, please come forward, my friend is a Life Mage and he will heal you."

A few shuffled some uncertain steps, their eyes studying

Farzin out of curiosity and fear, not sure what he was doing here.

"Trev'nor?" an uncertain voice called from the back.

It took a moment for him to recognize it, then Trev'nor bolted for the back of the spacious room. Or he tried to. It was so crowded that he had to hop, wriggle, and slither through people, rather like a snake after a proper warm up. He didn't care if it looked undignified—his heart clamored to put his hands on a missing friend. He vaguely felt someone coming in behind him, trying to keep up, but he couldn't force himself to slow down enough to even glance behind him. "Rikkana Sumi? Is that you?"

Huddled near the back corner, the aged Rikkana used a hand against the wall to brace herself as she creaked up to her feet. She bore almost no resemblance to the proud and clean woman Trev'nor knew, and she looked like she had aged a decade in slave chains, despite it being less than half a year since he'd seen her last. She reached out and caught his hands, giving him a tremulous smile.

"Rikkana Sumi." Trev'nor returned the grip, thankful beyond reckoning she had survived her ordeal. He'd worried about her more than the others because of her age.

She beamed back at him, the dirt highlighting every wrinkle in her skin. "Trev'nor. I doubted my eyes at first. Nolan's here as well? Becca?"

"Becca's up north in Riyu, managing things there," Trev'nor answered, carefully steering her away from the wall with an arm around her shoulders. He wanted to kiss her, so thankful she was still alive. Seeing her gave him hope that the rest might be alright as well, the questions burning in his throat. "But Nolan's here. What about the others? Is everyone from Rurick here?"

"No one's been sold," she confirmed for him. "We've been keeping track of each other. Have you really conquered all of Khobunter?"

"All but Von, we're working on them next," he answered a little ruefully, slowing his pace to match hers. Sumi had never moved quickly because of her aching knees, but he remembered her being more mobile than this. People shifted out of the way as much as they could, letting them through, and Trev'nor realized that Dunixan had followed him in, encouraging people to move. He gave them all a quick smile of thanks as he continued, "We'll have the whole country under control soon enough."

"Rikkana Sumi," Nolan greeted her, reaching out one hand to grasp hers. He had a child in his lap already, healing magic pouring into her, but he seemed to think he could do two people at once. Amir stood at his elbow, already making a list, taking in people's names steadily in lieu of Llona. Mose seemed to be taking his own inventory, although Trev'nor had no idea what his batman might be up to. "Here, let me handle your joints. Sit on the bench with me, that's it. Trev, I have this group, go to the next."

That sounded good to him, but he wanted help if he could get it. "Rikkana Sumi, I hate to ask, but can you come with me? Help organize everyone? I'd like to take them home today if I can."

A determined expression came over the old woman's face. "I insist on it, my young Warlord. Just let Nolan deal with my knees, I can't walk fast these days because of them."

"Two minutes," Nolan promised them both. "Mose, go with them, take in names. We'll combine the lists later."

"Of course, Raja," Mose agreed.

Clearing his throat, Farzin offered, "I can have these people led to another area, give them the opportunity to bathe and dress in something finer, in preparation for their journey?"

Trev'nor didn't know if he offered to somehow make up for these appalling conditions or if he meant it sincerely, but either way, Trev'nor would take it. "I would appreciate that,

Warlord. Thank you. If someone can lead me to the next area, Azin and I can handle it."

Humming noncommittally to himself, Dunixan turned and asked Farzin, "How many pens do you have in Rowe?"

Farzin might have winced as he answered, "Three."

"Then why don't I take the last one?" Dunixan offered to Trev'nor and Nolan. "I can at least get people out of chains and sort the ones who are going to Rurick from the magicians, get them ready to transport. We don't have a lot of daylight left and I assume you want at least some of these people settled by nightfall in their own homes."

"You assume correctly," Trev'nor confirmed, already itching to move. "Then, if someone can lead Roshan to the last area? Thank you, Warlord Farzin. Roshan, remember to get me a good headcount of the magicians, I need to contact Raile with a specific number so he knows what to prepare for."

Dunixan waved him away, attitude saying Trev'nor didn't need to state the obvious. "Magess Azin, come with me. I'll need your help."

"Of course," she agreed readily, following him out.

Nolan released Sumi and she stood, bending a little. Her tentative movement became more confident as she realized her arthritis had disappeared completely. She regarded Nolan with some astonishment. "I should have asked you earlier."

Grinning, Nolan agreed cheerfully, "You really should have."

"Thank you," she told him seriously, then grinned up at Trev'nor. "Well?"

Waiting on him, eh? "Let's go, then."

They trooped back out, and they must have made an odd group with a foreigner, a slave, a guard, and a mage all walking about together. People stopped and stared often enough that Trev'nor assumed it looked odd, anyway. Sumi took many a deep breath, enjoying the free air, and beamed at nothing in particular. "You'll have to tell me how you came here as warlord," she informed—no, ordered him. "I want all the details."

"I will be happy to tell you, but not today," he responded, his head full of logistics. "Soon, though, I hope."

"Answer me one question," Sumi tilted her face up curiously. "Young Becca, she is your consort?"

His head flopped back as he groaned. Did the woman never give up? "No, she is my co-ruler, and before you get it in your head that we're destined to be together, I have to tell you that Becca is currently being courted by a general."

Sumi's eyes nearly popped out of her head. "A general? Who?"

"He was a commander in Trexler when this all started, so you might not know who he is, but his name is Rahim Danyal."

Her lips pursed as she repeated the name silently, head shaking a little. "No, I don't know this man. He is respectable?"

"Highly so, and he adores Becca. We're all glad for the match."

Giving him a pitying glance, Sumi consoled him, "We'll find a nice girl for you."

Mose, striding along behind them, choked on a poorly disguised laugh.

Trev'nor thought about pointing out that at only seventeen, soon to be eighteen, he had all of the time in the world to find a nice person, and that he already had his eye on someone. Then he thought better of it. Sumi was one of those women you didn't challenge. It never ended well.

Their guard took another street and stopped in front of the slave pen, relaying the order to let Trev'nor free everyone inside. The guards let them through with considerable confusion, not at all sure about this order, but without the authority to countermand it. Trev'nor didn't even bother to convince them, just sailed on through and repeated his announcement from the first pen.

Mose grabbed a keyring and went to work on all the chains as Trev'nor talked and searched for familiar faces. He saw a few, people he recognized to be residents of Rurick. Sumi went forward to greet them with smiles and whispers of assurance as she urged them out of their caves.

He'd barely told them the essentials when he saw a man he knew very well. His friend from the slave pens in Rurick stood toward the middle of the room, eyes wide and stunned. Roskin had, for better or worse, made it into Rowe. Trev'nor beamed at him, happy to see the wizard still in one piece, and got an equally bright smile in return.

"—we'll transport all of you to safer places either today or tomorrow morning," Trev'nor finished. "If you're injured, don't move. I have a Life Mage in the first pen healing people and he'll come here to help you as soon as he can." That said, he moved through them, heading straight for Roskin and caught the man in a strong bear hug. "Roskin."

Roskin hugged him back just as hard, and what might have been tears dropped on Trev'nor's shoulder. "Trev'nor. I never in a million years thought I'd see the day. I thought you'd left."

"Well, we did leave and study the Ruins of Rheben, but we came back to Rurick a few days later only to find the city empty. We've been looking for all of you ever since." Trev'nor stepped back and looked him over, searching for injuries and finding none. Joy shook him so hard he nearly vibrated under the force of it. "You're well?"

"As well as can be," Roskin assured him, more than overwhelmed. "We're really free? We can leave?"

"You can, but please come with me?" Trev'nor knew that everyone inside watched and listened to this very interesting conversation, so he pitched his voice a little to carry. "I have a magical academy set up in Rheben right now. If you go there, you'll be trained for free, and then once you're properly trained you can go out into the world and make your own path in life."

Roskin stood stunned for a long moment, his dark eyes searching Trev'nor's face as if half-convinced he must be dreaming.

Perhaps Mose realized it, as he came to stand next to them, a gentle smile on his weather-beaten face. "He's not a dream, I promise you. He really means it. Go to the academy, please. I helped rebuild it and it's an amazing place with very kind teachers."

No better proof could be presented that Trev'nor spoke truth, as Mose was obviously Khobuntian and had all the bearing of a military man. "You helped build it?"

"Some," he answered truthfully, a little shyly. "Mostly Warlord Trev'nor and Magess Azin did the work. But even us soldiers found ways to help."

Trev'nor turned, spotted Sumi, and asked, "How many from Rurick do we have in here?"

"Two thousand four hundred and thirty-one," she rattled off promptly. "Half of Rurick's citizens are in here, but we were split up a little. We have another four hundred, I believe, in the last pen, and the rest are in Thais."

"Then we'll have to get them tomorrow. Everyone from Rurick, I'm taking you home tonight." Several gasped in disbelief, others started crying, and Trev'nor felt a pang for them. They must have thought they'd never see their homes again. "Don't worry, we repaired all of the damage, and there's gardens and aqueducts supplying food and water to the city. You won't be in a dire situation. Follow Rikkana Sumi, please, I need to gather all of you up in one place so I can transport you home tonight. Magicians, stay with Mose a little longer. We'll get you into baths and clean clothes tonight, and I'll take you up to the academy tomorrow with all of the other rescued magicians."

Mose stepped in closer to murmur, "I'll tell them about the Earth Path and try to figure out who might panic underground for you."

"You're the best," Trev'nor assured him in the same undertone. "Do that, please. And get me a good headcount. I'm going to step out, see where we stand with everyone else, and coordinate them. The sooner we can get Rurick's citizens home the better. We can't depend on Farzin coming up with all of the resources he needs to bathe, feed, and re-clothe this many people in a single night."

"I know it," he agreed readily, frowning as he studied the people around him. "Go, I have them."

Trev'nor turned to leave, then paused and watched him for a moment. How far Mose had come from the man he had first met. Now he dared to advise Trev'nor on what he thought should be done and didn't doubt that Trev'nor would listen to him. Was it war or just familiarity that gave the man so much confidence?

Shaking the thought aside, Trev'nor exited the pens, intent on settling people today before he lost all light.

13

Becca asked a favor of Sallah so that she could go down and spend at least a day with the returned citizens of Rurick. They had to retrieve Shad anyway, as Garth had ferried him up from Strae to Rurick the day before, his two weeks nearly over. It felt like the end of some grand quest they'd been on, a completion of a journey. She could barely stand still on the way down. Petting Tail helped some, and he settled in her arms, purring with half-masted eyes as she stroked his spine. She'd managed to convince Cat to stay behind in Riyu because they traveled by Earth Path and she'd be back within a day.

At Becca's elbow, Nahla looked around with wide eyes. "You say you normally travel like this?"

"Only if we're in a hurry," Becca answered, grateful for a distraction from her own emotions, "or if we're transporting a lot of people. Most of the time our dragons pitch a fit if we use this option. They like to be ridden. Amir hasn't talked about this? He's been down here at least once."

"He did, but he didn't describe it all that well." An indulgent smile spread across Nahla's face as she talked about her new husband. "For a man that speaks so many languages, sometimes he's terrible at explaining things. He mentioned that Rurick was important to you, but he couldn't tell me exactly how?"

Nahla's tone encouraged her to explain, but not in an oppressive way. Becca hadn't had her new batwoman very long, but she liked her well enough that she felt an obligation to explain. Otherwise Nahla would have no idea what she was walking into. "Rurick was the city where we were first enslaved."

Sallah's head snapped around, eyes wide. "What?!"

"Come to think of it, we don't normally tell people which city we were in when that happened. Huh," Becca mused. "It was Rurick's guards that captured us. We spent nearly two weeks in irons until we found the right moment to break free. We got to know the people there better than other places we've taken because of that. Rurick was the first place we conquered, but also the first place we lost."

Nahla's head drew back in confusion. "I'm not sure I understand."

"We weren't keen on the idea of taking over a country at that point," Becca sought to explain. "We just wanted to be free. We turned over the government, fixed up the walls, and then went north to the Ruins of Rheben to investigate. We knew at that point that all of the slaves we met were somehow Chahiran descendants, but we didn't understand how they'd come to be in this country. We wanted answers before we returned home. So we went to investigate."

Remembering those days, Becca's face turned bleak and taut in remembered pain. "Our plan was to go up, spend a few days, maybe get an idea of what was going on before calling home and reporting our findings. We never suspected anything would go wrong in our absence. When we got back, we found Rurick empty. Not a single soul was left. All of our new friends gone, the people we wanted to save, missing without a trace.

"We were heartbroken," Becca recalled, voice going soft and husky, the words bitter in her mouth, "and so angry with ourselves. We'd left them open to attack by killing so many guards. Why had we assumed they would be safe? It was then that we made the choice to save Khobunter from itself. If the people could do nothing better than prey on their neighbors, then they clearly needed better rulers."

Sallah reached over to clasp hands with her, a tight grip she returned, as she gave the listening women a lopsided smile. "Rurick was the beginning of everything. We've been searching for the city's people from day one. Frankly, we're relieved that Rowe had them. Not happy they had them in chains, but happy they had them."

Nahla shook her head, astonished. "That's incredible. I'd never have suspected that. Then when we arrive, we should have a festival to celebrate."

"That's not a bad idea," Sallah encouraged, glancing over her shoulder at the trio behind her. "They probably feel like throwing a party for regaining their freedom."

Pursing her lips in thought, Nahla considered that for a moment before nodding decisively. "A festival is a great idea. We'll try to pull it off."

Becca didn't disagree, although she wished Rahim could have come down with her and seen Rurick for himself, heard the story from the survivors. "I keep hoping we'll find Azin's family in one of these provinces but it hasn't happened yet. Frankly, it worries me. Our only other province is Von, and if they're not there…."

"Let's not borrow trouble just yet," Sallah counseled. "They might very well be in Von."

She prayed for that, as Becca really wanted the best for Azin. The woman had already suffered and come through so much already.

"Passengers, prepare to disembark," Sallah intoned. The earth around them shimmered and changed as they began their ascent. "We have arrived."

Becca held her breath as they rose above the earth, the sand sloughing away to clear their heads, spilling about them like a fountain. Her first look at Rurick didn't show much of a difference, as Sallah had brought them to the outside of the northern gate. They'd been through here twice before to fix the walls, station guards, and build up the gardens. Becca noted that they were actually on the main highway, the earth around them still green and thriving, orchards still only her height but growing. It looked leagues different than the first look she'd had of this country nearly half a year ago.

Then her ears caught the sounds of multiple voices, of people moving, a beautiful cacophony on her ears. It brought tears to her eyes to realize life had returned to the city. She tightened her hold on Tail as she headed straight through the gates, too impatient to wait even a second longer. She called out a greeting as she moved to the guards on either side of the gate. "Akash! Pallav!"

Both men jolted then saluted, which Becca automatically returned, although she had to transfer Tail up to her shoulder to manage it.

"They're all here, Raya," Akash informed them with a bright smile on his face. "The last of them came in yesterday. They've all been so happy to be home, and they're exclaiming over all the fruits and vegetables."

"Everything's still working right? Everyone has enough food and water?" Becca anxiously checked.

"It's all fine. Raja Nolan has been busy growing things since his arrival," Pallav assured him with a broad smile, teeth very white against his dark skin. Turning in place he lifted a hand to cup his mouth and boomed out, "MAHARAJA BECCA HAS ARRIVED!"

Maharaja? What was that about? Becca had no chance to ask before people swarmed them from all sides. Becca didn't claim she could recognize every single person from the city—she'd never met all of them—but she saw more than a few familiar faces and reached for them with a smile wide enough to hurt. With the women, she got actual hugs;

the men clasped hands with her; and all of them exclaimed how happy they were to be home again, asking how had they managed it, and offering to bring Becca home to feed her. It overlapped so badly Becca couldn't get three words out before someone interrupted her, but the outpouring of love and relief were clear and didn't really need words. It quickly became a press from all sides, and while Becca didn't mind, it did overwhelm her. At some point Tail decided to save himself and leapt for freedom, disappearing in the crowd.

Trev'nor swooped in from somewhere to try and save the day, only to be caught up in the enthusiasm. It took Dunixan arriving on scene, his arms around Becca and Trev'nor, before they could fight their way out to a clearer space. He kept a firm grip on both of them, maneuvering them with his own body, until they reached a low-rise fountain, then urged them up onto the lip. Turning, he announced in a loud voice, "We'll have a festival tonight to celebrate everyone's return! You can speak with your maharajas then! For now, let's prepare food and drink, and if you can play an instrument, get it in tune!"

Delighted by this news, the crowd scattered in different directions. Becca leaned into Dunixan's side, not surprised when Trev'nor did the same thing on the other side, and caught her breath. "I knew they'd be happy to see us, but I wasn't quite expecting that. Are they still pouncing on you, Trev?"

"More or less," Trev'nor admitted to her cheerfully. "I don't mind, actually, but it does make getting around challenging. Roshan's been my hero, acting like a barrier for me. Speaking of, since when did we decide to hold a festival tonight?"

"Only thing I could think of to buy you some breathing space," Dunixan admitted with a shrug. "But it's appropriate, don't you think?"

Becca did not miss that Trev'nor was now on a first

name basis with Dunixan. She caught his eye and waggled her eyebrows at him meaningfully. He read her expression perfectly well and made a face back at her, but she could tell he was pleased at the development.

Nolan came up with Nahla and Sallah, having escaped the crowd at some point as well. He'd apparently had to go to the women's rescue. "I'll encourage the trees to bear a little more fruit, maybe get some juice presses going. Miss Nahla—"

"Just Nahla's fine," she assured him, hands up in a warding motion.

Correcting himself, Nolan gave her a smile in thanks for the informality. "Nahla, can you help me with the food? I don't know the traditional dishes or what ingredients they require."

"Absolutely, assuming Becca doesn't need me," she promised with a questioning look at Becca.

Becca waved her on. "I'll be fine. Go, go. Sallah, you're welcome to stay for the party."

"I'd love to but need to get back." Sallah made a face and shrugged, resigned. "I barely had time to run you down here. Should I come back later?"

"You'll likely need to, I'm not done with Rowe yet," Trev'nor answered apologetically.

"That's fine," Sallah assured him. "I'll be back later, then." With a casual wave, she headed back for the gates, the earth churning under her feet as she went, the Earth Path already opening up for her.

As people split off, Becca returned to the very interesting question burning in her mind. Since she had Dunixan on hand, she posed the question to him. "Why am I suddenly a Maharaja and what does that mean?"

"A century ago, before greed tore this country apart, the five provinces you know were actually united under a single governing body," Dunixan explained, his hold loosening a little on her, but still supportive. "We, at that time, had a king over the warlords. A maharaja."

"It literally means great lord," Trev'nor tacked on, still leaning against Dunixan. "Or so Amir explained to me. Rowe started it. After the treaty was signed, he started addressing me that way. Technically, we really are, as we have the greater majority of Khobunter under our rule."

While that made sense, at the same time, it didn't. "But shouldn't there be a different form for me? They're calling us both maharaja?"

"There is no feminine form," Dunixan explained, patently amused. "Never before in the history of Khobunter have we had a female warlord. Consorts, wives of the maharaja, yes. His equal? No."

"Well doesn't that just take the cake," Becca grumbled to herself. Of course there was no feminine form. What had she been thinking?

"Think later," Trev'nor advised. "Let's get ready for a party now. And we have a few people here dying to see you, they made sure I understood that. If I don't bring you to them, they will skewer me, great warlord or not."

"Then let's go," she encouraged, happy to see old friends.

Dunixan trailed after them as she went around the city greeting people. They'd gone a whole street when Shad found them.

Racing forward, Becca caught him in a tight hug, relieved to have him back even as she pelted, "Shad. How's Aletha? The baby?"

Hugging her tightly to him, he breathed in, then let out a long breath. "All good. Aletha didn't even need a Life Mage's help to deliver, which relieved all of us, and our daughter is perfectly healthy. And by healthy, I mean loud. She can be heard on any battlefield, I guarantee this."

Snorting a laugh, Becca asked against his shoulder, "So did you get any sleep at Strae?"

"Only when the princess slept. Did you know newborns only sleep for three hours at a time?"

That really made her laugh, painfully so. "Poor you. Wait, are you saying you actually get more sleep here than there?"

"Sad but true."

"What did you name her?"

"Sabrina."

"Riicsabrinaan," Becca tried it and nodded. "It rolls off the tongue well enough."

Stepping back, Shad looked around. "So, this is where it all began?"

"This is the place," Trev'nor confirmed, stepping in for his own hug. "Come on, I want to introduce you to people."

It turned into a tour of sorts, with them pointing out things they had built, or events that happened in certain places, interrupted often by people greeting them. With all of the walking they did, Becca grew unaccountably warm so she brought in extra shade clouds, which everyone appreciated. Even for late fall, the weather held unseasonable warmth. As the day waned, more and more stone tables appeared in the middle of the city, stretching out through the streets, all due to Trev'nor's handiwork. Food appeared on them—large trays of sliced fruits, vegetables, breads, dipping sauces, and spicy foods she didn't recognize. Street lights came up as well, casting the city in a warm glow, and a few strains of music could be heard as people reacquainted themselves with guitars and flutes.

The festival more or less started without anyone making an official announcement. As the suns set, the music started in earnest, a more concentrated effort than before in a minor key that sounded haunting and lovely. Bells appeared on a few women's fingers, their small cymbals clashing as they started a long, sinuous line, weaving in and around the tables. A few men joined in as counterpoint, and Becca found herself following along, mimicking the other women to get a feel for the dance. Two claps, holding the hands in prayer fashion above her head, then kick her left leg out in an arc, bringing it back around in a half-lunge, rotate up on that leg, then gently rocking back to her back leg, hips twisting in a dip before taking three slow steps forward and repeating.

From the corner of her eye, she caught sight of several men on the side of the street, clapping along and shouting encouragement. Trev'nor and Dunixan were on the corner, Dunixan's hands on Trev'nor's hips as he demonstrated and tried to teach Trev'nor the moves. Trev'nor laughed like a loon as he tried to learn. Becca could have told Dunixan that putting his hands anywhere near Trev'nor's ribcage would get the man doubled over in giggles. Trev'nor was the most ticklish person to walk the planet. But it had been ages since she'd seen Trev'nor laugh like that and she chose not to interrupt.

Besides, she didn't want to stop dancing.

They changed tunes and dances, sometimes pairing off, sometimes dancing in a line, and Becca danced it all. When she didn't know the steps, someone would teach her, and then off she'd go. She danced and danced, until her feet protested and her smile muscles threatened mutiny. Then she sat, drank a full gallon of water, ate whatever people put in front of her, and got up to dance some more. Someone snuck Nolan a particularly spicy dish and he went seal again, diving into the nearest irrigation canal, which got everyone laughing. Becca felt like they'd slipped back in time somehow, to that first week of freedom in the city.

Emotions and joy ran high until Becca felt sensitive with it. She had to retreat, then, find a space to let herself settle and breathe. Somehow she ended up on top of one of the higher buildings, lying flat on her back and stargazing. It reminded her of when they traveled toward the Isle of Strae when she was eight, the first time Shad had her stargaze with him, and she learned she could ask him any question in the world. That hadn't changed, even now, and it comforted her. Shad no longer possessed all of the answers to her questions, but that didn't matter. She still felt comforted knowing he'd listen.

"There she is." Trev'nor's head came into view as he mounted the stairs. "I swear you have a seeking ability in you, Becca. You always seem to find the quiet spaces up high."

"I'm part cat, that's why," she answered, turning her head to watch as he and Nolan came into view. "You try being raised by a cat and see how that affects you. Speaking of, have you seen Tail?"

"Someone offered him milk," Nolan informed her, dropping down to lay next to her. "He was whisker deep and purring last time I saw him. Our meurittas were given some sort of elaborate mess of ribbons to play with, so I think we're safe for at least ten minutes."

Trev'nor snorted as he dropped down on Becca's other side. "Safe being a relative term."

"I'm surprised you're up here," Nolan said slyly, popping his head up enough to give Trev'nor an arch look. "I thought you were too busy flirting."

"I wanted to check on Becca," Trev'nor retorted primly. "I can go back to flirting later."

Becca giggled, as she had a suspicion who the boys referred to. "Strange, isn't it, that we had to go to another country to find people we want?"

"In your case, yes," Trev'nor responded, sighing as he got more comfortable with the stone roof. Becca felt a ripple of magic before her back and head abruptly became more cradled, the roof conforming itself to her shape. "In mine, not so much. The Gardeners likely had certain things in mind when they first awakened my magic. I don't think they went so far as to prepare a certain person to be mine, but they're also really meddlesome, so they likely encouraged it."

Snorting, Nolan agreed, "Oh, I know they did. Garth said they'd deliberately meddled with him and Chatta."

Becca snapped her fingers, the memory of it coming abruptly to mind. "I'd almost forgotten that story."

"No one say anything," Trev'nor warned them. "I do not want to add any pressure. I'm difficult enough to date as it is."

Understanding fully what he meant, Becca swore, "I won't utter a peep. Not until much later, assuming things work out well."

"Wouldn't dream of it," Nolan promised.

A comfortable silence descended for a stretch. Becca's eyes went back to stargazing. Strange, how much more vivid the sky was here without a lot of cloud cover and trees to block her view. Brilliant spots of white twinkled in an inky dark sky, causing parts of the night to shine a lighter navy blue, breathtaking in its display. A gentle wind brushed over her, warm and comforting, carrying with it the scent of sunbaked rock and sounds of the festival still in full swing below. They'd likely party all night. Becca might even rejoin them when she got her second wind.

"It feels like a decade ago that we were here in chains," Trev'nor whispered, words so soft Becca strained to catch them all.

"Doesn't it?" Nolan agreed, equally as soft. "I thought you two were crazy when you said that you'd stay. I couldn't imagine there was really anything in this country worth saving. As long as we could take the magicians out, and help everyone in Rurick make it back home, I thought that might be good enough. I never imagined Danyal, Dunixan, Azin, Ehsan, or any of the rest."

"None of us did." Becca's hands blindly sought out the boys', her fingers trailing over cool stone until she found their wrists. They turned their hands to grip hers in return.

She needed that physical anchor as memories returned like ghosts. Her chest felt heavy with remembered anger, twisted with grief. "I almost regretted that decision several times. Every battle we fought, it was so hard to walk into a city and face the distrust."

"Harder still to face their hope, their gratitude after they realized we weren't there to hurt them," Trev'nor responded, tears thick in his voice. "No one should be that thankful for basic human kindness. I never regretted the decision we made that night, although Guardians knows it's been difficult even at the best of times."

Becca thought about turning her head to see his expression, but she didn't need to. She had the feeling he found it easier to confess everything knowing they all looked toward the sky. "We took a very roundabout method of bringing our friends home."

Nolan choked on a laugh. "You can say that again. A very difficult method, no less. I know I haven't said this before, but you're both shaping up to be good rulers."

That praise meant the world to her and Becca squeezed his hand tightly, her emotions clogging her throat too much to speak.

"Thanks, Nol." A trace of worry in his voice, Trev'nor asked, "You always said you'd stay until we had Khobunter under control and got everyone home again to Rurick. We're almost at that point. Will you leave after we get Von?"

"Not immediately," Nolan responded, tone reassuring. "I've grown fond of the place and I feel like you still need me. I mean, I know you have excellent help now, not saying otherwise—"

"Still would like to keep you for as long as we can," Becca stated firmly. "Dunixan's a huge help when it comes to governing, but he doesn't quite get what we're trying to achieve. You're always the one that knows how to break it down and explain it to people."

A smile in his voice, Nolan promised, "I'll stay for as long as I can. If nothing else, I'd like to see you two properly settled first."

"Hey now, are you rushing me?" Becca riposted in mock outrage.

"Or me?" Trev'nor objected in the same teasing vein.

Tone very dry, Nolan said, "Perish the thought. Although, seriously, Bec. Your wedding is going to be a three ring circus. Do you even have an idea of how to manage it?"

"I'm trying really hard not to think about it," she groaned. "Rahim assured me that eloping is not a possibility."

"It really isn't," both boys told her firmly in near unison.

"Do you two realize a wedding in Khobunter—not a royal wedding, mind you, just a general wedding—takes four days? And Trev'nor, no matter what you might think, you're going to be right alongside me preparing for all of this."

Trev'nor groaned. "The price I pay for being your best friend. Seriously."

"I think she's banking more on the co-ruler bit," Nolan disagreed, amusement rich in his tone.

"Aha, there you three are."

Becca lifted just her head, chin touching breastbone, to find Dunixan standing at the top of the stairs. He leaned casually against the side of the stone railing, his smile barely distinguishable on his face in the dim lighting. "Busted."

Laughing, he strode forward, offering a hand to pull Trev'nor up. "Your meurittas are braiding people's heads together and apparently enjoying their reactions when they can't untangle themselves. Shad is encouraging this."

"Of course he is," Trev'nor sighed before turning and offering Becca a hand up. "I feel hair cutting looming in our immediate future."

Cocking his head, Dunixan queried, "You can't just unbraid it?"

All three instantly shook their heads with Trev'nor explaining, "In a fit of madness, I taught them Tonkowacon braids. They're hideously complex, at least the higher forms of them are, and if it's just hair they're braiding, it's impossible to untangle. Far easier to cut them out and then have Nolan regrow the hair."

Dunixan's eyes roved over Trev'nor's head in a new light of understanding. "Those braids of yours mean something?"

"A lot, actually," Trev'nor answered with a quick smile and shrug. "Come on, help me round up the victims. I'll explain as we go."

Becca stayed a day longer than she planned on, finding it hard to pull away from Rurick so quickly. She left the boys and Dunixan down in Rowe to finish things up. Sallah came to fetch her, Nahla, and Shad back to Riyu. She did stop by Rheben on the way up to check on the new batch of students. Raile kept assuring her that he wasn't at maximum capacity yet, although how he managed such a large student body while simultaneously restoring Rheben was anyone's guess. Becca suspected the man didn't sleep.

She'd expected Trev'nor to be back after a few days, but a week later she got a different message relayed through her dragon. "Trev'nor still wants more time down there?" she asked Cat dubiously. "But he's been there almost two weeks already. And he said himself that Rowe wasn't in as bad of shape as Trexler or Riyu."

"More time," Cat maintained, although she did flick her ears back and forth, the dragon equivalent of a shrug. "Gardens aren't in yet."

"I will bet you the left leg of my childhood teddy bear that the gardens are in and he's terraforming things he shouldn't be right now. And flirting," Becca grumbled. She looked to the sky, making sure she didn't lose track of the storm Trev'nor had requested. Sitting up here on the top of the fortress made it easy to see the sky in all directions, which made her job easier, but only if she actually paid attention while she worked.

A scrape of a boot against stone heralded Rahim's entrance. "You might be right, but even if he's not finished, he needs to come back."

Turning, she greeted her boyfriend with a smile that quickly faded. "Hi, honey. I don't like that expression on your face, that's your worried look. What's gone wrong this time?"

Rahim came around to kneel in front of her, their knees brushing. "I asked Ginger and Ehsan to scout the border of Von for me. They went and took a look at Brecon Watchtower since it's closest, and I don't like what they had to report. Ehsan says that all of the fields and gardens were ruined and he sensed poison in the wells. Worse, it looked like half of the town lay abandoned."

A deep sense of foreboding settled into the pit of her stomach like an oily snake. "Salted earth policy."

His brows twitched together in a frown. "I don't know that phrase."

"No, likely not. It's something that only Shad's ever used. They did this sometimes in the Magic War." Becca's mind whirled even as she sought to explain, thinking of logistics and timelines, wondering how she could send word to her friends to get them back to Riyu quickly. "You take all able-bodied people out of the area, then destroy any trace of food, and poison the wells so that the conquering force has nothing to live on. It forces them to either retreat or double the cost of maintaining supply lines. Either way, it puts the conquering force in a terrible position, as they face either starvation or bankruptcy."

Rahim swore under his breath. "We can't afford to waste any further time. If they've already done this to Brecon, then—"

"They're working on the other cities now. We must

send emergency rations immediately," Becca agreed whole-heartedly, already rising to her feet. A sense of panic rode up her spine, urging her to move quickly.

He gave her a hand up, then maintained his grip on her for a moment. "I'll organize troops and supplies. You don't think this a trap?"

That question amused her in a bleak way. "Rahim, if this were any other warlord, would they send in help to an enemy city?"

"I think…" he trailed off, then snorted in dark amusement. "I'm so accustomed to your ways now—of sending help where help is needed—that I sometimes forget what it was like before you came. No, no warlord would even consider it. I doubt they know you well enough through the reports to guess you would do this. Taking care of your own territory is one thing, helping an enemy another. You realize that at the very least, they'll pull both Brecon and Dilmun and retreat into Von."

"I just pray they haven't done it to all of their cities except Von," Becca responded grimly. "I can't afford to help four cities at once. Rahim, go. I'll sit here and send out a recall, maybe ask Raile to borrow his Life Mage as well, as I think we'll sorely need the help for the next few weeks."

Nodding understanding, he squeezed her hand once and then took off down the stairs at a fast sprint.

To the listening Cat, still curled up around the top of the building, Becca requested, "Send word to Trev'nor and Nolan, and use these words precisely: Von is using salted earth policy. Brecon Watchtower's first. Return to Riyu immediately. See if you can find Shad for me too."

Nodding her understanding, Cat lifted her head and did a sonorous call, cut up with guttural undertones that were so deep Becca couldn't even hear some of them, just feel them.

Ignoring that, she pulled her mirror free and called urgently, "Raile. Raile!"

"I'm here, I'm here, what's the fuss?"

"Raile, I've got an emergency on my hands and need immediate help. Von's using salted earth policy against his own cities, and at least Brecon Watchtower is in trouble—"

Raile cut her off with an oath so vile it turned the air blue and drew a blush to her cheeks—and this after spending most of her life around soldiers. "Those vermin scum. To their own people? It's unforgiveable. Alright, I'm sending you help immediately. Life Mage, Earth Mage, any witches or wizards I can spare, and what food we have in storage to help stem the tide. It will arrive by evening."

"I love you," she told him seriously.

That made him chuckle briefly. "Ah, if only I were two centuries younger, I'd give General Danyal a run for his money. What else can I do?"

"You're the only one with the means to send a comprehensive message to the other cities. Ask them to gather what food they can spare and request that Sallah swing by each and pick it up. We do not have enough ready food at hand to do more than feed them as a stopgap measure. I need to give our Earth and Life Mages time to get a garden in, which takes at least a few days."

"I'll do that next," he promised.

"I thought Von might be up to something because they didn't respond one way or another to our letter, but this?" Becca pounded a fist against her thigh, so mad she wanted to unleash a tornado at something. Or lightning. "I don't think any of us expected this."

"Evil men do evil things, unfortunately. The best we can do is stop them. I'll put the call out to the other cities immediately. Becca, one thing, do you know if they took all of the slaves out of Brecon?"

"Our intelligence isn't that detailed," she apologized, kicking herself for not thinking to ask Rahim that very question. "In fact, we're not even sure how many people there are to feed. Ehsan flew over it earlier and it's his eyewitness account we're going off of."

"I see. Then let's plan for the worst and hope for the best. I'll call you again when I have everything in motion. Try to get firmer numbers for me."

Becca nodded firmly even though he couldn't see it. "I will." She ended the call and immediately brought it up again. "Ehsan?"

The Water Mage responded almost immediately, the faint rush of wind around him, a sound she knew well. He'd just landed somewhere. "Here. Did Danyal speak to you already?"

"He did, just now. I have Raile sending up help and supplies. Rahim's also gathering troops and supplies, and we've got a call out to the other cities for supplies. Ehsan, I need firmer numbers of how many people are in Brecon and if there's any magicians left in the city. Can you take a Legend with you and see if you can give me at least an estimate?"

"I will, just let me get more water and some food; we'll take off within the hour. Becca, I'm worried about Dilmun."

"We are too, but I don't want you flying out that far, I might need you rather soon." Thinking fast, she promised, "I'll contact the dragons in Sha Watchtower, they're closer, and they can give us an idea of what's going on there."

"That's smart. Ah, Ginger says she'll ask them."

Bless his dragon for being quick on the uptake. "Tell her I owe her a cow."

"She'll hold you to that, don't think she won't."

Another voice, lighter and with the varied undertones of a dragon's speech, interrupted: "Big cow."

"I promise, big as I can find," Becca responded, trying not to laugh. What was it about dragons and beef, anyway?

"Shining Sand flying to city. Will look and report."

"Thank you, Ginger. Ehsan, don't push your luck and approach too close to Brecon. It's a very, very small possibility, but they might have done this on purpose to lure us in."

"I know, don't worry. Why do you think I'm taking water with me? I'll either use it to give some immediate relief or have a weapon on hand."

"You're a smart man. Alright, go, keep us posted." Becca ended the call, then took a minute to bury her face in her hands and scream. What was wrong with this country?!

Cat nudged her side, nuzzling in a comforting way that almost sent Becca straight to the floor. Tail wound around her ankles, also trying to give comfort. "Breathe," her dragon advised sympathetically. "Will be fine."

"It'd better be," Becca snarled, lifting her head again to stare northward. "Because if it isn't, they're going to pay the price."

As much as she wanted to fix the problem now, Becca couldn't. Too many other things had to happen, and it took time to pull even a temporary solution together. She spent her entire morning doing nothing but coordinating people, double checking how many supplies were needed, and reporting to someone else the status. Cat helped as much as she could by relaying messages back and forth from the other dragons, which sped the process along admirably. Shad hopped on a dragon and went for Jashni, coordinating a relief effort from there, as they had more food supplies due to their coastal location.

At noon Becca retreated to her desk to eat a hastily prepared sandwich, fielding calls and eating whenever she felt she could risk a bite. They'd made good progress despite only preparing for the past four hours, so she had hope they'd be ready to roll out by morning.

"Becca?" Of course Ehsan called when she had a mouthful.

She managed a garbled, "Here."

"I, ah, sort of landed in Brecon."

Groaning, she stopped chewing for a moment and closed her eyes in a fatalistic manner. Forcing herself to swallow what was in her mouth, she cleared her throat, then demanded, "Why?"

"Jetta is with me. She said there wasn't anyone guarding the walls, or in the barracks, just civilians. A few slaves, not many, and mostly the old and weak. Same goes for Brecon's populace. We landed outside and came in slow, but the people here were so glad to see clean water, they let us right in without a fuss. It's…pretty bad here, Becca."

So Jetta had gone in with him? Becca had to give that woman props. She had guts to waltz into enemy territory with only one mage and a dragon. "Give me details."

"They destroyed all of the food stores, the gardens, the fields, even people's personal garden beds. There's no water to be had except what I've brought with me and I distributed most of it already. They said this happened about three days ago, so they're starving over here. Literally. How fast can you get food in?"

"Three days?" she repeated incredulously.

"That's what they said. There's only the old, the infirm, or the very young left. Anyone between eight and fifty were taken. Jetta took a headcount and we have a little under two thousand."

Two thousand. "We actually planned for more than that, just in case. I have enough food to last them a day gathered now, but—"

"Send it. Immediately. Becca, when I say very young, I mean like infants."

She slammed her head against the desk and fought not to either lose her temper or cry. Right now she felt like doing both. Forcing her emotions back under control, she rasped out, "I'll send them now. Tell everyone to hold tight, just for a few more hours. I'll have to fly in what supplies we can via dragon. All of our Earth Mages are not in Riyu and unavailable at the moment."

"Understood, I'll tell them. I'll borrow Azin to uncover the wells here."

"Do they know if Dilmun is in the same situation?"

"We haven't heard from them yet?"

"I wasn't expecting to, Shining Sand likely won't arrive for another hour at the very least. He had further to fly."

"True. I sometimes lose track of distance when flying. No, no one here knows anything about Dilmun. I asked."

Typical. "Are you absolutely sure this isn't a trap of any kind?"

"Absolutely positive. If you could see what I'm seeing, you wouldn't even ask the question. The Rikkana here swore to me that if we sent help, everyone here would give you an oath of fealty. You won't have to fight for this place, Becca. You can just waltz in and take it."

While that would be a nice change of pace, Becca wished it hadn't come at such a high cost. "I'll come myself with the supplies. Tell them to just hold on for a few more hours, we're almost ready here and we can leave very soon."

"I will. See you soon."

She stared at the mirror in her hands for a long moment, reining in her temper. Only then did she call out, "Cat?"

The dragon coiled up on the roof slithered down, scales scraping against stone, until one eye came into view in the window. "Find Rahim?"

"It's like you read minds," Becca marveled, dredging up a faint smile for her. "Yes, please. Tell him to hurry, that Ehsan said infants are in trouble, so bring milk."

"Will." The dragon disappeared from view, and the building shook a moment later as she launched off of it. They really had to talk about that. This building was not designed to withstand that kind of force. Becca swore someday soon the building would be knocked right off its foundation.

Becca bit viciously into her sandwich even though her appetite had more or less fled. She likely wouldn't be able to eat much the rest of the day so she'd better make the most of this meal. As she ate, she daydreamed about hopping on Cat and flying to Von and then blasting the city to smithereens. Not that anyone would let her do that, nor should she, as she'd kill innocents in the process.

Still, she could dream, couldn't she?

Ehsan had not been exaggerating. Brecon was bad.

It reminded her eerily of Rurick—the second time they'd come back to the city to find it completely empty—the walls and parts of town destroyed. Only this was worse. Far worse. Buildings bore testament of fire damage in some areas, the fields scorched, and every well or fountain in town broken down to rubble. If not for half of the city still standing, and the people dragging themselves toward the center of town, she would have said the place past redemption.

But they had to save it, didn't they? Because now it was one of theirs.

She strode through town with two platoons of soldiers, all carrying cartons of food in their hands, overseeing supplies distributed. Half her attention rested on the storm overhead that she'd called. They needed more than a little rain to help wash the soot away, and Ehsan claimed he could remove the poisoned water, boil it, clean out the wells, then use rain to refill them with no damage done. As he was the water expert, Becca trusted his opinion. Trev'nor and Nolan wouldn't arrive in Riyu until tonight, so she had to do what she could until they could make it to Brecon.

A line formed in one area, people taking small bags of flour to make flatbread with. Ginger watched from her perch on a nearby rooftop. She lifted her head and announced to

Becca, "People coming."

"What people?" she asked, uncertain what the dragon meant by that statement.

"Magic people." Nodding decisively, Ginger lifted her head and called out a sonorous note.

Hopefully that meant her group from Rheben. She waited a few more minutes, saw the dragons land outside the main gate, crates and people quickly set on the ground. She went out to coordinate with the first wizard she saw, one of her Coven Ordan volunteers, and spent a few minutes directing people on where to go. With their orders issued, she retreated back into the city, leading the way to the next food station. She refused to let a single person go hungry and wouldn't rest until she knew everyone had at least a little food. As she walked down what must be the main street, she saw multiple dragons perched on rooftops or snugged into side streets, all of them talking to the citizens. Somewhat alarmed citizens, but people replied tentatively, their eyes wide at the experience of talking to an actual dragon. Becca gave it until tomorrow before her winged friends had charmed the whole town.

The one she most worried about was Starlight, as she had carried all of the milk and soft foods for the babies. Jetta had reported forty-six infants and one hundred and eighty children under the age of two, which included those found in the slave pens. Becca really didn't think they had enough adults on hand to deal with that many children at once.

Rounding a corner, she found Starlight, her midnight-blue skin a sharp contrast to the tan buildings and setting suns. In front of her sat two open crates, and elderly women quickly divvied out the milk to each other, passing it along until someone with a free hand could pick up a crying child and feed them. Becca saw children as well, none of them older than seven, with young babies or children in their arms, feeding them. Older siblings feeding younger, perhaps? She saw several old men as well, their hands full of infants. Grandfathers, likely. Nahla had beaten her there, a child already in hand, and she looked up with a plaintive expression that basically screamed for help. Becca saw a desperate scene, and even though her own experience with children was limited, she jumped right in. "Pass me a bottle."

The woman near the crate immediately did so, without even looking, then glanced her direction and blinked. Her dark eyes took in Becca's foreign looks and uniform and she did a double take before immediately dropping into a bow. "Maharaja."

"That's me," Becca admitted cheerfully, already heading for a little girl sobbing with hunger. "More help is coming, I promise, we just have to do what we can for now. Here now, shh, take the nipple. That's a good baby."

The adults didn't have the luxury to watch their warlord take a child into her arms and feed her, even if it probably did look like a strange sight. She'd asked Rahim to free the slaves while she oversaw the distribution of supplies and hoped he was done there soon, as apparently they needed the help here more than anywhere else. Only three dozen men, women, and children fed all of these babies. Everyone else focused on feeding themselves.

When the child in her hands finally got full, she fell instantly to sleep, and Becca stole a moment to just watch her. It felt immensely satisfying to feed her. Was this a little of what motherhood felt like? The thought pleased her and she couldn't help but grin. Then she looked up and realized she had no idea what to do with the baby now. They were in an open street, for pity's sake, she couldn't just put her on the ground, even if she had been there before.

"Becca," Starlight beckoned, her open paw on the ground twitching a single claw in a come-hither gesture. "Here."

"What, are you going to hold her for me?" Coming around, Becca saw in astonishment that she actually had a dozen children already, all of them lying side by side, comfortably sleeping. "Wow. Now that's a sight. Alright, well, have another one, I guess."

"Good babysitter," Starlight informed her smugly.

"Yes, you are," Becca agreed readily and made note of that for the future. Turning, she grabbed another bottle from the crate and headed for the next child crying its eyes out.

"No," one of the elderly women corrected, pointing to a child lying next to it. "Feed the quiet ones first. Children sleep more when starved."

So, the quiet ones were in a more desperate situation? "I see. Thank you." Becca went for the other child instead, the motion jostling the child awake so that it mewled, working up to a full cry. Hoping to thwart this, she coaxed the nipple into that tight mouth, relaxing a hair when the baby latched onto it immediately, two small hands coming up to help grip the bottle. Alright, one minor crisis averted.

This time she sat on a doorstep next to one of the elderly women who somehow juggled two children at once, feeding an infant with one hand while sharing bites of bread and cheese with a toddler perched on her feet. "Hello. No, no, don't stand. You're fine, keep going."

The woman managed a deferential duck of the head. "Thank you, Maharaja. We would have been lost without you."

Literally. Becca tried not to think too much on that. The thought of losing two cities to starvation sickened her stomach. "We're very glad we discovered the situation when we did. Is this all the children? Do you know?"

"Your subordinate, Carjettaan?" the woman stumbled over the foreign name a little. "She made sure all were gathered here."

"Oh, good. Thank you, I haven't been able to double check with her. What's your name?"

"Daru," the woman answered a little shyly. "These two

are my grandchildren."

"Are they?" Becca stared at the two and then kicked herself. Of course the grandmother would feed her own grandchildren first, that was just maternal instinct. "I see. Do you have any others?"

"One," Daru allowed, her chin pointing to the dragon babysitter. "She's sleeping there. It's a wonder to see a dragon so tame."

"They're naturally like that, actually," Becca corrected absently, wondering just how many grandmothers and grandfathers had made feeding their grandchildren a priority over eating themselves. "They're only fierce and bloodthirsty when something threatens their own. Daru, I've been searching for the Rikkana or Rikkan but haven't found them yet. Where are they?"

"Our Rikkana is there," Daru did the chin pointing thing again to a woman on the opposite side of the street, who also fed multiple children at once. "Niyati is her name."

"Thank you." And the baby in her lap was fast asleep, mouth still around the nipple. Poor thing probably hadn't slept well because of the hunger pangs. Becca popped up, put him (her?) down with the rest in the dragon's claw, then headed for the next child. She might as well feed someone while talking to the Rikkana. They didn't have the luxury of doing one thing at a time.

Becca, remembering the advice from earlier, went for the quietest child she could put her hands on. Lifting what seemed to be a one year old in her arms, she cradled him in the crook of her elbow and lifted a bottle to his mouth, which he latched onto fervently.

"Angle the bottle a little more," Rikkana Niyati recommended, juggling a plate of bread on her knee and a bottle in her free hand. "They won't suck in as much air that way."

Becca blessed her linguistic skills, as for once, she'd

comprehended the Khobuntish without a single issue in spite of the northern accent. Doing her best, she responded in the same language, "Thanks for the tip. I've rarely fed a baby before this."

"Takes practice, but you're young yet," Niyati responded with an encouraging smile. "Thank you, Maharaja. We were in dire need of help. We never once thought it would come from an enemy."

"The world is strange that way," Becca agreed, finding an open spot of ground near the woman and settling into it cross-legged. "Rikkana, do you have the authority to formally swear the city over to me?"

"The Rikkan and I both do, yes."

"Then let's do that officially after we get everyone fed," Becca requested, shifting the baby in her arms to a slightly more comfortable position. Holding something that weighed twenty pounds at the same angle for long lengths of time did wear an elbow out quickly. "And tell me, what do you suggest about long-term care for the children? I don't know who to send here to help."

"Your soldiers likely have fathers in the ranks," Niyati pointed out patiently. "Wouldn't they be useful?"

Becca really should have thought of that before. "I'll ask for volunteers, then. Or wait, I bet Rahim would know. The man knows everything."

"Patently untrue, Becca," Rahim stated as he picked his way toward her, avoiding all of the people on the ground.

"Is not," she snarked back, grinning up at him. "Hi, honey. How goes it?"

"Everyone's out of chains and being fed," he reported, coming around and sinking down to his haunches so they could converse comfortably. "I've unfortunately found a few bodies but not nearly as high of a count as we feared. We have enough food for tonight and the morning, but we'll need more supplies and help in before lunch, which I think we can manage. This is quite the sight. I've never seen you with children before."

"I don't have a lot of experience with them," Becca answered truthfully, eyeing the bottle and judging it to be about half empty. The child in her arms showed no interest in slowing down, chugging it for all it was worth. When the baby choked, she took the nipple away for a moment, urging the kid to breathe, as she didn't want it spewing on her. "I was one of the youngest in the academy, after all, except Garth's kids. And Kaya's brood, but they're dragons, I'm not sure they count. I never had to help feed them."

Starlight, listening in, found this funny and snorted a dragonish laugh.

Rahim, as a man of impeccable good sense, did not just sit there and look decorative, but grabbed a bottle and a baby and joined them. Becca beamed, her affection for him doubling, especially since he was obviously out of his element. He looked very uncertain about how to hold either baby or bottle and was aping their positions as best he could.

"Tilt her head up more," Niyati instructed patiently, eyes twinkling in mirth. "That's it. We'll make a father of you yet. Maharaja, this is your husband?"

"Not quite," Becca answered, finding Rahim's flush amusing. "This is General Rahim Danyal and also the man I'm courting."

"Ah," the Rikkana intoned knowingly. "I see. Harmony upon you, General. I am Rikkana Niyati."

"Rikkana," Rahim greeted with a respectful bow of the head. "I've been searching for you. Your Rikkan assures me that all are accounted for and that he is willing to swear the city over to us if you are?"

She nodded sadly. "I am."

"Good, we'll do that later tonight, when people are more settled." Rahim frowned, shifted the fussing baby so the bottle sat more comfortably near her mouth, and then smiled when she peacefully started eating. "Becca, Ehsan informs me he got all of the poison out of the wells, so if we can unbury them, we'll have fresh water here."

"Trev'nor will do it tomorrow," she responded, thinking hard. "Or Sallah, whoever gets here first. Bear with us, Rikkana, we have the right help coming, but they were on the other end of the country when we learned of this. Tomorrow morning is as quickly as they can get here."

"Tomorrow morning is fine," she assured them. "General, perhaps we can have further help from your soldiers? Fathers that have experience with children?"

"I had the same thought," Rahim responded in kind. "I've already passed the order to Riyu for volunteers. They will hopefully be here tonight, as they have a shorter distance to travel."

Becca looked at him wonderingly. "Now when did you think of that?"

"About the same time I heard children screaming their heads off," he answered, winking at her. "If I'm at a loss with a crying child, I know who I'd ask for first."

"A parent," she acknowledged ruefully. "Right. I suppose I was thinking about everything else, then, as the obvious didn't hit me until our Rikkana said it. Although I wish Nolan would get here tonight, as I have no idea if any of them are dehydrated after being without water and milk for three days."

"They likely are, but there's little we can do about that but feed them," Rahim observed. "Have you heard from Nolan or Trev'nor?"

"Not since this morning," she denied thoughtfully. "Nolan said he'd call when they got closer to Riyu, see if we needed immediate help tonight, and I rather expected a call before—" she cut off as a muted sound came from her breast pocket. Juggling baby and bottle, she reached for the mirror and just managed to ease it free with two fingers before lifting it to her mouth. "Say again?"

"Becca, it's Nolan."

"Ah, there you are! Rahim and I were just talking about you."

"Is that why my ears are burning?" Nolan teased. "I should have figured. We're a few minutes south of Riyu now. Do you need us up there?"

"Please?" she asked plaintively. "I know you're tired, but they buried all of the fountains and wells up here, I need Trev to unbury them. And they left a lot of children up here, and no one's been able to eat for three days, so I'm worried about the kids."

"Define children," Trev'nor requested uneasily. "How old we talking about, here?"

"The youngest is four months," Niyati answered in a hard, clipped voice. Her jaw worked under strong emotion, her anger clear to see.

"Great good Guardians, they left all of the infants behind?!" Nolan demanded incredulously. "I'm going to wring their filthy necks. Trev, speed up."

"Already am. Bec, should I swing by Riyu first and pick anything up?"

"No, we're set for tonight and we don't have enough supplies put together for tomorrow yet."

Rahim caught her wrist and leaned in to correct, "Actually, do that. Carjettaan went back to the city to gather up volunteers, so they should be ready to go about the time you hit Riyu."

"Alright, I'll do that. See you soon."

Becca saw that her baby was done, so she pocketed the mirror broach and put him down for a nap alongside the rest. She had this sneaking suspicion that by the time she finished feeding all the babies, Trev'nor would just manage to get the wells unburied, thereby missing the opportunity to feed anyone. Well, even if that did happen, she'd make sure he got a chance tomorrow.

For his own good, of course.

Trev'nor did not arrive within the next hour, nor did anyone else, and the supplies in Brecon went very low indeed. Becca actually picked up the mirror to call him when she heard a rising of voices near the main gates. It was a strange overlap of orders being called out, people wailing in relief, and the rumbles of dragons volleying back and forth. Not knowing what to expect, she rushed out into the main street to get a look for herself, only to stumble to an incredulous halt.

Every free dragon of Riyu and Jashni covered the buildings and along the top of the wall, crammed into the streets and the road outside. They carried crates and passengers, setting both gently to the earth, only shuffling aside to give the others room to enter the city. Becca expected soldiers to arrive with aid, and she saw more than a few uniforms, but most of the new arrivals seemed to be citizens. She recognized more than one face and felt the world tilt on her. Riyu's citizens had come?

She spied Shad and Jetta in the crowd and broke into a jog, waving a hand over her head to get their attention. Shad broke off speaking to Jetta to return the wave, meeting her halfway. "I brought what help I could. Trev stole half of it for Dilmun."

"Wait, he's here?"

"Here and gone again," Shad responded, his attention already drifting back to the people arriving. "Jetta had people mobilized in Riyu, so we passed the word via dragon to Trev and he swung by first to get me, then Jetta's group, before coming here. I don't even want to know how fast he was going, the earth was making some very strange cracking noises."

Since Shad grinned saying that, Becca knew he'd enjoyed the adrenaline ride. "I can't believe—Riyu's people came to help?"

"It took no effort to convince them." Jetta came to stand with them, a proud smile on her face. "I just spread the word that Brecon and Dilmun had people in trouble, the warlords had gone ahead. I didn't even ask. They immediately pulled together food and water and when they learned of the children, every young woman and grandmother that could responded as well. We—"

Impatient, one of the women rushed forward, coming straight for them. It took Becca a moment to put a face to name, then it came back in a rush. Jamila, the young woman who had the guts to ask about the marriage license fees when they'd first taken Riyu. "Jamila."

"Maharaja." Jamila ducked into a quick bow, or as much as she could manage around the bottles and blankets she had cradled against her chest. "Where are the children?"

Straight to business. Becca grinned at her as that was exactly the right attitude for this situation. "Straight down this street, at the major intersection, go left. No, better yet— Jetta, take all the ones that can care for the children and lead them, please."

"On it," the woman responded briskly, turning back and clapping her hands, calling out orders.

As people moved, Becca stayed Shad with a hand on his shoulder, needing more information before she also directed people. "Who's with Trev?"

"Nolan, Ehsan, Azin, Mose and about three dozen volunteers, including some soldiers."

"Dunixan?"

"Dunixan's still in Rowe finishing up," Shad informed her. "Where do you need the rest of us to go?"

"There's still people stuck in their houses, too sick to move, can you organize the troops to go house to house and get them all out? We've commandeered a hotel on the main square to put people there."

Nodding, he moved off in a ground eating stride, his voice booming out as if he were on a battlefield.

Becca rather felt like they were on one, with time as their enemy. It boggled her mind that her people had so readily pitched in to give aid. It might not be remarkable behavior in the rest of the world, but this was Khobunter. Anyone outside of a province was an enemy, not a friend. To see them so readily help the enemy stunned her.

Well. Maybe they were having more impact on Khobunter's culture than she realized. A smile on her face, Becca lifted the mirror to her mouth once more to make sure that Trev'nor had the help he needed.

16

Trev'nor had passed Rheben when the report came in that Dilmun had also been ravaged, most of its people taken, and the rest left to fend for themselves in an area turned inhospitable. Trev'nor didn't know whether to cry or rage—fought not to do both—as he frantically transported people toward Dilmun with what food crates they could scrape together. The hour had to be near ten in the evening, and normally Trev'nor looked for a bed about this point, but he couldn't even think of sleeping until he could at least offer clean drinking water to those poor people.

If, of course, they were willing to let an enemy in.

Unlike other places, Trev'nor did not just pop in wherever he wished, but rose just inside the gates, as he didn't know if they would be willing to let him in. As his head surfaced above the ground, he found that no soldiers were on station, like Brecon. No one lingered in the streets, either, although a few places had dim lighting, as if they had candles or something equally small to use for illumination. In his loudest voice, he called out, "MY NAME IS RHEBENTREV'NOREN AND I AM MAHARAJA OF KHOBUNTER. I'VE COME TO GIVE AID."

The dragons shook themselves behind him, shedding imaginary dirt as they always did after being underground, then hopped lightly on top of the walls, perching there and keeping watch. Priya hopped up onto a wall and joined them, watching the city avidly. Trev'nor paid no attention to them as someone tentatively poked his head out of a doorway, taking them in with wide eyes. "Who did you say you were?"

Striding to him, Trev'nor answered at a lower volume, "Maharaja of Khobunter, Rhebentrev'noren. Who might you be?"

"Amit, Rikkan of Dilmun," the man answered hoarsely, throat no doubt parched from days without water. "Maharaja, have you come to conquer this place?"

"I have," Trev'nor answered, stopping at his doorway and giving him a respectful bow. "Rikkan, harmony find you."

Bemused at this greeting, he bowed back, the motion jerky. "Harmony find you, Maharaja. There is nothing of value here. Warlord Von had everything removed, to stop you from taking it."

"I'll take it and save the people he left behind," Trev'nor answered steadily, meeting the man's eyes in the dim light of the moon. "I have with me a Life Mage, Water Mage, and Elemental Mage. We'll clean the wells, provide drinking water for you all tonight, and heal anyone injured. I have a few supplies on me, mostly flatbread, but we have more food being gathered up tonight that will arrive tomorrow. Help me gather the people, Rikkan."

The man cried unabashedly, tears streaming down craggy cheeks. He didn't even try to wipe them away. "I will. Thank you, Maharaja, I will."

Trev'nor clapped the man on the shoulder, squeezing gently before letting go. "It will be alright, I promise you. For now, show me to the nearest well or fountain, we'll start there. Then we'll gather the people. Are there any slaves left behind?"

"Some hundred or so," he answered, hurrying off his doorstep, then listing sideways.

Trev'nor caught him, putting a steadying hand around

his waist. Too weak from hunger to move quickly? It seemed that way. "Lean on me, it's fine. No, truly, it's fine. You're about to faint from hunger and dehydration. Nolan, can you—"

Anticipating what he needed before Trev'nor could, his friend stepped around and offered Amit a piece of flatbread, which the man hastily accepted with mumbled thanks and devoured in four bites. "Slowly," Nolan advised sympathetically. "If you eat too much all at once, your stomach will revolt. Ah, busted buckets, it's trying to already. Hold still for a moment."

Confused, Amit allowed Nolan to touch his stomach, then shivered from head to toe, eyes wide. "What are you doing?"

"Tweaking your digestive system so you don't throw up," Nolan responded absently.

"He's the Life Mage, Vonnolanen," Trev'nor explained so his friend could focus. "Think of it like having medicine pouring through you, as that's essentially what his magic does."

"Mage?" Amit repeated, dumbfounded. "Von? The Vons are mages?"

"Originally, yes," Nolan answered, then looked at him sharply. "Why?"

"There was a story, a legend, that a man named Von came from Chahir and created our capital city," Amit answered slowly, studying Nolan with open fascination. "A man as fair as the sun, with eyes like the sky, that's what the legend said. He wasn't a magician, though."

"I will bet you my eye teeth he was, and your history was changed to make it more politically acceptable," Nolan corrected gently. "The only members of my family that came north were mages."

While it was all fascinating, Trev'nor also recognized they had other emergencies demanding attention. "The history lesson can wait until later. Let's focus on feeding people now, alright?"

Nolan chittered at the meurittas, giving them some sort of order, and they darted ahead, air swooping around them as they flew down the street. Amit pulled back to the situation and urged Trev'nor forward. Acting as a crutch, he did so, straight for what had to be the downtown section, as it had decorative fountains set in an open courtyard. Or at least they likely had been decorative before someone took sledgehammers to them. Grimly, Trev'nor set about removing the rubble, putting them back into a working shape with little care for how pretty it looked. Square fountains worked just as well as round ones.

Turning his head, he found Ehsan right behind him and requested, "Can you work with the water now?"

"I can, and I just spoke with Becca, she's sending another storm my direction to help. If you'll fix that fountain, there? I'll put the clean water in it."

"Alright." Trev'nor followed directions, then let Ehsan focus as he went through the city, Amit at his side, calling for people to come out and drink, eat. People tentatively poked their heads out of their homes, or whatever buildings that still offered good shelter, asking few in the way of questions. All of them eyed Trev'nor warily, but their suspicions eased as he fed them.

Sadly, even the most paranoid person becomes more docile when on the brink of starvation.

Ehsan pulled more and more water out of the poisoned wells, boiled it in a roiling ball mid-air, then deposited the cleaned water in the fountains Trev'nor created for them. People felt a little skittish of magically touched water but were desperate enough to drink it anyway.

Mose took over directing their volunteers and soldiers, everyone spreading out through the city. They announced over and over that help had arrived, giving aid to any too weak or disabled to make it out of the houses under their own power. His and Nolan's meurittas went with them, unlocking any door necessary, proud of themselves for being so helpful. Priya darted in to rub up against his face, boastful and chittering, then flew off again as someone called for her help. Trev'nor gave her a quick grin but didn't have the energy to really keep track of her. He checked in on his volunteers as he worked, pausing to give orders only as necessary, but otherwise let Mose handle things.

Nolan tapped him on the shoulder and leaned in to murmur in Chahirese, "I found someone here who knows where the slave pens are. I'll head there next. What are we going to do about the infants and children?"

"At least get water in them tonight, bread if they have enough teeth to eat it," Trev'nor responded helplessly. "I don't know what else to do."

Grimly, Nolan nodded understanding, then went off at a quick lope.

Thinking quickly, Trev'nor fished his mirror broach out and tried hopefully, "Sallah? Dearest cousin?"

"Here. I just arrived in Riyu, where is everyone?"

"Becca's in Brecon, Nolan and I are in Dilmun. Sallah, please tell me you brought food supplies with you?"

"What we could quickly scrape up, which isn't a lot. I've got several mages and some witches that were able to come up with me. Where do I need to take everything?"

"Dilmun, please, and quickly. Also, grab whatever help you can from Riyu before you come. I have a lot of children up here that need to be fed and no real means to help them." He'd thought he'd stolen enough volunteers from Shad's and Jetta's group, but they'd proven inadequate to the task.

"Children. Define children."

"Ages infant to about eight."

"That whoreson abandoned children?!"

"Believe me," he said wearily, taking a moment to lean against a wall, "you're not going to say something we haven't already. Sallah, we're at our wit's end over here. We have a good three thousand people who haven't had water or food in about three days."

"I'll be there in an hour or less," she promised and abruptly ended the call.

He did love his cousin. Spying Amit near the fountain, he hailed the man and crossed to him. "Rikkan, I just heard from my cousin, and she's bringing more food and help with her in about an hour. I'm not sure how much she's brought, so we might still have to ration the food a little, but it should help cover more stomachs. Can you gather some volunteers, get all of the children together, so we can readily feed them when she arrives?"

"Of course, Maharaja," Amit responded in abject relief. "We were all worried for them. I'll handle it personally. Where do you want them?"

"Here's fine," Trev'nor answered after a moment of thought. "Let's keep people near a clean source of water, for tonight at least."

"I understand." Amit moved off, calling out to people as he did, mostly those that had already drunk their fill and were resting on the ground nearby. At his orders, they moved again, splitting off in different directions, heading for the children still lying abandoned in their homes. The very thought broke Trev'nor's heart and he clenched his eyes shut, feeling the urge to go directly to Von and beat the warlord to a bloody pulp. The man would pay dearly for this.

"Trev."

Lifting the mirror to his mouth, he took a moment to control his temper before responding to his friend. "Yeah, Nol?"

"I have family up here."

Trev'nor felt like something jolted him and he looked sharply down toward the mirror. "You're kidding."

"I'm really, really not. There's a Life Mage, a little boy

about six. I don't think they realized what he was, his magic isn't active enough to register on a triangle yet, and they left him here. He told me his secret name is Vonallenen."

Swearing roundly, Trev'nor spun in place. "Where are you?"

"Don't try to find us, this place is a labyrinth. I'm heading your direction anyway, you can meet him in a minute. But Trev, that means the Von line didn't die out up here. I actually have distant cousins too."

"I mean, we always thought it was a possibility, but—" Trev'nor's head swam with this news. "Get here, then let's talk about this."

"Alright. I only called because there's so many people, do you want to form benches or tables, something they can sit and eat at?"

"I'm an idiot and should have thought of that. Sure, I'll do so." Trev'nor ended the call and went to the more open space of the courtyard, using the paving stones and rubble to form square benches and tables in sections, the corners rounded just in case people bumped into them. No one was steady on their feet just now.

The inhabitants looked at these magical constructions uneasily, but Trev'nor charmed a few into trying them, and when nothing untoward happened to them, the rest slowly moved that direction. It helped when he and Ehsan put the food on the tables, people naturally gravitating to it.

Good to his word, Nolan arrived several minutes later with the rescued slaves in tow, and he herded them toward the second fountain Ehsan had cleared, having everyone drink their fill. In his arms was a skinny little boy that looked like a brunette version of Nolan at that age. The resemblance was striking. A direct descendant? It had to be.

Trev'nor forced his tired body to move, also directing people, shifting them so the magicians could sit and eat too. He saw a few citizens try and object, then look at him and bite back the words before they could fully escape. Smart of them to realize that going against their new maharaja's obvious wishes would not go over well.

Azin appeared from somewhere carrying metal crates of more food supplies with her, which she promptly placed near the food line and helped distribute. He saw her question the remaining slaves, no doubt asking after her own family. Trev'nor wished her luck. He wanted them found for her sake.

With most of the people either eating or in line to drink from the fountain, Trev'nor stole five minutes to meet the little boy clinging to his best friend. Ducking down a little, he put himself more on the child's level and gave him a winning smile. "Hello. I'm Rhebentrev'noren, an Earth Mage."

"He's my best friend," Nolan introduced to the boy, "and the new Maharaja of Khobunter. You can trust him with your secret name too."

A little doubtful, the boy whispered to Nolan, "Are you sure?"

"He glows to you, doesn't he?" Nolan responded patiently. "Anyone that glows can be trusted, no question. Some people that don't glow can be trusted too. I'll tell you who they are."

This apparently tied into some earlier conversation Trev'nor hadn't been privy to, as it convinced the child and he gamely faced Trev'nor. "My name is Vonallenen."

"A pleasure to exchange names, Vonallenen," Trev'nor responded with a slight bow. "It's always a pleasure to meet a Life Mage."

"Am I really?" Allen asked him curiously. "Nolan said I am."

"He's right. Your magic is still faint, 'cause you're growing, but I can see it clearly." And at this young age, it was a little stronger than it should be. Allen would be a powerhouse by the time he hit eighteen. "Did he tell you that you have family in Chahir?"

"Yes. He said I'd have to come live with him, 'cause we're cousins." Allen smiled up at Nolan, although the smile was sad. "I want my father to come too, though."

Nolan's head turned toward him sharply. "Your father? You have family up here still alive?"

Nodding sadly, the boy whispered, "They took him away with everyone else."

Trev'nor and Nolan exchanged startled looks, the idea of yet more family up here amazing to them. Rage briefly crossed Nolan's face as he no doubt realized how close he'd been to them—if he'd only known. Trev'nor put a hand to his friend's shoulder, steadying him, even as he tried to reassure Allen. "You know, I found a cousin up here as well. Her name is Parisa. It took us a while, but we found her parents about two months after I found her, and they're all living together now."

Allen looked heartened at this news. "Can you find my paha too?"

"We will do our absolute best," Trev'nor swore to him. "It should be doable, since we have a very good idea where he went. For now, though, why don't you stay near Nolan?"

Two small fists knotted into Nolan's shirt as he looked shyly up at his bigger cousin. "Can I?"

"I insist on it," Nolan answered firmly, trying to smile back, although it came out forced and crooked. "Trev, I think I feel Sallah?"

"She said she was about an hour out when she called," Trev'nor answered, already turning, his earth sense tracking his cousin's movement toward them and wincing. "She didn't say as much, but I believe Shad's with her. I know we're in an emergency, but she's going way too fast."

"Why don't you tell her that," Nolan suggested dryly.

"Do I look like I have a death wish?" Trev'nor shot back, already moving toward the front gates, where his cousin would likely stop and surface.

"Says the man that conquered a country because it pissed him off!" Nolan called to his back.

Trev'nor shot him a very rude gesture over his shoulder, making Nolan laugh.

From the opposite end of the courtyard, a wail of grief rent the air. Trev'nor turned sharply, locating the sound and moving towards it automatically. Azin? She lay crumpled on the ground, kneeling with her head pressed to the stone ground, shaking and crying. Had she been hurt? Trev'nor raced to her, dropping down and putting an arm around her shoulders, trying to draw her back up again. "Azin? Azin! Tell me what's wrong."

Llona crawled over the top of a building, coming in closer, her blue eyes sad, ears flat against her head. "Family gone."

Family gone. Azin's? Horrified, Trev'nor pressed, "You're sure?"

Despondent, Llona nodded, then lifted her head in a minor sound that spoke of nothing but grief.

Ehsan appeared at a dead run, dropping down to Azin's side so quickly that his knees clacked against the courtyard. He didn't seem to notice or care as he pulled Azin into his lap, smoothing hair away from her face, rocking her back and forth like an inconsolable child. Azin buried her face into his neck and clung to him, tears pouring down her cheeks, soaking them both. Ehsan had tears in his own eyes, his grief just as raw as hers.

Trev'nor couldn't think of a single thing to do. He watched helplessly, keeping a hand to her back, letting her know she wasn't alone. He looked up to see Nolan standing just behind Ehsan, anger and tears brimming in his blue eyes.

"The slaves never had a lot of water or food to begin with, they were half-starved even before people were carted out of here," he whispered, words choked. "Half of the slaves abandoned here didn't make it."

So, they'd literally starved to death before anyone in Riyu had even known something was wrong. Trev'nor felt a wave of fury rock through him, the emotion strong enough it took hold of his magic, the ground rippling out from him in a wave. The ground around him cracked under the pressure, splintering out in a round circle around him, making people leap back and screech in alarm. A stream of hot breath touched his neck before a warm, scaly head pressed up against his back.

"Breathe, fledgling," Garth counseled, his words also tinged with earth-rumbling grief. "Will punish bad men later. Grieve now."

Trev'nor folded himself over Azin's back, wishing he could take even part of her grief from her. His heart bled for his friend. He'd grieve, certainly, and help her bury her dead. But there would be a price to pay for her loss.

He'd make sure the price got paid.

17

"Wait, you found family over there?" Becca demanded incredulously. "Nolan, are you absolutely sure?"

"Positive," her friend confirmed through the mirror, his tone absolutely exhausted. "Unlike the others we've found, his family not only kept the name, but the Chahiran version of it. It was a 'secret' name, they kept it strictly within the family. When I introduced myself, he recognized it and felt comfortable enough to share who he was with me because of it. Vonallenen is his name. He's about six, but he tells me his father is still alive too, just taken to Von."

Becca let her head thump back against a scaly hide. It felt too heavy and full to support just then. "Oh, my giddy aunt. My head's swimming over here. What are you going to do? I mean, he can't be considered another heir to the throne, right?"

"No, he's not a direct line, no one would accept him. Still, he's family, and the Von family is very small in Chahir. I literally have two cousins, my grandfather, and my father. That's it. My family is going to be over the moon to learn we have yet more relatives over here."

"From what I know of your grandfather, he'll come up here himself to get them."

"He might do just that. I'm not kidding. At the very least he'll send Garth up here to fetch them. Bec, I'll be honest, it's a little overwhelming. I mean, we suspected a Von had to have built the city up here, but to have living relatives up here?"

"Now you know how Trev'nor felt when he first met Parisa." Becca wondered what it must feel like, but she'd never experience it herself, being the last of her line. Her only family still resided in southern Chahir, so far away as to be on the moon. Shaking the thought away, she looked up and found Danyal gesturing toward the mirror in her hands with a questioning cant of the head. "Hold on, Rahim wants an update."

"You can fill him in, I actually need to go. Becca. I hate to be the bearer of bad news, but we found Azin's family."

Why bad news? A sense of foreboding twisted in her gut. "Dead?"

"Unfortunately, yes. No one survived. Azin was the only mage in her family, so they were abandoned here. They starved before we arrived."

A wave of grief rippled through her chest, twisting her heart. Azin was more than an ally, she was a friend, one of Becca's first students—not that she'd been able to teach the woman much. They'd all prayed for her sake they'd find Azin's missing family. None of them wished for this ending. "You give her a hug for me and tell her that if she needs a few days to grieve, she has it."

"I sent her and Ehsan back to Riyu for now. Trev'nor buried everyone for her. It left us shorthanded but I just couldn't...."

"You made the right call," she assured him. "If I was over there, I would have done the same thing. Whatever she needs, she can have."

"That's exactly what I said. Anyway, I thought you should know. Just send more food and help over, please, we're running ourselves ragged over here."

"I will, as soon as I can," she swore and ended the call.

She'd been resting against Cat's side, taking advantage of the shade her dragon cast, but pushed up to her feet as Rahim approached. "That was Nolan. We've got bad news and good news. Which do you want first?"

"Bad," Rahim answered with open trepidation.

"Azin found her family, but not alive." Becca hated the words as they left her mouth but there was no way to soften this.

Rahim's eyes swept shut in understanding, sorrow pulling at his expression, aging him. "I never get used to news like that. Who grieves with her?"

"I think we all do, but Ehsan has her right now."

Nodding, Rahim allowed, "He is the one closest to her. I'll send word back to her to allow her time for her grief. If that's the bad news, what's the good?"

Becca felt relieved she actually had good news to share in spite of the disaster the past two days had been. "You won't believe this, but Nolan found a young cousin over there, another Life Mage."

Rahim's jaw dropped and he looked poleaxed for a moment. "Truly? That amazes me."

"It amazes all of us. We knew a Von ancestor had to have come up here at some point because of the city's name, but to have a living magician that's a descendant? It's mind-blowing."

Frowning, he turned to look northward, thoughts turning inwards for a moment. "I wonder how the founder's family lost control of the province enough to become enslaved themselves."

"It's a good question that I would dearly love the answer to, but I'm afraid it might remain a mystery. They would have purged that kind of history from the books." Becca was absolutely sure of that, as they still had no answer to who founded Sha, even after combing through all of the city's records. She'd actually put a bounty out on the information and still didn't have an answer. Shaking the thought off, she continued seriously, "It doesn't matter anyway, not as long as can find the rest of the Von family."

Rahim nodded agreement. "We'll do our best to aid Nolan in that. The dragons reported to me that Shad is over in Dilmun?"

"He is. As soon as we have people settled here, we need to pull everyone back to Riyu for a war council." Becca's smile spoke of torture racks and chains. "We need to have a little talk about how to handle a warlord."

Becca sat in the war room of Riyu's fortress for all of three seconds when her brother strode in, looking as exhausted as the rest of them. She put a hand to the table and pushed herself up and onto her feet, reaching for him. "Shad."

He enfolded her in a strong hug, then let out a long breath. "I don't mind telling you, the past few days have been horrible. Let's not repeat them."

"I could not agree more."

Drawing back, he looked at her, for once not the jokester, but a tired and very angry man. "I'm glad we were able to pull in enough help that we didn't lose anyone more, it's bad enough that we lost civilians in both cities."

Becca really didn't want to ask, the words promised to taste like ash in her mouth, but she had to know. "How many? What was the final count?"

"Two-hundred eighty-three combined," Shad answered blackly. "Mostly people that resisted, some from exposure or starvation."

She closed her eyes at the number. Becca had expected worse, but she wasn't really happy to hear it was less than she feared. Even one death upset her. "It could have been worse."

"It really could have but, Bec, are we sure about the other cities in Von?"

"No, but I asked two pairs of dragons to go and do a scouting run," she assured him, dropping back into her chair. She didn't have the energy to remain standing, not after three days of taking shifts to feed infants while running a country at the same time. "We'll know by the end of the day, perhaps tomorrow morning. I suspect they only pulled this trick with the cities on their southern border to prevent us from taking them."

"More fools, they," Rahim remarked darkly. "It only made it easier on us to claim them."

"I'd rather it wasn't easier, in a way," Trev'nor grumbled, collapsing into a chair on the opposite end of the table. "Bec, I have a message from Sallah: 'More help is coming from Coven Ordan, don't worry about them. We have this.'"

"I love that woman," Becca stated generally, relieved to hear it.

Nolan came to sit next to Trev'nor, responding in a voice rough with exhaustion, "We all would be lost without her. I'm convinced of this. Alright, are we all here?"

Panning the room, Becca did a quick headcount. Dunixan and Simin were still in Rowe, although they planned to return in the next few days. They had Rahim, Shad, Trev'nor, Nolan, Amir, Ehsan, and Azin present, all of them more or less slumped in their respective chairs around the table. "I think we are. Before we get started, quick question. Trev'nor, how long did Dunixan want to stay in Rowe?"

"He requested three more days to reorganize their tax codes and judiciary system before coming back to Riyu," Trev'nor answered readily, propping himself up with both arms on top of the table. "I promised to go fetch him when he was ready."

"Alright. I rather wish he was here, but all things considered, I'd rather not have problems developing in Rowe while we focus on Von." Taking in a breath, she focused on the immediate problem. "I'm calling for an immediate vote. All in favor of smashing Von into itty bitty pieces?"

Everyone raised their hands in agreement except Rahim, who stared at them in exasperation. "Be serious, all of you."

"Think we're pretty serious," Shad answered with a tight smile. "But the man's got a point, kids; there's a lot of innocent people in that city who don't want to be there. Let's not punish the innocent with the wicked."

She'd been half-joking anyway. Well, somewhat joking. Becca's rage demanded blood, but she found it hard to feel anything properly through the haze of exhaustion. "Then let's come up with Plan B."

Shad leaned back in his chair, head tilted back so he could stare thoughtfully upwards. "How much of a rush are we in, here?"

Becca didn't understand the point of the question and exchanged confused glances with the others before offering, "We'd like to win sometime this month? Why?"

"Let's try to smoke them out," Shad suggested with an evil gleam in his eye. "They did everything in their power to stock up on food and take all resources into Von. It's obvious they're expecting a siege. So let's give them a siege and then change the rules. Ehsan, you can draw all of the water out of that city, make sure their wells and fountains are useless, right?"

"Given enough time, sure," Ehsan agreed, an unholy smile spreading over his face, matching the one on Shad's. "It's a big city, but I think I can pull it off if you give me about two days."

"No one can survive without water for longer than a week," Nolan observed, a finger tracing an idle circle on the table's surface. "But that's under optimum conditions. In this kind of extreme heat? Three days is pushing it—as you've all seen—and within five they're dead."

"So in three days you think we can pressure them into surrendering?" Trev'nor grinned at his co-ruler. "I like this idea. A lot. Why didn't we try it before?"

"Because we aren't good at being sneaky," Becca sighed with a nod toward her brother. "Hence why we need Shad. I'm perfectly alright with trying this method, but I have to warn you—there's a slight possibility that it might not work as smoothly as you think it will."

Rahim cocked his head at her, not understanding. "Why?"

"Mage," the boys said in unison—well, growled would be a better term for it.

"What, now?" Shad demanded.

Groaning, Rahim also growled out, "I'd forgotten. The mage that keeps redirecting your storms. You think he's in Von?"

"I'm almost one hundred percent sure of it at this point. Von seems to have taken all of the stronger magicians into the city, which surely means he took this mage in as well, if he wasn't already there. Why keep such a powerful resource, someone that can help you keep storms in your area, in another city?"

Shad tapped a rhythm against the table with his fingers, frowning into the distance. "That does put a wrinkle in things. Becca, how hard would it be to keep storms out of his area?"

"In theory? Not. I'm more trained and thereby more powerful than he is. But Shad, I have to sleep at some point. If he waits until my guard is down, he can redirect any storm he likes, and I have to keep the rest of Khobunter well-watered or risk losing all of the gardens we put in."

"So he might be able to offset this by yanking your storms away in the middle of the night." Shad turned to Azin, who'd been very quiet thus far. She still carried signs of her grief in the dark circles under her eyes, the stiff way she carried her body as if it was ill-fitting, but she met Shad's gaze steadily. "Can you help with this?"

"Air is my weakest element," she responded apologetically, spreading her hands. "I wouldn't even begin to win such a tug of war."

"So can't count on that." Shad pondered for a moment before asking, "What about Tyvendor?"

"He's actually covering for Sallah at the academy right now," Nolan supplied. "We don't dare pull him out of there at the moment, we need her to help transport supplies quickly to our two new cities. The dragons do their best, but they can only carry so much at a time. And with the time it takes for them to transport, they can't carry enough in fast enough. It takes an Earth Mage to make up the difference. They'll starve without an Earth Mage transporting food in."

"And I can't be available for it," Trev'nor finished, then slowly sank to put his forehead against the table. "I hate it when we have no good options."

"Let's not jump to the conclusion that this won't work just yet," Rahim counselled. "I still think it has good odds of succeeding, as storms take time to cross the distance. If we have people on the lookout for clouds, we can alert Becca when one of her storms is nearby, and perhaps thwart him."

That was a very good suggestion and Becca should have thought of it. Thinking while half-asleep on her feet was challenging, to say the least. "He's right, you know."

"He is," Trev'nor agreed, lifting his head again to stare blearily at Rahim. "If we do that, you realize she's not going to get a lot of solid sleep."

"I think she'd prefer that over a battle of attrition," Rahim observed mildly before turning to Becca. "Is that not right?"

"That is completely right," she agreed, although part of her soul wailed in protest at the idea of even more sleep deprivation. She told the whiny part of herself to suck it up. Lack of sleep wouldn't kill her. "Alright, let's try it. I don't see anything to lose except a little time and magic if it doesn't work."

"I still give it very good odds of working," Ehsan opined. "Do we march the whole army to that area, just in case?"

"We'll need them on hand anyway to manage the city once we take it," Shad pointed out patiently. "So yes, we should. Danyal, I know things are a bit disorganized, what with the sudden reassignments you've had to do the past few days. How long will it take to pull everyone together and march for Von?"

"Five days?" Rahim offered, thinking hard with a slight crinkle in his forehead. He slowly nodded to himself, validating his own opinion. "Yes, I think I can manage in five days."

"So let's leave in six," Becca suggested. "We need to make sure there's enough food and water going up with us, all things considered. I can't call in storms readily, not that close, so we have to treat this like a normal campaign."

They all voiced agreement, and Becca knew that they should probably discuss more in the way of details, but when she looked around the table she just didn't have the heart to drag the meeting out any further. Everyone looked dead on their feet, even Amir, and he hadn't been in the two cities personally but coordinating everything from Riyu. In fact, now that she thought of it, she really shouldn't have called a council with them all this tired in the first place. Tired people were not well-known for making good decisions. "People, I feel like we should all go take long naps and then reconvene the meeting. We're too tired to see straight right now."

"Seconded," Trev'nor agreed immediately.

Becca waved a hand in a very sloppy salute. "Motion carried."

"Naps," Shad sighed wistfully, like a gourmet speaking of the perfect meal. "I do adore naps. Why do children hate sleep so much?"

"I really want that question answered," Becca groused, already pushing to her feet. "Not that I blame the kids, it's hard to sleep when you're hungry and missing your parents."

"Reconvene after a solid six hours of sleep and a late lunch?" Trev'nor asked. He probably meant it to be casual but it came off as begging.

"At the very least," Becca promised, already staggering for the door. If this was anything like being a parent, she would make sure she had lots of help lined up first before having children. This whole let's-run-a-country-on-no-sleep thing was not inspired.

18

Trev'nor had blessed his decision to leave the army up to Becca several times in the past, and he did it again now as he watched her pull together the army once more for their attack on Von. If not for Danyal and Shad helping her, she might have lost her sanity altogether, and even then she hung on by a thread. He did not need that headache, thank you very much.

He gladly escaped the anxiety and tension of Riyu to pick up Dunixan and Simin in Rowe. It gave him almost a full day of riding peacefully about in the earth, which Trev'nor had frankly needed. Warlord Rowe gave him a proper welcome and offered him dinner, which Trev'nor took him up on, and he received a verbal report on how matters stood in their new province while they ate. Garth kept his rambunctious meuritta out of trouble while Trev'nor played nice with his new ally, lingering around the outside of the city.

With it so late, he ended up staying the night and breakfasted again with Warlord Rowe in the morning. Only then did he reluctantly pick up his passengers and head back for Riyu, promising himself that he'd come back to Rowe after this and finish the job he'd started. The gardens still didn't have everything he wanted to include and Thais especially had only half of the aqueduct system he'd planned. And he hadn't even done most of it, Azin had.

If there was a way to duplicate himself, Trev'nor would have already requested Nolan do it.

Dunixan didn't seem to be in much better shape, but the man had likely been operating on short sleep as well in order to put Rowe to rights quickly. Catching Trev'nor's arm in a light grip, he queried anxiously, "Trev'nor, how bad was the situation? The dragons only gave me a general guideline."

"I hope to heaven that I never see anything like it again," Trev'nor answered frankly, anger threading his words. "People were literally abandoned in their sickbeds, all of the wells and fountains blocked by rubble, the gardens scorched—they even abandoned children. The people were left there to starve to death. We've all sworn we'll murder Von when we get our hands on him."

"It's very possible that Von didn't know about that order," Dunixan offered slowly. "It's precisely the sort of thing General Ajil would do without Von's knowledge."

Snapping his head around, Trev'nor demanded, "What kind of warlord wouldn't know that his people and cities had been abandoned to the fate of the enemy?"

"A weak one. Well, I say that, but in truth I think that Von focuses solely on managing his territory and businesses and leaves all military decisions up to his general. The few times I've interacted with him in the past gave me that impression, at least. I wouldn't be so hasty to place blame just yet." Dunixan rocked back on his heels, mouth pursed, and admitted, "Although you can certainly place negligence squarely on his head. Just because he's not comfortable with military matters doesn't excuse him for ignoring them completely. Even you have fallen into that trap a little. You often leave military decisions to your co-ruler."

"Yes, but I don't ignore them completely," Trev'nor protested.

Dunixan stroked his arm soothingly. "I know, I know. I'm just drawing a parallel. You're the responsible-type.

You'd never shove all concerns over on Becca."

"I don't dare, too much rides on our military, and Becca needs a supportive co-ruler, not an apathetic one." Trev'nor rubbed a tired hand over his face, reminded himself he was supposed to be taking them safely to Riyu, and focused once more. "I'm still inclined to murder them both."

"I doubt you'll encounter any resistance," Dunixan assured him darkly. "I, for one, have no intentions of arguing with you. When do we march on Von? Is that still set for the day after tomorrow?"

"Yes. We thought we'd try Shad's suggestion first of trying to force them out with a drought. If it doesn't work, we'll be parked outside of the city's walls for three or four days anyway. We'll have plenty of time to think of our next move." Trev'nor grimaced as he admitted, "And we're not really confident about the plan. Becca's convinced that the mage causing her so much trouble is in that city, which means he can possibly divert storms to help them. My main concern is that we have no record of what magicians Von has in there. If he has another Water Mage, or an Elemental Mage, he can undo any attempt of Ehsan's and draw water back into the city readily enough."

"So this plan has possible holes in it, and we won't know for certain until we try," Simin noted from behind them. She sounded more thoughtful than resigned. "But you still think it will work, otherwise you wouldn't try it."

Tilting his head a little, Trev'nor told her over his shoulder, "I give it even odds, honestly. And we'd like to try a non-combative approach first and save ourselves a siege if we can."

"Sensible," Simin approved.

"We need you because you know Von better than anyone else," Trev'nor informed Dunixan frankly. He absently ducked them down a little to avoid a ley line, then steered hard right to avoid an underground lake, although he made note of its location for future use. "An unknown enemy is hard to predict."

"I wish I had been in Riyu this past week instead of Rowe," Dunixan lamented, brows drawn together in a dark frown. "I might have anticipated abandoning the two cities if I'd had the spare brainpower to think strategy instead of economy. Did you check the status of the other cities?"

"We did, and fortunately they're fine, it was just the southern two they abandoned. Which, tactically speaking, makes perfect sense. Why abandon the others if you don't have to?"

"Their willingness to sacrifice territory this early on in the game speaks volumes in and of itself." Dunixan's expression turned shrewd and he stared sightlessly forward, lost to a vision in his own head. "They fear you greatly and had no confidence in retaining their smaller cities. They've gambled by focusing all of their strength in defending their capital city."

"It was a bad gamble." Trev'nor's hands clenched into fists, tight enough to hurt, and he had to force himself to relax again. "In better news, we learned two interesting things this week. First, the Von line—I speak of the Life Mage line, not the warlords—did not die out. Nolan found a young cousin in Dilmun by the name of Allen."

Dunixan's head snapped around. "They left a Life Mage behind?"

"He's too young, they likely didn't realize what he was," Trev'nor explained. "Nolan's over the moon. I'm not sure if you realize, but the Von family in Chahir is very small. I think they only have five members."

"No, I wasn't aware of that." Dunixan's interest sharpened. "Is this child another candidate for the throne, then?"

"Too far removed from the main branch, or so Nolan tells me, but they'll still bring him into Chahir as soon as they can. Allen's father, too, once we find him. We believe he was taken into Von."

Shaking his head in wonder, Dunixan had to sit with that for a moment. "Remarkable. If that's the first interesting thing, what's the second?"

"We have finally found an answer to who founded Sha. There was a record buried in Rheben that detailed who founded which cities. Our genealogist and historian from Coven Ordan nearly had a fit when they found it he was so happy. Or so Raile tells me. Apparently, when the forced evacuation happened during the Magic War, several soldiers went with the magicians to help protect them. One of them was married to a mage of the Sha family and he was the one who created the watchtower—one of the first—meant to act as a line of defense against Libendorf. We're still tracing the genealogy, but I have a sneaking suspicion Commander Talib is a descendent."

"Sneaking suspicion, or you're fairly certain?" Dunixan asked knowingly. "Because you look confident."

"Turns out his mother's full name is Kamira Sha." Trev'nor shrugged, as that adequately answered the question to his mind. "Not that anyone bothered to tell us that before this week."

"So, he's a direct descendent, or close enough." Simin looked very intrigued by this. "You said before he had to be, in order to look so Chahiran."

"Turns out I was right. It's a rare moment, I'm enjoying it," Trev'nor said cheerfully. "Once we have it confirmed, we'll have to tell Talib and his mother, explain their family history. It's too remarkable to leave it buried in the past."

"It's nice when the mysteries are explained. I wonder how the Life Mages lost control of Von?" Dunixan asked rhetorically.

"That's the question we're all asking but I doubt it will be a much different story than how the Rheben family lost control of Rheben." And Trev'nor preferred not to think about it. He had enough anger to deal with without focusing on what had started this madness. "Anyway, that's our news for the week. I consider most of it to be good, and Guardians, we certainly needed some good news after the week we've had."

"Maybe next week will be easier," Dunixan offered with a sympathetic smile. "Maybe your first battle plan will work and we'll have Von under control by this time next week."

"From your lips to the Guardians' ears," Trev'nor fervently prayed.

With his usual excellent organization, Danyal had all of the troops lined up and ready to ride on Trev'nor's earthen moving carpet by dawn. Trev'nor himself didn't feel completely awake, and he hid many a yawn behind his hand as he waited for everyone to get situated. Ehsan and Ginger flew ahead with the goal of shutting off the water supply into Von. He absently petted Priya, who lay around his shoulders like a woman's fur stole, purring in contentment, the tip of her tail twitching.

Nolan and Llona did not appear any more awake than Trev'nor felt and had in fact found a clear space nearby to curl up and nap with each other. Nolan's meuritta lay curled up on top of the dragon's head, as comfortably perched there as he would be on a cushion. Trev'nor couldn't help but feel they had the right idea, to steal what sleep they could while they had the chance to do so.

Danyal came to stand next to him, surveying the men lined up behind, and grunted satisfaction. "I think we're ready, Trev'nor. I'll ride with Becca."

"Danyal," Trev'nor responded, trying not to roll his eyes, "at this point I assume you're riding with Becca, trust me. It would be stranger if you chose to ride with me instead. In fact, if that ever happens, I'm going to assume that you two had a fight, alright?"

Chuckling, Danyal teased, "Like I can assume that Dunixan will travel with you?"

Shrugging, Trev'nor allowed, "Probably a safe assumption. Alright, see you there."

Trev'nor did his own check as the general strode off, making sure that he didn't have anyone still standing, then whistled at Nolan. "Wakey-wakey, Nol."

Groaning, Nolan turned over and cracked open an eye. "I'm flying with Llona. Go ahead."

"You're totally going to sleep another hour before even trying to catch up," Trev'nor accused him.

"Don't be jealous," Nolan responded with saccharine sweetness before rolling back over.

Some friend. Trev'nor ignored Garth's rumbling chuckle and got them under way, his own dragon gliding right above his head. At least that way Garth provided him with some nice shade to sit under.

Unlike most of the year, the weather now had a bite to it. The desert didn't differentiate well between seasons. The fall weather here had lasted a whole week, dropping them from blazing hot to slightly chilly with little transition. Trev'nor felt grateful for his coat and what warmth the twin suns offered as they had definitely arrived in winter. Although, winters up here didn't appear to be too brutal, not compared to the wet winters of Chahir at least. Still, at night it got cold enough to snow, as they'd discovered recently. Becca's attempt to bring in rain yesterday had not quite gone as planned. Trev'nor had arrived back in Riyu to a scene of a white carpet covering the ground and buildings, turning it almost fairytale in appearance. It hadn't lasted of course. The ground still had too much heat to it, so it all disappeared by morning. Still, it had been a revelation to Trev'nor that it could apparently snow in the desert.

"Fledgling," Garth called down to him.

Trev'nor lifted his face up, anxious, as Garth rarely tried to talk to him when they traveled this way. Conversations were too awkward to manage. "What?"

"Water ahead," the dragon warned. "Moving fast."

Water moving fast? Did he mean a river or—oh, wait. "You mean a flash flood?"

"Yes. Coming up quickly."

The normal response to that would be to find some way around, or detour along the bank until it died down to a calmer river of water, but Trev'nor wasn't about to do that. He had earth magic for a reason, right? "Got it, thanks!"

He reached out with his senses, found that the river lay just beyond his immediate line of sight, and slowed them a little so that he could stop readily when he got to the bank. It took a few minutes and then he finally understood why the desert people feared flash floods so much.

Water, choppy and forceful, flowed with all of the power of a riptide. He'd never seen water that filthy before. It looked like mud moving, although it hadn't the solidity of a mudslide. Random sticks sometimes appeared, bobbing up and down, before disappearing again in some sort of undertow. If an unwary traveler tripped into it, he'd be pulled under instantly with no ability to swim for the shore. Trev'nor bet that not even a dragoo would have the strength to fight its way free.

Slowing, he paused them long enough to build a wide bridge over the river, something sturdy enough to support the weight of all the troops behind him. He anchored it very firmly with several support pillars as well, not wanting to trust magic and will to keep it up after he left. Others would travel this way eventually and he wanted to offer them safe passage. Satisfied it would hold, Trev'nor got them underway again, smoothly crossing the danger.

Turning a little, he asked of his batman, "Mose? Is a flash

flood normally that strong?"

"More or less," Mose answered with a thoughtful glance behind them. "Maybe a little stronger due to all of Raya Becca's storms, but not by much."

"Huh. Interesting. I know Danyal warned us of the danger, but I expected something a little tamer."

"We fear them for a reason, Raja," Mose responded with a shrug. "Not that you need to fear them."

Trev'nor couldn't refute that. "One of the many perks of being an Earth Mage. Have you come out this direction before?"

"No, not once," Mose admitted easily. "Too dangerous to try and cross through Riyu's land. I only know what I've heard and what I can read on the map. The place is a little greener than I expected."

Trev'nor had observed the same thing. Not that they had grass, or anything of that nature, but more cacti lived up here and a few bushes with actual leaves on them. He saw more signs of life as well in the form of rabbits and mice. "Perhaps because of the winter runoff? There's enough water up here for things to grow?"

"Maybe?" Mose responded doubtfully. "Although we get the same amount of water along the coast and our land didn't look like this."

"That," Trev'nor turned to study the land more carefully, eyes narrowed in concentration, "is a very good point. It didn't, did it?"

Overhead, Garth let out a long call, followed by three dark, growled out sounds that bordered on barks. Trev'nor didn't speak much dragon, but he knew trouble when he heard it. "What happened?"

"Ginger sent crashing," Garth reported, tail lashing in the air strong enough to send cold air eddies over their heads.

Alarmed, Trev'nor demanded, "Is she alright? Ehsan?"

"Both fine. Bruised. Mad. Magic wind forced her down."

Trev'nor snarled a curse as he realized what his dragon meant. "Becca was right. The Air Mage or whatever he is definitely lives in Von. Did Ehsan manage to shut the water to the city off?"

Garth blew out a hot breath, more steam than fire, but it still spoke of anger and frustration. "No. Ginger says other mages stop him."

"So, our first plan will not work." Trev'nor let his head flop back on his shoulders for a moment, feeling like this day had just become a decade long already despite it not being lunch yet. "Can you pass that to Llona and Cat? Tell them I'll still bring the troops up, but apparently we need to sit down and come up with a firmer Plan B."

"Will," Garth promised.

Mose asked hesitantly, "Do we have a Plan B, Raja?"

"We certainly do," Trev'nor answered, sighing. "We do this the hard way."

Becca glared at the city with considerable heat, wishing for the first time in her life she could breathe fire like Cat could. Von had the same sort of impressive size to it as Riyu, spreading out in all directions with very thick walls protecting it from the outside world. That didn't matter to her much. What caught her attention was the line of magicians all along the battlement. Even from this distance she could see a few details clearly, and it didn't spell anything good to her mind. "Cat, correct me if I'm wrong, but they're not wearing chains, are they?"

"No chains," Cat confirmed, her head level with Becca's as she peered at the city.

"I thought so," Becca snarled, vexed by this. It should have been a good thing—under different circumstances she would celebrate at this news—but she had a feeling the lack of chains was nothing more than a manipulation.

Nolan and Trev'nor stood on her other side, Rahim, Dunixan, and Shad right behind her. To the non-magicians, Nolan explained, "The magicians all along the walls are much brighter than we're used to seeing. It doesn't look like they have the usual limiters on."

"Maybe two at the most for the mages, not even that for the witches and wizards," Trev'nor opined, words careful and slow as he calculated it out loud. "Isn't that interesting."

"Not the word I would have chosen," Becca huffed.

"This should be good news," Dunixan sighed, raking a hand through his hair. "But you know that he's got them controlled somehow. The lack of chains or amulets doesn't mean they're free."

"Far from it," Shad agreed darkly. "He's either got hostages to control them or he's manipulated them into thinking that they're better off with him. Either way, they're going to fight hard to defend the place. Kids, I hate to say this, but I think you'd better call in reinforcements."

Trev'nor acknowledged grimly, "We do not have the magical firepower necessary to take them on."

Rahim followed this conversation, his eyes bouncing back and forth between speakers, brows drawing together in an expression of confusion. For his sake, Becca explained, "This won't be like the previous battles. The amulets severely limit the magician's ability to tap into power. Say that a mage's normal power is like a bonfire. The amulet takes it down to a candle's flame."

He blinked at her, confusion deepening. "So every other time you've battled a magician, they didn't lift off the amulets?"

"Well, they might have lifted off one or two, it's impossible for a magician to fight otherwise," Nolan corrected. "But what we're seeing here is that the witches and wizards over there don't have a limiter on at all, and the mages might have only one on. Which means they're more or less at full strength. That changes the stakes completely."

Rahim regarded the people stationed on the wall with new eyes. "If a normal soldier faces them, he won't survive it."

"Cannon fodder is all he'll be," Shad confirmed, shifting back and forth on his feet, anxious and unhappy with the situation. "The army is here to deal with Von's army should he choose to send them out. We can't depend on him using only the magicians to fight."

"And if he does send out the army, then our magicians here would be quickly overwhelmed," Rahim completed the obvious with a grim nod. "Understood. I'll have them prepare temporary defenses and lock this area down. Becca, who can you call to aid you?"

"I'll start with Raile. He has a few people down at the academy that promised to fight with us if we needed them." Becca tugged at the braid over her shoulder, the slight pull on her scalp helping her to think. "And perhaps Raile can think of others that will help us too."

"Call him," Trev'nor stated, already turning. "I'll create some defensive lines with Sallah and start a camp. I have a feeling we'll be here a few days."

Becca hated to admit it, but Trev'nor was likely right. Very unhappy with everything in general, she yanked the mirror out of her pocket and growled into it, "Raile."

It took a few moments, with some sounds of rustling fabric and a thump of a body sinking into a chair, before Raile responded. "That does not sound like a happy Becca. What's wrong, child?"

"We're in trouble," Becca admitted and explained the situation as fully as she could.

"How many magicians are we speaking of?"

"Hundreds," she answered. "Our Legend is double-checking the count now, but her tentative number was seven hundred."

Raile fell into a ruminative silence for several seconds. "I know that these magicians are not well trained. I've seen the lack of control and knowledge in my own students. Still, they know a little, and with that kind of number…you'll be overwhelmed with just the magicians you have on hand."

"I know." Becca took in a breath and did the very thing she swore not to do. "Raile, is there anyone in Coven Ordan or at Rheben Academy willing to fight?"

"There is. And I will ask them and send them your way immediately. You said you're just outside of Von now?"

"Unfortunately."

"Then I will send them today. Do not try to fight by yourself, Riicbeccaan, do you understand me?"

"I wouldn't even dream of it," she promised him and faithfully meant every word.

"I can't promise that many will come. This is very much outside of their job descriptions, but even a few might turn the tide for you."

Becca understood that all too well. It could be that even if Raile sent people up, it still wouldn't be enough and they'd fall to a very difficult, costly battle. Still. "Send who is willing. That's all I can ask."

"I will. And keep your courage up, child; this isn't the end of the world."

The mirror went dark and silent once more and she gripped it in a tight fist, turning her skin white around the edges. She stared hard at Von. It wasn't the end of the world, Raile was right about that, but the thought of losing here made her ill. She absolutely could not afford to leave those two men in power.

Shad came up to stand beside her, leaning down so that he could rest his chin on her shoulder. Tail shifted to her other shoulder to allow him room, although the cat ended up almost precariously balanced in the process. Becca pulled him down before he could fall, as his balance wasn't what it once was, cuddling Tail against her chest instead. The cat purred, eyes closed as he pressed his chin against her chest.

"This reminds me of the battle around the Watchman's Pool," Shad mentioned casually to her, the vibration of his words leaving tingles in her skin.

Casting her memory back, she reviewed stories he'd told her over the years until she thought she had the right one. "The battle where you caught all of those Star Order Priests, stripped them naked, and forced them to walk away?"

"I left them with clothes," he protested mildly. "They just felt naked without their magic or weapons."

"What about this situation reminds you of that one?"

"Overwhelming odds and attacking a fortified stronghold is the same," he responded, tone nostalgic for a moment. "Before we got there, Huish had gathered some forty magicians, and they'd put in all sorts of traps and trigger spells in case they were attacked. They were half-trained too because they had the spell books and manuals stored in the Pool. Wifey and I tried to get in one night and ended up with singed hair. Most fun I had in ages."

Of course he found attacking a highly defended stronghold to be fun. "But you got through them eventually, right?"

"More like we were able to eventually talk them out. We didn't really want to attack, after all, and risk injuring people."

Becca leaned her head sideways, resting it briefly against his for a moment, drawing strength from his presence here. "We already tried talking once, though."

"It took more than one attempt for us to succeed back then, too. All I'm saying, kiddo, is that you shouldn't dig in for an enforced siege just yet. Try another attack, but if we can't win without severe casualties, I'd give talking another go."

The general in Von, though, had no intention of giving them time to gather reinforcements. As soon as Trev'nor put the first line of trenches in, the magicians on the wall started attacking. One magical spell after another came zinging their direction. Becca, Azin, and Ehsan all threw attacks right back at them while Nolan raised several magic barriers, anchoring them into the ground so that the soldiers had something to duck behind.

It dissolved into madness very quickly with magic being thrown about like dry lightning, forcing the dragons to either retreat well into the clouds or huddle with the soldiers behind Nolan's barriers. Becca could feel sweat prickle all along her spine and down the nape of her neck, her magic steadily draining as she either attacked or rebuffed a spell. The sand became pockmarked like a leper, some of the ground either melting or sizzling from the spells. This did not make Trev'nor happy. Fixing this later would be quite the headache.

Sallah strode up to stand at her side, sweat making her fair hair stick to her scalp, a thunderous scowl on her face. "We've got the front lines protected, for now at least, but I don't know how long we can maintain all of these barriers. Trev'nor wants to know how fast help is coming."

"Raile said he'd send them up today, which was—" she lifted her head to check the position of the sun, calculating "—six hours ago. So, anytime? Although I don't know how many people are coming."

"How many do you suspect?"

"We have at least two, as they promised help before. Tyvendor and Halcharlesen. Other than that, your guess is better than mine."

Sallah's mouth went into a flat line as she glared at the city. "I would think about a dozen willing to come up, likely not more than that. I don't know if another dozen trained magicians will be enough to turn the tide of this battle."

Becca gravely doubted it would. "If we can even suppress them long enough to get the dragons into play, I think we might have a chance. I realize the odds aren't good on that, but I want to at least try before we write the possibility off."

"We can't even try to sneak Nolan into the city as a scout, or Tail, because too many magicians are free and they'll be able to spot them immediately," Sallah bemoaned, planting a hand on her hip. "If we only had more intel to work with."

"You're not the first to make that wish," Rahim observed as he came up to them. He handed a canteen to Becca and silently encouraged her to drink.

It took no encouragement, really, as she felt parched. Lifting it to her mouth, she ignored the flat taste of the water and drained half of it in one long pull. Handing it back, she licked the few drops that had escaped onto her lips, then gave him a tired smile. "Thanks, honey. How is everyone else holding up?"

"Thirsty, frustrated, worried, just like you." Rahim indicated the area between the front lines and the wall. "I feel that if your reinforcements don't arrive in the next hour, we should withdraw out of their range of fire for the day and rest. We're losing daylight to battle in."

Truly, they only had about an hour of daylight left, as the encroaching winter days were shorter. Even if their reinforcements arrived soon, it might be wiser to just retreat for now and try again in the morning anyway. "We're all tired. Tired people make mistakes. It might be better to just retreat for the day. Rahim, spread the order."

Rahim lifted his brows an nth degree. "Don't you think you should confer with Trev'nor first about that?"

As if on cue, Trev'nor's voice rose above the sounds of battle in a long, creative curse that would make a sailor blush. Becca couldn't see him, but didn't need to, and tossed a gesture in his general direction. "You were saying?"

"Right." Rahim winced before moving off, his voice rising in a familiar bellow as he barked out orders.

"He's generally so quiet, you'd never think he could be that loud," Sallah commented, her eyes trailing after Rahim's back.

"I know, right?" Becca agreed a little absently. "It surprised me too, the first time I heard him on a battlefield.

Sallah, help guard our retreat, please. I'm going to move ahead and mark where our camp line should be so that everyone knows precisely where the safe zone is."

The mood among the army festered, a roiling mix of anger, fear, and frustration as they beat a timely retreat some quarter mile further south. Fortunately, they'd anticipated this trouble and their camp lay far enough away to be safe from nightly bombardments. Trev'nor left the earthen works he'd created that morning alone, aside from some patchwork here and there, leaving them ready for use the next day.

Becca's focus centered on her army and it took her a little too long to realize that she felt an Air Mage approaching quickly from the south. She turned her head, expectant, but could barely see anything at this distance. Still, she knew who it must be. Tyvendor had come, hopefully bringing help with him.

It took another half hour for him to actually land at the southern border of their camp. Becca and Shad went to meet him, partially to keep her jumpy soldiers from unduly attacking. Becca waved in greeting. She did a head count as she strode toward the group, ignoring the sand that buffeted her as Tyvendor brought his passengers gently down to earth. Nine people had come, most of whom she recognized, as they were all involved in Rheben's renovation or with the academy somehow. Nine people did not seem enough to manage a miracle but she greeted them with a smile anyway. "Thank you so much for coming, all of you."

"I'm not sure how much help we'll be, but we're all determined to stay until the battle's won." Tyvendor grabbed her up in a brief, fierce hug before letting go again. "I'm surprised to see you back here, though. Did we arrive too late?"

"We're losing light," Becca responded, tone reassuring. "We didn't feel it wise to fight anymore today. Everyone can get some good rest tonight and we'll attack in the morning.

Sallah, can you lead them to the tents we've prepared?"

"I'll be glad to," she answered, already waving people to follow her. "This way, I'll explain as we go."

As the magicians trooped past them, Tyvendor lowered his head to murmur near her ear, "I don't think this is enough help but I'm afraid no one else possesses the fighting skills. Do you think we can manage with just this group?"

No, she didn't. "I think it will be very difficult, especially as we're trying not to harm any of the magicians."

Tyvendor rocked back on his heels, blue eyes studying her face, his own expression one of concern. "Becca, can we actually take this city?"

"We have to," she responded bleakly. "We just have to."

20

Trev'nor eyed the sky with severe misgivings. Tyvendor had gone up with Becca so that he could focus on battling the Air Mage, or whatever they were to a standstill, giving Becca the necessary room to put her storm properly to work. Granted, two trained mages should be well up to the task, but they seemed to have assumed they only had one mage to deal with. Trev'nor didn't think that was the case.

In fact, he had severe misgivings about fighting a magical battle at all. His gut feeling said that they wouldn't win this battle, that the odds were stacked too highly against them, not with that many magicians against them. But he did agree with Becca in that they at least had to try. If it came down to a true siege, where it stretched out into months, then they'd have to reconsider what to do.

Orion, impatient as always, started the battle off by diving toward the city walls and spraying the bottom of it with a long line of fire. Azin had her hands full shielding the both of them from the magical attacks coming from the walls, the sparks of multiple spells clashing against her shields strong enough it looked like concentrated fireworks going off. They dove and flew past the city in seconds, serving as a diversion while the rest of the dragons approached at breakneck speeds.

Trev'nor rode Garth by hanging low over the pommel,

the wind rushing past his ears so loudly he couldn't begin to hear anything from below. His dragon breathed out in hot steams, charging the air so much that Trev'nor felt sweat dew his skin along his neck and spine. He prayed Garth didn't start flaming the city as well, as that would risk severe injury of the very people they hoped to save.

He had his own mission up here: to close off the battlements, make the walls tall enough that people couldn't see enough to fight from them. His magic flared in his chest, warm and live, as he called upon it. Front section of the city first, the top-tier section. Trev'nor spoke to the stone forming the walls, growing it straight up like a tidal wave to create a barrier. People threw themselves backwards in alarm, avoiding the stone, then standing again and shaking their fists at it.

Garth had to turn at that point, cutting Trev'nor's line of sight off as they came back around, and in those ten seconds, someone destroyed half of Trev'nor's work. The wall he'd created crumbled, falling to the ground below as if a giant hammer had crashed against it. Not an Earth Mage, or even a mage at all—it looked like a wizard or witch had thrown raw power at it. Trev'nor stared at it in dismay. They could retaliate to unexpected attacks that quickly? That meant they had at least some autonomy in fighting. They weren't waiting on specific orders from a commander.

That was not in the least bit helpful.

Growling a curse to himself, Trev'nor tried something different on the next pass. He couldn't block their view if they could destroy stone, but could they repair things? Taking a chunk from the ground, he threw it full force into the gates and punched through the heavy iron doors, blasting them aside with such force that he could hear it even through the wind.

Garth spun in the air, turning them quickly back around, and Trev'nor's heart sank as he realized that one of the gates had magically repaired itself already, the other one in process. So they knew repair spells. Well, no, that made perfect sense. Usually the slaves were used to repair things. Trev'nor himself had been used as a repairman at first. Stupid of him to forget that.

What else could he possibly do to impede them without causing anyone harm?

As he pondered the question, he took a look around, trying to gauge how everyone else was doing. Nolan had gone dragon at some point, fighting alongside Llona, attacking the far right tower and trying to dismantle it. They made some headway as he watched, the top part of it crumbling to the ground, although the magicians on the wall attacked so ferociously they were forced to retreat.

Trev'nor went through a mental list of options. He'd tried creating barriers along the battlements to split them up but they'd thrown a series of destructive spells at the stone, breaking it apart in seconds. It hadn't helped him. He could, technically, sink the walls into the ground and level the playing field a little, but that risked injuring the people on top of the wall. He also feared that doing so would drain the majority of his magical power, and he was running lower than he liked.

Becca and Tyvendor seemed to be in some sort of battle of the skies as the storm shifted back and forth in a chaotic swirl of dark clouds, the wind going first one way, then another. Definitely more than one mage with air ability over there to give them that much trouble. Garth seemed to be struggling with the air currents, as he grunted with effort several times. His wings abruptly snapped one way, then another as he fought to stay in the air.

Worried about them both, Trev'nor signaled for a landing, as he didn't see the point in staying up when he didn't know how else to attack anyway. Garth fell like a rock for several hundred feet before gliding in toward the back of their army, landing a little heavier than usual.

Turning his head, Garth inquired, "Alright?"

"I'm fine, I was worried about you," Trev'nor assured him, already unbuckling. "The air currents up there are so crazy I was afraid you'd crash trying to keep us up. And I'm out of ideas on how to attack anyway. I want to talk with Shad and see if he has any suggestions."

Relieved, his dragon nodded and hunkered down a little so Trev'nor could dismount easier.

Pushing his goggles up onto his forehead, Trev'nor moved rapidly through the men stationed behind their impromptu earthen barriers, and headed for the command tent. Without Garth's hot steam to warm him, he felt the winter chill readily and shivered a little in his riding leathers. The tent would hopefully be warmer, as it cut off the chilly wind. Stepping inside, he found Dunixan, Simin, Danyal, and Shad all gathered inside.

"You're back down already?" Dunixan asked in surprise.

"Ran out of ideas," Trev'nor admitted a little sheepishly. "Everything I can think of to do, they apparently know how to counteract. I need something sneakier."

"We're getting similar reports from all of our magicians," Danyal groaned, planting both hands against the table's surface and leaning heavily against it for a moment, shoulders slumping. "Short of physical harm, they can only do so much. I now understand why Becca was so uncertain about this working."

"We all had doubts," Shad allowed, stepping up to peer through the open tent flaps. "It's turning out worse than I feared, though. Hard to cage an enemy without injuring them. Harder still to do it when you don't know what they're capable of. Trev, what else did you see while you were up there?"

"They have soldiers standing at the ready along the base of the interior wall," Trev'nor answered as he headed for the brazier. Ah, warmth. "But I couldn't get a headcount, sorry. About twice the number of the magicians on the wall would be my guess, maybe three times? They seem to be on standby. Also, the counterattacks I experienced up there were very rapid, too rapid for them to have relayed a command to the magicians."

"So they have some autonomy in this fight," Danyal translated slowly, expression growing troubled. "That does not make me feel better."

Shad grunted sourly, still peering at the city. "I will bet you anything that their orders are something along the lines of 'protect the city at all costs, we don't care what you do.'"

"It wouldn't surprise me," Dunixan allowed, sinking into a chair like an eighty-year-old man. "Now you understand why I hate the general of Von so much."

Trev'nor really hated to ask, but couldn't seem to help himself. "Are we losing?"

"Yes, young maharaja, we are," Simin answered with a grimace and splay of hands. "Unless you choose to actually fight and not try to capture."

He really, really didn't want to do that. Turning to Shad, he asked helplessly, "What else can we do? What have we not tried yet?"

"Don't consider this battle lost just yet," Shad counseled. Turning from the city, he met Trev'nor's eyes steadily. "They don't have the training you do, or the magical stamina, remember that. You might be able to wear them down. You've only been fighting about an hour; I say if you can't wear their response time down by dinner, then that's when we take this as a loss and reconsider our options. What you were doing before was wrecking the gate and blocking off their battlements, right?"

"Yes."

"Do it again. And again, and again. Close up their arrow slits, their doors, block the stairs so no soldiers can attain the top. Punch holes through their walls. Do it over and over until they can't keep up with you. If we can manage that, we'll create just enough of an opening to get our own troops inside."

Trev'nor grimaced. "Has this become a battle of attrition?"

"Unfortunately, it looks that way," Danyal admitted sourly. "Your cousin Sallah is doing her best with the East Gate entrance, but she's reporting the same lack of results. Actually, all of the magicians are reporting the same results. Siege warfare is wearing your enemy's defenses down to the point that they fail and give you an opening."

He understood that in theory, but Trev'nor had never actually been forced into this position before. In every other city they'd had almost overwhelming force on their sides, or at least enough to punch through the enemy's defenses. He didn't like being on the reverse of that for once, not one iota. "Alright. I'll go back up. Just be aware that Becca and Tyvendor have their hands full up there. The air currents are so chaotic that it's obvious to me they're encountering severe resistance."

Danyal went taut with alarm, eyes flaring wide. "Is that why she hasn't called on her storm?"

"That's my guess. Garth had to seriously fight to keep us up in the air. Your plan to wear them steadily down might work," Trev'nor glanced at Shad as he said this, "but I'm honestly not sure how long the dragons can stay airborne without becoming absolutely exhausted. We might have to land and fight on the ground, which won't be nearly as effective."

"No, it won't," Dunixan agreed, head lolling backwards on his neck for a moment.

Shad urged him, "Try anyway. Try for as long as you can and land when it gets too dangerous to stay up there anymore. I'm not convinced they have the stamina to battle you to a standstill."

"Neither am I," Trev'nor admitted. "Alright, back up I go."

Garth didn't say a word to him as he returned to the dragon's side and remounted. Trev'nor tightened the buckles a little more than he normally did, worried about falling out because of the air battle going on overhead. He put his goggles back into place before tapping Garth's shoulder, asking for them to go airborne. With a powerful thrust of his back legs, Garth launched them into the air.

The air, if possible, had gotten even more chaotic and problematic in the twenty minutes since he'd landed. Trev'nor felt the force of it pull his lips back from his teeth sometimes, and Garth had to fold his wings tight against his belly more than once and drop to avoid being swept straight to Libendorf. Trev'nor had a feeling that Becca might be attempting some kind of dervish or windstorm against the city, only to have it batted away.

With the wind this strong, sand got picked up and swirled through the air, and the storm overhead started a light drizzle, no doubt to give Ehsan something more to work with. The combination dropped visibility even further, and Garth had to come in closer than before to give Trev'nor the line of sight he needed to work. That meant, of course, that the enemy had better range on them. Trev'nor kept a moving shield up around them both to protect them from magical attacks.

He tried to ignore the sparks and flares of heat against the shield as he worked, although having the random glares against his goggles proved immensely distracting. He soon fell into a headspace where nothing intruded but what action to do next.

Close up arrow slits and doors—everything in reach— magic held at the ready as Garth passed the city walls and came about for another pass.

Block all the stairs leading up to the battlements, flatten the stairs to a slide, interrupt their lines of communication.

Stop as they passed by the wall and had to loop about again.

Trev'nor took in the sight grimly. The Von magicians had already broken the arrow slits and doors free. As he watched, they frantically hit the stairs with multiple repair spells, some of them working better than others. He gave it five minutes tops before they had the stairs back to rights. He raised the walls on the battlements again, giving a reprieve to anyone flying by. No one could attack through solid stone.

Fly by, turn, dive back in. Trev'nor chose to punch holes in the walls this time, large chunks of it, wide and tall enough to shove a wagon through. On the next pass, most of the holes were closed up again.

Garth's steam hit his face, almost welcome in this cold air that danced a permanent shiver along Trev'nor's skin. He didn't think his dragon did it for Trev'nor's sake, though; more a sign of mounting frustration. Trev'nor hit the city again with his magic, tampering with the stairs again, as they seemed to struggle the most with fixing those for whatever reason.

They did it again, and again, and again. Trev'nor's frustration mounted with each pass. The human mind didn't like repetition without results. In fact, wasn't that the very definition of insanity? Doing the same thing over and over again while expecting a different result? He felt insane, at least, though he knew that a battle of attrition meant doing precisely this.

The suns climbed steadily in the sky, hit their zenith, then started for the other side. Trev'nor could feel his magical strength start to wane. Not at dangerous levels yet, not nearly, but still nowhere near what he had started out with this morning. He could feel Garth's strength drop as well. His breath came hard and quick in his lungs, muscles sometimes trembling with effort underneath Trev'nor's legs. He didn't give either of them more than another hour before common sense forced them to land.

The magicians in the city might be tiring as well, but not by a significant amount. Trev'nor couldn't swear to it, but it seemed as if they took shifts, which was smart of them. Unfortunate for Trev'nor, though.

Tired, hungry, frustrated, and feeling like a stretch of leather baking too long in the sun, Trev'nor signaled for them to land. Garth promptly turned, sending them briefly upside down, then glided back and around behind the front lines. His feet impacted with the earth so forcefully that Trev'nor wasn't sure if they'd actually landed or been shot down for a moment.

Stroking a hand along his dragon's side, he asked in concern, "You alright?"

"Tired," Garth admitted with a gusty sigh, head dropping.

"I'll find you a cow," Trev'nor promised him. "After today you totally deserve a cow."

Garth's ears perked up at this. "Cow is good."

"Cow is always good to you," Trev'nor teased, although his tone came out a little flat. He, too, felt fatigue draining at him. "I'll put in a request with the cooks before I report in. Let me unsaddle you real quick."

Mose came jogging up, calling to them as he moved, "I'll handle the saddle, Raja. Raja Trev'nor, there's food and drink available in the command tent."

"Bless you, Mose," Trev'nor groaned as he dropped heavily out of the saddle. He had not realized how much strength he'd exerted to keep his balance up there until just now, when his thighs and lower back ached. "Can you find Garth a cow?"

"I certainly will, sir," Mose assured him.

Clapping the man on the shoulder, Trev'nor moved past, calling to Garth over his shoulder, "Go rest, we won't fly again today!"

Garth let out a low breath, settling onto his belly right there. That tired, eh? Trev'nor wished that he'd landed earlier but really, he couldn't have been sure until after lunch if they'd make any headway or not.

He made his way to the red command tent with a heavy tread, ducking a little to get through the flaps only to discover that he wasn't the first mage to abandon the battle. Ehsan sat at the table with Danyal, also looking bone weary. He turned at Trev'nor's entrance, a scowl on his face that aged him a decade. "This isn't working."

"I totally agree," Trev'nor returned, heading for the tray of breads, cheeses, fruits, and the pitcher of water set off to one side. After fighting all day, he was beyond famished. "Can someone recall everyone? We're just exhausting them for no reason."

Ehsan pulled out a mirror broach from his pocket and started muttering into it.

"Well," Shad stated with false brightness. "I think it's time to implement Plan C."

Trev'nor paused with a date halfway to his mouth. "We have a Plan C?"

"We certainly do." Shad beamed at him.

"Am I going to like Plan C?"

Shad shrugged and allowed, "Probably not. I'll have fun, though."

That worried Trev'nor. That worried him a lot, as he knew exactly what Shad thought of as 'fun.' "Will Plan C work?"

"You better hope it does," Danyal responded grimly. "We haven't been able to come up with any other plan."

"It's just all kittens and rainbows today," Dunixan observed darkly. "Alright, Shad, what's Plan C?"

"We issue a call to quarters." Shad's jokester smile didn't fade, but it never reached the very serious set of his eyes.

"Kiddos, we have very capable allies willing to help us. We know this. I think it's time to call them in."

Trev'nor stared at him for a long moment, battling with himself. They'd sworn in the beginning they wouldn't drag anyone into this mess, that they'd fight this battle with their own people, but…he looked to Becca and found her jaw set in determination. "Bec?"

"He's right." Blowing out an exhausted breath, she met Trev'nor's eyes levelly. "Trev. We either call in help or we demolish the city trying to extract people from it. I know which I would prefer. You?"

"You know, it's really hard to argue that." Trev'nor ran a hand over his face, feeling forty instead of a teenager. "Alright. Let's call for reinforcements and see who responds. Becca, will you do the honors?"

"Why am I always the one making the call?" she asked, not confrontationally, just curious.

"Because the first time I sent you out for reinforcements you came back with Raile." Giving her a crooked smile, he lifted a shoulder in a shrug. "Obviously you get good results. Excellent leadership is knowing who to send out to garner the best results, right?"

A twinkle in her eye, she preened, head tilted at a mock demure angle. "He does say the sweetest things sometimes. Alright. Let's call for help."

"It's all well and good to say that, but how?" Nolan looked between all of them, head cocked in challenge. "We don't have the means to reach that far, we'd need a stationary pool to pull it off."

"Watch and learn, young grasshopper," she responded airily. Lifting the mirror to her mouth, she called through it, "Raile? My favorite wizard, are you there?"

"Funny how I'm always a favorite when you need something," Raile responded dryly. "Yes, child, I'm here. Now what do you need?"

"I need you to connect me to every pool, every mirror, of every country that you can reach." Becca's expression settled into one of fierce determination, standing straight and rigid as if she expected to go back into battle any second. "I'm issuing a call to quarters."

Dead silence on the other end lingered for a small eternity. Then Raile's voice rasped back, "Are you saying that even if I send you more of us from Rheben, it wouldn't be enough? You're that hard pressed?"

"I've got a good seven hundred half-trained magicians up here with no amulets on," she informed him bluntly. "They're fighting tooth and nail to keep us out of the city. Another dozen magicians isn't going to be enough. Will you connect me to my allies?"

Raile blew out a gusty sigh. "Great good Guardians, that's overwhelming odds. Alright, Becca, give me five minutes."

Nolan let out a low whistle. "He can really do that? Becca, how did you know?"

"Garth mentioned he'd seen Raile do something similar," she explained absently.

Trev'nor leaned in and warned her, "You'll have to repeat everything in different languages, not everyone speaks a common language."

She nodded in agreement. "Chahiran is the most universal language in the magic community, I'll start with that."

"Alright, Riicbeccaan, you are connected. Speak."

The formal announcement put her back up and she stood at full attention as she spoke distinctly, crisply. "This is Riicbeccaan, Weather Mage and Maharaja of Khobunter. I am at the city of Von and require assistance. We have seven hundred magicians enslaved in the city who are being forced to fight us. We can't get through their defenses with the magicians we have on hand, not without destroying the city itself. I'm issuing a call to quarters. To anyone who is our ally, anyone willing to fight, please come immediately to Von. If we can't subdue them peacefully in the next three days, we'll be forced to destroy it." Switching languages, she slipped into Hainish, "I repeat—"

Trev'nor caught sight of Danyal's face as he watched her. The man stared at Becca in awe, as if she were the most amazing thing he'd ever seen. Shad beamed at her, as proud as any parent would be in his shoes.

Leaning into Trev'nor's side, Dunixan whispered, "You really think people will drop everything and come?"

Tilting his head toward him, Trev'nor responded in a low voice, "You have to understand, the magical community is very tightly knit. Part of it is because we're mostly all related to each other, either through marriages or adoption. Take me, for example. I'm a Rheben, but also a Tonkowacon, and a Jaunten because various people adopted me and raised me. It's actually not that uncommon. Becca's strength is actually her ties with Shad, as he helped rescue a lot of magicians, and her relationship with Tyvendor, as she's his student. She'll draw a lot of Chahiran and Hainan magicians just by asking."

"How many?" Dunixan asked seriously.

"Enough," Trev'nor responded grimly. "Hopefully enough."

21

With the call issued, they couldn't do anything else. Trev'nor called the meeting to an end and staggered out. Dunixan caught him before he went more than five steps, then reached back to support Nolan as well, half-carting both exhausted mages to bed. Relieved Dunixan had them in hand, Becca ceased to worry about them and stood, intent on finding her own bed. Before she could even clear the flaps, Rahim caught her with an arm around her waist, not so much cuddling as pulling her strongly into his side. Bemused, she turned her head to look at him. He normally didn't do this sort of thing in full view of the entire army.

"You're weaving," he informed her, well able to read the question on her face.

"Am I really?" She didn't feel unbalanced, just tired, and like a strong wind could knock her down.

Frankly worried, he lifted a hand to her face, eyes roving her from head to toe and back again. "You said you weren't injured."

"I'm not," she assured him, leaning heavily into his side. "I think my balance got a little disoriented up there, that's all. Tyvendor and I took the brunt of the wind attacks, so Cat had to do all sorts of barrel rolls and spins to keep us from being sent straight into the ground. It so nauseated Ty that he's had to lie down for the past hour with a cold cloth over his eyes."

"Then you, too, should lie down." That decision made, he steered them both for her tent.

Belatedly, Becca realized that the tension she could see in his face didn't only stem from this losing battle they fought. "Did I worry you? While I was up there fighting, I mean."

For a long moment he didn't answer her, his face pointing straight ahead. "You are an amazing fighter. I know this."

"Fear is not usually rational." She put a hand over the one gripping her waist, wishing he would look at her. "Rahim. I'm sorry I scared you."

Heaving out a gusty sigh, he stopped dead, pulling her also to a halt. Only then did he look at her, his face drawn and pinched in an unhappy way. "No, dearest, I don't need an apology from you. It was just hard on my pride and nerves to see you off this morning, to let another man protect you. Harder still to be stuck on the ground and only able to watch as you fought. I badly wished I could do something but there wasn't anything to be done."

"I was in the air and didn't actually manage to accomplish anything, so trust me, I understand that all too well." Was it just that? Most of the time he was honest with his feelings, but sometimes he had this stubborn way of keeping things to himself. Becca didn't know at this point and really didn't have the energy to pursue it, either. Later. She'd deal with it later, if it came to that.

Rahim sighed and put them in motion once more. As if confessing some grave sin, he spoke in a low tone. "You are vital to the world. I know this. But sometimes I wish I could argue, explain that you're vital to me as well, and that you shouldn't be sacrificed for the world's betterment."

Sometimes the way he spoke to her sounded like the sweetest of love confessions. Unable to help herself, she caught his head and pulled him down enough that she could put a kiss against his cheek, whispering against his skin, "I love you, too."

The look in his eyes changed to one of hunger and high emotion, his eyes dark and dilated with it. Rahim pressed in close, capturing her mouth and kissing her with gentle thoroughness. She did her best to kiss back and found it difficult, as he effectively turned her brain off.

Someone let out a wolf whistle. Rahim slowly released her, lifting his head, and threw out a very rude gesture to the whistler. Becca recognized the laugh all too well and called out, "Just wait until it's your turn, Ehsan!"

Laughing, the Water Mage didn't respond.

With a last dark look at the interfering man, Rahim walked them the last stretch toward her tent, where Nahla stood patiently waiting for them. An indulgent smile sat squarely on the woman's face even as she held out both hands. "Give her to me. I'll put her to bed."

Becca wanted to argue that she wasn't a child, and would have if the notion of being put to bed didn't sound so delightful. Rahim handed her over a little reluctantly. "Good night, dearest."

"Night," she responded with a loopy smile in return, allowing Nahla to pull her inside the tent.

Her batwoman closed the flaps as Becca sank onto the pallet. She tried untying the laces of her boots but they fought back, the vicious fiends, and she ended up with her fingers caught in the laces. Becca had sensed herself crashing for the past hour but she hadn't realized how badly she tottered along that knife edge until she sat there arguing with her shoes like a five-year-old child.

"You're done in," Nahla observed, kneeling in front of her and gently untangling Becca's fingers. "And while that kiss looked lovely, I don't think that's what did it."

"Fighting all day drains me," Becca acknowledged around a yawn. "The kiss was lovely, though, wasn't it? I love that he will finally do that in public."

Nahla gave her a strange look, the first boot half off her foot. "Of course. He had to wait until your engagement."

Becca returned that expression with one of her own, caught flat footed. "Engagement? Ah, Nahla, the man hasn't exactly proposed."

Her eyes crossed, hands fumbling. "And you let him kiss you in public?!"

"Culture gap," Becca sighed, now more or less resigned to instances like these. "A kiss isn't as all-inclusive in Chahir as it is here. Don't be alarmed, Nahla, I'm sure we'll eventually sit down and talk weddings, it's just hard to do so with a war going on. We have plans for both of us to meet each other's families, and if that isn't pre-proposal stage, I don't know what is."

Nahla put a hand over heart and let out a sharp breath of relief. "Sometimes the things you say alarm me."

"I do that a lot to people in this country," Becca acknowledged, grinning. "You should have seen me when we first arrived, and they kept piling all of these rules on top my head. I felt like some hellion child."

"I'm just as happy to have missed that stage," Nahla assured her dryly, going back to removing the boots. "The whole country assumes the two of you will marry. Do you understand that, at least?"

Becca rolled her eyes expressively. "They haven't exactly been shy about sharing their opinion. And I'm very, very happy about that option, trust me. But bringing Von under control takes precedence at the moment."

"We all understand that as well," Nahla assured her. She still seemed somewhat unbalanced by the casual way Becca treated the prospect of being married, but this woman had spent five years engaged, struggling to earn enough to marry. She likely had a very different perspective on the matter.

Becca wiped off the worse of the sweat with a wet cloth, then sat still as Nahla patiently combed through her hair.

By the time she climbed into a nightdress, Becca resorted to willpower to keep herself upright and awake.

Nahla bid her goodnight, stepping out and tying the flaps shut behind her. Becca just toppled straight over, barely managing to wiggle her way under the covers. Eyes dropping shut, she pondered Nahla's statements to her. The whole country expected her and Rahim to marry? Kissing her in public meant they were basically engaged? Did Rahim understand all of that?

No, silly question, of course he did. He understood this culture far better than she did, having grown up in it. So, when he moved to touch her in public that first time, had he already made his decision? Likely so.

Definitely so.

The thought made her smile as she slipped into an exhausted slumber.

Even if the requested magicians dropped everything and immediately rushed to the rescue, no one could possibly get there in a single day. Becca didn't start scanning the skies until after noon on the second day, Trev'nor just as anxiously studying the ground. They stayed out of range in an uneasy stand-off with Von. No one from the city was willing to leave the walls to attack them, and her army had strict orders to not move.

Just because they waited didn't mean they could sit around sucking their thumbs, however. They had to plan for every eventuality so they'd know how to act. For lunch they reconvened in the command tent and Becca stood, still feeling tired even after a full day of rest. She used the table to support most of her weight. "Alright, let's talk about what to do when people get here. Assuming we have enough magicians to force them into a standstill, then what?"

"Then you use the ultimate weapon," Shad informed her, lounging on three thick pillows nearby, for all the world at his leisure. "Words."

"You want us to talk," Becca repeated dubiously.

Shad tsked her, wagging a finger. "No, I want us to be charming and persuasive. And don't take that tone with me, every battle ends with a treaty, doesn't it?"

"Normally the losing side doesn't try to force the winning side into a treaty, though," Dunixan observed dryly. Out of everyone in the command tent, he seemed to have held onto his sense of humor the best.

Becca wasn't in the mood to discuss anything. But she also recognized that frustration made her feel that way, and as a ruler, she couldn't afford to let frustration get the better of her. She sidled over to stand right next to Rahim, catching his hand under the table. He always calmed her down in moments like these. He squeezed her fingers gently but otherwise gave no sign.

Leaning back in his chair, Dunixan crossed his ankles, mimicking Shad's very relaxed pose. "I do have a thought, however. Perhaps we should treat this more like a business negotiation."

Trev'nor stopped consuming everything on his plate and looked up. "How?"

"Von has always had a reputation of being more generous with his people," Dunixan explained. "He gives them slightly more freedom than most of the other warlords. You've seen it yourself with the magicians. But what if we make his standards a lie? What if we can prove to them, somehow, that what we offer is true freedom?"

Becca pondered that, her thumb rubbing absent circles on Rahim's skin. "You know, it sounds difficult, but I think we can actually do it. Quite a few people in that city were forced to leave loved ones behind. The young parents, especially, that couldn't take their infant children with them have to be worried sick."

"I'd murder the warlord myself if he forced me to abandon my children," Sallah input with a hard gleam in her eye. "I bet if we go down to Brecon and take some of the children, bring them up here as proof that we saved the ones Von sacrificed, they might revolt."

"It's a good start," Shad allowed. "What if we start a garden right outside of the city walls as well, like we would with a conquered country? Nothing elaborate, just enough to be a show and tell."

No one in Khobunter really understood what a garden was, not the way the rest of the world thought of one. Becca could describe it until she was blue in the face and not relay the image of it accurately. A garden, even a small one, would be a good way to make the point without talking.

"Llona says that she will recite the names of the ones we've saved," Nolan remarked, then turned his head to say something in the low, haunting tones of Dragonese. He paused, listened to the short response, and grinned. "She promises to be very loud."

Simin cleared her throat before speaking, drawing their attention her. "Maharajas. Listen to your advisor. The general and warlord of Von have no doubt made airy promises to their people. 'We could only save so many of you.' 'There's more freedom here than what your conquerors will deliver.' 'You must fight to keep the lives you have now.' You can prove them to be liars."

"No one trusts a liar," Shad acknowledged with a grin at her. "I'm with Simin on this. Besides, kiddos, you just spent two full days attacking the city while carefully not hurting anyone. I'm sure they've realized that you don't want to do actual damage, and that's going to say a lot by itself."

Becca pondered all of that, and while it still seemed ludicrous on some level—to try and talk an enemy into surrendering—she didn't see what they'd have to lose by trying it. "Alright. I'm not convinced this will work, but if nothing else it might buy us some time to come up with another plan. Trev?"

"I'm for it," Trev'nor informed her, exhaustion bleeding into his voice. "If it means avoiding another day like that one, I'm all for it. Sallah, which would you rather do? Plant a garden or go down and fetch some of the kids?"

"I'll fetch," Sallah answered forthrightly. "They know me better than you."

"Good point," he acknowledged. "Becca, can you get any rain out of that storm overhead?"

"It'll be difficult," she admitted. "The minute I start to do anything, I have a fight on my hands."

Ehsan stirred from where he sat cross-legged in the corner, a cup of water in his hands. "Don't worry about that, Trev'nor. I'll water the soil for you."

"You do make my life easier," Trev'nor said by way of thanks. "Then I vote we wait for tomorrow morning, give us all a little more time to magically recover before we start. Let them really watch what we're doing. How much garden should we plant before we try to talk to them?"

"What can you plant and harvest in the same morning?" Rahim countered. "If we bring them fruit and vegetables, it provides even more physical proof it's not a mirage."

The magicians wouldn't need to see such physical proof, of course, but Rahim probably thought of the common people when he suggested this.

Nolan rattled off the information without any forethought. "Cucumber, zucchini, peaches, apples, pears, cherries, apricots."

"Some of those are trees," Rahim approved, nodding. "Good, that makes them easier to see from a distance. I suggest planting an orchard. Such a thing doesn't really exist here, not the way you plant it."

"Orchard it is." Nolan swept his eyes across the people

in the tent, mouth turning in a lopsided smile. "And who's going to be charming and persuasive first?"

"Llona," several voices said in near unison.

Nolan snorted a laugh. "Well, she is the loudest out of all of us. And she can certainly get their attention. Sallah next, then, to prove we have the people that Llona names?"

"After that, play it by ear," Shad advised. "Depending on how they respond, we might not have to say much else, or we might have to try something totally different."

Becca didn't see how they could plan any of this out in detail, so she agreed with Shad's statement with a one-shoulder shrug. "Everyone alright with this plan? Yes? What if we don't get enough people in?"

"Oh, I wouldn't worry about that," Shad said with an enigmatic smile. "I would worry about how you're going to transport all of those people near the city. In terms of speed, you'll have some disconnect. Some of you are mounted on dragons, others will be on foot, and that's going to cause deployment problems."

Nolan shook his head, grinning. "You're behind the curve, Shad. Garth already realized this problem and called home for help. We have another thunder of dragons on their way."

"When did this happen?" Becca demanded, twisting to see her friend seated next to her.

Shrugging, Nolan admitted, "Not quite sure. He just informed he'd already called for help and not to worry about it."

"That's my dragon, alright." Trev'nor shook his head in amusement. "So, we'll be able to mount people when they get here. Assuming I can create that many saddles. Sallah, I don't suppose you'd help?"

"Sure?" Sallah cocked her head at him, leaning her elbows on the table so she could look around Dunixan to see his face. "I have no idea what I'm doing, I've never made a saddle."

"It's not complicated. If you watch me do it once, you'll get the hang of it," Trev'nor assured her. "And I hate to ask, but do you think any of our family from Coven Ordan is coming?"

"If Aral isn't, I'll divorce him," Sallah informed him bluntly, making Shad chortle. "Don likely will come as well. But someone's got to watch the kids, so likely that will be all that can come in our immediate family. I wouldn't be surprised if we got a healthy group of people from home, though."

Becca just wished she could put a number to them. "Well, let's see who comes."

Late in the afternoon, help arrived. Becca heard Trev'nor let out a whoop and she immediately ducked out of the command tent, eyes searching until she found him standing at the back of the camp, right in the middle of the road. He did something with his magic, like a signal flare, and then did a happy dance.

Sprinting to him, she demanded loudly, "Who's coming?"

"Aunt Kayden!" Trev'nor whirled around, a wide, happy smile on his face. He spied Dunixan nearby and waved the man over. "Come here, I want you to meet everyone."

Becca skidded to a stop near Trev'nor's side, anxious to see who else Kayden had brought. To her complete lack of surprise, Rahim, Shad, and Sallah all quickly joined them, also peering impatiently at the horizon.

It took more than a few minutes before Becca spotted the tell-tale signs of an Earth Path opening up. As multiple people came into view, Becca quickly counted them, astounded at the number. Sixteen. Sixteen had come from Hain, far more than she anticipated. She recognized most of their faces but not all, the majority of the group Trev'nor's side of the family.

Kayden stood at the head of the group and she went straight for Trev'nor, arms thrown wide in invitation. "There's my rebellious little cousin."

Laughing, Trev'nor caught her up in a strong embrace, nearly lifting her toes from the ground. "Aunt Kayden, you are a sight for sore eyes. All of you are." Letting go, Trev'nor offered a hand to Kayden's wizard husband standing behind her. "Uncle Roarke."

Roarke Kartal grabbed his cousin in a quick embrace, as darkly handsome and serious as always. "We were glad you called. This is too much for even you three to manage."

"Can't argue there," Trev'nor agreed, making a face.

Becca lost track of them as she moved forward, making her own greetings. "Jarod! Hayden! I didn't know you were still in Hain."

"We were actually packing up to return to Chahir when we heard your call," Jarod admitted. Still big as life, he had to bend down to give her a quick hug. "Hayden and I had just finished repairing a bridge in southern Hain, so your timing is good."

Hayden reached around to give her a quick kiss on the cheek, blue eyes twinkling. "That and we were feeling left out. Everyone else gets to play with you and we don't? For shame."

"What, I never said you couldn't come," Becca sassed back, returning his grin. She half-turned, catching Rahim's hand and drawing him forward. "Rahim, this is Lonjaroden and Rhebenhaydenen, both Elemental Mages. This is General Rahim Danyal."

The men gave each other appropriate bows of greeting, and from the expressions on their faces, they obviously knew that Becca and Rahim were courting. Someone had been carrying tales it seemed. Likely Kayden.

Catching Rahim's confusion, she explained, "Hayden's actually adopted into the Rheben family."

"Garth found me twelve years ago in Chahir and rescued me," Hayden picked up the explanation smoothly, a nostalgic smile on his face. "He took me into the family. I was actually raised by his parents. Trev's more a brother than a cousin, really. Of course we had to come help. Bec, do you know Wizard Waetomlinen?"

A shorter, stockier man with a baby face and pale skin stepped around Jarod's bulk and offered a quick bow. "We've never met, but I certainly know of you, Riicbeccaan."

"Same," Becca admitted. "Thank you for coming, Wizard Waetomlinen."

"I owe both Shad and Garth a serious favor for rescuing me out of Chahir." Tomlin gave her a lopsided smile. "I figure this is a good chance to repay it. Quite a few of us are responding for that reason, actually."

Becca looked out over the crowd, recognizing practically everyone else. Wizards Kamik Dassan, Saman, Clason, all of them guest lecturers over the years about Blood Magic at the academy. Rheijennaan, another Elemental Mage, and her sisters Rheiveraan and Rheinellaan. Two more Life Mages had made it up, Jillian and Cora, Cora making good on her earlier promise to help. It might have taken Cora longer than expected to get here, but Becca couldn't begrudge the time. She'd made it when Becca needed her most. Sinhelenan stood in the midst of them, as serene and calm as usual, one of the few that wore her mage robes. When she caught Becca looking at her, she offered a wink and smile, to which Becca winked back, making the woman laugh.

The last three she didn't know. The two wizards and witch stood a little apart from the family, watching indulgently as the reunion played out. Shad moved around to greet them, a happy bounce in his stride. "Bornemeier, Loewy, Huish! It feels like Act II, doesn't it?"

"It does," Loewy—surely that wasn't actually her name—responded with a sharp smile. "How is it that I only meet you on a battlefield?"

"Because I'm fun that way," Shad responded with an outrageous waggle. "Come meet my Becca."

So Shad knew these people from some prior conflict? Becca tried to place the names with a particular scene and came up with a vague memory. Hadn't they helped him protect a city in Chahir from the Star Order Priests? She came to him and Shad put an arm around her shoulders as he made the introductions. "This is Wizard Bornemeier, Witch Loewen, and Wizard Nihuishen. I'm not sure if you remember, but that story Garth and I tell about the Watchman's Pool in Chahir with all of the magicians in it? The ones gathered up by a single, very determined wizard? Huish did that."

The memory clicked into place and Becca greeted him with a very respectful bow. "I'm very glad to finally meet you."

"So am I," Huish responded, smiling back at her. Until she had the name, she wouldn't have suspected him to be a Chahiran magician, as he had the dark brown hair and coloring usually associated with Hain. "And glad to finally return the favor."

"Well, I don't actually have a reason to come up here except I can't trust this one to make sane decisions," Loewen declared, poking a long finger into Shad's side. He flinched and chortled like a drunk elf. "Really, do you never grow up?"

"Never," Shad denied, beaming at her.

"The first time I met your brother," Bornemeier confided to Becca, "I was so incredibly green to real combat. He pulled me aside and explained all about fatal funnels and how doors are not our friends. That knowledge has saved my life on multiple occasions."

Shad's chest puffed up. "I did."

Blinking, Becca cocked her head as something failed to jive in her head. It took a moment, but she remembered Shad saying the complete opposite to her when they were breaking into Riyu's fortress. Pinning her brother with a look, she demanded, "Now wait a minute. You told me that doors were our friends!"

"When?" Shad asked, confused and innocent.

She knew better than to trust that expression. "When we were breaking into Riyu's fortress!"

"Ah, but that's different, darling. When you're sneaking, doors can be friends. When you're fighting, they are not. Very capricious things, doors." Releasing her, Shad pirouetted away, clapping his hands together loudly and calling to them, "Now, now let's not stand here. Come in to the camp, we can catch up with each other while we wait to see who else comes in!"

Throwing her hands into the air, exasperated, Becca followed after him.

Trev'nor started in on the soil conditioning just after breakfast of the next day, taking advantage of what warmth the suns radiated as they rose in the sky. He conditioned the soil as he always did, removing the harsher minerals and modifying it so that the ground would properly receive moisture. For good measure, he worked on a large patch on either side of the main road leading into the main gates of Von. As he worked, he kept sneaking glances back at the camp, still not able to believe how many people had responded to Becca's call for help.

Fifty-six people. They had fifty-six trained mages, witches, and wizards ready to fight with them. He didn't know all of them, some of them were here just to repay a favor for either Garth or Shad, but some of them came solely to help. Of the ones that Trev'nor did recognize, he felt more than awed, as these people carried serious reputations. Two of the Remnant Mages had come, arriving barely a half hour after Aunt Kayden's group—Terran Far'Auchmage and Hayel D'Auch. They'd carried with them multiple magicians from Coven Ordan, which included Aral Bender, Sallah's husband, her brother Don, Eliza Far'Auchmage, Tara, a Fire Mage, and two dozen others Trev'nor had never met.

Garth arrived late last night with his own people in tow, most of them former students who Trev'nor recognized but couldn't always put a name to, and word that Krys was on his way with Kaya and her brood. Which would mean not only more dragons to help carry magicians into battle, but it would bring their total up to two Fire Mages. The support they received nearly overwhelmed Trev'nor.

Their dragon foster-father—after this, Trev'nor couldn't think of him as anything else—sent another fifty dragons to help, and they'd arrived in the pre-dawn hours this morning. All of them had been fed and were lying about in the cool suns, taking naps, recuperating from their long flight.

He'd known they were loved, but not like this. Not when people from around the world instantly came to help. It humbled him, how quickly they'd responded, and Trev'nor had no idea how he'd pay any of them back for their unconditional support in this dark hour.

Ehsan ambled up to stand next to him, his magic coming to bear as he pulled water from some underground source and into the topsoil. "I can practically see their unease from here."

Following Ehsan's gaze, Trev'nor studied the magicians lined up along the top of the wall. They watched like wolves, ready to defend their territory at the slightest hint of aggression, and not sure if the strangers at the gate intended to start the fight or not. Trev'nor had deliberately chosen the spot he did to work with, as it sat in that no man's ground of close enough to see but far enough out of comfortable range. "I'd say something like let's be careful to not make any aggressive moves, but there's nothing threatening about putting in an orchard."

"Thankfully true. Although I think it's watching multiple magicians arrive that's put them so on edge. Becca said we're waiting on one more—a Fire Mage from Mellor?"

"Haikrysen is his name. He's sort of an adopted big brother to most of us. He was the first dragon rider of this generation, as he was adopted by a dragon in Libendorf. He's a formidable fighter. I'm really glad he's coming." Trev'nor paused to stare at the sky, searching again for any hint of Kaya. "He called this morning to say he would be here shortly. He stopped off at Rheben to rest last night, so it shouldn't be much longer."

"I'm stunned at how many people came." Ehsan shook his head, bewildered but in the best of ways. "Is that why you had Becca call? You knew she'd pull this many people?"

"Honestly? Shad's got a huge pull with the magical community, as he helped Garth rescue a lot of people. That was part of it. And as the only Weather Mage, she's very famous in magic circles. I figured her word would carry more weight than mine." Trev'nor didn't mind that in the least. He did not seek fame.

"It looks like you were right." Ehsan idly swirled a hand, playing a little with the water. "Is this enough?"

"For now, sure. Not sure how much Nolan will need when he actually starts planting. He's going to force the trees to semi-maturity to get good fruit off of them."

Ehsan accepted that with a judicial nod and drew up some more water just in case, leaving it sitting in a barrel-sized shape without the physical structure of an actual barrel. Show-off. "Trev'nor, do you really think this will work?"

"I have no idea. But Shad keeps pushing us to try, which says a lot. Even Roshan seems to think that there's a chance we'll succeed if we lay our cards out right. I don't have as much battle experience as they do, so I'm trusting their instincts on this." Privately he added, "I just really hope it does. I'm deathly sick of casualties, and if we push this battle any further, that's what we'll have. Lots and lots of casualties."

Grimacing, Ehsan agreed, "It's what we're all afraid of. That taking the city will destroy it."

"Hopefully it won't come to that."

Nolan strolled up with a mug of steaming tea in his hand, looking a little bleary and mussed around the edges. It suggested he had not gotten as much sleep as the rest of them, but then Life Mages always seemed to sacrifice sleep to one medical emergency or another. "Morning."

"Morning," Ehsan greeted. "Right side is ready for planting. Is this enough water?"

"For the right side, maybe."

Taking the hint, Ehsan promised, "I'll draw up more for the left."

Green sprouts started out of the ground in regimented rows. Trev'nor's part was done at this point but he lingered, ready to throw up a shield to protect the other two so they could work without worrying.

"Fledgling." Garth's long neck turned to point. "They come."

Trev'nor stopped all work immediately and lifted a hand to shield his eyes from the morning sun so he could see better. They were nothing more than specks against a blue sky at first but they came quickly into view, Kaya leading the way with her children in a flying V formation behind her. She went straight for Trev'nor and landed several feet away, politely giving him enough space that she didn't knock the three puny humans over.

Trev'nor strode straight for them, beyond relieved to see Krys. With him here, they were ready to face Von, and Trev'nor's nerves couldn't stand the suspense any longer. He wanted to move, get this over with. "Krys."

Lifting his goggles up to rest on his forehead, the Fire Mage waved and unbuckled himself in three efficient moves before tossing a leg over Kaya's neck and dropping neatly to the ground. He made it look like one sinuous motion, but then, he'd had ten years of experience doing it. "Trev. You scamp, you were knee-high and helping me break up water towers and then I turn my back for five minutes to find now you're conquering countries."

Hugging the man tightly, Trev breathed in the scent of leather, sunlight, and dragon, feeling more confident now that he had Krys with them. He'd seen this man take on the impossible and come out on top. If Trev'nor had a choice of who to ride into battle with, Krys's name would feature at the top of the list. "I blame Shad."

"We all blame Shad," Krys assured him dryly. With a final pat on his back, Krys let go. "Hello, Water Mage, who might you be?"

"This is Ehsan," Trev'nor introduced, then continued the introductions as Krys, of course, hadn't met either Llona or Garth properly. Kaya came from the same clan, so the dragons greeted each other like the old friends they were.

Becca appeared during this, got her own hug in, then went straight down to business, her demeanor professional and collected. "Krys. I know you just got in, but we want to try to subdue the city today. Much longer, and we invite trouble."

"We are perfectly ready to go," Krys assured her just as seriously. "The kids want to help carry magicians in, so whoever doesn't have a mount can borrow one of them. Trev said he'd made up saddles?"

"Not just him, several others helped, and I believe we have enough. Come with me, we'll get everyone organized. Trev, Nol, how much longer do you need for the orchard?"

Nolan regarded his own handiwork for a moment before offering, "Another hour?"

"Then we'll be ready to go in an hour." Determined, Becca strode off.

Trev'nor apparently had his marching orders. He went

back to work, speeding up a little, as Becca had a game plan that he had no intention of messing with.

An hour crept by as Trev'nor worked until he finally just called it good and stopped, as he couldn't do anything more in the time allotted. Jogging back toward the front line, he caught Priya's eye and motioned her firmly to stay back in camp, ignoring her mournful chitter. Spying Garth and Aral ahead, he headed for them. The two men paused as he approached, Aral asking, "Did Becca fill you in on our plan?"

"Is this different from the plan we came up with yesterday?" Trev'nor canted his head in question, as something about the way Aral asked this question suggested plans had changed.

"We told her something that changed her mind," Garth explained, hands coming up to illustrate in wide gestures toward the city. "We've been in a situation rather like this, where we had to face off with a city. Granted, we were on the defensive side, but I think the principal will still work. Aral coordinated all of the magicians in a cohesive ward that made it impenetrable to magic. We were able to hold it for a considerable amount of time."

"The cities' sizes are about the same," Aral continued, brown eyes narrowed as he calculated things. "And our intent is similar. I think we can use the Four Corner Ward to contain all attacks. We can approach the city without fear that way. Becca explained your plan to get close enough to talk?"

It sounded like a question, so Trev'nor nodded confirmation.

"This will enable you to do it." Aral gestured toward the city. "I don't think we can hold it all day, but certainly I can buy you several hours. What do you think?"

"I think it's so, so much better than you causing a distraction and we somehow sneaking up onto the walls."

Which had been Plan A. "Let's do it. Aral, can you coordinate the warding?"

"I've been volunteered to do it." Aral gave Garth a sidelong glance to make it clear who exactly had volunteered him.

Shrugging innocently, Garth said mildly, "You're an expert, aren't you? I've seen you do it already. Trev, Becca wants to do this now, and I think everyone is almost in position. Are you and Nolan done over there?"

"Nolan's literally harvesting things. So yes. Aral, where do you want me?"

Pointing to a spot, Aral turned him gently by one shoulder, orienting him to the right area. "Straight down the middle of the road. I'll be on your left, Garth on your right. Everyone will be mounted, so get on Dragon Garth first."

Sighing, Garth complained to Trev'nor, "How hard did you try to talk him out of my name? Really."

Grinning cheekily, Trev'nor admitted, "Not that hard. It was too funny." He dodged the playful swipe Garth aimed at him and skipped out of range, heading for his dragon.

"Trev!"

Turning, he waited for Dunixan to catch up with him. Dunixan came in close enough for their arms to brush, speaking in a low tone not meant to carry. "We're almost ready to begin. Are you sure this will work?"

"Not at all, but I do think it will give us a very good chance of reaching them." Trev'nor prayed that would be enough. Trying to reassure the man, he gave him a playful nudge with his shoulder. "Either way, you'll like what happens next. You've never seen a full warding circle before, right?"

Slowly, Dunixan shook his head, brows lifted in curiosity. "No, just heard what happened in Trexler."

"The warding spells are ancient, the oldest of all magic. They're so old they're in song form and we literally sing the spell to put a ward in place. The magic is strong enough that even without any magical talent, everyone can see it as the ward forms. It's awe-inspiring, even for magicians. We don't do this kind of coordinated magic very often."

"Then I'll look forward to it. Just…" worry tightened the corners of Dunixan's expression, "be careful? Please."

Garth turned his head to nudge Dunixan's side gently. "Fledgling be fine, Roshan. I will protect."

Dunixan rubbed at that giant snout before scratching under Garth's chin in the perfect spot, sending the dragon's eyes to half-mast in pleasure. "I'm counting on you, Garth."

Trev'nor squeezed Dunixan's shoulder once in reassurance before slinging himself up and into the saddle, buckling in. Not that he would need to while they stayed on the ground, but if Garth had to abruptly launch them into the air, he wanted to be firmly strapped in.

Dunixan retreated, giving everyone enough room to mount their dragons.

As Trev'nor stood at the ready, Llona came up and bumped against Nolan's side affectionately before turning her big blue eyes on Trev'nor. "Talk now?"

Trev'nor considered that. Everyone in Von seemed to be on the walls, watching avidly, and he didn't see why Llona couldn't start her part of the campaign now. "Can you be sure that the whole city will hear you?"

Llona gave him a look that said 'please, as if that's a concern.' "Am sure."

Of course she was. Trev'nor gave her a grand wave of the arm. "Then as soon as the ward is up, please start, my lady. Ah, maybe stand a little away from us so we have some hearing left in our old age."

Snorting amusement, she nodded in a very human gesture, then paced off in a few dragonish bounds with Nolan to their assigned spot. Trev'nor readied the mirror broach in his hands and waited, nerves jangling, for Aral's signal.

23

Aral hummed out the first note, the sound deep and in the minor key of the spell. Every magician matched his pitch, their voices overlapping and blending, from the lowest bass to the highest soprano. Trev'nor's throat vibrated with the force of his hum and he held the note steady for several beats before Aral launched into the song.

Sixty voices sang with him, the song pulsing strong, the mirrors echoing it back and forth to cocoon the entire city. The air shimmered with magic, like dust motes in strong sunlight, gathering strength and presence. They swirled together, moving forward, connecting to other motes of magic as they moved, coalescing into a dome of light and power. Every fiber of Trev'nor's being felt the force of it singing along his veins—not just under his own magic, but everyone else's. He could feel them all as they blended magic and intent into one powerful spell, and it threatened to take his breath away.

The dragons couldn't take just listening and they pitched in as well, their voices lifting in a counter-harmony, deep and low. Trev'nor had a split second to be afraid that the addition would disrupt the spell, but instead it enhanced it. The ward went from shimmering light to something an opaque gold, barely thin enough to see through. He had no idea why their voices would have that effect on the spell but suspected it had more to do with the magicians. Having a powerful set of voices supporting the less confident singers would explain the boost.

It painted such an amazing picture that Trev'nor swore to himself he'd have this memory dumped into a crystal and a painting commissioned. He wanted this moment preserved for history.

Everyone on Von's walls stared, half-entranced, half-terrified as the dome pressed in. The dragons moved in unison, taking their magicians closer to the walls, and the ward moved with them, closing in around the city on all sides. Trev'nor could hear the screams of alarm even from here and wished he could explain to them that the wards wouldn't hurt them.

Garth kept to a slow pace with the other dragons, no one wishing to jar the singing magicians, his gait smooth as silk. A stone's throw from the walls, everyone stopped, again in perfect unison, the last note of the spell echoing and fading. Trev'nor craned his neck up to look at the watching magicians and found them staring back in utter terror. The braver ones tried throwing out a spell, only to have it ricochet. The few soldiers on the wall threw a few attacks as well with more conventional weapons, only to be equally rebuffed.

Not knowing what to do, they withdrew instead, putting what distance they could between themselves and the ward.

Llona took this as her cue and lifted herself like a cat sitting on its haunches and boomed out. "I AM LLONA, DRAGON OF MAGE VONNOLANEN, KEEPER OF RECORDS. I WILL RECITE THE NAMES OF THOSE MAGICIANS NOW FREE. FROM TREXLER—"

She certainly knew how to broadcast her voice. Trev'nor blessed, again, Llona's precise pronunciation. Even at extreme volume, everyone could understand her perfectly. He really wished he could see the reactions of the people listening to her, as his view was limited to the ones right in front of him. Trev'nor couldn't decipher what anyone said as they listened to that recitation of names. Llona's voice effectively drowned them out. But he saw more than a few tears of relief fall, some people putting a shocked hand to their mouths, others sinking down to their haunches, openly stunned and disbelieving. The people here knew those rescued, be they friends, family, or just acquaintances.

With the ward in place, a select few left their positions to join Trev'nor in front of the main gate. Being the closest, Ehsan and Ginger arrived first and came to stand next to Trev'nor. The dragons' hides brushed up against each other, and Ehsan let out a low gasp, more felt than heard.

"Ehsan, you recognize anyone up there?"

A strange expression on his face, Ehsan nodded. "I do. Two, in fact."

Trev'nor perked up at this. "Some of the friends you were missing?"

"Yes. But…" his voice stumbled and choked, "I was told one of them was dead."

Stilling, Trev'nor fumbled for a response but couldn't think of what to say. 'You sure?' seemed stupid and anything else smacked of being insensitive. His mouth popped out, "Obviously someone lied to you."

Ehsan lifted a palm to his eyes and swiped at them, masking tears before they could fall. "Trev. When you go up to talk to them, I'm coming too."

"Of course you are," Trev'nor agreed instantly. "Wouldn't dream of doing otherwise."

Trev'nor focused again on the people above him, how they cupped their hands around their mouths and shouted out something he couldn't begin to hear over Llona. The trick of learning a foreign language was that while you could understand the spoken word just fine, lip reading proved to be near impossible. "Ehsan, what are they saying?"

"I'm only making out a few words here and there," Ehsan apologized, eyes narrowed with intensity, "but they seem to be demanding details. When they were freed, where they are now."

He had the gut feeling it was time to approach and try talking more directly. "Ehsan, get the others, let's try approaching." Lifting the mirror to his mouth, he yelled into it, "Nolan! Ask Llona to pause and come up with us!"

Llona abruptly ceased speaking and the silence felt deafening in comparison.

It took several minutes to draw everyone together. Shad, Becca, Danyal, Dunixan, Simin. He looked for Sallah and belatedly realized she was already speeding for the camp to fetch the kids from Brecon. She obviously didn't need him to give any orders.

So many dragons meant not much room, so they dismounted and let the dragons back up several paces, giving them enough space to stand together.

Shad bounced lightly on his toes, a wide smile on his face. "Time to have fun?"

"Time to calmly and slowly walk toward enemy walls, yes," Becca stated repressively. It bounced right off Shad's smile without making a dent. Rolling her eyes in a prayer for patience, Becca formed them up and walked calmly toward the walls. Well, outwardly she looked calm. Trev'nor knew her well enough to see the rigid muscles, and he didn't miss how she shook out her hands and arms three separate times, forcefully keeping herself from locking up.

Huish came with them, not offering a reason why, and Trev'nor didn't question it. A wizard of his caliber would prove useful no matter which way this went. Besides, he could do sound amplification spells, which would be very handy shortly. All of the other magicians with them stayed in the camp on standby, some of them mounted on dragons, ready to dive in if this took a turn for the worse.

In an effort to not appear threatening, they didn't bring their magic into play at all. Llona paced along right behind them like a well-trained hound, her head up, staring at everything avidly. Trev'nor thought she appreciated the vocal break if nothing else after shouting for a full half hour.

For the first time in days, no one on the wall tried to stop them. Trev'nor spied several officers yelling, gesturing toward their approach, but not one magician lifted a hand toward them. They wanted answers before they would attack. Either that or they knew fighting the barrier would be utterly futile.

No one dared to say what they all were thinking: that this had worked better than they thought it would. A handful of attacks to test the strength of the barrier and then they gave up? It was too easy. And they didn't try anything at all after Llona started her recitation. That spoke of underlying problems. Just what had Von told them? That all of the other magicians had been killed, or further enslaved? What lies had he used to manipulate them into fighting? Trev'nor had a feeling that the lies weren't in the man's favor any longer.

As one, they stopped near the wall—far enough away to see without craning their necks too badly and close enough that they could hear.

Ehsan put a hand to Becca's shoulder, staying her, before stepping in front and calling up hopefully, "Laxmi! Murali! Do you know me?"

"EHSAN?!" two voices called back in shock.

Trev'nor had to take a moment to pick them out from the crowd, but then he saw them, leaning over the edge at an almost dangerous angle, a man and woman of roughly Ehsan's age.

Tears stood in Ehsan's eyes as he nodded. "It's me. I've come to free you, truly free you. Won't you come down?"

"But why are you with them?" the woman, Laxmi, demanded, her voice rising in pitch. "And that list of names that was read off earlier, what was that about?"

"The mages with me, they're freeing all of the magicians, including me. Everyone's name that Llona listed off is in the Ruins of Rheben right now getting training. They're full citizens of Khobunter." Ehsan swallowed hard, expression so hopeful it nearly hurt to look at him. "I don't know what you heard, what you were promised, but it's not worth it to protect this city. You can be anything under the new Maharajas' rule. Go anywhere. Please, please, come to me. Let me get you out of that city."

"Wait," another magician called down, shoving an officer out of the way so she could peer at them suspiciously. "You mean every other city in Khobunter is under their control? You've turned every other slave loose? Why would any ruler do that?"

"Because they're family," Becca answered calmly. "All of you are family, in one way or another."

"We can prove that," Nolan added, his eyes roving over the listening magicians. "I am Vonnolanen. I have Vonallenen. Is Vonallenen's father here?"

People rippled as someone shoved forward from the back. A man with sandy blond hair nearly fell off the wall in his attempt to press between people. "You have Allen?!"

"I do," Nolan assured him with a bright smile. "Are you Vontanviren?"

Even from this distance, the man seemed flummoxed to be addressed by his true name. He hesitated for a long moment before his father instincts overrode his caution. "I am. Allen is alright?"

"He's perfectly fine," Nolan assured him. "In fact, he's back in camp playing with the dragons and trying to keep the meurittas out of trouble. You understand that he told me your true names because I'm your cousin? You have family in Chahir as well."

Tanvir sank against the wall, expression beyond

confused. "I was told he died. My son…my son is alive and you're my cousin? From Chahir?"

"Nearly everyone that you were forced to abandon in Dilmun and Brecon is alive," Nolan announced firmly. Then he leaned sideways and requested, "Wizard Huish, might I impose on you and ask for a voice amplification?"

"Of course, Prince Nolan," Huish assured him and deftly snapped out his wand to lay the spell around his throat.

Assured that everyone could hear him, Nolan repeated, voice carrying to the far reaches of the city like a thunderclap: "Nearly everyone abandoned in Brecon and Dilmun is alive. We took over both cities and fed them, replaced the food stores stolen or destroyed. The trees I grew this morning? That's an example of how we fed them. Here, see for yourselves."

Huish opened a small window in the barrier and levitated the fruit to the top, where people cautiously reached out to touch it. One person, particularly bold, bit into an apple and chewed. When he didn't immediately topple over, others tried it, sharing the fruit about, proving it to be juicy and harmless. Several officers tried to stop this, yelling out commands or forcing their way forward to seize the fruit. The magicians would have none of it, some of them using what binding spells they knew to force the commanders against a wall and stay there with magical bonds.

Trev'nor let Nolan explain that they all hailed from Chahiran descendants, that they were related in a somewhat distant manner, and all the rest. He paid less attention to what Nolan said and more on how receptive the magicians took this in. Some of them seemed doubtful but others—likely the ones that recognized Llona's list of names—appeared sold. Or sold enough to want immediately out of Von so they could reunite with loved ones.

Taking a deep breath, he tapped Shad on the shoulder and murmured, "I'm going to try something risky. Cover me."

"I knew you were my student for a reason," Shad murmured back, shifting with him, ready to cover.

Lifting the mirror to his mouth, Trev'nor issued quick instructions through it. "Everyone, I need to form a doorway in the barrier at South Gate. Adjust power flow." He could see the power divert and change, altering so that the bulk of power anchored along the base, giving him the opening he needed to create a large doorway in the barrier. Borrowing the broken stone lying about the base of the wall, Trev'nor reformed it to create uniform stairs leading up to the top of the wall. Then he maneuvered to the base of the stairs, extending a hand up in invitation. "Please. Free yourselves of this place. Don't fear the barrier, it won't harm you. You can exit through this doorway."

No one seemed to know whether they should move or not. Trev'nor stayed steady and prayed. They were so close, so close, to winning this without having to fight again. If he could just get one person to move, others would follow.

From behind he heard the familiar sound of wings and displaced air. Turning, he found Dawn Rising had glided in, something clutched protectively to her chest. She set down with more control than Trev'nor had ever seen from the bulky dragon, then just as carefully lowered her burden to the ground. Allen popped out of the claw with a wide smile on his face, running automatically to Nolan.

People parted to let him through, Nolan extending an arm and catching the kid handily as Allen climbed him like a tree. Lifting his face, he spied his father and called out, "Paha! Come down, come down!"

Swearing, Tanvir lost no time in pushing people aside, racing toward Trev'nor's staircase and taking them with such speed that Trev'nor watched his descent with his heart in his throat, afraid the man might stumble and end up half broken at the bottom. Miracle of miracles, he didn't, nor did he hesitate to sprint for Allen.

Nolan stepped forward and held the boy out, grinning as he handed son to father. Tanvir clutched him tightly, shoulders shaking in a sob.

How had Allen…? Well, even as an underdeveloped Life Mage, he no doubt could communicate just fine with the dragons. Trev'nor eyed Dawn Rising suspiciously and got the dragon equivalent of an innocent shrug in return. Riiiight. Not for the first time, Trev'nor blessed the fact that Dawn Rising wasn't his dragon.

Although, it appeared Dawn Rising might have done them all a favor with this timing.

With living proof that they really had rescued a magician abandoned to die in Dilmun, the doubts and suspicions holding the rest back broke. Ehsan's two friends started for the stairs and multiple people followed their lead, descending quickly only to stop uncertainly at the bottom.

Trev'nor grinned as they reached him, taking any amulets he spied off and casually crushing them with a wisp of power. "It's alright, come on. Just follow the road to camp, there's people that will help organize you there so we can transport you to your friends and family."

Shad took up the mantra, repeating that on the other side and also removing any amulets he found. Not many wore them, most being wizards or witches, but a few mages appeared in the mix. Some of them ignored his directions and instead went to Llona, peppering her with further questions about people she hadn't named off, and she lowered down to her belly and answered them in her light voice.

Quite a number of magicians abandoned Von without even a backward glance. Not all, however; some hovered on top of the wall, blatantly uncertain. This worried Trev'nor and he caught one man's arm, staying him. "Wait, honored elder, I must ask, what about the other magicians in the city?"

"Some are being held in the city," he answered cautiously, not sure how to react to Trev'nor, although he seemed pleased at the respectful way Trev'nor addressed him. "Others are still guarding the other gates."

"No one's in chains? Or being held captive in any way?"

Making a face, the man admitted, "The general said that we should stay in a holding yard. It would be safer that way. We thought because he removed the chains, we were free… but seeing you walk about like this, it changed my mind. The others inside the city, will you get them out too?"

"I will," Trev'nor vowed faithfully. "Thank you."

With a duck of his head, the man moved off. Trev'nor eyed his stairs and realized that of the ones that hadn't come down, most seemed young enough to be parents, or old enough to be grandparents. Worried about leaving family behind?

A hand landed on his shoulder and he turned to find Danyal staring up as well. "You've gained all you can right now. Let me try."

Of all their plans, not once did they consider having Danyal speak. Trev'nor didn't know what to make of this, but he recognized the steely determination in the man's expression and chose not to argue. "Of course. Let Huish put a spell on your voice so that all can hear you."

"I will." Turning, Danyal hailed the wizard, gesturing toward his own throat.

Shad stepped in to whisper to Trev'nor, "Have you ever heard Danyal speak publicly?"

"A few times," Trev'nor admitted. "He's a decent orator, especially when he gets a mad on. It's why I'm willing to let him try. Besides, he might be able to reach the troops. He knows what to say to get their attention. And if he can get the army to defect—"

"The battle's more or less won." Shad pondered this before asking, "Why didn't anyone suggest he speak yesterday, then?"

"Because we were all tired and stressed and thereby made poor decisions?" Trev'nor offered guilelessly.

Snorting, Shad allowed the possibility with a nod of the head. "True enough. Well. I'm going up to guard him. You?"

"Me too," Trev'nor assured him. "I don't think we'll get any more magical attacks, but you should have a magician handy just in case. Besides, if something happens to Danyal, Becca will skin us."

"Don't remind me."

24

The magicians of Von might not have the will to fight anymore—at least, not at this gate—but the soldiers were a different matter altogether. They pulled what magicians stood on the walls down, forcing them to make way so the soldiers could scramble up to defend their position. Danyal made it to the top but only just, Shad and Trev'nor close on his heels. Seeing the situation, Trev'nor threw up a quick weapon's barrier like a dome over their heads, forcing people back. It only took two soldiers attacking the barrier to convince everyone else to leave it alone, although that grated. They glared at Trev'nor with clenched teeth, eyes wild with anger and bloodlust.

Danyal watched them for a moment in pity, took in a breath, and spoke to each soldier in turn. His voice echoed out, sounding as if he spoke to every individual soldier in the army. "I am General Rahim Danyal of Khobunter's Armed Forces. I hail from Trexler, where I served as a commander for many years before it was conquered by Maharaja Riicbeccaan and Maharaja Rhebentrev'noren. Before we were conquered, the army suffered under Warlord Trexler. For years, we were forced to work for half-pay, denied leave, and fight battles we didn't know the meaning of. We had no freedom to leave, to see loved ones, to marry, not even to mourn the fallen. We were enslaved, but because no chains bound our hands, we thought ourselves free."

The soldiers standing just outside the barrier no longer had that blood-crazed lust in their eyes. They stood silently, listening intently as they met Danyal's eyes. Not in sympathy, but in empathy, as if they understood exactly what conditions he'd lived through. Trev'nor imagined it wasn't much different than the rules imposed on them now.

"I had no idea what a good ruler was until we were conquered," Danyal continued, voice going raspy with emotion. "Suddenly, I had a ruler who valued my opinion. I was a lowly commander, but she sought me out, asked for my advice, cared about our lives. She learned that we couldn't afford to marry and it enraged her. She changed the laws that very day so that we could. She learned we hadn't been home in years, so she released us, let us return home for weeks so that we could see loved ones. She learned we'd been on half-pay for years and instantly stopped it and even now does her best to give us the back-pay we are owed.

"I have two maharajas that don't treat the life of a soldier like cannon fodder. We serve and are rewarded for that service. We fight and are honored for our sacrifices. We don't need to ask for mercy because it's freely given to us. We ask for help knowing that it will be given. Our maharajas do not hide behind the front lines of battle but fight alongside us, sharing the same dangers and victories. Even now," Danyal put a hand on Trev'nor's shoulder, hot even through the cloth of the uniform, "my maharaja stands next to me, protecting me so that I might speak to all of you. Would your warlord do the same?"

No. None of the soldiers dared answer that question out loud, but Trev'nor could read their expressions easily enough. No, their warlord would not. Danyal's description of how much his life had improved under their reign swayed quite a few of them—they looked wistful, as if they wished they could say the same.

But Danyal wasn't done. "I walked through the streets of Brecon and Dilmun. I saw what you were forced to do. I tended the people you were ordered to abandon. They were in those cities without water, without food for three days before we realized their peril. Grandmothers, grandfathers, infants, people too weak to fend for themselves. You did not slaughter them by sword, but they would have died because of the orders you followed, if not for our intervention. Some of them still died despite our best efforts."

All of them looked away at that, ashamed deeply, some openly flinching as if Danyal had taken hold of a dagger already thrust into their hearts and twisted it.

"I watched my maharaja take the children your warlord callously abandoned into her own arms and feed them. She cared for them in place of the mothers ripped away into this city. This maharaja next to me brought in supplies and help, and between them, they made sure that we didn't lose another soul in either city."

"They're alive?" a young lieutenant demanded breathlessly, starting forward before remembering he couldn't touch the barrier. It left him hovering, antsy, and shifting from foot to foot as he stared intently at Danyal. "They're alive?"

"Most of them," Danyal answered firmly. "I know, because I helped feed some of those children myself. I brought those too sick to move out of their sickbeds so they could have water and food. You were ordered to take only the best and most capable, to destroy the food and water supplies, to salt the earth and poison the wells, but it was all to naught. Because this—" Danyal flung a hand behind him to indicate the patch of orchard grown this morning "—is what they are. They are gardeners. Builders. They carry the future with them and they share it with us. They want to turn all of Khobunter into a garden, a safe haven for the people to live in. Every city they take immediately has gardens and water fountains put into it. It is green and thriving, a paradise to my eyes. Don't you want that?"

"Give us proof," another man, a sergeant, demanded. He held tight onto his spear with both hands in a white knuckled grip. "Prove to us that they're alive."

Trev'nor sensed a story there, one that he would deeply love to hear, but it would have to wait until later. He turned and looked down, but Sallah hadn't quite arrived yet, although he could sense her. "I can prove it. Give me a moment." Fetching the mirror out of his pocket, he called, "Sallah."

"Almost there."

"I know you are, I see your path, but can you come directly to the wall? The soldiers want to see for themselves that we really did save people out of Brecon and Dilmun."

"I brought the Rikkana from both cities and some of the kids, but I only grabbed about six people. Is that alright?"

"Should be fine," Trev'nor assured her. He hoped it would be, anyway. Would numbers matter at this point?

A commotion started at the base of the stairs, the ones leading up from the street level, and Trev'nor had an idea that the general of Von headed their direction. He asked the stairs on the other side to become a slide, halting that advance. They couldn't afford an interruption just yet. Judging from the cursing he could faintly hear, he'd done it just in time.

Sallah popped out of the ground a moment later, two kids on either hip, the Rikkanas and four other children in tow. They ascended the stairs with some difficulty, as the elderly Rikkanas didn't really have the knees for such a steep staircase. Trev'nor, eyeing the surrounding soldiers, dared to think he could drop the barrier for a moment. He lifted it but kept his magic poised, ready to drop it again in a split second. One soldier, after a cautious look at Trev'nor, went down the stairs and offered a supportive hand to both women, which they gratefully took.

Huish belatedly followed them up, supporting the other Rikkana and speaking rapidly with them both. Trev'nor had an idea of what he said, as he put an amplification spell on both of their throats. Good thinking. The whole city would need to hear what they would say.

He seriously owed that man a favor for being so quick thinking.

As they waited, he whispered a quick status check via the mirror. "Becca, how are things going down there?"

"Not everyone is convinced. Makes sense, they only hear our voices, and they can't see all the evidence we're presenting."

"Some are swayed at North Gate," Jarod reported in a deep rumble. "But not everyone, not by a long shot. We're repeating things over here, offering our own evidence, but we're not making a lot of headway."

"Same problem at West Gate," Kartal reported, sounding irritated. "And someone up there keeps battering at the barrier, trying to break through."

Trev'nor wished he could be surprised, but it made sense that not everyone could be convinced that easily. He'd actually have been more surprised if it had worked on the first push.

When the Rikkanas finally came into view at the top, they greeted Trev'nor properly first, then Shad and Danyal. Every soldier watching took note of that, and it solidified their case as no amount of words could.

Only then did Rikkana Niyati address the soldiers directly. She stood there, short and wizened, with a blazing fire in her eyes that belonged in a warrior's face. Several men shrank from her, cowed and ashamed. "I am Rikkana Niyati of Brecon. I testify that we were saved by Maharaja Riicbeccaan and Maharaja Trev'nor. They sent their army and dragons in with food, with supplies, and then they came themselves and served the people. This young maharaja," Niyati reached back to catch Trev'nor's arm and dragged him forward to stand next to her, "came himself and unblocked the fountains so we could drink. He put in new wells, built tables and benches for us, went and fetched more supplies as we needed them. He built us gardens with Raja Nolan and Raja Ehsan—gardens like I've never seen before. They fed us, their enemy, and showed us compassion that our own rulers deemed we were unworthy of. Why are you standing here? Why are you serving those greedy men? You think your lives are worth more than ours were in their eyes?"

The lieutenant that had demanded proof of their welfare approached her with a deep bow. "Rikkana Niyati. I ask you only one question. Akhila Ghan, is she...?"

"Akhila Ghan walks," Niyati answered him forthrightly. At his startled double take, she moderated her tone a little to sound more compassionate. "Raja Nolan saw what was wrong with her legs and healed her. She walks."

The lieutenant folded in on himself, both hands over his face, and openly wept.

Trev'nor didn't know if this woman was a sister, fiancé, or what, but he could tell she was deeply close to the lieutenant somehow. He looked to Sallah, silently asking, as he had no idea who they spoke of. Sallah shrugged her ignorance. So only Nolan would likely know in this group, eh?

"General." A commander stepped forward, his thick brows drawn together, not in anger but extreme tension. "You speak a good case for your maharajas. May I address your maharaja?"

Danyal gave a curt nod. "Permission granted."

They needed permission for this sort of thing? News to Trev'nor. He faced the man squarely and gave him an encouraging smile. "Please speak to me comfortably."

"Maharaja, I am Commander Deodan," he introduced himself. "What are your terms if we surrender to you?"

"We do not wish for concessions, Commander," Becca answered, coming steadily up the stairs to stand at Trev'nor's side. "I am Maharaja Riicbeccaan."

Trev'nor blew out a breath of relief. He much preferred for Becca to handle the military matters. Even if she had stayed on the ground to coordinate the magicians, he felt better having her up here with him. Trev'nor dared only to say one thing before turning this whole conversation over to his co-ruler. "When we take a city, Commander, the people become our own. We do not punish them for formerly being our enemy."

"If you swear fealty to us, you maintain the rank and position you did before," Becca assured him. "Any back-pay owed to you is paid. We grant you leave whenever possible. You become full citizens under our rule. We do not believe in slaves."

Someone shouted in a harsh voice, "DO NOT LISTEN TO THEM!"

Every soldier up top started guiltily. Trev'nor didn't need any guesses on who was shouting down there, not from their reactions.

Becca glided forward, capturing the commander's attention—all of their attentions—once more with the sympathetic smile on her face. "I conquered this country to free the magicians. That was what prompted me in the beginning. But when I took Trexler, I realized that these people were enslaved as well. You've been denied so many basic freedoms, it hurts my heart to look at all of you sometimes. Won't you let me free you, too?"

Deodan's expression firmed into one of rock hard resolve. He snapped out a salute. "Maharajas, I offer my oath of fealty to you. I will remain loyal until I am placed into my grave."

As she had done so many times, Becca snapped out a returning salute, just as crisply given. "Accepted,

Commander. Thank you for your oath."

Every other soldier up top immediately followed example, swearing fealty, and Trev'nor did his best to salute back and accept them. Becca took charge at that point, requesting their help in reaching the rest of the city, and Danyal mobilized them. Trev'nor didn't dare fix the stairs just yet, so they ended up scattering along either side of the wall.

"Trev."

He pulled out his mirror and answered, "Cora?"

"Yes. East Gate just opened and more than just soldiers have poured out, but a lot of the common citizens as well. They're demanding the right to swear fealty. What do I do?"

Wow. Danyal's speech had worked better than he expected. "I'm on my way. Shad, you got Becca?"

"Got her," Shad assured him, already on the move, following as Becca went west along the wall.

"Sallah," turning to his cousin, Trev'nor stole a moment to request, "I'm absolutely positive that anyone from Brecon or Dilmun will want to go home and reunite with people shortly. Can you ferry them back and forth for me?"

"Consider it done," she assured him, shooing him on.

He really had the best family ever. Trev'nor grinned at the thought before scampering down the stairs. Or he intended to, at least. Garth caught him halfway down in a massive claw and glided about the city until they reached the East Gate. Trev'nor really should have expected that his dragon would not be able to stay put with Trev'nor in that kind of volatile situation.

Trev'nor made it to the East Gate in seconds flat, Garth settling them to the earth. Cora had made it sound as if there were perhaps a hundred or so people, but in fact, Trev'nor guessed it to be more like several hundred. Mouth dry, he stared incredulously about. People were apparently more upset with Von than he'd anticipated. Then again, sacrificing two generations of people just to keep yourself in power likely didn't endear you to the rest of the populace.

Moving forward, he took people's oaths as he could, unable to spend one-on-one time with any of them for more than a few seconds, but they seemed astonished he'd make the effort to do even that. Sallah appeared shortly and called out an offer to magically transport anyone to Brecon or Dilmun that wanted to go, and she had several hundred takers in seconds.

Cora leaned in close to murmur, "Is it always like this?"

"No," Trev'nor answered in a daze, "it's never like this. Normally we have to be super nice and friendly for several weeks before they'll even try to talk to us."

"General Danyal is persuasive," Cora noted. "But I think Von stabbed himself in the foot when he abandoned those two cities."

"Probably the stupidest decision made to date. I mean, tactically it made sense. He couldn't have defended those two from us, but politically speaking? Suicidal. The man did us a favor without even realizing it." Trev'nor wanted to thank him for being an imbecile, but that likely wouldn't go over well.

"Speaking of stupid leaders, what are you going to do about them?" Cora gave an illustrative gesture towards the city. "Surely not everyone is going to jump ship to your side, right?"

"I really wish they would, but no, likely not," Trev'nor agreed with a sigh. It would make his life so much easier, but people were rarely that convenient. "As for the leaders, Roshan's requested the first crack at them. The man's a pro negotiator. Odds are good he can bargain most of the government into working with us."

"And if that doesn't work?" Cora didn't challenge him on this, just sounded curious.

Trev'nor shrugged. "I sic Becca on them."

"She's terrifying," Cora agreed with an understanding nod. "That's a good backup plan. Where is she, anyway?"

"Dealing with the army. Most of them are defecting. Can you go fetch Dunixan for me? I want to see if we can deal with the government while she's doing that."

"Sure," Cora assured him, already backing away to turn dragon.

Having other trained magicians around sure was handy.

"I need help on the West Gate," Becca's voice suddenly proclaimed through the mirror. "I repeat, help on the West Gate. The general has mobilized the soldiers and magicians and is counter-attacking."

25

Becca blessed that she had gone west while Trev'nor went east, even as she cursed it. She hadn't really expected that the entire city would be convinced in one fell swoop, hence why she had taken troops with her as she went. She knew the instant things took a turn for the worst, as a powerful wind attack battered at her. If not for Tyvendor's quick reflexes, they'd all have been knocked off the wall.

"Why are we still getting this kind of resistance?" Tyvendor demanded, more frustrated than anything.

"I will bet you on that kitty-shaped cloud over there that Von's general went for the West Gate when he couldn't reach South Gate," Shad said. "This is going to get rough, kiddo. Maybe we need to get more reinforcements up here."

Becca saw his point at once and lifted the mirror to her mouth, snapping out orders. "I need help at the West Gate. I repeat, help on the West Gate. The general has mobilized the soldiers and magicians and is counter-attacking."

"Hostages," Shad reminded her.

Bless him for keeping track, she couldn't keep it all readily in her head. "Someone grab Carjettaan and rescue the magicians still in the holding yards in the city. I need them out immediately."

Garth's smooth tenor stated with false calm, "On it."

She felt fiercely glad that she had four Earth Mages. She

apparently needed all four for this battle. "Someone create a doorway at the West Gate and a set of stairs. We need to give people a way to flee."

"We did that," Kartal's deep voice sounded rough with anger, "and that base whoreson had anyone who went for the stairs shot in the back. We've got three possible fatalities."

Becca bit out a curse that would make a sailor blush. "I'm halfway there, someone give me options."

"Keep the doorway open," Hayden requested. "Helen and I are almost there. Kaydan, don't block them off, I need to see as I come in."

Come in? Something about the way he said that indicated to Becca her honorary uncle had a plan up his sleeve. She had little chance to ask as she sprinted along the wall. This section had few people, most of them having already left the wall, but as she approached the West Gate that changed. Layers upon layers of shields stacked up on top of each other in a living barrier, soldiers behind it. They created narrow slits so that the magicians standing behind them had enough sightlines to attack with.

And attack they did.

She and Tyvendor both threw up personal shields protecting them against arrows and the hot zings of magical spells thrown at them. They deflected those easily enough, but the air attacks intensified, battering at her group with all the force of a summer gale. Becca's few escaped tendrils of hair whipped around her face like mini lashes, sometimes threatening to blind her. She pushed back just as ferociously, snarling. "That idiot is seriously messing with my weather patterns. I'll murder him if he doesn't stop soon."

Over the roar of the wind, she barely caught some garbled voice from the mirror. Pressing it close to her ear, she shouted, "SAY AGAIN?"

The wind abruptly stopped and she heard yelling from other side of the shields.

"Can Shad hear me?" Bornemeier repeated, half-yelling.

Shad put a hand to her shoulder blade and leaned in to respond. "Right here, bucko."

"Does this count as a door?"

"It does."

"It doesn't look friendly."

Shad grinned manically. "This one is definitely not a friend. Treat as a hostile."

"Roger roger. Loewen and I are going in."

Another voice joined into the conversation. "Becca, Helen and I have the back."

That statement made no sense to her. "Hayden, what do you mean you have the back?"

"We got this. Go."

She had seconds to question but in the end, she had to trust that an Elemental Mage and a Water Mage could handle whatever thrown at them, especially with a witch and wizard backing them up. "Tyvendor, let's end this madness. Concentrated air attack on three. One, two, three."

Their magic built around them in a rich crescendo, sharp and loud, a miniature tornado above their heads. Tyvendor released it with a sharp gesture of the hand, knocking every soldier in their path flat onto their backs, scattering them like flower petals. They impacted against each other, most fetching up against the stone on either side in a hard crunch, aborted screams and yelps ringing out as they came to a painful halt.

The newly cleared path opened her view to the conflict on the other side of the gate, distracting her momentarily.

When Hayden said he had the matter in hand, he wasn't kidding. The blond whirled like a dervish, Helen at his back, and between the two of them they'd managed to disarm every soldier within reach of them and a little beyond. Not a weapon or shield was within sight. Helen kept up a water barrier between the soldiers and the magicians, blocking them and encouraging the magicians to take advantage and rush for the stairs. Bornemeier and Loewen seconded this, adding in their own voices, using Solish as they didn't know enough of the native language to manage. A few of the bolder ones bolted for the stairs while the offer stayed safe. Others huddled at the back wall, staring at the magicians as if they wore second heads.

Busted buckets, Becca didn't want any potential hostages up here, she wanted people to move.

Kartal and Kaydan came up the stairs, tackling the wizards and witches still fighting, subduing them quickly. It took the brunt off of Hayden and Helen, thankfully, as even two mages with their experience and training could be quickly overwhelmed under these odds.

She looked around for the Air Mage she'd felt before, but didn't spy him up top. She didn't see the general either, which boded ill. One of the few still actively fighting was the Elemental Mage ahead of her. Becca had felt the powers of an Elemental Mage before while trying to take this city, but she finally had a face to put to the magic. The woman looked even thinner than the others, nearly skeletal, and she fought like a tigress. Desperation? Did she have people to protect?

Becca didn't know, only that she had to stop her. "Tyvendor, which side do you want?"

"Right."

"Then I'll take left." Becca strode forward, Shad right in her shadow, and she decided to end this quickly. She still had that thrice-cursed Air Mage to hunt down and deal with; she didn't have the luxury to dally up here.

The Elemental Mage threw any and every attack she could, her raw power making up for any lack of training. Becca and Tyvendor moved to either side in a pincher movement, struggling to defend while subduing the woman and avoid injuries all around. The next attack she threw at them, Becca caught the wind and diverted it sharply up, letting it spin off harmlessly into the sky. Tyvendor's attacks battled with the Elemental Mage's but Becca ignored the wind as it brushed hard up against her skin and clothes, focusing on her own attacks. The roar of wind, shouted commands, pleas for help, all beat against Becca's ears in a cacophony. She pushed it aside as well, trusting her allies to keep the situation contained and her Guardian to protect her rear.

The Elemental Mage gave up on wind, calling toward the metal around her, hurtling it at Becca. Most of it struck harmlessly against her weapons shield and the few that tried to sneak around her flat barrier, Shad efficiently dealt with. The Elemental Mage looked beyond exhausted, her magic dipping crucially low, and for a moment she faltered in her attacks.

Tyvendor took prompt advantage of the opening and subdued the Elemental Mage, the woman pinned in place by a ferocious band of moving air. She looked like a caged wildcat, desperate to get free. "Stop it," Tyvendor barked at her. "You'll injure yourself if you keep struggling. We don't intend to harm you!"

The woman glared at him and continued fighting the hold, bruising herself in the process. Becca repeated in Khobuntish: "Stop. We don't wish to hurt you. The world won't end if we win, I promise you."

That stopped her for a moment, eyes still wild, panting for breath. "You've no idea the price we pay if you get through!" she spat, her voice raw and dry from dehydration.

Becca's heart sank at these words. They never preceded anything good. "Who's being held against you?"

Startled, the woman stared at her, stilling. "How do you know?"

"It's unfortunately a common tactic up here," Becca responded grimly. "Who's being held to ensure your cooperation? Tell me so I can rescue them."

"Who are you to guarantee anything?" the woman shot

back.

"Maharaja Riicbeccaan, Warlord of Khobunter," Becca responded cordially. She could see it when her title impacted with the woman, along with every enslaved magician listening nearby, as they froze like startled deer. "If you will tell me who they are, where they are being held, I swear to you we will rescue them and let you reunite. My word as a Riic."

"My..." she gulped in breath, swallowed, and tried again. "My name is Jera. My husband Derhan and daughter are dead if I don't defeat you here."

Kaydan strode up, her mirror in hand. "Garth. You have everyone out of the city yet?"

"Not quite, but we're underground and on our way. Why? What's happening up top?"

"We've got a very worried mother up here." Coming in closer, she held the mirror near the Elemental Mage's mouth. "Call to your group, see if you have a Derhan, husband of Jera in the crowd."

It took a minute as Garth yelled out the names, but Becca could faintly here someone respond, and she had a sense Garth was arranging it so the mirror got near the right man. Then Garth's voice came back. "He's here."

"Call to them," Becca encouraged. "They can hear you."

Expression filled with distrust, her mouth worked for a long moment before saying tentatively, "Derhan?"

It took a long minute before a male voice responded, husky and thick with a northern accent. "Jera?"

A sob caught in the woman's mouth and she slapped a hand over it, stifling the sound.

"Jera? Are you alright? The man that rescued us out said you should be, that no one wants us harmed. Love, are you alright?"

Nodding, Jera swallowed multiple times before

whispering, "I'm alright. They told me—the general told me that you were dead if I failed. You and the baby were dead."

Becca felt like killing something. So she'd been fighting desperately to prevent her family from being executed. She'd murder the general when she finally got her hands on him. Casting about, she tried to spot him, but every insignia she saw was that of a captain or lower. Had he escaped back into the city during their distraction? Retreated when this attempt to rally the troops failed?

Another witch, who'd been huddling against the wall, tentatively stood. "What about my children? Does he have them too?"

"Anyone in the holding yard has been rescued by my brother," Kaydan assured her. Raising her voice, she offered with a charming smile, "Anyone who wants to reunite with their friends and family, come with me. I'll take you to them."

Becca waited with baited breath, watching to see what would happen. One moved, then another, all rushing down the stairs.

The Elemental Mage stared at the scene with perplexity, not understanding, but her wariness had dropped, replaced by the faintest hint of hope. "You're really here just to stop us?"

"And free you, because what you have here certainly isn't that," Becca repeated herself, trying to stay patient. Taking off her own canteen, she handed it over as Tyvendor dropped the restrictive band of air. "And will you please drink?"

Eyes on Becca's, the mage lifted it took a swallow, then took another, longer pull.

"Good." She looked about, spotted Kartal, and motioned him closer. "Kartal, can you manage things here? I need to check the last gate and make sure they're not having similar trouble there."

Kartal shooed her on with a wave of the hand, slightly arrogant as usual, his words stated with an aristocratic lilt.

"We can manage this. Go on."

As she moved, Becca lifted the mirror to her mouth once more. "Who has Carjettaan? I need her."

"I do," Garth responded. "Here she is."

"What is it, Becca?" Jetta answered.

"Jetta, the general and Air Mage have both disappeared on me and I have a bad feeling they're up to something. Can you find their location for me?"

"Give me a minute." It took more than one, as Becca made it halfway back to the South Gate and the staircase Trev'nor had tampered with earlier before Jetta responded grimly, "They're holed up in the fortress with about a thousand soldiers. Not many other magicians, though, a few witches and wizards."

At her elbow, Shad muttered, "He gathered up whoever he could in a quick retreat, sounds like."

Yes, so it did. "Thanks, Jetta. Garth, as soon as you have people out, bring her back to us. We'll need her."

"Will do."

Becca lowered the mirror for a moment, thinking hard. "Shad, who would you suggest storming the castle with?"

"Well, I mean, Garth's the expert at breaking buildings. But Krys and Jarod are a fair hand at it too. And if Kaya doesn't get to break something soon, she'll be downright peeved."

She probably should worry about collateral damage, but with four Earth Mages around, why should she? Lifting the mirror, she called, "Krys, Jarod, Kaya, you all hear me?"

"I do." "We do." Both mages answered near simultaneously.

"Meet me at the fortress. We have a building to break into."

26

Becca stared at the fortress with considerable vexation. Of course he'd barricaded the place thoroughly. Every window had either weapons or shutters blocking it, the doors were barred, and someone over there knew how to do a magical shield, as a rudimentary one stood guarding the main door.

She stood in the main courtyard with Shad on her right, Cat and Tail on her left, the other three mages circling overhead on their dragons. Tyvendor was at the ready to keep the Air Mage from bolting. Becca considered calling in more help, but really, the five of them should be able to manage this, especially with four dragons doing some of the heavier lifting. "Brother dearest?"

"Yes, my cute little flower?" Shad responded sweetly, his eyes never leaving the fortress, his body in a fighting stance.

"That door does not look friendly."

"Definitely not a nice door," Shad agreed promptly. "It's alright, we don't have to make friends with every door we meet. Let's just pummel this one."

"I had a feeling you'd say that." She shared a fierce grin with him before requesting of Cat, "Tell Kaya she has dibs if she wants the first pass at it."

Cat lifted her head as she called up to the sky, then gave a dragonly chortle at the response. "Kaya says duck."

Becca didn't, instead throwing up a thick shield around

them to protect from debris and flame. Just as well she did, as Kaya came in hot and fast, the air screaming in protest at her speed, both wings tucked in tight against her body as she dove. Krys rode in low to her neck as well, his magic coming into play, and when they grew dangerously close to crash landing, they both spat out massive fireballs before Kaya threw out her wings, veering them sharply away from the buildings. The fireballs impacted like a meteor, destroying the entire front of the building and leaving parts of it singed and melted. If there had been any wood nearby, it would have caught fire, but stone couldn't. Becca blessed that, as she didn't want a fire spreading in the city.

Pandemonium ensued as the people inside the fortress panicked, abandoning the lower level and racing for the broad staircase in the back to try resetting a defense line on the upper floors. With Krys leading the charge, Jarod came in hot and ready too, his dragon mount also spitting fireballs. Cat shifted, obviously wishing to join the charge, but she stayed planted at Becca's side, unwilling to leave her post.

Becca strode in through the ruined front, skirting around the larger pieces of debris as she moved, some of it still flaming hot to the touch. The braver ones still within sight of her tried shooting arrows, to which Shad took personal offense. He whirled in front of her, sword coming up and into play, cutting down anything shot at them. Of course, he also laughed like a lunatic doing it, but Becca expected that.

The building rocked, trembling as if an earthquake struck it. Or a dragon. She couldn't see either Jarod or Krys from this angle but assumed one of them was behind the attack and didn't pause. They knew not to really bring the building down around her head.

Cat bounded in ahead of her, clearing the way, the opening large enough that she fit her front half in easily before the interior walls prohibited her from going in any further. Becca walked in under her belly, winding around her legs to reach the main foyer. Soldiers stood on the first landing of the staircase, shields at the ready, spears pointed at them, but even from here, she could see the whites of their eyes. They knew this was suicidal, they just didn't know what else they could do.

"General!" Becca called out. "I'm Riicbeccan, Warlord and Maharaja of Khobunter. I've come for your surrender!"

Silence.

"So that's how he wants to play it, huh?" Shad muttered out the side of his mouth. "Has desperation made him stupid?"

"No, that doesn't jive with the man we know," Becca denied slowly. A tendril of unease curled up at the base of her spine. "Shad, does this look like a trap to you?"

"It's got that vibe to it, doesn't it?" he agreed blackly. "Cat—"

The dragon abruptly yelped in pain and jerked backwards, her head dislodging a loose chunk of stone overhead as she pulled sharply free of the building. Becca swore as she realized how foolish she'd been to just charge in here. Of course it would be a trap.

"Becca, look alive in there!" Jarod warned. "You've got soldiers closing in from behind you."

"We need to work on his early warning system," she snarled, magic whirling about her as she called upon the heat in her core. "Cat, you alright?"

A roar answered her as Cat swung into battle mode.

Trusting her dragon to have their rear, Becca faced on the group ahead of her and let lightning fly, her voltage low enough to knock people unconscious and injure them, but not permanently. Men screamed and thrashed as they were hit, going down like wilting damsels in a heat wave. She could hear other soldiers fall outside, Cat's tail lashing like a whip and taking out chunks of the building and people in equal measure. More than a few bones broke and Becca winced in sympathy. Good thing they also had three Life Mages up here.

The building rocked again, hard this time, fine dust scattering in the air. Becca choked on it briefly but didn't pause, still fighting her way inside. She just knew the general and the Air Mage had to be in here somewhere. Jetta had kept tabs on at least the Air Mage—he definitely was in the building. The few soldiers she didn't subdue on the stairs retreated frantically upwards, putting as many walls between them as they could manage. Becca let them go, not interested in pursuing any of them. Shad could play with them if they found the nerve to try engaging her again.

Second floor, no one stayed behind. By the third, Tail ran ahead of her to scout, then doubled back to give her a deliberate head shake—no one—before darting up to the third floor.

"I haven't seen him scout in years," Shad observed idly as they moved at a trot to the staircase. "I see he hasn't lost his touch."

"I'm glad he hasn't," Becca agreed. She'd seriously missed Tail in the previous battles before Shad had brought him up for that reason. Tail was a wonderful scout.

"This smacks of being too hastily done." Shad looked around in disapproval as they moved. "He should have at least a few snipers stationed on these floors to try and take you out."

"Shad, are you complaining while your enemy is making a mistake?"

He shot her a wink. "Perish the thought."

The fortress stood five stories tall and, of course, they finally found the last bastion for the general on the fourth floor. Becca half expected it, as no one sane stays on the top floor when being bombarded by dragons, and they'd already abandoned the main floor as indefensible. Fourth floor made the most sense, although he should have put more manpower in between the floors to try sneak attacks with. Shad was right about that.

The floor opened up into one large room that had all the earmarks of being a War Room with maps on the walls, multiple tables, and a semaphore station off on the balcony that she could just see from this angle. Of course, the tables now lay on their sides acting as improvised shields with two hundred men huddled behind them and archers standing at the ready. They fired as soon as Becca fully cleared the staircase.

Shad, laughing again like a lunatic, whirled into motion, arrows splintering as he knocked them aside with his sword. Becca didn't bother to pay any attention to them, letting her weapons shield take the brunt. Instead, her eyes searched out the Air Mage. Behind the soldiers stood the Air Mage in question, the air swirling around him a little, ready to attack. He looked of an age with Ehsan, although leaner, clothes ill-fitting and sagging on him.

The Air Mage barely met her eyes before he flung the first attack at her. Tail dodged it lightly with his normal cat reflexes, smoothly heading to Shad's side. Shad also dodged with catlike reflexes, leaving Becca to deal with the magical attack. She took it head on with a grunt, using wind to deflect it toward the side, opening a cutting slice through the outer wall. The stone made an eerie, high pitched sound as it split, daylight streaming through the new opening.

Becca barely noticed it, already defending against the next attack. The Air Mage desperately sent sharp, cutting edges at her, which she either avoided or deflected. Multiple holes appeared in the walls, in the ceiling, the structure of the building groaning as it took so much damage. Shrieking hinges, if she didn't put a stop to this soon, the building really would collapse around their heads.

She was done. Just flat done. A different tack was in

order. She'd been fighting like an Air Mage all this time. Time to fight like a Weather Mage.

Using more than wind, she called upon the lightning, flinging it out with a sharp huff. The Air Mage dodged, but not all of the soldiers with him managed to do the same, and the ones she did hit went down with grunts of pain or screams. Shad closed in next to her for a moment, checking her status, then darted out again, making sure that no one flanked her. From the corner of her eye, she saw Tail dart with him, twining in and around people's ankles, tripping the soldiers neatly. Between him and Shad, soldiers fell like dominoes.

Desperate, the Air Mage threw another attack at her, coming in from the side this time, putting more power and ferocity into it. She caught this, too, throwing it up again, the wind whistling as it moved under her will. Becca kept marching steadily toward him as he flung one spell after the next at her, growing increasingly desperate when nothing seemed to affect her. Ten feet away, she could see the whites of his eyes, the perspiration streaking down his cheeks, dripping from his chin. He still glared at her fiercely, not ready to quit and show her his belly just yet.

She flung out more lightning, aiming not really at the mage, but the man hovering behind him. She couldn't see his insignia, but the middle-aged man kept barking out orders to the other soldiers, and if he wasn't the general, he was at least the most superior officer in the room and thereby the first person they needed to stop. With him down, she had a chance of stopping this madness before it went any further.

"STOP HER!" the man screeched at the mage.

The Air Mage jolted and renewed his attacks, each one more ferocious than the previous, although sloppier now. He didn't have the time to execute anything properly while dodging Becca's lightning. She gritted her teeth, frustrated that she couldn't properly hit him. One bolt grazed his thigh, and he yelped, but didn't go down. Instead he found a shield to hide behind and kept attacking.

Alright, fine, the lightning might not work in this situation. If she couldn't use spells to stop him, she'd use brute force. She'd show him exactly how ineffective his wind was with her.

The next attack he threw, she caught it and flung it up, hard enough that it went through the ceiling above their heads and the fortress's roof. Sweat poured down her back, along her sides, but Becca didn't falter or lose concentration as she handled each successive attack, flinging them all upwards, pockmarking the ceiling like a leper's face.

Between her, Shad, and Tail, most of the soldiers were injured or unconscious. Only a tightly knit core of a half dozen remained, acting as a living shield as they stood around the officer in a rough half-circle. The Air Mage had little magical power left. With his lack of training, everything he did required brute force and he had no idea how to pace himself. He had one, perhaps two magical attacks left in him before he had nothing left to fight with.

"What are you doing?!" the officer screeched at him. "Kill her!"

Becca pointed in that direction. "Shad, kindly deal with that."

"I SAID KILL HER!" the officer roared.

Chortling, Shad bounded forward, caroling, "Won't take but a moment!"

Becca saw the Air Mage's magic flare as he gathered up the strength for one last attempt, felt the air vacuum around her as he pulled it toward him.

Frustrated beyond belief, she lunged straight for him and smacked him sharply on top of the head. "Stop that."

Astonished, he spluttered and lost all control of the wind. He stared at her with wide grey eyes, not understanding her, taut and wary like a cornered wolf. "What?"

The man sounded completely parched. Becca's throat ached in sympathy even as she resisted throttling him. "You idiot, when you're drained that badly, the last thing you should do is attempt another spell. The last three days didn't stop me, you think anything you throw at me will work? Just stop."

Staring at her hard, he demanded hoarsely, "You're my enemy, why are you...you're stronger than I am."

"I realize might-of-arms rules this country," she responded tartly, crossing both arms over her chest before she could smack him again, "but there's limits, alright? I'm not fighting you because you're my enemy, I'm fighting with you to get you away from here and because you're an idiot."

His anger flared to match hers, magic struggling to match.

Jabbing a finger at him, she used the vilest Khobuntish swear word she knew. "Inta mavish mukh! Stop that this instant!"

He startled more at the swear word than the command, disbelieving that a woman would dare say such a thing to him.

"You throw one more spell, you'll be comatose and out cold," she snapped at him, angry that he'd drive himself into a corner even as she offered him a way out. "I'm not your enemy, but if you mess with my weather currents more than you already have, you'll become one. I'm constantly re-routing storms, pulling the air streams back into alignment and altering the hot-cold ratio to prevent tornadoes thanks to your monkeying about."

"What are you?!" he demanded finally, just as frustrated and confused.

"Weather Mage." She stared him down as he chewed on this answer. "Now, show some sense and stop fighting. Drink this."

He stared at the canteen as if it contained poison.

Rolling her eyes, Becca took a quick swig out of it, then thrust it at him again. "Drink it."

He took the canteen from her slowly, expression perplexed and wary. He didn't understand what she was doing. Becca didn't really either, this was not how she planned things to go. Instinct drove her now. "I came up here to stop you messing with the air currents. You're seriously messing with my storms. Until you're properly trained, no more tampering with the wind for you."

"You came up here to stop me from diverting your storms," he repeated in his rough voice, tone going up incredulously.

"And to free everyone," Becca added truthfully before pointing at the canteen. "Drink. You'll recover faster if you're hydrated."

The Air Mage stared at her hard. "You could kill me right now."

"I could. I don't want to. You're only fighting because you don't think you have a choice."

He stared at her some more, perplexed and suspicious. "What happened to my friends? The other slaves?"

"Freed. They swore fealty to us, became full citizens, and are reuniting with friends and family right now." Becca cocked her head at him, examining his expression. He didn't seem quite as battle-ready as before, his hold on his magic loosening so that it dissipated. Of course, that might not be by choice, he had precious little fight left in him. Willpower alone probably kept him from swaying on his feet. Aletha always counseled that when someone's back was against the wall, the trick was not to up the pressure, but to lower the wall. Becca didn't see the harm in trying and conjured a charming smile she hoped didn't carry too much ire. "Wouldn't you like to do the same?"

"Who are you to offer it?" he countered immediately, still not sure if he believed her.

"Maharaja Riicbeccaan."

"The warlord?" he responded incredulously, spluttering. "You're a mage?!"

"My co-ruler is too. Although he's an Earth Mage. See? Your new rulers are magicians. You'll be a free man under our reign."

Several thuds had the Air Mage looking over his shoulder to find that Shad had quickly subdued the remaining soldiers, all of them disarmed and facing the wall with their hands above their heads. Even the belligerent officer stayed lined up with them, although he glared venomously at Shad as he did so.

Seeing this, the Air Mage let out a breath and said, "My name is Patric. Give me your word, Maharaja, that if I surrender to you, I will be a free man."

She held out a hand, beaming when he clasped it. "My word as a Riic. Patric, one question before we go down. General Ajil, where is he?"

"He escaped through the tunnels after the first dragon attacked the building," Patric answered somewhat apologetically.

Becca growled, half-resigned. "Of course he did. Shad, let's wrap this up, we have to go general hunting."

"What, again? Is he part weasel?"

"Or snake, take your pick," she groused, already lifting the mirror. "Jarod, Krys, Tyvendor, we're all clear in here. Let's not shake the building anymore, our Earth Mages are going to be peeved enough as it is."

27

She could not leave General Ajil just running around loose in Von, even if he had precious little to work with. The man was conniving and desperate, a deadly combination, and she didn't want him wreaking havoc more than he already had. She set Jetta and Don Blackpool to searching for him, one of the Von soldiers assisting Don so the man would know who to look for.

Becca didn't technically have control of the city yet, but when roughly half the city's army swore fealty to her, she considered it good enough to start issuing orders. The last gate had crumpled at the first push and by the time she got there, Jarod had it all well in hand. She found Commander Deodan again and pulled him along with her, coordinating as she made her way back around to the North Gate. Commander Deodan strode at her right hand, almost hovering, offering her insight into the city's layout and where everyone was stationed. Halfway around the city walls, she spotted the East Gate's gathering of soldiers and citizens, Trev'nor down below with Cora assisting him. So even the citizens had rebelled due to Danyal's speech?

Her not-quite-a-fiancé was quite the orator.

Shad put a hand on her shoulder and leaned in to murmur near her ear, "It would help if we could lower the potential hostages."

Her brother made an excellent point. Turning, she requested, "Commander Deodan, do you think we can take the rest of the slaves out of the city? I'd like to lower the potential hostages before I negotiate with Von."

"I think we can get at least most of them, Maharaja," Deodan answered respectfully. "There's not many left at this point in the city. I can dispatch someone to oversee the operation."

"Do so, please." Pulling out her mirror, she asked, "Nolan? You're still with Dunixan, aren't you?"

"No, he's with Trev, but I think you'd better get down here. General Ajil has made his appearance."

A feral smile traced its way over her face while a zing of anticipation flicked through her system. "Has he, now."

"He's standing at North Gate demanding to speak to a warlord. He won't talk to anyone else, he said. Trev's at East Gate accepting oaths from people, he's stuck there. You want to handle this?"

"I can. Give me five minutes and tell Don and Jetta they don't need to search anymore." Pocketing the mirror, she requested, "Tyvendor, can I ask you to handle matters here? If anyone else wishes to switch sides, they're welcome to go to East Gate and speak with Trev."

Tyvendor nodded instantly, expression betraying concern around the edges. "I can, of course. What will you do about General Ajil?"

"Nothing pleasant." Becca's preference was to turn the man into a burnt crisp but she had to give the people of Dilmun and Brecon Watchtower first crack at him, she supposed. They deserved that much. "I'll keep everyone posted. Cat!"

Her dragon's head popped over the top of the wall, followed slowly by the rest of her as she scaled up the stone like an overgrown gecko. Becca swung into the saddle, then extended a hand to Shad, giving him a boost he likely didn't need. He took it anyway, snugging an arm tight around her waist as Cat dropped down into a lazy glide that took them around the city and back to the gate they'd just left a half hour ago. She touched to earth with a slight bounce, strutting and showing off with a flick of her wings and tail before settling so Becca could dismount. She eyed her dragon suspiciously. Strutting? For who, the enemy commander? Or had some male dragon nearby caught her eye?

Becca would have to investigate this later.

She counted eight men inside the open gate, all of them in uniform, none of them dressed like a warlord. That did not bode well. Ignoring them for a moment, she headed instead for her own people, as they stood on the main road several paces outside of the walls. She noted Dunixan's presence with some surprise, as she thought him at East Gate. Had he doubled back to help her deal with this situation?

Azin noticed her first and greeted, "He refused to speak with anyone. Said he would only speak with either you or Trev'nor."

She went to Dunixan, speaking low, even though the others couldn't possibly hear her from the gate. "Dunixan. What's your take on this?"

"He's deliberately come ahead without his own warlord, which says one of two things to me. Either Warlord Von is frantically trying to pull troops and personnel together in a last ditch effort or he deems the warlord useless in negotiations. My bet's the latter."

A year ago, she was a novice in negotiations and would not have been comfortable bartering with someone else when thousands of lives were at stake. Now she stared at the general's group and tsked chidingly. "He thinks he can negotiate with some green, power-hungry teenagers and come ahead, does he? Dunixan, you're my backup. Let's get rid of this idiot."

Shad whistled an airless tune. "Remember, if I need to

accidentally-on-purpose kill the dastard, you only have to say the word."

Part of Becca felt like she shouldn't use her own brother as an executioner. But this general was also guilty of genocide several times over, so it didn't really matter what she thought about it. Shad would not forgive that kind of soulless atrocity and he'd be itching for an excuse to separate the man's head from his shoulders. "Oh, I'm sure you'll recognize the right timing for that, brother dearest."

A glint in Shad's eye spoke of macabre humor. "What if I make a mistake?"

"The man's guilty of democide," Dunixan drawled with a snort. "No one's going to shed any tears on his grave."

"Now, now," Becca dissuaded in a mild tone, already striding for the gates. "Don't encourage him. He likes offing bad guys."

Shad snickered and nearly skipped in her wake. "I certainly do. I sleep better at night afterwards. Now that I'm a father, I strangely find myself even more keen on killing every bad man I see. I wonder if Aletha feels the same?"

Nolan choked. "Great merciful magic, I hope not. Just one of you is bad enough."

Silently seconding that, Becca decided not to comment. Hopefully this manic urge of Shad's would pass. It generally did.

Fifteen feet away from the group, Becca came to a stop, everyone with her naturally coming to a halt as well. Cat stayed directly behind her, breath steaming a touch too hot out of her mouth. Llona and Orion perched along the tops of the walls, half over the edge, surrounding the man on all sides.

Her eyes roved over the soldiers' shoulders, reading their insignias with ease. A captain, two majors, three colonels, one commander with a translator's stripe underneath his rank, and of course a general. She looked General Ajil over with a cynical eye. Forties, dark eyes burning bright with anger and greed, a thick musculature not hidden by the tailored uniform, rigid posture radiating stress. He did not possess anything in the way of good looks, but she might be too biased to fairly judge him on that score.

"I'm Maharaja Riicbeccaan," she introduced herself, voice clipped. "With me is my ally, Warlord Dunixan, First Simin, Advisor Riicshaden, Prince Nolan, and Magess Azin."

"I am General Ajil," he announced in a rough voice. A pipe smoker, no doubt, with a voice like that. He didn't openly sneer at her, but he relaxed his shoulders, as if no longer viewing her as a threat. "I am open to negotiations."

"Lovely," Dunixan responded with a bright smile. "Bring forth Warlord Von so we may do so."

A vein twitched in Ajil's head. "There is no need."

"There is every need as you don't have the authority to surrender or negotiate for this city." Dunixan spoke briskly, confidently, not at all cowed or deterred by the other man's demeanor.

Ajil bristled like a wet cat. "I am the leading general of Von, of course I have the power to negotiate with you!"

"When the warlord of a city is present, he trumps all other officers of the state, and must be present for negotiations between foreign states or countries." Dunixan had a wicked glint in his eye and his smile had a distinct edge to it. The man enjoyed this hostile banter enormously. "Come, come, man you don't really expect us to just take your word for things? We're not that naïve. The only one that can bargain with a warlord is another warlord, which you are not."

The general of Von ground his teeth audibly. Shad snickered softly behind her, enjoying the show. Becca had to bite the inside of her cheek to keep from joining him. Dunixan knew the laws well and gave his opponent no quarter. She blessed the Gardeners, again, for preparing him as their ally.

"Fetch him," Dunixan ordered, not unkindly, "or we'll bring him out ourselves. I promise you, General Ajil, you won't like it if we have to retrieve him."

Both men stared hard at each other, each waiting for the other to give up: Dunixan smiling enigmatically, Ajil glaring as if the man had insulted his mother. Finally, Ajil nodded curtly, then barked a command at his translator. The commander saluted and immediately sprinted for inside the city.

Becca felt no need to entertain the other party as they waited, so she lifted the mirror broach out again to get a status update. Deliberately speaking in Chahirese, she inquired, "Trev. How goes it?"

Trev'nor thankfully picked up on her hint and responded in their native tongue. "I have lost count of how many people swore fealty to us. The Rikkanas assure me that basically everyone from Brecon and Dilmun have come out at this point. Sallah's taking the third group home as we speak. Garth and Aunt Kayden have already gone ahead with their first two. Your Commander Deodan brought out two groups of magicians, but he says there's more still in the city, and he thinks he can get everyone out."

"Good. How is Rahim doing? Have you seen him?"

"Not as of twenty minutes ago. He went further into the city with a full squad of our soldiers. But don't worry, Ginger and Ehsan are keeping track of him from overhead. If anyone even looks at him sideways, Ginger promised they'd go squish."

"I do love that dragon."

"We all do. Don't worry about your cuddle-honey, we've got his back."

"Cuddle-honey?" Becca squawked, then elbowed Shad in the ribs when he laughed. Nolan disguised his laugh under a cough, not very successfully.

"Snuggly bear?" Trev'nor offered, a grin in his voice.

"Trev'nor. Stop."

"Sugar muffin?"

"You stop or I will hurt you," Becca threatened. "Seriously, you have the worst timing for teasing people. I'm standing here in front of an enemy general, waiting on Von to show up, and you start throwing absurd nicknames at my head."

"But it's not like you're actually negotiating, right? Speaking of, what terms are you offering? Surely not the same as Rowe's."

"Good gracious, no, I don't trust them. They give me Von, I let them live. That's my terms."

"You know, I'm good with that. Uh-oh, here comes another wave. Yell if you need me." The mirror went abruptly dark.

Becca wondered at this strangely upbeat mood of Trev'nor's, but it could be a byproduct of exhaustion. Or perhaps he felt relieved that they could take the city without bloodshed? She didn't know which and it hardly mattered anyway.

Another group approached the gate, the commander from before leading them, this time with a full complement of bodyguards and the warlord's banner carving out a path ahead of them. Becca hadn't actually expected him here that quickly. Perhaps the Warlord's Residence sat close to this gate?

In her time, Becca had seen every warlord in Khobunter aside from Rowe's. They'd always been confident, powerful men, striding through the world as if they owned it. Trev'nor had described Rowe as a quieter man, but still with that confidence and authority. So it took her a moment to process that the nervous, fidgeting man standing in the circle of his bodyguards wore the formal dress of a warlord. It took her another moment to realize that he couldn't be more than five years her senior, perhaps even less than that, as he seemed to still have some baby fat in his cheeks. Well, perhaps not, he had a plump build and he moved in a slovenly way, as if he didn't really feel comfortable moving about in his own body. Lifting a sword would likely cause him to fall over.

Becca shared an astonished look with Shad and Nolan. This was Warlord Von? Surely not. Had they quickly stuffed someone into the warlord's clothes to pass him off as a decoy?

Leaning in, Dunixan whispered against her ear, "That's really him. You see now why I said the general of Von was the real threat."

"Yes, I do," she responded softly, still not quite able to believe her eyes. Well. If he really proved to be as soft willed as he looked, this should be a snap. Approaching a step, she gave him a slight inclination of the head, barely civil. She couldn't force herself to do more than that, impatient and frustrated in turns at how long this battle had already dragged out. "Warlord Von? I am Maharaja Riicbeccaan."

He ducked into an awkward bow. "Maharaja. I, uh, thought there were two of you?"

"My co-ruler is elsewhere dealing with other matters." Becca hated to judge someone on first impressions but what sort of spineless twerp was this? Swallowing that down before it showed on her face, she spoke with as neutral a tone as she could muster. "Warlord, I ask for your unconditional surrender."

General Ajil slashed a hand through the air. "No! That is completely unacceptable!"

Von started, staring at Ajil with wide eyes, nodding along like a puppet. "Yes, of course it is—"

"Warlord," Dunixan took over with a smooth tone, "I don't think you're quite aware of the situation. Half of your standing army in the city has already sworn allegiance to Maharaja Riicbeccan. All of your citizens from Brecon and Dilmun have sworn allegiance to us and most of them are already home again. All of your magicians are gone as well, in our hands. You have three gates standing open in this city, half of your force has deserted you, leaving you with no adequate defense. On what grounds are you denying our right to take this city?"

Dismayed, Von demanded of Ajil, "Is he right? How did that happen? I did what you told me to!"

Ajil hissed at him to be still, fuming.

And that adequately summed up that relationship quite well, telling Becca everything she needed to know. Becca addressed Von as if he were a child and a particularly slow one at that. "Warlord Von, I promise you that I won't exile or execute you upon your surrender. In fact, let's do this: if you surrender to me now, I promise you a suitable house with its own guards and staff so that you may peacefully live out the rest of your days. How does that sound?"

Licking dry lips, Von raised his eyebrows hopefully. "Really?"

"Warlord," Ajil rounded on him, voice scalding, "don't you dare agree to that!"

Pouting at him, Von argued, "You said that if we abandoned Brecon and Dilmun, pulled the people out, we'd be able to fend them off! Well, you were wrong, and now they're in my city! And with half my army! I can't fight with just half an army, I'll lose, and be executed, and I don't want that!"

Could he sound any more like a five-year-old child throwing a tantrum? Tilting sideways, she murmured from the side of her mouth, "I thought you said Von was good at business-oriented management?"

"I said he was good at following the business plan of his predecessor," Dunixan corrected blandly. "He's excellent at following orders, one might say."

"Ah. Got it."

Von and Ajil fell into a whispered argument that peaked, getting louder with each word, until Dunixan tired of it and clapped his hands together sharply, as loud as a thunderclap.

"Do cease, your behavior is unseemly. Von, whatever the general thinks, you've no prayer of keeping your position or remaining cities. We literally have you surrounded. The woman standing at my side is a formidable mage, and it's only her patience that keeps her from killing you all outright and simply striding inside. I suggest not testing that patience and accepting her offer before it expires."

Ajil whispered something to Von, fast and urgent, but the warlord pushed him off, nervous and agitated. "Maharaja Riicbeccaan, you swear I can live in comfort?"

"You will not agree to this!" Ajil thundered at him, expression as dark as a mother storm. Stepping right into Von's personal space, he snarled, "I don't care what I have to sacrifice, you won't surrender to these magicians—"

Becca's own tenuous control of her temper threatened to snap. She took a half-step forward, ready to tell the man off, when instinct sent her ducking instead. Several thin, sharp bars of metal flew in from almost every angle, impacting with Ajil's body, stabbing into him like pins in a pincushion. He jerked as they sliced through him, gasping in pain, unable to utter a single word as one of them went through a lung.

Whirling, Becca searched for the source, and found it not two feet away from her. Azin lowered her hand slowly, breathing a tad fast, expression one of vindication. She'd extracted her revenge for her family, and nothing in her face suggested the tiniest ounce of remorse.

Von, aghast, hastily retreated from the general by two steps. "Wh-why did you do that?!"

"He killed my family," Azin answered with cold finality. "He doesn't deserve the right to surrender. I'm not sure you do either."

Becca rubbed at her forehead, not sure how to handle that. She didn't blame Azin whatsoever for her actions, but it did put something of a damper on negotiations. "Nolan?"

Nolan smiled at her with a questioning cant of the head.

"Yes?"

The man was playing deliberately obtuse. "Do you want to, I don't know, keep the man from dying?"

The Life Mage regarded the general bleeding out at their feet and gave a mournful shake of the head. "I'm afraid I don't have enough magic to heal that."

Eyeing his magic level—which could handle healing a thunder of dragons—she drawled, "Riiiight."

Shad drew Nolan in for a quick hug. "You're my favorite."

For her own sanity, Becca wrote off any help from that quarter. From what she could tell, Ajil was basically dead at this point anyway—even if she called another Life Mage, they wouldn't get there in time. And did it really matter? Dilmun and Brecon would have called for the man's execution regardless.

Ignoring the body on the ground, Becca regarded Von, who stared at his general with alarm and a decidedly green cast to his skin. "Von. Warlord Von!"

He snapped his head around, throat working convulsively.

"Does that disturb you?" she asked, pointing at the body. "Have you never seen a dead body before?"

Shaking his head no, he went back to staring.

"Do you realize that your two cities, Brecon and Dilmun, had thousands of people left to die because of this man's orders? Because of your orders?" Becca watched his face, alarmed when he looked confused at her words. "Great good magic, man, are you that blind to what he was doing? He abandoned infants, children, and the elderly in two cities. He sacrificed thousands of people to keep his position and murdered anyone that tried to escape him. Hundreds are dead in Brecon and Dilmun because of his carelessness."

Von, shaken, kept staring for the longest moment, pale as a corpse and with about as much expression to him.

Did anything she say actually make an impact in this moment? Becca somehow doubted she could penetrate the shock. Going to him, she grabbed him by the shoulders and forced him around so that his back was to the body. "Ignore that. Now, answer my question. Will you surrender to me?"

A fine tremor ran through is frame, but he pulled himself together enough to ask, "What about my family?"

He had a younger sister and a much older, senile grandmother, Becca recalled. "They can live with you, of course, as long as they sign over all rights of power to Von. You will not want for comfort throughout the days of your life. My word as a Riic."

"Then I accept," Von stated weakly, expression relieved.

Becca almost argued for him. What kind of an idiot walked into a gilded cage of their own volition? She mentally shook off the temptation and drew up a smile from somewhere. "Thank you, Raja Von. We will have a formal agreement written up for you to sign presently. For now, please walk with me and announce your surrender to all relevant personnel to help speed matters along. We don't wish for unnecessary bloodshed, do we?"

"No, of course not," Von assured her, eyeing the dragons still perched around him, silent and threatening. He almost gave a backwards glance at his fallen general, then apparently thought better of it and offered her his arm instead. "Allow me to escort you."

She didn't actually want to touch the idiot but hid the impulse to slap him. Play nice, play nice. "Why, thank you. Dunixan, will you attend to, ah, other matters for me?"

Dunixan gave Ajil a dark look, lips pulling up over his teeth. "Of course. Cat will assist me."

Von didn't even spare a backwards glance at the general he'd abandoned.

She kept her hand in the crook of Von's elbow, mostly to ensure the idiot didn't try to run, and lifted the mirror to her mouth. In a rare moment, she didn't address the call to any specific person, but instead broadcasted out to any person who might be listening. "This is Riicbeccaan. Von has surrendered. We've won. I repeat—" tears of relief threatened to choke her and she had to pause, clear her throat, before she could speak again. "I repeat, the war is won."

Shad put a hand to the nape of her neck and pressed a quick kiss against her temple. That silent gesture said more than words and she shared a bright-eyed smile with him. Despite all the odds stacked against them, they'd managed the impossible.

Khobunter was theirs at last.

Von took a full two months to stabilize into a manageable level. Their wonderful families and friends stayed as long as they could, some of them lingering a full two weeks after Von was conquered. They eventually had to return home but not before they were all personally invited to come back for an official coronation ceremony and Becca's wedding later that spring.

With all of the additional help, they managed to put Von to rights faster than normal. Trev'nor left Becca to manage it and hailed a call for help in Rheben a month in, as the dragons needed proper nesting grounds. Since he'd seen what they should look like, it only made sense he build the new ones. It took more time than it should have, as it basically meant building a mountain near the city. Even with Sallah's help, that took a solid month's work to manage.

Nolan assisted with planting as many redwood trees as he could possibly fit around the mountain's base and along the eastern border of the city. Redwoods, he informed them authoritatively, worked better in desert environments as they had the right root system to survive well in arid climes. That and they grew to tremendous sizes, which could accommodate a dragon's needs.

Trev'nor didn't mind the work so much as he missed Dunixan fiercely. With Khobunter now under their own control, Dunixan had hitched a ride for his own territory to check in and deal with administrative things a couple of days after the battle had finished. And granted, the man hadn't been home in almost two months—he likely had a backlog of work to do that would rival a hoarder's house—so Trev'nor knew he had legitimate reason. He still missed him.

The minute Trev'nor finished here he was heading straight for Dunixan.

By the time they had a proper nesting grounds at Rheben, Trev'nor had completely forgotten that Garth promised to bring up exchange students at the beginning of the new year.

Oops.

Trev'nor showed up at the academy cold sweating under his jacket, hair a mess and cheeks red from the cold because Dragon Garth had flown him down from the mountain without him putting on his riding gear first. Not exactly the best first impression he could make on young students. Well, not that young, most of them were only four or five years younger. Although looking at their innocence and naivety, he felt unaccountably old.

Pasting a smile on his face, Trev'nor introduced, "I'm Rhebentrev'noren, Maharaja of Khobunter. Yes, I realize I don't look like it, I was building a dragon's nest. First lesson: dragons are very, very particular about their nests and they will hold you hostage until you have built it to their exact specifications."

A few nervous twitters from the crowd. Trev'nor did a rapid headcount. A baker's dozen? Was he supposed to have that many? He pulled his professional smile out and aimed it at the group in general. "Welcome to Rheben. A few facts for you before I show you the academy: First, the city was not named after me. A very distant ancestor came here directly after the Magic War and built this place. There's a memory stone nearby that tells the history. Please, please don't touch it, it will keep you captive for about two days if you do. There's little creatures running around in the city that look like furry eggs with tails called Fuzzies. They're perfectly harmless, cute little fluffballs that get into everything. And I do mean everything. Safeguard your snacks carefully. Also, be aware that before we took the city on as our capital that it was in complete ruins. We've made great progress in renovating it but there's a few places still roped off. If you see rope cordoning off an area, respect it and don't enter. And don't think you can just skip through and have an adventure, the dragons will notice, and they're the worst tattle-tales on the planet."

"He means it," Garth assured his group. "The warnings he gives you are won through hard experience. Be wise. Don't learn the same lesson the hard way."

Trev'nor appreciated the backup. This group didn't seem to know what to do with a teenage ruler. "Well, come in, let me give you a tour of the place. You're in the main courtyard now, but there's three in total for the academy's compound—"

He led them inside, through the main doors and into the academy itself. Every magical academy Trev'nor had ever seen looked completely different. Even Khobunter's did, based more on ancient Chahiran architecture and largely formed of sandstone. The magicians of Coven Ordan had taken the basic repairs Trev'nor and Azin had done and gone the extra mile. It no longer looked like a very large box, but it had arches, towers, water fountains, the trim and detail work bringing it almost to the level of a mansion.

In fact, the Maharajas' Residence didn't look as grand as this place.

Halfway through the tour, Trev'nor spied Tyvendor heading out of the cafeteria and flagged the man down. "Tyvendor! These are our exchange students. Can you show them to their dorm rooms, get them signed in, all of that?"

"Be happy to," Tyvendor assured him.

He blew out a breath as the students left and felt Garth's hand land on his shoulder.

"You forgot we were coming," Garth stated knowingly, a wicked curve to his mouth.

"Dragons," Trev'nor responded with mock dignity. "I blame the dragons. Very distracting."

Chuckling, Garth let that one pass. "I almost brought Parisa and her parents with me, but they're actually quite happy at Strae. If it's all the same, I think I'll keep them with us a little longer."

"That's fine," Trev'nor assured him, leading the way back out of the academy. He wanted to sit down, eat a belated lunch, and catch up with his cousin. "Your timing is actually good, we have the major parts of the city pulled together. It's the outlying corners and a few random pockets that still need some help. And we got an answer yesterday morning about who founded Rheben."

"Really?" Garth's interest sharpened. "Who?"

"There's actually a list—" he paused as he heard the mirror talking in his pocket and he pulled it out, lifting it near his mouth. "Hello?"

"Trev! There you are. I've been trying to reach you all morning." Becca sounded quite put out about it.

"Dragons," Trev'nor promptly answered. "Very distracting dragons who had specific requirements for their nest can be blamed. What's up?"

"I'm coming to Rheben with Shad and Rahim now. Actually, I called for a ride, but Sallah came and got us. We're almost there."

"Ah. Well, Garth is here too with his exchange students. You probably haven't had lunch yet, why don't you meet me at the bakery? We're heading there ourselves."

"Sounds perfect, I'm famished. Be there in a few minutes."

"Excellent, this way I don't have to make an extra trip,"

Garth observed as Trev'nor put the mirror away again. "I'm supposed to take Shad home. Or at least, Aletha informed me that if I failed to return with her husband, she would quit on me."

"He's really due to go back," Trev'nor admitted. "I think he was lingering until Becca and Danyal became officially engaged. Which happened right before I came down to build for the dragons, so really, he has no excuse to linger. Time for him to go home."

"I understand how hard it is to let go of someone," Garth stated a bit wistfully. "But Becca's grown now, he needs to let her walk her own path. Now, about that list of founders, what did you mean?"

"We unearthed a memorial stone yesterday morning, buried in some rubble near the east end," Trev'nor explained, then paused to get his bearings. He'd been so caught up in talking he hadn't been paying attention and almost took the wrong street. Indicating they take the next right, he continued, "Eight people were listed on the stone as the founding members. They apparently named it Rheben to honor Rhebenashlynan, who transported them all safely out of the Isle of Strae and into Khobunter. I'm not up on my genealogy, do you recognize the name?"

Garth nodded slowly, eyes narrowed in concentration. "I do. I believe she's our great-great-great grandfather's younger sister? I might have missed a great in there somewhere, but she's listed in the Magical Index. So we have the descendants from her line?"

"I wish I could tell you," Trev'nor answered with a helpless splay of the hands. "We've only found two partial Magical Indexes and they didn't cover much of the Rheben line. Our historians are going slowly insane trying to piece the lineage together. They've pestered our students, forcing everyone to list every single family member they can remember, but their memories generally only go back about four generations. Anything beyond great-grandparents gets a little murky. The only exception to that seems to be the Von family, but they had some kind of ditty or rhyme they'd made up as an oral tradition."

"So we're missing whole generations and have no record of them anywhere," Garth sighed in resignation. "Well, I suppose in the long run, it doesn't really matter. We know they're all related, they're all family."

"That's exactly what Nolan keeps saying. I agree." Reaching the bakery, Trev'nor ushered him to his favorite table, the one next to the indoor garden area, calling out to the owner, "One of everything on the menu! I'm expecting three more people."

The door opened right behind him, Nolan stepping in, his eyes still reverting from dragon's eyes. "And an extra apple pie, Master, thank you."

Turning, Garth gave him a quick hug. "Good to see you, Nolan. I have a message from Allen: 'When you come home, teach me to go dragon.'"

Snorting a laugh, Nolan answered, "I promise I will."

With an arched brow, Garth inquired, "And just how long are you planning to stay up here, anyway?"

"It's excellent princely training up here," Nolan responded mildly.

"So not anytime soon," Garth translated dryly. "Your grandfather and father keep pestering me to fetch you. Perhaps you should talk to them directly about this?"

"I will, later," Nolan promised airily.

Trev'nor knew good and well his friend had no intention of going back to Chahir for at least the next year, probably longer. He felt immensely grateful for it because while they might have the basics in each of their cities established, their rule was too new still to be really called 'stable.' Nolan pitched in with governing and troubleshooting on a regular basis and Trev'nor really didn't want to consider what he'd do when his friend decided to finally go home.

They settled around the table, catching Garth up on what all they'd been doing, and getting news from home in return. Becca sailed through the doorway with Shad, Danyal, and Sallah in tow, a smile on her face as she greeted Garth.

Trev'nor watched as Garth greeted Danyal as a cousin would, recognizing the man who would soon be family. Danyal warmed under the greeting, the bright smile he always wore when reminded he'd soon have Becca as a wife blooming across his face. They'd set the wedding date for late spring, giving them time to plan, and Trev'nor didn't envy either of them. He didn't know which would be more daunting: conquering a country or pulling off a royal wedding. He suspected the wedding.

Worse, Becca and Danyal didn't have the option of eloping, either.

They all lingered over lunch, enjoying each other's company while they still could, as it might be months before they saw each other again. Before they'd started a rebellion in Khobunter, Trev'nor had known that would be the case, that he wouldn't easily be able to visit and see family. But he knew they'd always be there for him, as he would be for them, and that's what was truly important.

Duty interrupted, as it always did, with Azin calling to ask Nolan questions. Nolan left the table and stepped outside to answer her, and they all took that more or less as their cue, standing as well. They left the bakery for the open air courtyard and paused there to say their goodbyes.

Garth and Shad gave everyone hugs, Shad lingering longest with Becca.

"I promise we'll be here for the wedding," he told her, for once serious. "Aletha and your sister too."

"I'll bring them," Garth tacked on. "As we'll all come too. Rahim, brace yourself, you're about to inherit quite a bit of family."

"Looking forward to it," Danyal assured him with a grin.

Reaching out, Garth drew Trev'nor into a strong embrace, which Trev'nor returned just as firmly. He felt his eyes burn and blinked, refusing to lose control of his emotions here. Shad would never let him live it down. "If you need anything, you let us know, alright?"

Chuckling, Garth stepped back, green eyes sparkling. "I think that's my line, kiddo."

"I'm maharaja of a country now," Trev'nor reminded him smugly. "You're not the only one with political pull in this world."

"True enough. I'll keep your offer in mind, Maharaja Rhebentrev'noren. Becca, thank you so much, by the way."

Becca pointed a finger toward her own nose, head canting in confusion. "What did I do?"

"I'm no longer the most destructive one. You now hold that title." Garth waggled his eyebrows at her mischievously.

"What!" she squawked indignantly. "Why, because of the fortress?"

"Precisely," he purred at her. "I destroyed a few storefronts. You destroyed a whole fortress. So, thanks for that." With a wink, he turned to Shad and inquired, "That bag your only luggage?"

"This is it," Shad confirmed. "But Garth, before we go, I have a burning question."

Garth eyed him warily. "I know that expression. It never spells good things."

Grin edging toward manic, Shad asked earnestly, "Aren't you curious how a Jaunten dragon would work?"

"No, Shad," Garth ordered firmly.

"Think about it," Shad insisted, grin now infectious. "Their memories are already amazing, what if—"

Garth's hand darted out and snagged Shad quite firmly by the ear. The Earth Path opened up under their feet, and Garth hauled a protesting Shad down with him.

AUTHOR'S NOTE

The Advent Series is a very special one to me. It literally launched my career, as Jaunten was the first book I published. I never expected it to be more than the original four books, but I had so much fun with this world that I kept expanding on it. My original intention was to only do six books, actually. After I'd finished the main arc of the series with Garth's story, I thought to write one with Shad and Becca, then another book with Trev'nor and Nolan to finish off all the loose ends.

Having nine books in this series is as much a surprise to me as anyone else, as I certainly did not intend to have this many. It's taken me ten years to write this series from start to finish and I must say I loved the journey. I'll miss them a little now that the series is complete, but I'm glad that I'm able to bring the story to such a satisfactory ending.

I hope to see you in the next world.

-Honor

Honor Raconteur grew up all over the United States and to this day is confused about where she's actually from. She wrote her first book at five years old and hasn't looked back since. Her interests vary from rescuing dogs, to studying languages, to arguing with her characters. On good days, she wins the argument.

Since her debut in September 2011, Honor has released almost 30 books, mostly of the fantasy genre. She writes full time from the comfort of her home office, in her pajamas, while munching on chocolate. She has no intention of stopping anytime soon and will probably continue until something comes along to stop her.

Her website can be found here: http://www. honorraconteur.com, or if you wish to speak directly with the author, visit her on Facebook.

Made in the USA
Monee, IL
26 December 2022

19452285R00173

Made in the USA
Monee, IL
26 June 2023

37374347R10095

POEMS, TALES AND WISDOM

For Daily Inspiration

Table of Contents

When in school, I studied every subject as if it were my major in order to make good grades in order to qualify for a scholarship.

To make a long story short, in 9th grade, I took Book of American Short Stories, my first literature class. In the 10th, I explored American Literature and in the 11th grade British Literature.

During my senior year, Mr. Walker, the schools Industrial Art teacher was invited to speak to the students in the regular morning assembly. I clearly remember he ended his speech with the "If" poem by Rudyard Kipling. From that moment on I wished to be a poet. Then I attended college and took the required World Literature class as part of my Bachelor of Arts degree in Business & Economics.

After graduation I worked in accounting and research, but returned to school for both a Master of International Management and a Master of Education degree. I subsequently worked for several years in accounting including a position as the Director of Education of Bentonville Boys & Girls Club. During that I had time to write short poem about topics such as The Importance of Coming to the Learning Center and the Usefulness of the Computer.

I taught for over five years as an adjunct instructor at the Northwest Arkansas Community College. Then a local museum offered me a position with benefits I could not refuse. For more than two years now, I have been serving as guest attendant while taking my poetic skills to the next level.

The poems attached are just few of my first poetic expressions. The poems are about my role models, friends, acquaintances, and family.

STORIES

NOVEMBER 21, 2012

Among those in my father's and mother's family,
I am the only one with a completed college education;
Among the boys that James J. Cooper helped to educate,
I am the only college graduate,
Among the boys that my uncle Chief Guyan raised,
I am the only boy he sent to school.
These fortunes make me humble and thankful,
With no room to be doubtful.

I am married to a lady of perfect choice and love.
She is a lady of tough love though also like a dove,
She is my good friend for better or for worse, forever and ever,
I trust her. No room for separation, no, not ever.

She and I are blessed with a beautiful daughter and a handsome son,
Our daughter and her husband have two handsome boys
And are dedicated to their children's education,
With no room for procrastination.

My wife is both healthy and an angel.
We are lucky to be with the best doctors for any everything.
We have instructors for every medical problem who offer sage
advice.
What a blessing to have right doctors with every needed excellence
and method and device!

From the Lofa County tribal villages and towns, I have become very conservative and religious,
including an aspiration to the priesthood before the end of my life pious.
Perhaps I can become the religious servant representative, maybe even President.
Those happenings for the Liberian people will never be coincident.

These blessings and dreams could only come from the Almighty above
With me as an instrument of the Lord's wave.
Those who repent for their sin will be in line for Jesus to save.
Undoubtedly, humankind must always be thankful for the present and every future move.

— **Moses Sao Sumo Cooper of Deignmai**

AUGUST 8, 2013

My dad starts every meal with chopped fried onion for the aroma of
a fine dish
And cooks with hot spices that taste delicious rather than like fish.
Meals are usually a green or bean vegetable dish cooked with
chicken or steak.
His creation looks appetizing with no ingredient that is fake.

He tells everyone that he is a true and sincere vegetarian.
When they say "Really?" He says, "Yes with some chicken or steak
for a Liberian!"
Nonetheless, his cooking is always tasty and nice,
And every meal comes with lots of steamed rice.

He also likes to cook a huge pile of beans with chopped chicken or
steak for flavor.
This meal has my mother's highest favor.
My father's meals and regular exercises make my parents look
healthy,
Younger than their age. There is in their home no room to be filthy.

My two boys and husband have learned to eat and enjoy his meal,
And that to me, as their only daughter, is surely a great deal.
Even better, my mother is a city lady who cooks on special occasion
So she does the holiday cooking with perfection.

When I take my family home to visit my parents, I give back and do
the meal preparation.
I guess because my mother trained me, I cannot depart from the
family tradition.
My mother also served in a beauty salon a long time ago before
nursing school
So now I cut hair for my family and my father and my mother for the
joy of sitting on her stool.

My parents now encourage me to become a professional beautician,
To be like Koto Momolu, a professional designer who is also a
Liberian.
I guess I am like my parents in the ways of aspiration because
My parents and I are always advancing forward without
procrastination.

Now I pray for my boys to be ambitious and do the same
So that they can work hard and advance in the school game.
Then they will be prepared for career advancement
Which would allow me and my husband to retire some day with
proud enjoyment.

– **Moses Sao Zumo Cooper of Deignmai**

MY LEFT HAND WRIST

JUNE 20, 2010

When my left hand wrist was broken,
I thought that it was just a dream and not of sugar or cream.
I had just stepped out of my car with the engine running
When the door locked with the transmission screaming.
My two feet slipped from the icing ground to high in the air.
With no hold for my weight to bear, I was in despair!
I used my left hand for support,
And landed on a crash deport.

Then I was taken to the St. John's Emergency Regional Center.
Hoping to get care, I sat in a position no better.
No doctor on duty was assigned.
While waiting, I realized that I did not worry about the pain because
I could have lost what my wife had expressed in our marriage
counseling: love.
Love was also the first feature I heard her express
On the day before our matrimony.
which turned out to be a happiness ceremony.

Therefore, I remember this memorable wrist experience as father's
day wishes.
This morning, I thought of my departed father's and his brothers'
absence.
They left a vacuum unfilled.
Therefore today, on Father's Day, I was thinking of a Mother's Day
present for my wife:

To teach my children, grand children and their children to come that family comes first,

That love of family should always be the most important job in life.

Happy Father's Day and Happy Mother's Day Everyone!

— **Moses Sao Zumo Cooper of Deignmai**

JANUARY 7, 2012

Perhaps thought of and perceived as a casual joke,
 I used first class service with no room to fake.
I materialized and realized her favorite flavor of cake,
A privilege for this humble gentleman to bake.

Serving as an honor to have and enhance opportunity
For her joy felt with delighted continuity,
Revealing surely her delightful smiles,
With millions of carefully driven miles.

The gesture would find place in the gallery of artistic kindness,
Always sharing literary boldness
By the many who love literature
And an affirmative approved signature.

Her delight would be mine to cherish.
Surely it would never diminish.
In happiness she would share
With no one yet never anyone to dare.

"In short, driving Miss Caroline would give her the joy of happiness
and allow me the reward of kindness."

– **Moses Sao Zumo Cooper of Deignmai**

FEBRUARY 28, 2013

A search for lost love can be an exciting or a trivial pursuit.
You fly or travel miles and miles to find a dream attractive or
handsome love in a suit.
The discovery may surprise you or be less surprising than exciting.
This is just a friendly reminder for landing in an environment so
inviting.

I must find the love that I won among many and let it fly through my
fingers.
I may have been undecided but never, ever in danger.
It does not matter how far I must fly or travel to the destination.
Surely I do not and will not allow anything to hold me back,
not even looming procrastination.
I never knew how pleasant memories can be, much less how
emotionally powerful.
I can feel in my bones and especially in my sincere heart the past
memories
For which I am grateful.
God, please help me to manage the challenging feeling of the
intangibles that I lost.
For many years I have been at the disadvantage of lost love's cost.

When I hopefully find my love again, I intend not to lose it, no
matter what it takes.
 I could share that true and only one: I have no other choice to make.
Lord, have mercy on my soul and that of the beautiful or handsome
one who my heart stole.
She or he innocently captured my heart with my permission and put
it under the cart.

The focus of my search is narrower because I do now know my
love's location,

with this knowledge being very clear and good for my self-actualization.
The challenge is that I may not see what I expect to see
As compared to the memory that I hold.
The wise saying is that "blessed are those who do not expect
For they will not be disappointed" or told.

The thought process has been refreshing and exciting for my soul's desire.
I will cherish the pleasant thoughts; and anyone who tells me anything different, I will dare.
The pursuit of my heart's desire should and will be primary in all my life's happiness
Because determination would be a lot better than accepting depression or sadness.

Long live the pursuit of happiness for any man's or woman's satisfaction,
Life would be meaningless without the pursuit of one lost love to be found with proper direction.
The lost heart will be settled for better or for worse or good.
What everyone needs is satisfaction and soul food.

    –   Moses Sao Zumo Cooper of Deignmai

HOUSE HOPPING IN AN ICE AND SNOW STORM

DECEMBER 7, 2013

I pray for you to be house hopping in a severe ice and snow storm,
So you could land and sit by my fireplace on a cozy love seat.
I would make you a sweet cup of hot chocolate or a mug of mulled wine,
While resting in my love seat waiting to dine.

I would put on my snow boots and take my ax to cut more wood from my yard,
To keep the fire burning forever and ever like never before,
but especially to keep you from leaving for somewhere else in mobility,
in the hope you would taste the kind of love you could have with me, a warming possibility.

The forecast has already been made for Northwest Arkansas in early December.
Surprisingly, the museum is closed to everyone, even a member.
I pray weatherman to be 100% right this night.
I am hoping for no room on any flight.

Your happiness would be my duty to fulfill,
Please call your Mom and Dad. Tell them that you are doing well; your joy is mine to fulfill.
With no school and with no work, the night tastes like a pancake sweetened with honey.
 I would wait for that time to come in a future of your choosing when I have more money.

The futures of your job and that of mine are promising.
That kind of news sound very good without any messing.
Will you please tell me if I am crazy or if I am a true dreamer?

Truly, I am an economist and a a business man who lives in the pleasant land of a farmer.

I am sincerely farming for a harvest of true love.
And eager to work hard for the plentiful harvest to share with someone like you.
Are you interested in tasting a true and once in a life time chance?
If you are not sure, please ask your mother for some advice.

Although thousands fall in your way, please do not give up on love,
Love is the key to the whole wide world.
Will you be mine true and true mine forever and ever?
For you, I promise that I will be waiting in an ocean or just in the pool of a love diver.

    – **Moses Sao Zumo Cooper of Deignmai**

POEMS

APRIL 19, 2013

From the day I spied you, I knew that you were in serious good trouble.
I also knew that I was the only one chosen to rescue you without a fumble.
The day was exceptional, a sunny and beautiful afternoon.
That night, I dreamt about you standing in the glow of a bright shining moon.

Then with my humble charm, I took you to a pan-cake dinner;
You were happy and the easiest to please in the best manner.
I always was at ease with you, confident of your rescue.
I got along with your sister, your friends and especially with your mother's manqué.

Then I tried to be alone with you, but your cousins and friends were always around.
I joined the group and everyone called me good friend with a positive sound,
Each time I tried to impress you with my future plans, you were intimidated.
The past needed to be buried in order for us to focus on the future estimated.

Then my female friends were getting jealous about your role in my life.
Two of them often offered me serious commitment proposals for strife.
Along with my studies, I accepted a week-end, part-time job offer.
My busy week days and week-ends left me with no room for a buffer.

I felt that my rescue strategy was not going as planned. It was nowhere.

I was ready for help from the only one in good trouble or from anywhere.
I would not fight a losing battle, and so I had to take flight;
And in the name of academic pursuit, I left town without a fight.

Many years passed and unlike my nature, I had to give up on my rescue efforts.
I achieved my main goal by acquiring another academic degree of distinction of sorts.
Then the lady in the good trouble called me and said,
"You stole my heart once and for all with your deeds,"
And she politely asked for no commitments for the seeds planted by my needs.

For the sake of our children, our relatives and friends we must always be as peaceful as possible.
Love means giving to others and to the world of nations and homelands, always able.
I am grateful and thankful for the love you have shown me and it makes me more humble, I pray for thankfulness, repentance and for God's mercy for our endings to be more honorable.

   – **Moses Sao Zumo Cooper of Deignmai**

AFRICA WILL HAVE THE ANSWER

NOVEMBER 16, 1999

The Map of Africa is shaped like a Question Mark.
The answer from Africa, the continent of beauty though dark,
has no more justifiable complaint than colonialism should not exist.
Still the realization that a problem is well defined is already halfway
solved.
Africa must have all the conflicts resolved.

When government overthrows and their counters are no more,
Voters can choose what will be in-lieu of guns.
In-justice will not be used in the presence of justice;
The powerless can become the mighty.
Mothers and childrenwill be able to stand up tall,
Without a worldwide, crying call.

World Bank and donor nations can finance infra-structure,
Pave the way for adequate schools,
And for adequate public health,
With other cares to follow for all to know.
Each can enlighten their children and grand progeny,
That all mankind will be one for the too many.

United Nation and OAU and the like will have dealings no more
With governments of soldiers and dictators
Who demolish the will of the people.
No head of government will fatten and rot
With corrupt practices
That birth hidden many traces.

Solidarity & Trust will be the norm in every African country;
The Catch-Up Theory of economic development will truly hold.
There will be enforcement of rules of law
While public education and public health will improve
Along with high rates of investments and savings

To foster a real, visible higher standard of living.

Then most, if not all, of those in exile will return home
To build their lives and homes once for all,
To stand up in every way tall,
With dignity and elegance
Now and in the future,
To provide the answers for Africa's question-mark.

– **Moses Sao Zumo Cooper of Deignmai**

JANUARY 30, 2012

May we be free like a bird for a while, for even a moment?
Then I will invite you to my nest of contentment,
To sleep in my feather bed of self-actualization
With peace of mind for civilization.

We can fly in December and January with no return date
To a warmer climate in a tropical paradise,
To be pampered and spoiled,
Though our memories will never be forgotten.

Then I will be a servant to fulfill your wishes
And always do your dishes.
This sound too good for true promises,
But they will truly come to you with roses.

Never again will your desire be unattended,
And I will always be reminded
That love surely is the key of the whole wide world
And will fulfill your tender heart so it can unfold.

— **Moses Sao Zumo Cooper of Deignmai**

AUGUST 5, 2014

Immediately after our meeting, I went with a group to a Missouri
Fish Hatchery,
And what I am about to express here is not mere flattery.
I was very impressed to meet with you today in your elegant office.
Moreover, you were again as observant and observed, you and me,
as ever
Though you looked even more beautiful and elegant and even
younger.

The thought of meeting you caused me to email my thoughts and
aspirations.
Again you impressed me with the extent to which you considered
my inspirations.
Indeed, your technological analysis of my wishes was skillfully
wrought without bargain.
I felt that you and your resources and team were on my innocently
moving train.
I pray together we will travel many miles to leave behind the world's
drain on our souls.

These vehicles of my excited endeavors are ready to move on
With your hands, lucky and skillful;
And I am very happy to note that your expertise would be at my
disposal.
Never before have I been so enthusiastic about my wishful chances.
Now with your skillful support I will thoughtfully be in a mood for
many dances.
With your skillful expertise, we will mend even unforeseeable
fences.

Now I am mentally in the mood to read and digest the offered
constructive advice;
I truly will consider each as real methods of humankind service.

The current challenge is where will I start these enterprising endeavors so nice?

My prayer of "Lord direct my paths and guide my ways" will enrich these endeavor survivors.

Long live dreamers who will settle for nothing less than being winning warriors.

– **Moses Sao Zumo Cooper of Deignmai**

DECEMBER 25, 2009

You protect the homeland
With your brave band
For freedom without you is meaning-less.
You do it with all you have to offer.

You pay for loyalty with your blood,
like a water flood,
In a foreign land with cavalry of numbers untold.
You are truly a giant to behold.

Your job is noble
And you too humble.
What a just course to take
With no room to fake.

    —   **Moses Sao Zumo Cooper of Deignmai**

WISDOM

AN ACHIEVER'S DREAM

JANUARY 10, 2013

True and effective achievers have the habit of dreaming many times.
To make their dream come true, they set short and long term goals
like digging from mines.
Then they set daily steps to make themselves and others happy
And do not behave like a thoughtless puppy.

When they go to bed and cannot sleep, they reject sleeping pills
In favor of reading or doing some practice drills.
Obviously, they try to make tomorrow's tasks easier
And in the process make themselves and those around them happier.

If the achievers' goal is school, they plan again in short and long-
terms
So those plans and academic goals will be more than merely dreams.
The next step of classes or final graduation can be fulfilled with a
blessing of benediction
As the true journey of life begins with un-ending continuation.

Have you ever said to yourself, "What have I achieved after high
school graduation?"
The simple answer is not to worry about the past because you cannot
change that situation.
However, you can start planning for your future and prosperous
goals,
which is not made of magic or a bunch of bumbling boars.

Are you a parent like many who worry about your teenagers?
Trust me, they are in the company of best of army non-dodgers,
Is your young man or woman struggling with what to do next?
There will be no and never ever answer for now or for tomorrow's
quick text.

The mother of a younger friend of mine told him that if you pray,
you should not worry;

And if you worry, then you should not pray but always be sorry.
This wise saying brings me to the conquest of my inspiration,
And brings me home to the attributes of individual achievement and aspiration.

–   **Moses Sao Zumo Cooper of Deignmai**

MARCH 27, 2012

Sir Patrick Henry said, "I know not what course others may take, but as for me, give me liberty or give me death!"

I know some people think to be an American is a privilege.
As for me and my house, to be an American is a responsibility,
To be an American comes with unquestioned duty.
Responsibility, in lieu of a privilege, makes me responsible for my positive and negative actions.

I wake up in the morning with Maslow's Need Hierarchy to help plan the next level.
Then I try to study so hard in school, teaching and working that others marvel.
That makes me feel more of an asset than a liability to my community of America
While I nonetheless dream pleasantly of playing my favorite traditional songs on a harmonica.

Most people in American and around the world could not make it without good education,
Thus emphasizing the importance of youths' education and graduation,
The only fundamental and solidarity solution that makes a difference.
Therefore welfare in America or anywhere should lead to self-independence,

With independence comes the joy of success or the chance to succeed or fail.
Let us count on the happiness of expertise to do better next time in life's trail.
The good book says that it is more blessed to give than to receive;
Therefore, I truly believe that it is more of a joy to give and retrieve.

You and I and a few others believe that to be an American is a privilege.
Truly the current monarch of England cannot survive on privilege
So the monarchy works hard to earn the support of the citizens of the majority.
Any monarchy or a leader must have a purpose of dedication and a sense of priority.

Whether you are a political or not, please consider the icing on the cake by saying dearly,
Thus, all of us Americans and everyone in the world should aspire to our full potential.
We must solidify and magnify our indelible credential.

BEING AN AMERICAN IS A RESPONSIBILITY

If you are like few others who believe that to be an American is a privilege,
Please think twice that the current monarch of England cannot survive on privilege
So the monarchy is working hard to earn the support of the citizens of the majority.
Any monarchy or a leader must have a purpose of dedication and sense of priority.

John F. Kennedy put the icing on the cake by saying clearly,
"Ask not what your country can do for you but what you can do for your country," sincerely.
Thus all of us Americans and everyone in the world should aspire to our full potential.
We solidify and magnify our indelible credential.

   – **Moses Sao Zumo Cooper of Deignmai**

NOVEMBER 16, 1999

A step in the Boys & Girls Club Learning Center is worthy.
It is a step in the right direction,
It is a step for a better grade,
And undoubtedly a step for a marketable trade.

It is a step leading to deserved promotion,
Because these steps are not for social promotion.
They are for a genuine progression,
Indeed not steps toward economic or personal recession.

I can feel better in school
When I do the work
And am not being lazy,
But sincerely busy.

I do set goals in life to reach.
I am going to college or to a trade school and not sleep on the beach.
Yes, I will survive,
And, I believe, that I am sharp and always ready to stay alive.

– Moses Sao Zumo Cooper of Deignmai

DECEMBER 20, 1999

For the young and the old
Who have hunger untold?
Rid the old deficiency
With proficiency.

You must enhance education to the fullest,
And make the weak strong
To be able to aspire
In all the known and healthful desires.

You can be full of entertainment,
With cultural enrichment.
For the betterment of us all,
Be strong and tall.

— **Moses Sao Zumo Cooper of Deignmai**

MAY 31, 2013

I do not know about you, but I am aging in love like a bottle of good wine
Because I am still breathing.
Many of my elementary, high school or college classmates are gone
And no longer can say anything.
There are many reasons why you and I should be thankful
For the many blessings we have been given.
If you have the motivation to age like a good bottle of wine,
You are rightly motivated and driven.

Aging comes with many benefits like a gray hair,
And wisdom comes only with experience.
If you are married, healthy and have children,
You are self-actualized and diligent.
Perhaps everyone wants to age like a good tasting bottle of wine.
You are the beauty ad artistry of a twist of twine.

If you are not satisfied with your condition,
Please remember that you are lucky to be alive.
That is the experience you have earned without being a diver that dived.
If experiencing the adverse side-effect of a drug,
First exercise and eat well regularly.
Then have a talk with your doctor to recommend another step
To reverse the adverse effect positively.

May I suggest that we go to church regularly
With prayer for your health and those of other loved ones?
Then let us be active in church and in the community
With no boastful runs.

Make sure to improve your relationships with friends
And especially with those who definitely matter the most.
For better or for worse, they will always be your genuine,
Helpful, lawful and loving hosts.

Let us love our enemies for we do not know for sure
Who we will need to be our friend in time of need.
My first name is Moses.
However, let us avoid practicing the Mosaic Law of an "an eye for
eye" in-deed.
These are the remarkable attributes of anyone
Who wants to be more stress free and to age like good wine.
We need to practice two of the quotations of Mother Teresa's
expressions of good God's kindness.

Mother Teresa: "Kindness in your face, kindness in your eyes and
kindness in your smiles."
These are integral energy which will drive many aging people to
many and many more miles.
Again mother Teresa is quoted: "Let no one come to you without
leaving better and happier."
We can realize our full potential as productive, responsible and
caring citizens," to live life merrier.

Then we shall age and feel like a good bottle of fine wine with no
room for pessimism
Because we shall live and influence others with our heartfelt joy and
optimism.
We will thank God for his blessings and leave behind a legacy for
our friends and progeny to celebrate.
Once for all, we must repent of our weakness and the immoral deeds
we committed so we remain fortunate.

— **Moses Sao Zumo Cooper of Deignmai**

JULY 19, 2014

From my son TJ: "No pain, No gain."

Exercising for many months now has shown me that there is no better way to start the year.
In this 2014 New Year resolution, we should be submitting to a "Good Healthy Habit."
I do hope that millions of people in America and around the world will realize
The miracle of exercise. As my athletic son said, "No pain, No gain,"
Which is the step to actualize.

Miracles of exercise, especially for the aging, are beyond human comprehension
So for every aging man and women there should be no room for procrastination.
For anyone who is required to take a drug with a serious side-effects battle,
A good healthy habit promotes aging like a good wine bottle.

The first step is to take some time to listen and measure your blood pressure,
recording the results regularly for your physician's measure.
That would show a sign of how well your health is gauging
and lead you to proper managing.

Every morning and every evening one must check and record vital signs;

The above and below recordings are indeed winning signs.
To avoid increasing the dosage, the best thing to do is to do a lot of exercising.
The requirement is also for body strengthening.

The upper and lower body strengthening are steps in the right direction.
However, there must also be exercising for sticking out stomach reduction,
One should exercise regularly,
But from my experience also frequently.

    −   **Moses Sao Zumo Cooper of Deignmai**

SEPTEMBER 22, 2012

[KEEP YOUR FAMILY UNITED]

Have you ever felt un-appreciated by your children, relatives or spouse?
You may say sincerely that you have not done the same against someone.
Have you ever been un-appreciated with your mother or dad sleeping in the guest room?
Please do not let father or mother sleep in dog house gloom.

Have your mother and father shown to you and everyone else some degree of solidarity?
Through a thousand falls, let not family solidarity be described as in-sincerity.
Is she or he always ready for un-expected forgiveness with memory blackout?
Good hands and ears should also be open to the poor who are often left-out.

Though a thousand falls do not lead you to fail,
Do not let yourself go in a place where you need to make bail.
The United States of America is a land of opportunity,
And we must aim to be ranked first in a first class community.

It does not matter how your skin color looks.
To succeed, we all need to know many books.
Let us always work hard on the up-ward bound of achievement
Because that will always serve as our record of compliment.

We must not be classified as someone who did not try hard enough. Success, especially in the United States of America, comes easy for those who are tough.

We must be tough in the body and in the mind with an eloquence for good.

Let us feed our family and the many with motivation and with nourishing food.

   – **Moses Sao Zumo Cooper of Deignmai**

PRAYER

AUGUST 12, 2014

Lord please helps me to change the wishes that I can change.
I know I believe in you and know you can influence my wish to manage.
Please help me to manage the wishes of my heart
like shooting the right dart
And to begin a good start.

I want to be the perpetual trainer of the love of my heart.
Please bring her at least one inch closer to my arm,
And I would hold to that love and let not her wander onto another's farm.
That closeness would be the true source of my sincerity and charm,
and I am definitely true in my desire to prevent harm.

The challenge is that she goes everywhere but to my destination
Though I have patience to wait for her procrastination,
Hopefully not waiting in vain.
In the meantime, I will be in calm mood, not like a rushing train,
And I wish to be a true love pouring life and love giving rain.

I would like to retire with her and be the best possible trainer,
And also be a writer of economics, management and poems, though not a miner.
Then, I would truly be an owner of my academic achievements and the people's winner.
True happiness would definitely come with a life more joyful than ever.
In the swimming pool of true love, I would be an experienced diver.

And I would share the rewards with the love of my life, my progeny
and my people for ever.
Most importantly, I will ever be a servant of God through the Lord
who is our Savior.
I truly believe that my life, to direct and to guide, is in His Hand,
And I want to live and die in the strongest Christian band.
I pray we all pray to live and die in a Christian land.

– **Moses Sao Zumo Cooper of Deignmai**

JUNE 18, 2013

What a blessing we had when one of us dreamed about re-unification.
That gesture must have taken genuine love backed by a good reputation.
Let us count our blessings because we are alive on healthy feet and in fine mood.
Many of our adversaries and our loved ones are gone, never to come back and bring good.

We are happy for the good Lord saves us in time of accident and unexpected situations.
You see someone in a wheel chair who is smiling with much appreciation and
You often see God's kindness in the faces of those giving to others.
Please appreciate God's caring people, including sisters and brothers.

Everyone in the whole world is determined to come to the United States of America.
Opportunity is more reachable here while limited in other places like Africa.
Hence, all Americans should not complain about being rich or poor
Because every citizen here has a better chance to reach opportunity's door.

Everyone in every land has reasons for appreciation and thankfulness.
The abundant blessings in every land are the result of God's rich kindness.
Therefore, no reason exists for any faithful people to feel disappointment
Because apparent failure can grow into abundant blessings for further improvement.

We all need to be thankful for our loved ones still alive.
There is the generosity of good people from which we benefit and for which we did not dive.
There are donors and missionaries whose contributions show to others kindness.
"Let no one ever come to you without leaving better and happier."*
Avoid birthing meanness.

Mother Teresa

— **Moses Sao Zumo Cooper of Deignmai**

FRIENDSHIP

ODE TO MY TRUE GOOD FRIEND

JANUARY 1, 1974

Let me let you know from the bottom of my heart
That you are a very attractive and beautiful lady.
The compliment pouring from my heart is aptly descriptive.
I consider myself to be a lucky lad and take a note that you are a
lovely treasure.
One of my spiritual desires is to be a spiritual measure.
So I would pray for me and you so dearly.
That would make me a lucky man, standing tall and bravely.

Long live our genuine and sincere friendship.
The opportunity is that we both love education and teaching and
have the attributes of leadership.
Thus, we have a common bond which needs enrichment;
The challenge is for you and me to go further.
I believe that we have a mutual interest to go forever and ever.
 I sincerely pray for both of us to become even happier.

True and sincere friendship is one of the world's greatest treasures.
For such a worth-while course, there should be no measures.
We must allow the precious love seeds to grow graciously;
We must give the feeling a chance to flourish very sincerely.
The love reward for us would be flowering endlessly.

You said that you will not let me down no matter what happened.
That is indeed a comforting assurance with no room to bend.
I am very fortunate to hear from you that you will never let me
down,
And everyone would support us in my home-town.
Everyone in my hometown would be happy to know there is no
room to frown.

–   **Moses Sao Zumo Cooper of Deignmai**

THE ROBOT WILL HAVE LIFE

SEPTEMBER 25, 2014

The robot shall and will have successful and happy moods to live.
I will swim, work hard if necessary for the robot, and I will dive.
The challenge is obvious, but I will, with the cooperation of the robot, make it probable.
Together, we can make it as real as possible.

Where there is will, it is said, there is a way.
No matter how hard and difficult the journey will be, I am willing to pay.
However, it takes two to tango, as the saying goes, and will be the main case.
If necessary, I am willing and determined for the right reason to chase.

I see the genuine beauty in the robot that no one sees as much as I do so clearly.
Therefore, I am willing to do the chase and persuasion even more dearly.
I pray for the blessing to be with me in my attempt to make the life of a winner.
I am determined and willing to be more than a mere dreamer.

With my African instinct and skillfulness, I wish to make the dream come true.
Never have I been ever an empty dreamer of failure.
With many charming skills, I would be humbled to be a winner
With the robot emphasizing my crazy attempt to qualify me as a true dreamer.

My artistic orientation makes me live in the land of dreamers and wishful thinking for
The poetic dream, and when tempered by writing skills, the dream can become a making.

The main goal is not only the writer's happiness but to make the main character of Robot happy.
The beauty is for the writer to save the Robot's joy on a disk that is floppy.

    — **Moses Sao Zumo Cooper of Deignmai**

APRIL 05, 2013

After over thirty years of lost love, I found it in a condition of better
perfection.
At the end of my search, I was ready for better or for worse,
And to be frank, I was ready for rejection.
The Good Lord came out of nowhere and blessed me
With what I met on the second day of my arrival.
My lost love looks better than ever when I opened my hotel door
And my eyes were in denial.
There she/he stands and told me she/he has taken some time off
work
To be with me on my vacation.
I said without doubt, "You are the love of my heart," without
procrastination.
She/he responded politely and in a lovable tone, "I am humbled."
She/he continued, "I will run with this ball and never fumble."

I confessed to her/him that everyone except me knew that you were
the choice love of my heart.
In spite of my mother's warning about you, she loved you from the
start.
I said, "My past blinded me to let you slip through my fingers.
I needed to hold you fast and keep you out of danger."

Then I said what normal gentlemen or ladies are wont to say, "I am
all yours to hold."
In response, she/he stepped towards me and hugged me in her/his
arms with a gesture so bold.
My heart beat too fast with joy but also with reservation to resist
however helplessly.
I said to myself that I must be in my habitual dreaming land
completely and hopelessly.

From there, every day of my vacation was taking activities to the next level of excellence.

The experiences were ever and ever beyond what I expected without my usual role of diligence.

I said to myself, "What did I do to deserve such lovable moments like these I wonder?"

This is the life for lucky lovers like us who will ever be full of ponder.

Then, in my pleasant dreaming she/he said. "This is our belated honey moon."

From that moment, it was beyond and above the dream of real and true love like a full moon.

She/he said in a lovely voice to me, "Thank you for coming to find me in lovers' 'paradise.'"

I replied, "Thank you for accepting me and for selling me lovers' merchandise.

On the last day of my vacation, reality started creeping in my thoughts with sad tone.

When I returned home and I emailed her/him the caption: "No Regret," alone.

She/he replied and stated that the title of my email should be: "I am Thankful."

Our endeavor was indeed a mission for lovers who are truly lucky to be grateful.

— **Moses Sao Zumo Cooper of Deignmai**

BIRTHDAY APPRECIATION

SEPTEMBER 17, 2012

Happy birthday to you and many, many more returns,
With good health, prosperity and no burns.
Words are not rich enough to express my appreciation for your
friendship
With no room to send an ounce of it to you by electronics, air, or by
ship.

Your kindness to all is without measure,
And that is indeed invaluable treasure.
Long live you and the great man in your life
With blessings and goodness and with no strife.

Sometimes I am tempted to call you mother Teresa in good faith.
You enjoy Sunday morning services before you come to work and
that is no myth.
You are a blessing to your parents, to your spouse and to all of us
your colleagues.
Indeed you are a model for all of us who serve in the life of little or
big leagues.

The honor is mine to express few lines for the silent majority:
They wish you well on your birthday with sincerity.
You are always your brothers' and sisters' keeper.
Do you wish for no room to tell on any of us like a beeper?

Long live you with many and many prosperous years to come,
And may your wishes find comfortable home.
On behalf of the many that I know who know you well,
We wish you many good years and pleasant stories to tell.

Long life may you with have with many memorable years to live,
With good health and happiness and no misfortune looming,
I pray for many blessings,
In any time of testing.

    — **Moses Sao Zumo Cooper of Deignmai**

YOU MAKE IT SO GOOD

AUGUST 11, 2013

In many things that I watch you do, you do it and make it so good.
You do it like a French chef who makes very appetizing and tasty food,
Perhaps, you do it like a Frenchman preaching to the Africans that the British are colonizers.
On the contrary, the French in Africa are the true civilizers.

I often see you smiling and looking like you are aging like a good bottle of wine.
That attribute of yours for many of us your friends do not reflect the passage of time.
Indeed, you show an example of humankind with true blessing.
This must be a reminder to all of us who admire you without seeing you under fire-testing.

Your humility as a son of a chief whose father was a king makes all of us humble.
Therefore, we your friends and those of your children and grandchildren must avoid trouble.
Some of us wonder about where you get your inspiration to perform at the best of your ability.
Our observations of your interactions with us leave
No room for procrastination, and irresponsibility.
Such gestures on your part show to us your friends and humankind the very kind best.
Obviously you, like many of us, have some flaws hidden by your fineness.
Long live your talents after you have served well and are departed.
We pray that your faith in the Lord will take you to heaven strongly firm and united.

Good humankind like you and others out there should
Lead the world for better destination and further.

The rooms for such great people with good education to lead our children in the world are better.
I am very humbled for the kind compliments, and,
I must confess, the secret of my so-called lucky fortune.
My passion for everything shows I try to be very strong with positive tune.

Guilt gets into me. For example when I miss a church on Sunday for some reason,
I feel like I have committed some kind of treason,
And I look forward to reading in church when I am assigned to do the lector reading.
I could do it every Sunday like I was assigned in the church choir singing.

My secret of good health is my inspiration from God to exercise strenuously
Every morning with sweat.
In addition, I eat quarter slices of orange and one banana and a glass of milk
After my regular exercise.
The count of my rigorous exercise must be precise.
To summarize, at my current age, I am more grateful with much promise.

— **Moses Sao Zumo Cooper of Deignmai**

I WANT TO SEE THAT LOVE LOOK IN YOUR EYES

JUNE 18, 2013

The innocent love looks were hidden from my blind eyes, from the sounds of my ears.
I am not sure if you intentionally hid them from me, or I was too busy those years.
I only saw it when you let me know that you missed me for long and long periods of time.
I was lucky and wise to be in a condition of self-actualization prime.

You invited me to see it, and, at first, I did not believe in the invitation sincerely.
However, the urge to search for true and genuine love led me to taste it dearly.
The question that I am asking myself is am I worthy and capable of such luck?
It is priceless and worth more than gold, diamonds, or a twenty point buck.

The taste is ever-lasting, sincere and so enriching, that one can experience it only in a dream.
It makes me more humble and thankful to you and to the good Lord
For a taste like nice ice-cream.
It is a kind of ice-cream that tastes better not only in summer,
But in frozen weather as well.
It wakes me up like a school bell that has a genuine ring and an expensive knell.

It is so great that I am not sure that I am able to harness it and keep it for-ever and ever.
It is the kind of luck that comes once in life time and not only to those who are clever.
I must not forget that I truly and sincerely want your love look,
Something that cannot and never can be found in any kind of well written book.

It comes from the heart for the blessed and innocent very lucky people.
The luck is for people who cannot and should not afford to be in any kind of bad trouble.
Do I think that I am a candidate for such fortune and treasure?
I think not though I thank the Almighty for becoming a candidate for such a blessed measure.

I feel lucky for you to let me be the chosen one to see it in your eyes.
I was not even around but away for many years and miles without signs.
The looks are scared and of the best quality.
The chance and the opportunity for anyone to taste it is a slim possibility.

The challenge is for me to ask the good Lord to help me keep it forever.
And I will learn and relearn to never again say never.
I will surely live for full of signs of opportunity,
Even for those of us who are in the minority.

— **Moses Sao Zumo Cooper of Deignmai**

THE END.

THANK YOU

Dear friends :

In high school, when I listened to Mr. Walker, an Industrial Art Director, recite the poem "If" by Rudyard Kipling, I was inspired and wished to be a poet too.

First, I would like to thank my family for the unconditional support during this project. In the swimming pool of true love, I would be an experienced diver.

Secondly, thanks and appreciation go to Denise Brooks of Alexis Information Systems, who noticed my aspiration for writing poetry and recommended that I compile at least twelve copies of my poems for publication. Thus, she inspired me to undertake this project. Before then, it did not occur to me the saying of "working smarter" is better than working too hard.

Finally, I am grateful to my friend Dr. Mike Bauer, PhD in Literature, who agreed to proof-read the first manuscript, especially so when English is a second language for me.

Also, I thank everyone who helped me bring this publication to life.

Sincerely,

Moses Sao Cooper of Deignmai

Moses Sao Zumo Cooper was born on Christmas Day in Vezala, Liberia, West Africa. As a young man, his dream was to come to the United States to pursue graduate studies and he accomplished it in 1977.

He holds a B.A. in Economics and Business Administrations from the University of Liberia. First, he earned Master Degree in International Management from Thunderbird Global School of Management in Glendale, Arizona followed by another Master Degree in Education from Drury University in Springfield, Missouri; which led Moses to one of the most rewarding professional career: teaching.

Moses is a dedicated family man, his family and friends describe him as a "people's person."His life's work and passions has been to educate students around the world.

His hobbies include writing poetry which he taught himself. Moses' other hobbies include listening to Classical and Country Music, cultivating his love for art history and listening and watching the World News.

He currently resides in Bentonville, Northwest Arkansas with his family.

Find out more at www.writercooper.com.

Made in the USA
Middletown, DE
05 July 2017